THE WEDDING CHALLENGE

CANDACE CAMP

THORNDIKE
CHIVERS

This Large Print edition is published by Thorndike Press, Waterville, Maine, USA and by BBC Audiobooks Ltd, Bath, England.
Thorndike Press, a part of Gale, Cengage Learning.
Copyright © 2008 by Candace Camp.
The moral right of the author has been asserted.

The text of this Large Print edition is unabridged.
Other aspects of the book may vary from the original edition.
Set in 16 pt. Plantin.
Printed on permanent paper.

LIBRARY OF CONGRESS CATALOGING-IN-PUBLICATION DATA

Camp, Candace.
  The wedding challenge / by Candace Camp.
    p. cm. — (Thorndike Press large print core)
  ISBN-13: 978-1-4104-1104-4 (hardcover : alk. paper)
  ISBN-10: 1-4104-1104-4 (hardcover : alk. paper)
  1. Large type books. I. Title.
PS3553.A4374W43 2008
813'.54—dc22   2008037780

BRITISH LIBRARY CATALOGUING-IN-PUBLICATION DATA AVAILABLE

Published in 2008 in the U.S. by arrangement with Harlequin Books S.A.
Published in 2009 in the U.K. by arrangement with Harlequin Enterprises II B.V.

U.K. Hardcover: 978 1 408 42163 5 (Chivers Large Print)
U.K. Softcover: 978 1 408 42164 2 (Camden Large Print)

Printed in the United States of America
1 2 3 4 5 6 7 12 11 10 09 08

Dear Reader,

The Wedding Challenge is the third book in the MATCHMAKER series and was probably the most fun to write. (And, yes, there are books that, no matter how much I love them, are not fun while I'm writing them.)

However, this book was like telling a story about old friends, since I've written about Callie and her brother and Francesca in the first two books. Callie is a little younger than most of my heroines, and I enjoyed presenting her youthful enthusiasm and joie de vivre. And even though it's set long ago and far away, with customs and manners that are years removed from us, I think that the challenges Callie faces will be something that most of us women can relate to.

So choose your favorite reading place and settle down for a few hours with some good friends. Happy reading!

Best wishes,
Candace Camp

For Leslie Wainger,
editor extraordinaire,
for her wisdom and
her talent for sharing it.

CHAPTER ONE

Lady Odelia Pencully's birthday ball was the event of the Season — even though the Season had not yet begun. Not to have been invited was a cause for deep social embarrassment. To have been invited and not attend was unthinkable.

Either by blood or by birth, Lady Pencully was related to half the most powerful and wealthy families in England. The daughter of a duke and a countess by marriage, she was a pillar of Society, and it was rare that anyone dared cross her. During her heyday, she had ruled over the *ton* as she did her family, with an acid tongue and an iron will, and even though she had, with age, remained more and more at her country estate, rarely coming to London even for the Season, she was still a force to be reckoned with. A prodigious correspondent, she kept up to date with the latest scandals and news, and was never averse to dashing off a note to anyone whom she felt needed the benefit of her advice.

So this year, when she announced that she would celebrate her eighty-fifth year of life with a grand ball, it immediately became the one event that no one of any social standing or pretenses thereof could risk missing, even if it was in London in January, the most unfashionable and difficult time of the year. Neither snow nor cold nor the difficulties of opening up a town house for a brief visit could hold back the ladies of the *ton,* who comforted themselves with the fact that at least it would not be true, as it usually was in January, that no one would be in town, since everyone who mattered would be coming to Lady Odelia's party.

Among those who drove into London from their country estates was the Duke of Rochford, along with his sister, Lady Calandra, and their grandmother, the dowager Duchess of Rochford. The duke, one of the rare few who would have dared to refuse Lady Odelia, had been disinclined to do so. He was, after all, her great-nephew, and he was a man who believed in carrying out his family responsibilities. Besides, there was business he needed to attend to in London.

The dowager duchess had come because, while she had never really liked her late husband's older sister, Lady Pencully was one of the few people left of their generation — though, the duchess was careful to point out, Lady Pencully was a number of years older than she — and was, moreover, one of the even fewer number of women whom the duchess considered of equal standing. Lady Odelia was, quite simply, one of the duchess's set, despite Odelia's sometimes rather shocking lack of manners.

Of the three in the carriage waiting in the long line of carriages creeping along Cavendish Crescent toward Lady Pencully's door, only the youngest, Lady Calandra, was looking forward with eagerness to the evening.

At twenty-three years of age, Callie, as she was known to those close to her, had been out for five years, so a London ball, especially one given by an octogenarian relative, would not normally have been cause for excitement. However, she had just spent several long months at the Lilles family country estate, Marcastle, months made even longer and drearier by an inordinate number of drab rainy days and the constant presence of her grandmother.

In the usual way of things, her grandmother was accustomed to residing a good part of the year in her home in Bath, happily reigning over the slow and genteel social scene of that community, and only occasionally, particularly during the Season, coming up to London to make sure that her granddaughter was conducting herself properly.

However, at the end of the last Season, the dowager duchess had decided that it was well past time for Lady Calandra to be married, and she had taken it as her primary occupation to get the girl engaged — to the proper sort of gentleman, of course. To that end, she had sacrificed her usual winter course in Bath for the cold drafts of the historic family estate in Norfolk.

Callie, therefore, had spent the last few months cooped up by the inclement weather, listening to the old lady's strictures on her behavior, admonitions of her duty to marry, and opinions regarding the suitability of the various peers of the realm.

As a result, the prospect of a real ball, with dancing, friends, gossip and music, set her stomach fluttering in anticipation. To make it even more interesting in Callie's opinion, Lady Odelia's party was a masquerade ball. This fact had not only allowed Callie the added fun of devising a costume, it also provided the evening with an intriguing air of mystery.

She had, after much careful consideration

and consultation with her seamstress, settled on the guise of a woman of the reign of Henry VIII. Not only did the close-fitting Tudor cap look quite fetching on her, but the deep crimson color of the gown was a perfect foil for her black curls and fair skin — and a welcome change from the usual white to which an unmarried young woman such as herself was limited.

Callie glanced across the carriage at her brother. Rochford, naturally, had eschewed any disguise, wearing his usual elegant black evening suit and white shirt, with a crisp, perfectly tied white cravat, his only concession to the evening a black half mask worn across his eyes. With his dark good looks, of course, he still looked sufficiently romantic and faintly sinister enough to have most of the ladies at the ball gazing in his direction and sighing.

He caught Callie's glance and smiled affectionately at her. "Happy at the thought of dancing again, Callie?"

She smiled back at him. Others might find her older brother a trifle distant and cool, even forbidding, but she knew that he was not at all cold. He was merely reserved and rather slow to warm to people. Callie understood his manner; she, too, had learned that when one was a duke, or even a duke's sister, any number of people wanted to ingratiate themselves with one not for friendship, but for the social and monetary benefits they hoped to receive. She suspected that Sinclair had had even more bitter experience with this phenomenon than she, for he had come into his title and wealth at a young age, and had not had the protection and guidance of an older brother.

Their father had died when Callie was only five, and their mother, a sweet woman with a perpetual air of sadness, had gone to her grave nine years later, still mourning their father. Her brother was Callie's only real family, except, of course, for her grandmother. Sinclair, fifteen years older than Callie, had assumed the role of guardian as well as brother, and as a result, he had been more like a young, indulgent father to her than a brother. She suspected that one of the reasons he had been willing to come to London for their great-aunt's party had been because he knew how much she herself would enjoy it.

"Indeed, I am looking forward to it," she answered him now. "I don't believe that I have danced since Irene and Gideon's wedding."

It was well known among Lady Calandra's family and friends that she was an active sort, preferring a ride or a brisk walk through the country to sitting with her needlework beside the fire, and even by the end of the Season, she never tired of dancing.

"There was Christmas," the duke pointed out, a twinkle in his eye.

Callie rolled her eyes. "Dancing with one's brother while Grandmother's companion plays the piano does not count."

"It has been a dull winter," Rochford admitted. "We shall go to Dancy Park soon, I promise."

Callie smiled. "It will be wonderful to see Constance and Dominic again. Her letters have been brimming over with happiness, now that she is in the family way."

"Really, Calandra, that is hardly the sort of thing one mentions to a gentleman," the duchess commented.

"It's only Sinclair," Callie pointed out mildly, suppressing a sigh. She was well-used to her grandmother's strict views of appropriate behavior, and she did her best not to offend the woman, but after three months of the duchess's lectures, Callie's nerves were beginning to wear thin.

"Yes," Rochford agreed with a grin for his sister. "It is only I, and I am well aware of Callie's scapegrace ways."

"It is all very well for you to laugh," his grandmother retorted. "But a lady of Callie's station must always act with the greatest discretion. Especially one who is not yet married. A gentleman does not choose a bride who does not conduct herself appropriately."

Rochford's face assumed that expression of cool hauteur that Callie referred to as his "duke's face" as he said, "There is a gentleman who would dare to presume to call Calandra indiscreet?"

"Of course not," the duchess replied quickly. "But when one is seeking a husband, one must be especially careful about everything one says or does."

"Are you seeking a husband, Callie?" Rochford asked now, turning to his sister with a quizzical glance. "I was not aware."

"No, I am not," Callie told him flatly.

"Of course you are," her grandmother contradicted. "An unmarried woman is always seeking a husband, whether she admits to it or not. You are no longer a young girl in her first Season, my dear. You are twenty-three, and nearly every girl who made her come-out the same season as you has gotten engaged — even that moon-faced daughter of Lord Thripp's."

"To an 'Irish earl with more horses than

16

prospects'?" Callie asked. "That is what you called him last week."

"Of course I would expect a far better husband than that for *you*," her grandmother retorted. "But it is vexing beyond belief that that chit should have become engaged before you."

"Callie has plenty of time for finding a husband," Rochford told his grandmother carelessly. "And I can assure you that there are any number of men who would ask me for her hand if they had the slightest encouragement."

"Which, I might point out, you never give anyone," the duchess put in tartly.

The duke's eyebrows sailed upward. "Surely, Grandmother, you would not have me allow roués and fortune hunters to court Calandra."

"Of course not. Pray do not act obtuse." The dowager countess was one of the few who did not stand in awe of Rochford, and she rarely hesitated to give him her opinion. "I am merely saying that everyone knows that should they show an interest in your sister, they are likely to receive a visit from *you.* And very few men are eager to confront you."

"I had not realized that I was so fearsome," Rochford said mildly. "However that may be, I fail to see why Callie would be interested in any man who was not willing to face an interview with me in order to pay suit to her." He turned to Callie. "Are you interested in any particular gentleman?"

Callie shook her head. "No. I am quite happy as I am."

"You will not always remain the most sought-after young woman in London," her grandmother warned.

"Then she should enjoy it now," Rochford stated, effectively ending the conversation.

Grateful for her brother's intervention, Callie turned her attention to the window, peeking past the curtain at the carriages disgorging passengers before them. It was not, however, quite as easy to ignore her grandmother's words.

Callie had spoken the truth: she *was* largely content just as she was. She enjoyed the social whirl of London during the spring and summer months — the dancing, the plays, the opera — and during the rest of the year she could also keep herself well-occupied. She had friends she could visit. She had grown especially close, over the last few months, to Constance, the new wife of the Viscount Leighton, and when the duke was at Dancy Park, Callie spent a great deal of time with her, for Redfields, Dominic and

18

Constance's home, was only a few miles from Dancy Park. The duke had a number of other residences which he periodically visited, and Callie often went with him. She was rarely bored, for she enjoyed riding and long walks in the country, and she did not disdain the company of the local folk or the servants. She had been almost entirely in charge of the duke's household since she was fifteen, so there were always things to do.

Still, she knew that her grandmother was right. The time was approaching when she would need to marry. In two more years she would be twenty-five, and most girls were wed by then. If she remained single after that, she would soon be regarded as a spinster, which was not, she knew, a particularly pleasant position to occupy.

It was not that Callie had anything against marriage. She was not like her friend Irene, who had always declared that she would never wed — a conviction that she had recently given up when she met Lord Radbourne. No, Callie expected to marry. She wanted a husband and children and a house of her own.

The problem was, she had never found anyone whom she wanted to marry. Oh, there had been a time or two when she had fallen into an infatuation, when a man's smile had made her heart flutter, or a set of broad shoulders in a Hussar's uniform had increased her pulse. But those had always been fleeting things, soon over, and she had yet to meet a man whom she thought she could be happy to see over the breakfast table every morning — let alone give herself up to in the vague, darkly fascinating and slightly frightening rites of the marital bed.

Callie had listened to other young women enthusing over this gentleman or that, and she had wondered what it must be like to tumble with such seeming ease into the deep chasm of love. She wondered if those girls had any idea of the opposite side of such love — the tears she had seen her mother shed, even years after her husband's death, the soft sad ghost her mother had become long before she actually died. She wondered if it was because she was aware of the sorrows love could bring that she found it more difficult to fall in love . . . or was it simply something lacking within herself?

She pushed aside such gloomy thoughts as the ducal carriage pulled up to the front steps of the brightly lit house and a footman sprang forward to open their door. She was not about to allow anything, either her grandmother's criticisms or her own doubts, to spoil her first evening out in London.

Reaching up, she made sure her dainty half mask was in place over her eyes; then she took the hand her brother offered and climbed down from the vehicle.

They were greeted inside the ballroom by Lady Francesca Haughston, easily recognizable despite the narrow blue satin mask she wore. Lady Francesca, a vision in cream and gold and blue, was masquerading as a shepherdess — not the actual sort, of course, but the romantic ideal. Her blond curls were caught up by blue ribbons that matched the wide ribbon wrapped around her white shepherd's staff, just below its crook. She wore a blue satin overskirt, draped to reveal a froth of white flounces on the skirt beneath, each draping point pinned by a rosette. Her feet were shod in golden slippers.

"Bo Peep, I presume," Rochford drawled, bowing over Lady Francesca's hand, and she curtseyed to him.

"You, I can see, did not bother to don fancy dress," she retorted. "I should have known. Well, you shall have to answer to Lady Odelia. She was quite set on the idea of a masquerade, you know."

She gestured toward the woman who sat across the room. On a raised dais, Lady

Odelia sat enthroned — there was no other word for it — in a high-backed chair padded in blue velvet. On top of her hair she wore an orange wig, and her face was painted white. A circle of gold was thrust into the mass of bright curls, and a high starched ruff rose up from her dress behind her head. Ropes of pearls hung from her neck down over her brocade stomacher and skirts, and rings bedecked her fingers.

"Ah, Good Queen Bess," Rochford remarked, following Francesca's gaze. "The aging one, I presume."

"Don't let her hear you say that," Francesca replied. "She cannot stand for long to receive guests, so she decided to hold court instead. Rather appropriate, I think."

Francesca turned toward Callie, holding out her hands and smiling with affection. "Callie, my dear. At least I can count on you. How lovely you look."

Callie greeted the other woman with a smile. She had known Lady Haughston all her life, for Francesca was Viscount Leighton's sister and had grown up at Redfields, not far from the duke's own Dancy Park. Francesca was several years older than Callie, and Callie had regarded her with awe and affection when she was a child. Francesca had married Lord Haughston and moved from Redfields, but Callie had continued to see her now and again when Francesca came to visit her parents. Later, when Callie had had her own coming out, they had associated frequently, for Lady Francesca, a widow for the past five years, was one of the leading ladies of the *ton.* Her sense of style was impeccable, and even though she was now in her early thirties, she was still one of the most beautiful women in London.

"I am completely in your shadow, I assure you," Callie told Francesca. "You look absolutely beautiful. But how did Aunt Odelia manage to trap you into receiving guests?"

"Oh, my dear, she did much more than that. She did not feel that she could put on a ball in her own honor, so that fell to her sister Lady Radbourne and, of course, the new Countess of Radbourne — you know Irene —" Francesca swiveled to include the woman standing beside her.

"Of course," Callie answered. The *ton* was not a large group, and she had known Lady Irene superficially for some years. A few months earlier she had come to know her better when she had married Gideon, Lord Radbourne, who was in some collateral way related to Lady Calandra and the duke.

Irene smiled in her frank way and greeted her, "Hello, Callie. Good to see you. Is Francesca telling you how I imposed on her good nature?"

"Hardly an imposition," Francesca demurred.

Irene laughed. She was a tall woman, with thick, curling blond hair, and she looked stunning dressed in the white drapery of an ancient Greek. Her odd golden eyes were lit with laughter. Marriage, Callie thought, agreed with Irene. She was more beautiful than ever.

"What Francesca means is that it was worse than that," Irene explained, glancing at Francesca with affection. "You know how hopeless I am at parties. The entire thing fell to Francesca, so you must compliment her for the fact that it has come off so well. Or at all, frankly."

Francesca smiled amiably and turned to greet the next partygoer as Callie moved down the receiving line to Irene and her husband, Lord Radbourne. Gideon, Lord Radbourne, had come to the party tonight dressed as a pirate, and it was, Callie reflected, a guise that suited his rather unconventional looks. With his dark, slightly shaggy hair and powerful build, he looked more like someone who might stop one's ship and rob it than like a gentleman, and he did not seem at all uncomfortable to have a cutlass thrust through his wide sash.

"Lady Calandra," Gideon greeted her, executing a brief but serviceable bow. "Thank you for coming." A smile warmed his hard features for an instant. "It is good to see a familiar face."

Callie smiled. It was common knowledge that Gideon was not at ease in the company of his peers — bizarre events in his childhood had caused him to be raised from childhood in poverty in London, and he had survived and even prospered solely by using his wits. When he was returned to his proper station as an adult, he had fit in poorly with the other members of the *ton*. He was not much given to talking, and he had so far managed to avoid most social occasions. But he had found a proper fit with Irene, whose blunt speech and disregard of other's opinions were equal to his own. On the occasions when Callie had been around him, she had found him quite interesting.

"It is a pleasure to be here," Callie assured him. "I fear that winter at Marcastle has grown quite monotonous. And, in any case, one could hardly *not* attend Aunt Odelia's birthday ball."

"That seems to be the case with half of

25

England," Gideon opined with a glance at the crowded ballroom.

"Let me take you over to visit the guest of honor," Irene suggested, linking her arm through Callie's.

"Traitor," her husband said in a low voice, though the warmth of his smile as he looked at his wife belied his caustic word. "You are simply seizing the opportunity to get out of this damnable receiving line."

Irene let out a laugh and cast a teasing smile at Lord Radbourne. "You are quite welcome to join us if you wish. I am sure that Francesca will be well able to handle the new arrivals."

"Hmm." Lord Radbourne adopted a considering pose. "Greeting guests or facing Aunt Odelia — a difficult choice indeed. Is there not a third, more attractive, alternative — perhaps dashing into a burning building?"

Gideon smiled at his wife in a way that was almost a caress and went on, "I had best stay here, else Aunt Odelia will no doubt take me to task again because I did not come as Sir Francis Drake as she suggested, a globe under my arm."

"A globe?" Callie repeated sotto voce as she and Irene strolled away.

"Yes. For sailing all over the world, you

see — though I'm not entirely sure that Sir Francis Drake actually circumnavigated the globe. But that would scarcely matter to Aunt Odelia."

"Little wonder that Radbourne did not care to come in that costume."

"No, but it was not the globe that put him off so much as those puffed short pants."

Callie laughed. "I am surprised you were able to get him to come in costume at all. Sinclair would not consider it, beyond a mask."

"Doubtless the duke has more dignity to lose," Irene replied lightly. "Besides, I have found 'tis quite amazing the persuasive power a wife can exert on her husband." Her eyes glittered behind her gold mask, and there was a soft, provocative curve to her mouth.

Callie could feel a faint blush rising in her cheeks at the implication of the other woman's words, and she felt a not unfamiliar twinge of curiosity. Women were usually quick to cease any discussion of the marriage bed if an unmarried girl was around, so Callie had heard very little about what happened in the privacy of a couple's bedchamber, although, as was usually the case in a girl who had been raised in the country, she had some degree of knowledge of the basics of the act, at least among horses and dogs.

Still, Callie could not help but wonder about the feelings — the emotions and the physical sensations — that were involved in that very private human act. To ask a direct question was, of course, unthinkable, so she had had to glean what she could from conversations she overheard and, sometimes, an inadvertent slip of the tongue. Irene's comment tonight was, she thought, different from most that she had heard from married women. Though lightly humorous, there was a *pleased* tone to her voice — no, more than that, there was the almost purring sound of someone who thoroughly enjoyed participating in that wifely "persuasion" about which she spoke.

Callie cast a sideways glance at Irene. If there was anyone who would talk about such a thing to her, she thought, it would be Irene. She cast about for some way to keep the conversation going in the direction Irene had taken, but before she could think of anything to say, she glanced across the room, and every thought left her head.

A man stood leaning against one of the pillars that marched along either side of the room. He looked negligently at ease, his arms crossed, one shoulder to the pillar. He was dressed in the style of a Cavalier, his wide-brimmed hat pinned up on one side and with a sweeping plume on the other. Soft leather gloves with wide, long gauntlets encased his hands and lower arms. His fawn breeches were tucked into soft boots that were elegantly cuffed just below the knees, and slender golden spurs hung at the heels. Above his trousers he wore a matching slashed doublet, bare of any ornamentation, and over that was a short round cape, tied casually at the neck and caught on one side behind the elegant thin sword hanging at his waist.

He could have stepped from a painting of the nobles who had fought and died for their doomed king, Charles I — elegant, and whipcord lean and tough. The dark half mask that hid the upper portion of his face only added to the air of romance and mystery that hung about him. He was glancing about the room, his expression arrogant and faintly bored. Then his eyes met Callie's and stopped.

He did not move nor change expression, yet somehow Callie knew that he had become instantly, intently alert. She gazed back at him, her steps faltering. A slow smile spread across the lower half of his face, and, sweeping off his hat, he bowed extravagantly.

Callie realized that she was staring, and, with a blush, she took two quick steps to catch up with Irene. "Do you know that man?" she asked in a hushed voice. "The Cavalier?"

Irene glanced around. "Where — oh. No, I don't believe I do. Who is he?" She turned back to Callie.

"I do not think I have ever seen him before," Callie replied. "He looks . . . intriguing."

"No doubt it is the costume," Irene told her cynically. "The most impossibly dull sort would look dashing in the clothes of a Royalist."

"Perhaps," Callie agreed, unconvinced. She was tempted to turn and look back at the man, but she resisted the urge.

"Calandra! There you are!" Lady Odelia exclaimed in her booming voice as they approached the dais upon which the old lady sat.

Callie smiled as she stepped up to greet her great-aunt. "May I offer you my felicitations, Aunt Odelia?"

Lady Odelia, a formidable-looking woman even when she was not dressed up in the manner of Queen Elizabeth, allowed a regal nod and gestured Callie forward with a gesture worthy of that monarch. "Come here, girl, and give me a kiss. Let me look at you."

Callie obediently bent and kissed her great-aunt's cheek. Aunt Odelia took both Callie's hands in hers and stared up at her intently.

"Pretty as ever," she announced in a satisfied voice. "Prettiest of the lot, I've always said. Of the Lilles, I mean," she offered in an aside to Irene.

Irene nodded her understanding, smiling. She was one of the few women in the *ton* who held no fear of Lady Pencully; indeed, she rather enjoyed the old woman and her blunt ways. She had, in fact, engaged in a few lively discussions with Odelia that had sent everyone else scurrying out of the room and left the two women flushed, eyes snapping, and quite pleased with themselves and each other.

"Can't imagine what is wrong with young men today," Lady Odelia went on. "In my day a girl like you would have been snapped up her first year."

"Perhaps Lady Calandra does not wish to be 'snapped up,' " Irene offered.

"Now, don't go putting your radical ideas into her head," Lady Odelia warned. "Callie has no desire to be an ape-leader, do you, my dear?"

31

Callie suppressed a sigh. "No, Aunt." Was she *never* to get away from this topic today?

"Of course not! What intelligent young girl would? 'Tis time you put your mind to it, Calandra. Ask that chit Francesca to help you. Always thought the girl had more hair than wit, but she managed to get this one to the altar." Lady Odelia gestured toward Irene, who rolled her eyes comically at Callie. "I would not have taken odds on that happening."

"Indeed, Aunt," Irene put in. "To hear you and Lady Radbourne speak of it, one would assume that your grandson and I had nothing to do with the matter, only Lady Francesca."

"Hah! If I had left it up to you two, we would still be waiting," Lady Odelia tossed back, the twinkle in her eyes counteracting the bite of her words.

The two of them continued to bicker in a playful fashion, and Callie realized with a rush of gratitude that Irene had skillfully led the obstreperous old woman away from the subject of Calandra's own unmarried state. She cast her friend a look of gratitude, and Irene responded with a smile.

Callie stood, idly listening as her companions strayed into an apparently endless and comfortably familiar list of items about which Irene and her husband's great-aunt enjoyed crossing swords. She glanced up at Irene just as her words suddenly came to halt and saw that Irene was looking over Callie's shoulder. Just as Callie started to turn around to see what had caused the sudden interest on Irene's face, a masculine voice sounded behind her.

"Pardon me, Your Highness, but I come seeking the favor of this fair maiden's hand for the next dance."

Callie swung around, and her eyes widened as she found herself staring up into the masked visage of the Cavalier.

CHAPTER TWO

The man was, Callie realized, even more intriguing up close than he had been at a distance. The black half mask concealed the upper portion of his face, but it also emphasized the strong, chiseled jaw and well-cut, sensual mouth that lay below it. The eyes that looked out through the mask were fixed on her with a gaze that was decidedly warmer than was polite. He was tall, with wide shoulders tapering down to a narrow waist, and he exuded a powerful masculinity that owed only part of its aura to the dashing costume he wore.

She should have given him a setdown, Callie knew, for she was certain that she did not know the man, which made it quite forward of him to ask her to dance. However, she found she had no desire to snub him. Indeed, what she desired was to put her hand in his and let him lead her out onto the floor.

However, Callie was certain that she would not be able to dance with him, for Lady Odelia would doubtless blister his ears for his impudence. Callie waited, with an inner sigh of regret, for that lady's words.

"Of course," Lady Odelia said — nay, almost purred, Callie thought, as she glanced at the old lady in surprise.

Irene's face registered a similar sense of shock as she, too, turned toward Lady Odelia. But Lady Odelia was smiling with what could only be called pleasure at the Cavalier, and when Callie did not move, she waved her hand in a shooing motion toward her.

"There, girl, do not stand rooted on the spot. Get to the floor before the orchestra starts again."

Callie did not need to be told twice to do what she wanted. If Lady Odelia had given her blessing to dancing with this man, it would satisfy the requirements of propriety — and prevent any upbraiding from her grandmother. But there was nevertheless a whiff of something illicit about dancing with a perfect stranger that she found enticing.

She quickly placed her hand on the arm the stranger held out to her, and they went down the step of the dais and onto the dance floor. Callie was very aware of the man's arm beneath her hand, the muscle hard under the soft material.

"I should not dance with you, you know," she told him, a little surprised at the flirtatious tone that bubbled up in her words.

"Indeed? And why is that?" He looked down at her, his eyes twinkling.

"I do not know you, sir."

"How can you be sure?" he countered. "We are masked, after all."

"Still, I am certain that we are strangers."

"But is that not the point of a masquerade? That you do not know who anyone is? And so, surely, it is only to be expected that one would dance with a stranger. The usual rules do not apply," he told her, and his gaze slid down her face in a way that made Callie feel suddenly warm.

"None of them?" she asked lightly. "Indeed, sir, that sounds dangerous."

"Ah, but that is what makes it exciting."

"I see. And it is excitement you seek?"

His smile was slow. " 'Tis pleasure I seek, my lady."

"Indeed?" Callie arched one brow, thinking that she should probably nip this conversation in the bud. It was growing altogether too familiar — and yet she could not resist the tingle that ran through her at his words, his smile.

"Indeed, yes — the pleasure of dancing with you," he went on, the light in his eyes telling her that he was aware of exactly where her mind had strayed.

The lilting strains of a waltz began, and he held out his hands to her. Callie moved into his arms, her heart beating a trifle faster. It was even more daring to waltz with a stranger than it would have been to take to the floor for a country dance. She had to stand so close to him during a waltz, her hand in his, his arm almost encircling her. It was a much more intimate dance. It was often not even allowed at the more conservative assemblies in the countryside, and even here in London society, she had rarely shared a waltz with a man with whom she had not at least danced before. Certainly she had never done so with a man whose name she did not even know.

But Callie could not deny that despite the strangeness of it, she liked the way she felt in his arms, and she knew that the flush moving up her throat was due only in part to the exertion of the dance.

At first they did not speak. Callie concentrated on matching her steps to his; she felt almost as she had when she had first made her debut — anxious that she might make a misstep or appear awkward. She quickly found, however, that her new partner was an excellent dancer, his hand on her waist steady and firm, his steps in perfect rhythm to the music. She relaxed and settled down to enjoy herself, glancing up at him for the first time.

Callie found the Cavalier looking down at her, and her breath caught in her throat. His eyes were gray, the color of a stormy sky in this low light, and so steady upon her that she felt herself lost in his gaze. She was near enough to him that she could see the lashes that ringed his eyes, thick and black, shadowing his expression. Who could he be? He seemed completely unfamiliar; surely no costume could disguise someone she knew so well. Yet how could it be that she had not met him sometime in the past five years?

Was he an interloper, someone who had seized the opportunity a masked ball offered to intrude upon a party to which he had not been invited? But Lady Odelia had apparently recognized him, so surely that was not the case. She supposed he could be a recluse, someone who disliked Society and usually shunned it. However, in that case, why was he here at an enormous party? Certainly his manner was scarcely that of one who was shy or solitary.

Could it be that he had been abroad for

the past few years? A soldier or naval officer, perhaps? Maybe a member of the foreign office. Or simply a dedicated traveler.

She smiled a little to herself at her fanciful thoughts. No doubt the explanation was something perfectly ordinary. After all, she did not know everyone in the *ton.*

"I like to see that," her companion said.

"What?" Callie asked, puzzled.

"The smile upon your face. You have been frowning at me so steadily that I was afraid I must have fallen headlong into your bad graces without even knowing you."

"I am sor—" Callie began, then realized the man's admission. "Then you agree that we are strangers."

"Yes. I admit it. I do not know you. I am certain that I would recognize a woman who looks as you do . . . even in a costume. You cannot hide your beauty."

Callie felt her cheeks go warm and was surprised at herself. She was not a schoolgirl to be so easily cast into confusion by a gallant compliment. "And you, sir, cannot hide that you are a terrible flirt."

"You wound me. I had thought I was rather skilled at it."

Callie chuckled in spite of herself and shook her head.

"The fact that we are strangers is easily enough remedied," he went on after a moment. "Simply tell me who you are, and I will tell you who *I* am."

Callie shook her head again. Curious as she was about this man, she found it enjoyable to dance and flirt with him, knowing that he did not know who she was. She did not need to worry about his motives or his intentions. She did not have to weigh each statement for the truth of it or wonder if he was flirting with *her* — or with an heiress. Even those men who did not need her fortune or pursue her for the sake of it were still aware of it. Her lineage and her fortune were as much a part of her to them as her laughter or her smile. She could never know how any of them might have felt about her if she had been merely a gentleman's daughter rather than the sister of a duke. It was quite pleasant, she realized, to know that when this man flirted with her, he saw only *her,* was attracted only to her.

"Oh, no," she told him. "We cannot tell each other our names. That would end all the mystery. Did you not just tell me that that was the whole point of a masquerade — the mystery and excitement of not knowing?"

He laughed. "Ah, fair lady, you have

pierced me with my own words. Is it fair, do you think, for one of your beauty to possess so quick a wit, as well?"

"You, I take it, are accustomed to winning your arguments," Callie countered.

"There are times when I do not mind losing. But this is not one of them. I should regret it very much if I lost you."

"Lost me, sir? How can you lose what you do not have?"

"I will lose the chance to see you again," he replied. "How shall I find you again, not knowing your name?"

Callie cast him a teasing glance. "Have you so little faith in yourself? I suspect that you would find a way."

He grinned back at her. "My lady, your faith in me is most gratifying. But, surely, you will give me a hint, will you not?"

"Not the slightest," Callie retorted cheerfully. There was, she was finding, a wonderful freedom in not being herself, in not having to consider whether what she said would reflect badly on her brother or her family name. It was quite nice, actually, for a few moments to be simply a young woman flirting with a handsome gentleman.

"I can see I must abandon hope in that regard," he said. "Will you at least tell me who you are dressed to be?"

41

"Can you not tell?" Callie asked with mock indignation. "Indeed, sir, you crush me. I had thought my costume obvious."

"A Tudor lady, certainly," he mused. "But not the time of our Lady Pencully's queen. Her father's reign, I would guess."

Callie inclined her head. "You are quite correct."

"And you could not be aught but a queen," he continued.

She gave him the same regal nod.

"Surely, then, you must be the temptress Anne Boleyn."

Callie let out a little laugh. "Oh, no, I fear that you have picked the wrong queen. I am not one who would lose my head over any man."

"Catherine Parr. Of course. I should have guessed. Beautiful enough to win a king. Intelligent enough to keep him."

"And what of you? Are you a particular Cavalier, or simply one of the king's men?"

"Merely a Royalist." He wrinkled his nose. "It was my sister's idea — I have the uneasy feeling she may have been jesting when she suggested it."

"But you need the hair, as well," Callie pointed out. "A long curling black wig, perhaps."

He laughed. "No. I balked at the wig. She

tried to talk me into it, but on that I was firm."

"Is your sister here tonight?" Callie asked and glanced out across the ballroom. Perhaps she knew his sister.

"No. I visited her on my way to London. She will not be here until the Season begins." He studied her, his eyes alight with humor. "Are you trying to guess who I am?"

Callie chuckled. "You have caught me, sir."

"I must tell you that you can easily extract the information from me. My name —"

"Oh, no, 'twould not be fair. Besides, I will find it out once you have discovered who I am and come to call."

"Indeed?" His brows went up, and his eyes glowed suddenly with a light that was not laughter. "I have your permission to call on you?"

Callie tilted her head to the side, making a show of considering. In truth, she was a little surprised at what she had said. She had not thought about it before the words had popped out of her mouth. It was rather audacious to give someone she had just met permission to call — especially before he even asked. It was, well, *forward* on her part. Her grandmother, a stickler for rules, would be horrified. She probably should tell him no.

But Callie found she had not the slightest desire to take back her words. "Why, yes," she replied with a smile. "I believe you do."

The dance ended soon after, and Callie was aware of a pang of regret as her companion led her off the floor. He left her with a bow, raising her hand to briefly brush his lips against it. And even though she could not feel his lips through the cloth of her glove, heat rushed up in her anyway. She watched him walk away, quite the most dashing figure in the room, and she wondered again who he was.

Would he call on her? she wondered. Had he felt that same surge of attraction that she had? Would he go to the trouble of finding out who she was? Or was he merely a flirt, passing the time with flattering banter? Callie knew that it would take only a few judicious questions to the right people to discover his name, but, oddly enough, she found that she liked not knowing. It added to the anticipation, the little thrill of excitement, wondering if he would indeed come to call.

She did not have long to think about the Cavalier, however, for her dances were soon all spoken for, and she spent most of the next hour on the dance floor. She was taking a much-needed rest, sipping a glass of punch and chatting with Francesca, when she saw her grandmother making her way toward her, gripping the arm of a solemn sandy-haired man.

Callie groaned under her breath.

Francesca glanced at her. "Is something the matter?"

"Just my grandmother. She is bringing over another prospect, I warrant."

Lady Haughston spotted the dowager duchess. "Ah. I see."

"She has become obsessed with the idea that I must marry soon. I think she fears that if I do not become engaged this next Season, I will spend the rest of my life as a spinster."

Francesca glanced again at the pair walking toward them. "And she thinks Alfred Carberry would suit you?" she asked, frowning slightly.

"She thinks Alfred Carberry would suit *her,*" Callie replied. "He is in line to inherit an earldom, though given the fact that his grandfather is still alive and hale, not to mention his father, I shouldn't think it will be until he is in his sixties."

"But he is such a dreadfully dull sort," Francesca pointed out. "All the Carberrys are. I do not suppose they can help it, living all together up there in Northumberland. But I should not think you would enjoy being married to him."

"Yes, but, you see, he is so respectable."

"Mmm, that is one of the things that makes him so dull."

"But that suits my grandmother."

"And he's nearly forty."

"Ah, but men my age are apt to be flighty. They might go haring off and do something that isn't respectable. No, Grandmother prefers them stodgy and dull — and from a good family, of course. Wealth would be nice, but she is not utterly wedded to that."

Francesca chuckled. "I fear your grandmother is doomed to disappointment."

"Yes, but I am doomed to her lecturing me. She has been doing so all winter."

"Oh dear," Francesca said sympathetically. "Perhaps you should come visit me. My butler has instructions to turn away all dull and stodgy men — or women, for that matter."

Callie laughed, opening her fan to hide her mouth as she murmured, "Do not let Grandmother hear that, or she will forbid me to call on you."

"Calandra, dear, there you are. Not dancing? And Lady Haughston. How lovely you

46

look, as always."

"Thank you, Duchess," Francesca replied, curtseying. "I must return the compliment, for you are in excellent looks tonight."

It was true, of course, for Callie's grandmother, with her upsweep of snow-white hair and slim, ramrod-straight body, was still an arresting-looking woman. She had been, Callie knew, quite a beauty in her day, and Callie counted herself fortunate that at least the duchess had excellent taste in clothes and had never quibbled about Callie's choice of wardrobe — aside from a time or two in Callie's first Season when her grandmother had put her foot down firmly against a ball gown that was other than white.

"Thank you, my dear." The duchess smiled in a regal way, taking the compliment as her due. "You know the Honorable Alfred Carberry, do you not?" She turned toward the man at her side, unobtrusively maneuvering things so that the duchess stood facing Francesca and Mr. Carberry was closer to Callie.

The duchess went on, introducing the women to Carberry. "Lady Haughston. My granddaughter, Lady Calandra. Tell me, Lady Haughston, how is your mother? We must have a nice coze together, for I dare swear I have not seen you since Lord Leighton's wedding."

She laid a hand on Francesca's arm and glanced over at Callie and Mr. Carberry, effectively separating the two couples. Smiling indulgently, she said, "No doubt you young people would rather not listen to us gossip. Why don't you ask Lady Calandra to dance, Mr. Carberry, while Lady Haughston and I catch up with each other?"

Francesca's brows lifted slightly at being put in a group with the duchess while the honorable Alfred, at least seven or eight years older than she, was termed a young person. However, she knew when she had been outmaneuvered, and she could not help but admire the duchess's expertise, so, casting a single sparkling glance at Callie, she let the duchess steer her aside.

Callie, smiling somewhat stiffly, said, "Pray do not feel you must dance with me, sir, just because my grandmother —"

"Nonsense, my girl," Mr. Carberry said in the hearty jocular voice that he commonly adopted with his younger relatives. " 'Twould be my honor to take a twirl about the floor with you. Enjoying yourself, eh?"

Callie resigned herself to a dance with the man, reasoning that it would be easier to avoid conversation with him while they were dancing. She was pleased to find, when they took to the floor, that it was a sprightly country dance, which allowed little breath or time for talking, though it was unfortunately a good deal longer than a waltz. She found herself glancing around the floor as they went through the steps, looking for the curving plume of a Cavalier hat.

Then she had time to do no more than smile and listen to his thanks for the dance before her hand was claimed by her next partner, Mr. Waters. She knew Mr. Waters only slightly, having met him once before, and she had the faint suspicion that the man was probably angling for a wealthy wife, but at least he was a witty conversationalist and a smooth dancer.

When their dance ended, Mr. Waters suggested a stroll around the room, and Callie agreed. It was almost ten o'clock, which meant that the dancing would shortly cease and soon the guests would start making their way to the supper that would be laid out in the smaller ballroom across the hall. Callie feared that her grandmother would approach her with some "appropriate" escort to lead her in to supper, so she would just as soon stay out of the duchess's sight for the next few moments.

They started around the periphery of the

room, with her escort making polite conversation about the grandness of the ball, the liveliness of the music and the warmth of the room after the dancing. He paused at one of the doors, open to the terrace to let in some of the refreshingly cold evening air.

"Ah, that is much better, is it not?" he said. "One can grow quite heated dancing."

Callie nodded absently, thinking that perhaps Mr. Waters was not so interesting a conversationalist as she had thought. She glanced around the room and finally spotted her grandmother. The old lady was engaged in conversation with Lord Pomerance, and Callie stifled a groan. Surely her grandmother would not inflict that insufferable windbag upon her! He was younger than Mr. Carberry and less stodgy, but his sense of self-importance was overreaching, and he was certain that everyone around him was deeply interested in all the minute details of his existence.

"Those two have the right idea," Mr. Waters continued.

"What?" Callie's gaze was fixed on her grandmother.

Her companion nodded toward the terrace beyond them. "Stepping outside for a bit of fresh air."

"Yes, I suppose."

The duchess turned her head, searching the room, and Callie knew that she was looking for her.

Callie whipped around so that her back was to her grandmother. "Yes," she said quickly. "You are right — a breath of fresh air."

She slipped out the door. Her surprised escort hesitated for a fraction of a second, then grinned and hurried out after her.

Callie walked swiftly away from the ballroom toward the darker reaches of the terrace. The winter air was chilly against her bare arms and neck, but, warmed as she was from dancing in the stuffy room, it was at the moment quite welcome. She stopped when they reached the railing that marked the end of the upper terrace, well beyond where her grandmother might see if she looked out the door from the ballroom.

"I am sorry," she told her companion with a quick smile. "You must think me quite mad, rushing out here this way."

"Not mad. Impetuous, perhaps," Waters replied with a smile and reached out to take her hand in both his. "I can only assume that you were as eager as I to be alone."

As Callie watched in stunned amazement, he raised her gloved hand to his lips and kissed it, then said, "I had not realized — I

51

had hoped, but I did not dream that you might return my affection."

"What?" Callie tried to tug her hand from his, but Waters was holding on to it too tightly.

She saw now the mistake she had made in her impulsive rush to escape her grandmother's manipulations. With some other gentleman, one whom she knew better, it would have been all right. He would have laughed about her predicament with the duchess and promised to come to her aid. Mr. Waters, obviously, had jumped to the wrong conclusion . . . or perhaps he had simply seen a golden opportunity to advance his suit with her. Callie could not forget her suspicions that the man was an opportunist.

She took a step back, but he followed her, still holding her hand and gazing down fervently into her face as he said, "You must know the depth of my feeling for you, the love that burns in my heart. . . ."

"No! Mr. Waters, I fear that you have misunderstood," Callie replied firmly. "Pray, let go of my hand."

"Not until you have answered me. Lady Calandra, I beseech you, make my dreams come —"

"Mr. Waters, stop!" With a heave, Callie

tore her hand from his grasp. "I am sorry that I inadvertently gave you the wrong impression, but, please, let us put an end to this conversation."

She started to walk past him, but Waters grabbed her arms, holding her in place.

"No, hear me out," he said. "I love you, Calandra. My heart, my soul, burns for you. I beg you, say that you care for me, too, that there is in your heart a spark that —"

"Stop this at once," Callie commanded. "Let us go back inside, and we shall forget that this ever happened."

"I do not want to forget," he told her. "Every moment with you is precious to me."

Callie gritted her teeth. His flowery words grated on her, and with each passing moment she was more convinced of his insincerity. This man did not care for her, only for her large dowry, and she no longer had any concern over hurting his feelings.

"I would wager that you would like to forget this moment if I tell my brother about it!" she snapped, and tried to jerk away from him.

His fingers dug into her arms, keeping her from leaving. He grinned, the loving mask dropping from his face as easily as it had come. "Your brother?" he asked derisively. "You intend to tell the duke that you have

53

been dallying with a man on the terrace? Go ahead. Tell him. I imagine he will insist on an engagement immediately."

"You are a fool if you think that," Callie shot back. "I have not been dallying with you, and when I tell him what has happened, you will be lucky if he does not hand your head to you."

"Really?" His eyes brightened with a dangerous light. "And will he be so ready to dismiss me with your reputation compromised beyond repair?"

He jerked her to him and bent to kiss her.

"Oh!" Callie let out a low cry of anger and frustration, and brought her hands up, pushing at him as she twisted and squirmed, turning her face away from him. She kicked out, landing a shot square on his shin.

Waters cursed as he struggled to control her, dragging her across the terrace to pin her against the wall. Callie felt the rough stone through the thin material of her dress, and she dug her fingers into the man's shirt, gripping whatever flesh she could and twisting. He let out a gratifying yelp.

Then, in the next instant, he was jerked away from her, suddenly gasping for air, as a large hand wrapped around his throat and squeezed, pulling him back against the broad chest of the Cavalier.

"What?" the Cavalier asked in a dangerously soft voice, tightening his grasp. Waters' eyes bulged as he flailed ineffectually backward. "Nothing to say? No brave words when it's someone other than a woman you are attacking?"

"No, pray, do not choke him," Callie said a little shakily, moving away from the wall.

"Are you sure?" Her rescuer looked over at her. "I think the world would not miss this one."

"Lady Odelia might object to a dead man on her terrace at her birthday ball," Callie responded dryly.

He grinned, and his hold on the other man loosened. "All right. If you wish it, I shall let him go."

Waters sucked in a gulp of air. "You'll be sorry," he began.

The Cavalier's hand tightened on his throat again, cutting off his words. "I am already sorry," he said flatly.

He let go of Waters' throat and grasped him by the shoulders, whipping him around and shoving him back against the railing. Digging his hand into the neck of Waters' shirt, he bent him backward.

"Perhaps you are not familiar enough with Lady Pencully's house to know that there is a twenty-foot drop from here to the garden below, but I am. I would consider that, if I were you, before I decided to threaten either me or this young lady again. Lady Pencully would dislike having someone take a nasty fall from her terrace on the night of her birthday ball. However, I assure you that she would quickly get over it, and no one would question an inebriated guest tumbling over the railing to the stone walkway below. And there would be no one to dispute my version of the events, since you, alas, would be dead. Have I made myself clear?"

Waters, his eyes huge in the darkness, nodded mutely.

"Good. Then we understand each other." The Cavalier stepped back a little, allowing Waters to stand again, but he did not release him just yet. Looking the other man straight in the eye, the Cavalier went on. "If ever I hear a word about this incident or the slightest whisper of a scandalous rumor concerning this young lady, I will know where it came from. And I will come deal with you. So I would suggest that you keep your lips tightly sealed. In fact, I think it would be a good idea if you left London immediately. A long stay in the country would definitely be in your best interests. Am I clear?"

Waters nodded quickly, not daring to look at the man or at Callie.

"All right, then. Now go."

The Cavalier let him go and stepped back, and Waters scurried off, never glancing behind him. Callie's rescuer turned back to her.

"Are you all right? Did he hurt you?"

Callie nodded and shivered, realizing suddenly how very cold she was. "Yes, I am fine. Thank you. I —" Her breath caught raggedly.

"Here. You are cold." He untied the cape that hung behind him and wrapped it around her shoulders.

"Thank you." She clutched it to her and looked up at him.

Her eyes were luminous in the faint light, swimming with unshed tears. He sucked in a quick breath.

"You are beautiful. 'Tis no wonder that a cad such as he would try to take advantage of you. You should not let that sort inveigle you outside."

"I know. I was foolish." Callie gave him a watery little smile. "I am not so naive as to step outside with a man I hardly know. I was — I was just trying to evade my grandmother, and I acted on impulse."

"Evade your grandmother?" he asked, his eyes lighting mischievously. "Is she a wicked grandmother?"

"No, just a matchmaking one."

"Ah." He nodded. "I understand. Almost as bad as a matchmaking mother."

Callie smiled. "I am very lucky you came along when you did. I am forever in your debt. Thank you for coming to my rescue." She held out her hand solemnly to shake his.

He took her hand, his long fingers wrapping warmly around hers, and he raised it to his lips, pressing them softly against the back of her hand. "I am pleased that I was able to help you. But it was not luck. I saw him lead you out the door, and I did not like the look of him."

"You were watching me?" Callie asked, warmed a little by the thought that he had looked for her just as she had looked for him.

"I had started across the room to ask you for another dance," he told her. "But then the music stopped, and I realized that it was time for supper. Then he whisked you away."

"Still, it was good of you to come after us."

"Any man would have done the same."

"No," she demurred with a smile. "Not all." She glanced down at their joined hands. "You still have my hand, sir."

"Yes, I know. Do you wish me to give it back?" His voice deepened sensually.

Callie looked up, and her insides quivered at the look in his eyes. "I — no, not really."

"Good, for neither do I." Softly his thumb stroked the back of her hand, and though it was only a small movement, Callie felt its effect all through her.

"And now that I have sent that blackguard packing . . . I think it must be worth a small favor, don't you?"

"What favor?" Callie asked a little breathlessly. He seemed very near her; she could feel the heat of his body, smell the faint scent of masculine cologne. Her heart hammered in her chest, but it was not from fear as it had been moments earlier. It was anticipation that welled up in her now.

"Your name, my lady."

"Calandra," she answered softly.

"Calandra," he repeated softly, lingering over the syllables. " 'Tis a magical name."

"Not so magical," she said. "And those who are close to me call me Callie."

"Callie." He lifted his other hand and slid his thumb along her jawline. "It suits you."

"But now we are unequal, for I do not know your name."

"Bromwell. Those who are close to me call me Brom."

59

"Brom," she breathed. Her flesh tingled where his thumb touched it, sending delicious tendrils of sensation spiraling through her.

"It sounds much lovelier on your lips." He brushed his thumb over her bottom lip, and warmth blossomed deep in Callie's abdomen. His eyes followed the movement of his thumb, and the light in them sparked higher, his own lips softening.

He leaned closer, and Callie was certain that he intended to kiss her. But she did not hesitate or pull away. Instead, boldly, she stretched up to meet him.

His lips closed on hers, and heat seemed to explode within her. She trembled, every nerve in her body suddenly alive and attuned to the slow, delicious movement of his mouth on hers. She had never felt anything like this before. Though one or two men had dared to steal a kiss from her, none of those kisses had felt like this — so soft and hot, her lips so sensitive to the velvet pressure of his. And none of those men had ever moved his mouth against her, opening her lips to his questing tongue, startling her and sending a wave of intense pleasure through her.

She made a low noise of surprise and eagerness, and her hands slid up instinctively around his neck, holding on to him as his arms wrapped fiercely around her, squeezing her against his long, hard body. The elegant plume of his hat brushed against her cheek, and that touch, too, aroused the sensitive nerves of her skin. He made a noise of hunger and frustration, reaching up to jerk the hat from his head and toss it aside as his lips pressed harder against hers.

Callie's fingers dug into the rich material of his doublet. She felt as if she were falling, tumbling into some wild maelstrom of hunger and desire, and she was all at once eager and frightened and more vibratingly alive than she had ever been before. She could feel his body surge with heat through the material of his clothes, enveloping her with his warmth.

Suddenly he lifted his head, sucking in a deep breath and staring down at her. Reaching down, he took her half mask between his fingers and pushed it up, revealing her face.

"You are so beautiful," he breathed. Then he reached up and took off his own mask, holding it dangling in his hand.

Callie gazed up at him, realizing with some surprise that his face was even more arresting without the dramatic mask. Sharp,

61

high cheekbones balanced the strong jaw, and the straight dark slashes of his brows accented his wide gray eyes. It was the face of an angel, she thought with a poeticism uncommon to her — not an angel of harps and fluffy clouds, but the fierce sort, standing guard at the gates of heaven with a fiery sword.

"So are you," she answered him candidly, then blushed at the naive candor of her words.

Something flared in his eyes, and he let out a shaky little chuckle. "My dear Calandra . . . it is much too dangerous for you to be out here alone with me."

"Do you think I cannot trust you?" she asked, the tone of her voice making clear her own belief.

"I think 'tis dangerous to trust any man when you look as you look . . . and feel as you feel." His voice turned husky on his last words, and he ran his palm down her arm slowly, reluctantly, and pulled his hand away, taking a step backward. "We should go inside."

He returned her mask, and Callie took it. She hated to turn away from him, away from this moment and the new feelings that were surging through her. Yet at the same time, his urging her to do so only strengthened what she felt for him. She smiled at him.

"Perhaps you would like the rest of my name."

" 'Twould make it easier," he admitted, grinning. "But, believe me, I will find you anyway."

"Then you should come to —" Callie broke off, turning, as her brother's voice sounded from the terrace behind them.

"Callie? Calandra!"

She whirled and looked back up the long terrace. The duke stood just outside the door, looking around. He started forward, scowling, once again calling her name.

"The devil take it!" Callie said under her breath, and her companion's brows shot up at the unladylike curse.

He smothered a laugh. "Not whom you wanted to see?"

"My brother," Callie said. "He is sure to fuss. Ah, well, there is no use in waiting. We might as well get it over with." She started forward with the confidence of one who had never received anything stronger than a scolding.

Her companion shrugged and strode after her, catching up to Callie as she called out, "Here! It is all right, Sinclair. Pray do not bellow."

Rochford hurried toward them, his face relaxing in relief. "What the devil are you doing out here? Are you all right?"

Beside Callie, as they came forward into the light, she heard her companion suck in a sharp breath and stop dead still. She half turned toward him questioningly, then glanced back at her brother, realizing that he, too, had come to a sudden halt.

Rochford stared at the man standing beside Callie, a black scowl drawing up his features. "You!" he snarled at the Cavalier. "Get away from my sister!"

CHAPTER THREE

Callie gaped at her brother, amazed at his uncustomary rudeness. "Sinclair!" She went forward, reaching out a hand to her brother in a calming gesture. "Please, no. You misunderstand the situation."

"I understand it perfectly well," Rochford retorted, his eyes never leaving the other man's face.

"No, you do not," Callie retorted sharply. "This man did nothing to harm me. He *helped* me."

She turned back to her companion, who was gazing at the duke with an expression as stony as Rochford's. Suppressing a sigh at such masculine behavior, Callie said, "Sir, allow me to introduce you to my brother, the Duke of Rochford."

"Yes," the Cavalier said coldly. "I know the duke."

"Oh." Callie looked from one man to the other, realizing that some other, stronger, undercurrent of feeling lay here, something unrelated to her being on the terrace with a man.

"Lord Bromwell," Sinclair responded, his manner, if possible, even stiffer than before. Without looking at Callie, he said, "Calandra, go inside."

"No," Callie answered. "Sinclair, be reasonable. Let me explain."

"Callie!" Sinclair's voice lashed out, sharp as a whip. "You heard me. Go back inside."

Callie flushed, stung by his peremptory tone. He had spoken to her as if she were a child being sent off to bed.

"Sinclair!" she shot back. "Don't speak to me that —"

He swung to face her. "I told you — go back inside. Now."

Callie drew a breath, hurt and anger piercing her with equal sharpness. She started to protest, to take her brother to task for treating her this way, but she realized even as the thought came to her that she simply could not create a scene at Aunt Odelia's party. Someone might step out of the door at any moment; there could even be someone in the garden now, listening. She had no desire to be caught in a blazing argument with her brother. She was embarrassed enough as it was, having been taken to task in front of this man, whom she barely knew.

Her eyes flashed, but she swallowed her words. She gave a short nod to Lord Bromwell, then whirled and stalked past her brother without a word.

The duke stood, watching the other man in silence, until Calandra had disappeared inside the ballroom. Then he said in a quiet voice as hard as iron, "Leave my sister alone."

Bromwell looked amused as he crossed his arms and considered the man before him. "How deliciously ironic . . . to hear the Duke of Rochford so concerned over the honor of a young woman. But, then, I suppose, it is different when the young woman is the *duke's* sister, is it not?"

With a sardonic look at Rochford, he started to walk around him, but the duke reached out and caught his arm. Bromwell went still, his gray eyes icing over. He looked down at the other man's hand on his arm, then up at the duke's face.

"Have a care, Rochford," he said softly. "I am not the boy I was fifteen years ago."

"Indeed?" Rochford asked, letting his hand fall to his side. "You were a fool then, but you're ten times a fool now if you think I will allow you to harm my sister in any way."

"I believe Lady Calandra is a woman grown, Rochford. And you are the fool if you think that you can keep her heart from going where it chooses."

An unholy fire lit the duke's dark eyes. "Damn it, Bromwell. I am telling you — stay away from my sister."

Lord Bromwell gazed back at him, his expression unyielding, then turned without a word and walked away.

Callie was furious. She could not remember when she had been so angry with her brother — indeed, so angry with anyone — as she was now. *How dare he speak to her as if he were her father? And in front of another person! A stranger!*

Her throat was tight, and tears pricked at her eyelids. But she refused to cry. She would not let him see, would not let anyone see, how Sinclair's words had affected her.

She walked through the ballroom, looking neither left nor right, not even sure what she intended to do, only walking as fast as she could away from what had happened on the terrace. Through the red haze of her anger, she noticed that the ballroom was virtually empty and that the musicians were absent from their positions on the small stage at one end of the room.

Supper. The guests were all at the casual midnight buffet in the small ballroom across the hall. Callie started toward it, remembering at the last second that she still wore Lord Bromwell's Cavalier cloak around her shoulders. She reached up and untied it, hastily folding it into a compact pad of material as she entered the small ballroom and looked around.

She saw her grandmother at last, sitting at a small table with Aunt Odelia and another elderly woman, their plates of delicacies still on the table before them. Lady Odelia, of course, was holding forth. The duchess listened politely, spine as straight as ever, not touching the back of her chair, and her eyes blank with boredom.

Callie walked over to the table, and her grandmother turned, seeing her. "Calandra! There you are. Where have you been? I could not find you anywhere. I sent Rochford to look for you."

"Yes, he found me," Callie answered shortly. She glanced at the other two women with the duchess. "Grandmother, I would like to leave now, if you don't mind."

"Why, of course." The duchess looked, frankly, relieved, and immediately started to rise. "Are you all right?"

69

"I — I have a headache, I'm afraid." Callie turned to her great-aunt, forcing a smile. "I am sorry, Aunt Odelia. It is a wonderful party, but I am not, I'm afraid, feeling at all the thing."

"Well, of course. All the excitement, no doubt," the old lady responded, a trifle smugly. She turned toward her companion, giving a decided nod that caused her orange wig to slip a bit. "Girls these days just don't have the stamina we did, I find." She swung her attention back to Callie. "Run along, then, child."

"I will send a footman to find Rochford and tell him we wish to leave," the duchess told Callie, turning and gesturing imperiously to one of the servants.

"No! I mean . . . can we not just go?" Callie asked. "My head is throbbing. And I am sure that Rochford will be well able to find his way home on his own."

"Why, yes, I suppose." The duchess looked concerned and came around the table to peer into Callie's face. "You *do* look a bit flushed. Perhaps you are coming down with a fever."

"I am sure Lady Odelia is right. It is simply too much excitement," Callie replied. "All the dancing and the noise . . ."

"Come along, then," the duchess said,

nodding in farewell to her companions and starting for the hall. She glanced down at Callie's hand. "Whatever are you carrying, child?"

"What? Oh. This." Callie glanced down at the folded cape in her hand, and her fingers clenched more tightly upon it. "It's nothing. I was holding it for someone. It doesn't matter."

Her grandmother looked at her oddly but said nothing more as they continued toward the cloakroom. As they passed the wide double doorway into the main ballroom, they heard Rochford's voice. "Grandmother, wait."

The duchess turned, smiling. "Rochford, how fortunate that we met you."

"Yes," he replied shortly. He no longer looked quite so thunderous, Callie noted, but his face was set and devoid of expression. He glanced toward her, and she looked away from him without speaking. "It is time to go."

"So now we are to leave just because you say so?" Callie flared up.

The duchess gave her granddaughter a curious look and said, "But, Callie, dear, you just told me that you wished to go home."

"I should certainly think so," Rochford

put in with a sharp glance at his sister.

Callie would have liked to protest his tone, as well as his peremptory order that they leave the ball, but she could scarcely do either without looking foolish, she knew, so she merely inclined her head and turned away without another word.

"I am sorry, Sinclair," her grandmother apologized for her. "I fear she is not feeling herself."

"Clearly," the duke replied in a sardonic tone.

A footman brought them their cloaks, and they went down to their carriage. On the way home, the duchess and Rochford exchanged a few remarks about the party, but Callie did not join in the conversation. Her grandmother cast her a puzzled look now and then. Her brother, on the other hand, looked at her as little as she looked at him.

Callie knew that she was behaving childishly, refusing to speak to Rochford or meet his eyes, but she could not bring herself to act as if everything were all right. And she was not sure she could say anything to him about the feelings that roiled inside her chest without bursting into tears of anger — and she refused to do that. Far better, she thought, to seem childish or foolish than to let him think that she was crying because he had hurt her.

When they reached the house, Rochford sprang lithely down from the carriage and reached up to help the duchess, then Callie, who ignored his hand and walked past him into the house. She heard her brother sigh behind her, then turn and follow her up the steps into the foyer. He paused to hand his hat and gloves to the footman as Callie headed for the wide staircase leading up to the next floor, her grandmother moving more slowly behind her.

Rochford started down the hall in the direction of the study, then stopped and turned. "Callie."

She did not turn around, merely took the first step up the stairs.

"Callie, stop!" His voice rang out more sharply, echoing a little in the vast empty space of the large entryway. As if the sound of his own voice had startled even him a little, he continued in a more modulated tone, "Calandra, please. This is ridiculous. I want to talk to you."

She turned and looked down at him from her place on the stairs. "I am going up to bed," she told him coldly.

"Not until we have talked," he replied. "Come back here. We shall go to my study."

Callie's dark eyes, so like her brother's,

flashed with the temper she had been keeping tamped down for the past half hour or more. "What? Now I cannot even go to my bedchamber without your permission? We must obey you in every detail of our lives?"

"Damn it, Callie, you know that is not the case!" Rochford burst out, scowling.

"No? That is all you have done for the last hour — order me about."

"Callie!" The duchess looked from one to the other, astonished. "Rochford! What is this about? What has happened?"

"It is nothing to be concerned about," Rochford told her shortly.

"No, nothing except that my brother has suddenly become a tyrant," Callie lashed out.

Rochford sighed and ran his hand back through his dark hair. "The devil take it, Callie, you know I am not a tyrant. When have I ever been?"

"Never until now," she retorted, blinking away the tears that filled her eyes.

It was, indeed, Rochford's past history of kindness and laxity that made his present actions so much harder to bear. He had always been the most loving and easy-going of brothers, and she had treasured their relationship all the more whenever she heard other girls talk about their brothers or fathers, who issued orders and expected obedience.

"I am sorry, Callie, if I offended you tonight," he said stiffly, with an expression of patience and reasonableness that only served to grate on his sister's nerves. "I apologize if I was too abrupt."

"Abrupt?" She let out a short, unamused laugh. "Is that what you call your behavior this evening? Abrupt? I would have called it high-handed. Or perhaps dictatorial."

The duke grimaced. "I can see that you have taken it amiss, but I must remind you that I am here to protect you. I am your brother. It is my responsibility to take care of you."

"I am not a child anymore!" Callie exclaimed. "I am quite capable of taking care of myself."

"Not that I can see," he snapped back. "Given that I found you alone in the garden with a strange man."

The duchess sucked in a shocked breath. "No! Callie!"

Callie flushed. "I was not in the garden. We were on the terrace, and there was nothing wrong. Bromwell was a perfect gentleman. Indeed, he helped me. He sent another fellow on his way who had not been a gentleman at all."

"Oh!" Callie's grandmother raised a hand to her heart, her mouth dropping open in astonishment. "Callie! You were alone with two different men in the garden?"

"It wasn't the garden!"

"That makes little difference," Rochford replied.

"I may faint," the duchess said weakly, but, of course, she did not. Instead, she marched forward a few steps so that she stood right below Callie, between her and her brother.

"I cannot believe what I have heard," she told Callie. "How could you have done something so scandalous? Have you no care for me? For your family? Sinclair is right. Of course he has responsibility for you. He is your brother and the head of this family. He has every right to tell you what you should do, and you should do as he says. What possessed you to go out onto the terrace with a man tonight? What if someone had seen you? You should be grateful that your brother was there to rescue you. I shudder to think what might have happened if he had not been."

"Nothing would have happened. I told you, I was perfectly all right. I did not create a scandal," Callie replied, color flaming on her cheeks.

"Until you are married and have a home of your own, you are under your brother's control," the duchess said flatly.

"And then I will be under my husband's control!" Callie tossed back hotly.

"Now you sound like Irene Wyngate."

"There is nothing wrong with Irene," Callie replied. "I would be glad to be like Irene. At least she has a spine, unlike most of the women I know."

"Grandmother, please . . ." Rochford said, knowing full well that the duchess was not helping his case with Callie.

"At any rate, it does not matter, as I will never be married as long as my brother treats my suitors like criminals," Callie went on angrily.

Rochford let out a humorless bark of laughter. "Bromwell will never be your suitor."

"I am sure not," Callie responded, "now that you have humiliated me in front of him."

"Bromwell?" The duchess asked, looking startled. "The Earl of Bromwell?"

"Yes."

Their grandmother's eyes lit with interest, but before she could speak, Callie went on, "What is wrong with Lord Bromwell? Why is it so terrible that I was with him?"

"You should not be on the terrace alone with any man," Rochford answered.

"But why did you say that he would never be my suitor?" Callie pursued. "Why did you say, 'You!' the way you did when you saw him? Why is he so particularly unsuitable?"

Rochford said nothing for a long moment, then shrugged. "The man is not a friend to me."

"What?" Callie's brows sailed upward. "He is not your friend? I cannot marry someone unless he is your friend? Who would you have me marry? One of your stuffy old scholarly friends? Mr. Strethwick, perhaps? Or maybe Sir Oliver?"

"Blast it, Callie, you know that is not what I meant," Rochford ground out. "You do not have to marry one of my friends. You know that."

"No, I don't know!" she shot back. "Right now, I feel as if I hardly know you at all. I would never have thought you could be so domineering, so careless of my wishes or feelings."

"Careless?" he repeated in an astounded voice. "It is precisely because I *do* care for you."

"Why? What makes the man unsuitable?" Callie asked. "Is his family not good enough? His rank not high enough?"

"No, of course not. He is an earl."

"Then is he a fortune hunter? Is he after my money?"

"No. He is quite wealthy, as far as I have heard." Rochford's mouth tightened in irritation.

"The Earl of Bromwell is considered quite a catch," the duchess put in. "Of course, he is not a duke, but there are so few of them, after all. And one could not want you to marry one of the royals. An earl would do quite well for you, really, and the family is an old and distinguished one." She turned toward her grandson. "Are they not related to Lady Odelia somehow?"

"Yes, distantly," Rochford agreed. "The problem is not his pedigree."

"Then what is the problem?" Callie persisted.

The duke looked from his sister to his grandmother. Finally he said, "It is an old matter. And that is not the point." He set his jaw. "I was acting in your best interests, Callie, when I warned him off."

"You actually warned him off?" Callie asked in a horrified tone.

He nodded shortly.

"How could you?" she demanded. She felt as if the breath had been knocked out of her. "I cannot believe that you would humiliate me in that way! To tell him that I could not see him, as if I were a child or — or deficient in understanding. As if I had no will of my own or any ability to make judgments."

"I did not say that!" he exclaimed.

"You did not have to," Callie retorted. "It is implicit in saying who I can or cannot associate with." Tears sprang into her eyes again, and she angrily blinked them away.

"I did what was best for you!"

"And I, of course, had nothing to say in the matter!" Callie was rigid with anger, her fists clenched at her sides. She was so furious, so hurt, that she could scarcely trust herself to speak.

She whirled and stalked up the stairs.

"Callie!" Rochford shouted and started after her, then stopped at the foot of the stairs, looking after her in frustration. He turned toward the duchess as though seeking an answer.

His grandmother crossed her arms in front of her and stared back at him stonily. "It is your fault that she acts this way. It is because you raised her so laxly. You have always indulged her and let her do exactly as she pleased. You have spoiled her terribly, and this is the result of it."

The duke let out a low noise of frustration, then swung away from the staircase and started toward his study. He stopped and turned back to his grandmother. "I will finish my business in London quickly. Please get everything ready, so that we can return to the country the day after tomorrow."

Callie stalked into her room, fuming. Her maid Belinda was waiting for her there to help her undress, but Callie sent the girl to bed. She was too irate to stand still while Belinda unfastened her buttons. Anyway, she certainly could not lie down meekly and go to sleep.

The maid gave her an uncertain look, then slipped out the door. Callie strode up and down her room, stewing in her own anger. As she paced, she heard her grandmother's slow steps go past her door, but she did not hear her brother's heavier tread. No doubt he had retired to his favorite room, his study. He was probably peacefully reading some book or letter, or going over a set of numbers in preparation for visiting his business agent tomorrow. *He* would not be grinding his teeth or boiling with injustice and rage. After all, as far as he was concerned, the matter was over.

Callie grimaced at the thought and flung herself down in the chair beside her bed. She would not allow herself to be put in this position. She had thought herself a young lady who lived her life on her own terms, at least within the general limits of society's rules. Had anyone asked, she would have said that she was free to do as she liked, that she directed her own life. She gave in to her grandmother a great deal, of course, in order to keep peace in the household, but that, she knew, was a decision she made. It was not something she had to do.

She went where she liked, received whom she wanted, attended or did not attend plays or routs or soirees as she chose. The household staff came to her for instructions. She bought what she pleased, using her own money, and if it was the agent who actually paid the bills for her, well, that was simply the way things were done. Sinclair's bills were usually paid the same way. And even though Sinclair invested her money for her, he explained everything to her and asked her what she wanted to do. If she always went along with what he suggested, it was only because it was the sensible course. Sinclair had been running his own affairs for years and did so extremely well.

But now she could see that her vision of

her own freedom was merely an illusion. She had simply never before crossed her brother. Who she saw, where she went, what she bought, the decisions she had made, had not been anything he disputed. But what she had presumed was freedom was not; she had simply been living in so large a cage that she had not touched the bars.

Until now.

Callie jumped to her feet. She could not allow this to stand. She was an adult, as old as many women who had married and had children. She was five years older than Sinclair had been when he came into his title. She would not give in meekly to his orders. To do so would be tantamount to granting him authority over her. She would not just go to bed and get up tomorrow morning as if nothing had happened.

She stood for a moment, thinking, then turned and went over to the small desk that stood against the wall. Quickly she dashed off a note and signed it, then folded and sealed it, writing the duke's name across the front before leaving it propped against her pillow.

She grabbed up her cloak from the chair where she had tossed it, and once more wrapped it around her shoulders and tied it. Easing open her door, she stuck her head out and looked up and down the hall. Then, moving silently, she hurried down the hall to the servants' staircase and slipped down the stairs. All was quiet in the kitchen, the scullery lad curled up in his blanket beside the warm hearth. He did not stir as she tiptoed past him nor even when she opened the kitchen door and stepped outside.

Callie closed the door carefully behind her and crept along the narrow path that ran down the side of the house to the street. She looked up and down the wide, dark thoroughfare. Then, pulling up the hood of her cloak so that it concealed her head, she started off boldly down the street.

Across the street and a few doors down from the ducal mansion sat a carriage. It had been there for several minutes, and the driver, huddled in his greatcoat, had begun to doze. Inside, two men sat. One, Mr. Archibald Tilford, sat back against his seat, a bored expression on his face as he turned his gold-knobbed cane around and around in his fingers. Across from him, staring out the open window of the carriage at Lilles House, sat Archibald's cousin, the Earl of Bromwell.

"Really, Brom, how long are we going to sit here?" Tilford asked somewhat peevishly.

"I've a bottle of port and some very lucky cards waiting for me at Seaton's right now. And the brick the driver put in here is growing cold. My feet will be like ice in ten more minutes."

The earl flashed him a cool look. "Really, Archie, do try to bear up. We have scarce been here a quarter of an hour."

"Well, I cannot imagine what you are doing, watching a dark house," his cousin went on. "What the devil do you expect to see at this time of night?"

"I'm not sure," Bromwell replied, not taking his eyes from the house.

"It is clear no one will be coming or going so late," Archie pointed out. "I cannot imagine why you took it into your head to see Rochford's house right now. Good Gad, it's been fifteen years, hasn't it? I thought you had finally forgotten about the duke."

Bromwell gave the other man a long look. "I never forget."

Tilford shrugged, ignoring through long experience the fierce gaze that would have quelled most other men. " 'Tis long over, and Daphne got married anyway." Bromwell did not reply, and after a moment, Tilford went on. "What are you about?"

Bromwell countered his cousin's question with one of his own. "What do you know about Rochford's sister?"

Archie sucked in a sharp breath. "Lady Calandra?" He hesitated, then said carefully, "You're not thinking of . . . some sort of game involving the duke's sister, are you? Everyone knows the man is devilishly protective of her — as you would know, too, if you had not spent the last ten years of your life buried up on your estate making money."

Bromwell grimaced. "I've never known you to complain about the money that I have made for the family."

"Heaven forbid," Archibald responded mildly. "But you have made an ample amount, surely. You can enjoy some of it now. Live a normal life for a change. Isn't that why you came to London — to enjoy yourself for a while?"

Bromwell shrugged. "I suppose."

"Well, a normal life does not include sitting about in cold coaches, spying on dark houses."

"You were going to tell me about Lady Calandra."

Archie sighed. "Very well. The lady is young and beautiful and wealthy."

"Suitors?"

"Of course. But she has rejected them all — at least all the ones who were not too scared of the duke to even try to court her. Rumor has it that she will never marry. They say that the Lilles are simply a cold family."

The corner of the other man's mouth quirked up a trifle, and he murmured, "I saw nothing cold about the lady."

Archibald shifted uneasily in his seat. "I say, Brom, what exactly are you thinking?"

A half smile played on Bromwell's lips. "I was thinking how nervous it made the duke tonight to see me with Lady Calandra. It was most amusing."

His words did not appear to reassure his cousin, who looked even more alarmed. "The duke will have your liver and lights if you harm Lady Calandra."

Bromwell sent the other man a sideways glance. "Do you really think that I am afraid of anything the duke might do to me?"

"No, the devil take it. I am sure you are not. But, frankly, I am scared enough of him for both of us."

The earl smiled. "Do not fret yourself, Archie. I do not intend to harm the girl. Indeed . . ." His lips curved up in a smile that was anything but reassuring. "I plan to be quite charming to her."

Tilford let out a low groan. "I knew it. You *are* planning something. This is bound to end badly. I am sure of it. Please, Brom, can we not just drive on and forget all this?"

"Very well," Bromwell replied absently. "I have seen all I wanted to, in any case."

He started to drop the curtain that covered the window, but then he leaned forward, peering out, and held up a hand to his cousin. "No, wait. There is someone coming out. A woman."

"A servant? At this hour?" Even Archibald sounded interested and turned to lift the other side of the window curtain. "An assignation, do you think, with some footman or —"

"The devil!" Bromwell's exclamation was low but forceful. "It is the lady herself."

He watched as the woman pulled up the hood of her cloak, concealing her head and face, then set off down the street. Taking Archie's cane from his cousin's relaxed hand, he raised it to open the small square window beside the driver's head and give him a terse set of instructions.

Then he leaned back against the seat, pulling the concealing curtain into place, as the carriage rolled forward, following the woman.

"You think that is Lady Calandra?" Archie asked disbelievingly. "What would she be doing out? Alone? And at this time of night?"

"What indeed?" his cousin repeated, tapping his forefinger against his lips thoughtfully.

Archie pushed aside a sliver of curtain and looked out. "We've passed her."

"I know."

At the next street their carriage turned right and rolled slowly to a stop. Bromwell opened the door and stepped out of the carriage.

"Brom! What do you think you are doing?" Archie asked.

The earl replied lightly, "Well, I can scarcely let a lady walk alone at this hour, can I?"

With a smile and a tip of his hat, Bromwell closed the door and walked off.

CHAPTER FOUR

Callie walked quickly, her footsteps echoing in the empty street. When she had conceived of her plan, she had not really thought about how dark and empty the night would be. It had seemed relevant only in that there would be no one about to see that she was walking out boldly without a maid or other companion. But now, as she hurried past the dark hulking shapes of the other houses, it occurred to her that a companion, even one as slight as her maid, would be reassuring.

She was not in general someone who frightened easily, but as she walked, the anger that had sent her hurrying out into the night began to ebb away, replaced by the realization that night was the time when thieves and other evildoers were afoot, going about their business. This was, of course, the best area of London and therefore should be much safer than any other place, but she could not help but remember the stories she had heard of gentlemen being followed home from taverns and attacked in their inebriated state. And surely, if someone was going to rob a wealthy household, now would be the time when the thief would be breaking in.

Moreover, even if there were no such robbers around, she knew that gentlemen, especially those in their cups, could be dangerous enough — and likely to assume that a woman alone on the street at night was not a decent woman at all, but in all likelihood one who sold her virtue on a routine basis. Callie had no desire to be mistaken for a barque of frailty plying her trade.

The sound of a carriage behind her made her start, but she did not look around, merely walked with as confident a stride as she could muster. Perhaps the occupant of the carriage would assume she was a man in a long cloak, not noticing the hem of her dress beneath it. Or perhaps he would not look out at all.

She let out a breath of relief as the carriage passed her, rattling over the bricks down the next block and disappearing around the corner. Callie hurried across the next intersection and on down the sidewalk.

The few blocks to Lady Haughston's home, so short a distance in ordinary circumstances, seemed frighteningly long now. Callie thought about turning back, but she told herself not to be a goose and forged on ahead.

In front of her, at the end of the block, a figure came around the corner, heading toward her. Callie hesitated, her heart leaping into her throat, and then she walked on slowly. If she were to turn and run now, she thought, it might cause the stranger to pursue her, if only because it would stir his curiosity.

Besides, there was something very puzzling about the man, something that made her go forward, squinting to see him better in the dim light. The man walking toward her did not wear a greatcoat or cloak or — how strange — even a hat. And though clearly he was a man, there was something odd about his manner of dress. His jacket was puffed at the sleeves, and his trousers were rather wide above his cuffed boots. He was not wearing the usual evening attire of a gentleman — or, indeed, the clothes of any sort of man she could identify. And he seemed to have stuck his cane through the side of his belt.

Her first thought was that he must be

several sheets to the wind, and her second was that . . . but *no, that was impossible!*

Callie came to a dead stop.

The man continued toward her at the same steady pace, and with each stride she became more and more certain that her eyes were not playing tricks on her.

"Lord Bromwell!" she exclaimed.

In the next moment she wished that she had not let out the words. She should, she thought, have turned around and headed straight back for her house. He would think she was a lunatic. No, worse than that, he might assume that she was a woman of loose morals. No sister of a duke would be suspected of selling herself, of course, but she knew that the likeliest reason for her to be out at this time of night was for some sort of romantic rendezvous. In a married woman, such behavior would be scandalous, but for a girl not yet married, it would be disastrous.

Her stomach sank at the realization that this man would probably now look upon her with contempt. And if he told anyone that he had seen her in these circumstances, her reputation would be ruined, her brother and family shadowed by the disgrace. Someone who knew her well would, she hoped, not assume that she was engaged in something reprehensible, and even if he thought poorly of her, many a gentleman would keep the story to himself in order to spare her family the shame.

But this man scarcely knew her. And, worse, Sinclair had treated the earl in an unfriendly manner; indeed, Callie would characterize her brother's attitude toward him as angry, even contemptuous. She hated to think how Sinclair had spoken to him after she left. Bromwell would have little reason to shield her or her brother; worse, he might gleefully seize this opportunity to get back at the duke.

And why had her brother acted that way? Sinclair's meddling and his cool assumption that he could tell her what to do had irritated her so much that she had not really stopped to wonder what reason he had had for being so upset that she'd been alone with this particular man. Was it Bromwell's reputation that alarmed her brother? Had the duke warned him off because he knew that the man had a history of seducing young females?

Her mind leapfrogged from one thought to another, each more disastrous than the last, in the instant that she stood there frozen. Her last thought, one that was purely wishful thinking, she knew, was that perhaps he had not recognized her voice and could not see her face inside the deep hood of her cloak. She could still turn and flee.

But in the next instant such hope vanished, for he started toward her, his face registering shock. "Lady Calandra? Is that you?"

Callie swallowed hard and squared her shoulders. She had to face this, whatever came; she must do what she could to keep the family name from being tainted by her impulsive behavior.

"Lord Bromwell. 'Tis no wonder that you are surprised." Her mind raced, trying to come up with a reasonable excuse for being there.

"Indeed, at first I thought my eyes were deceiving me." He stopped a foot away from her. "This cannot be right. You should not be out at this hour. Where is your family?"

Callie gestured back down the street. "They are in their beds. I — I could not sleep."

"So you came out for a stroll?" he asked, his raised eyebrows revealing the disbelief that his polite tone did not.

"I know you will think me very foolish," she said.

"Oh, no." He smiled. "I have a sister, and

I am aware of how confining the restrictions of Society are, how the rules weigh upon a young woman of spirit."

Callie could not help but smile back at him. Her fears had been foolish, she told herself. He seemed not at all disapproving of her actions; indeed, his smile, his face, his voice . . . all seemed both kind and understanding. Nor was there anything about him that bespoke the roué — no leer, no suggestive tone or improper suggestion.

"Then you will not . . . tell anyone . . . ?"

"About coming upon you walking?" he finished. "Of course not. There is little to remark on in meeting a young lady who is taking a stroll, is there?"

"No, there is not," Callie agreed, swept with relief.

"But, please, allow me to escort you back to your home." He politely offered her his arm.

"I am not going there. I am bound for Lady Haughston's house."

He looked a bit puzzled, but to Callie's relief he did not pursue the oddity of her deciding to take a stroll to Francesca's house at this time of night, but merely said, "Then I shall be happy to escort you to Lady Haughston's, if you will but show me the way. I am not, you may have guessed, well acquainted with London."

"I did not think that I had seen you before," Callie admitted, taking his arm and starting once more down the street.

"I have spent nearly all my time at my estate since coming into the title," he told her. "I am sorry to say that it was in a rather sorry state of affairs. I have not had a great deal of time for . . ." He shrugged.

"Frivolities?" she suggested.

He smiled, glancing at her. "I do not mean to imply that a life spent here is frivolous."

Callie grinned. "I take no offense, I assure you. Indeed, I know that a great deal of it *is* frivolous."

"There is nothing wrong with a little frivolity."

There was something quite exhilarating about walking along this way with this man — even their rather ordinary words seemed tinged with a feeling of daring and excitement. It was extremely rare for her to be alone with a man other than her brother for any length of time. And to be alone with any man at this time of night on a dark street was simply unheard of. Callie had never before done anything that would so shock everyone she knew. Yet she could not find it in herself to regret it. She did not, she realized with a little bit of surprise, even feel guilty or wrong. What she felt was free and fizzing with excitement.

Because she was a candid woman, she also knew that the way she felt inside did not come entirely from the adventure of being in this time and place. Indeed, most of the exhilaration bubbling up inside her had to do with this particular man.

She stole a sideways glance at him, taking in the hard straight line of his jaw, the upward swoop of his cheekbone, the faint shadow of beard that colored his cheek this late at night. There was something hard and powerful about him, not just in the obvious physical strength of his wide shoulders and tall frame, but in the air of confidence and competence he exuded. She sensed that, even as he smiled and talked to her, he was alert and watchful, his gray eyes always searching, his muscles tensed and ready. He was, she thought, the sort of man to whom people naturally turned in a crisis. But, conversely, she suspected that he was also not a man whom it was advisable to cross.

It occurred to her, with a little jolt, that in that way he was rather like her brother. Not as urbane as the duke and with a more roguish sort of charm. Still, she sensed that there was in him that same hard core that lay in Sinclair, a dark and immutable center that belied the aristocratic trappings and British gentility.

As if he sensed her eyes on him, he glanced over at her, his own eyes shadowed and dark. He did not smile or say anything, just looked at her, but Callie felt a sizzle of intense attraction snake down through her.

She looked away, afraid that her eyes would betray the sheer physicality of what she felt. Lord Bromwell unsettled her; she responded to him in a way she could not remember with any man. But the uncertainty, oddly, seemed to draw her rather than repel her. She wished that she knew what Sinclair disliked about this man, why he had reacted so sharply to seeing him with her.

"I must apologize for the way my brother acted," she began, again looking over at him.

He shrugged, seemingly unconcerned. "It is only natural for a brother to worry about his sister. To want to protect her. I understand, having a sister, also."

"I hope that you are not so heavy-handed about protecting her," Callie replied with a smile.

He chuckled. "Indeed not. I fear she would have my hide if I tried to tell her what to do. She is a little older than I, though she would not like to hear me tell anyone so, and she is more accustomed to telling me what to do than the other way 'round." The twinkle left his eyes, and there was steel in his voice, however, as he went on. "Still . . . I would despise any man who tried to harm her."

"I love my brother and my grandmother, but sometimes they can be a bit smothering," Callie admitted.

"Is their smothering why you are walking to Lady Haughston's by yourself so late at night?"

Callie hesitated, then answered noncommittally, "I am going to Lady Haughston's to ask her for a favor."

She was relieved when he did not point out that she had not actually answered his question . . . or that it was rather an odd time to be asking for a favor. She was all too aware of that fact herself. It had been foolish of her to strike out on her own as impulsively as she had. It had been only her good fortune that it was Lord Bromwell she met and not some ruffian.

"You must think me young and silly," she said, flushing a little. "Clearly I acted in the heat of anger."

"No." He smiled down into her face. "I find you young and very beautiful." He paused, then added, the mischievous sparkle once more in his gaze, "And perhaps something of a trial to your overprotective relatives."

Callie laughed. "No doubt I am."

She looked up and found it was terribly hard to look away. It took a conscious effort to pull her gaze from his, and she knew that she had stared at him far too long for politeness. Her throat was dry, and her mind seemed astonishingly blank. She cast about for something to say, telling herself that she was acting like a schoolgirl at her first dance.

"I see you are not wearing your hat," she said at last, groaning a little inwardly at the inanity of her comment.

"No, I left it behind. I found I could not bring myself to look quite that foolish on the street."

"Foolish! No!" she bantered. "I thought your hat was quite dashing."

She realized, with a little skip of her pulse, that she was flirting with him again, as she had earlier this evening. He responded in the same way, his voice light, yet laced with an underlying warmth and meaning, his eyes bright as he looked at her.

"You have not changed out of your attire, either." He reached out with his forefinger and pushed her hood back a little, exposing the downward dip of her Tudor cap in the front. "I am glad. 'Tis a fetching hat."

Callie realized that they had drifted to a halt, standing quite close together. His fingers still lingered at the edge of her hood.

"But I am glad you took off the mask," he continued, his voice turning husky. "Your face is far too lovely to hide even a part of it."

His fingertips brushed down her cheek, and Callie's breath caught in her throat. She thought that he was going to kiss her again, and her heart began to pound in her chest. She thought of the heat that had flared between them, the pressure of his lips on hers, velvet smooth and enticing, yet demanding, as well.

But then his hand fell away, and he turned, starting to walk again. Callie fell in beside him. Her pulse was racing, and her knees were a little wobbly. She wondered what he had felt, if desire had raced through him just then, or if it had been only on her side.

It did not take them long to reach the elegant house in which Francesca lived, and Callie's heart sank a little as they approached it. She forced a smile as she stopped at the foot of the steps before Francesca's door.

"We are here," she told him and extended her hand politely. "Thank you for escorting me. I hope I have not taken you too far out of your way."

"It was a pleasure," he assured her, taking her hand. But instead of bowing over it, he simply stood, holding it and looking down into her face. "But you must promise me not to do anything so dangerous again. You must send me a note if you plan any more midnight rambles. I promise I will come with you. To keep you safe."

"I assure you, I will be quite careful in the future. I will not need you."

"Are you sure?" He raised an eyebrow teasingly; then, with a swiftness that surprised her, he wrapped his other arm around her and pulled her to him, bending his head to kiss her.

Bromwell's kiss was everything she remembered, and more. His teeth were hard against her mouth, his tongue soft as it insinuated itself between her lips. He tasted a little of port and more of dark, beckoning hunger. Callie felt her knees sag, and she flung her arm around his neck, holding on, as she kissed him back.

His hand let go of hers and went to her back, sliding down along her cloak to the soft curve of her buttocks. His palm glided over the fleshy mound, fingertips digging in a little and lifting her up and into him. She felt the hard ridge of his desire against her softer flesh, and she was both startled and intrigued — even more so when she felt the wet heat of her own response blossoming between her legs.

She made a soft, eager noise, and heard the groan of his response. He lifted his head and stared down at her for a long moment, his eyes bright, a faint surprise mingling with desire on his face.

"No," he murmured. "I think I have it wrong — 'tis *you* who are dangerous." He took a breath and released it, letting her go as he stepped back. "I will bid you *adieu,* my lady." He removed himself another step, then flashed a grin at her as he said, "We will meet again. I promise it."

With that he turned and walked away, though Callie noticed that he paused in the shadow of a tree two doors down and turned back to watch her. It warmed her to realize that he was waiting to see that she got safely inside, while at the same time protecting her reputation by not appearing with her. Hiding a smile, she trotted up the few steps to Francesca's door. Taking a breath to calm her racing heart, she reached up and knocked.

Silence followed her knock, and for the first time it occurred to her that Francesca might not be at home. She could, indeed, still be at Aunt Odelia's party. After all, clearly Lord Bromwell had just been walking home. Or, of course, everyone in the house could already be asleep.

She reminded herself that eventually someone would hear the knock and answer the door, even if the household was abed. Francesca's butler would recognize her and let her in, however odd he might find her appearance on their doorstep at this hour.

Still, she was relieved when the door opened after a moment to reveal a slightly disheveled footman. At first he opened the door only a few inches; at the sight of only a young woman on the doorstep, his eyebrows flew up and he pulled the door wider.

"Miss?" he asked, looking bewildered.

"Lady Calandra Lilles," Callie told him, putting on her most dignified face.

He appeared a trifle dubious, but at that moment Francesca's butler appeared behind him, nightcap on and wrapped in a dressing gown. "My lady!" he exclaimed, then said sharply to the footman, "Step back, Cooper, and let her ladyship in."

"I am sorry to appear at such a late hour, Fenton," Callie told the butler as she stepped inside.

"Oh, my lady, do not even think such a

thing," Fenton replied. "You are always welcome in this house. Cooper will show you to the yellow sitting room while I inform Lady Haughston that you are here."

With a bow for her and a sharp nod to the footman, the butler bustled off up the stairs. Callie followed the footman into the small sitting room down the hall. It was not the grandest of the receiving rooms, but she knew that the small room was Francesca's favorite, its windows facing the tiny side garden and open to the morning sunlight. Also, because of its size, it was still rather warm from the banked coals of the evening fire.

Callie went to the fireplace to take advantage of its lingering warmth. Only a few moments passed before Francesca hurried into the room, tying the sash of her brocade dressing gown as she came. Her long blond hair tumbled down her back, and her pretty porcelain face was marred with a worried frown.

"Callie? What happened?" she asked, striding forward, hands outstretched. "Is something the matter?"

"Oh! No!" Callie answered, abashed. "I am so sorry — I did not think. I did not mean to alarm you. There is nothing wrong."

Relief washed over Francesca's face. "Thank heaven! I thought — well, I am not sure what I thought." Her face pinkened a little, and she let out a deprecatory chuckle. "I am sorry. You must think me foolish."

"Oh, no," Callie hastened to reassure her. "Indeed, it is I who is foolish. I should not have come here at this hour. 'Tis only natural to assume that there is something wrong. I apologize for alarming you."

Francesca airily waved her apology away. "Come, sit down. Would you like some tea?"

"No, I have already put your household in enough of a stir," Callie answered. "I am fine."

She sat down on the edge of a chair, and Francesca took the end of the love seat at right angles to her, looking at her with a concerned air.

"Are you really?" Francesca asked astutely. "I take it there is not an emergency, but . . ." She looked around speakingly. "Did you come here alone?"

Callie nodded. "Yes. I know it was not the safest thing to do, but I just — I could not stay in that house a moment longer!"

Francesca looked startled. "Lilles House?"

Callie nodded. "I am sorry to burst in on you at this hour. You must wish me at the devil, but I did not know where else to turn."

"But of course you can come to me," Francesca told her, reaching out to take her hand. "And do not worry about the hour. I had not retired, anyway. I was just brushing out my hair. And there is nothing Fenton loves like a little excitement. I shouldn't wonder if he will come in here in a few minutes with tea and cakes."

"You are very kind." Callie smiled, then added, a little shyly, "You know, I have always thought of you as, well, almost a sister."

Francesca's face softened, and she squeezed the younger woman's hand. "Why, thank you, dear. I am touched. I have often felt the same way about you."

"Once," Callie told her somewhat ruefully, "I actually thought that you were going to become my sister. I cannot remember why, precisely, but I thought so for some weeks — until Sinclair set me straight, of course. I was very young."

A silence fell on them. Callie knew that Francesca was puzzled but politely waiting for her to explain her appearance after midnight.

Callie sighed. "I am sorry. Now that I am here, I'm not sure what to say." She paused, then went on, "The fact is, Sinclair and I had a terrific row this evening."

Francesca's eyes opened wide. "You and Rochford? Why, what happened? I thought that the two of you got along so well."

"We do, generally," Callie allowed. "But tonight . . ." She stopped, reluctant to air her family disagreements, even to someone she had known all her life.

"You need not tell me if you don't want to," Francesca assured her kindly. "We can just talk about — oh, Lady Odelia's party, for instance. It was quite a success, wouldn't you say?"

"Yes, it was." Callie grinned at the other woman. "And you are the consummate hostess. But I need to tell you. I must tell someone, and I — I think that perhaps you could help me, if you are willing to."

"Why, of course," Francesca replied, her curiosity fully aroused now. "Just tell me, then. Do not worry about dressing it up nicely. I have known your brother even longer than I have known you, and I dare swear nothing you tell me will shock me."

"Oh, it is not shocking," Callie hastened to tell her. "It is all quite ordinary, really. It is just that I have never known Sinclair to be so, well, so high-handed."

"Ah."

"Well, at least, not with me," Callie went on. "He was excessively rude to a gentleman with whom I danced, a man whom even Grandmother said was a perfectly acceptable suitor. And he treated me — he treated me as if I were a child!" Heat rose in Callie's cheeks at the memory, and her voice roughened with the remembered shame and anger. "I know I should not have been out on the terrace with him, but it was not the earl's fault. Indeed, he helped me with a man who was being importunate. But Rochford would not even let me explain. He just told me to leave, as if I were a five-year-old being sent to her room without supper. I was humiliated."

"I am sure you were," Francesca sympathized. "No doubt Rochford will realize, when he has had a chance to calm down —"

"Oh, pray, do not take his part, too!" Callie cried.

"No, dear, of course not. I am sure he acted abominably. Men frequently do, I have found. But surely, when he reflects on it, he will be sorry he was so hasty."

"I sincerely doubt it," Callie responded with some bitterness. "I tried to talk to him about it when we got home. But he still refused to give me any sort of explanation.

All he would say is that he acted in my best interests — and I am supposed to be content with that!"

"Mmm. Most annoying," Francesca agreed.

"Then my grandmother joined in, telling me how he was right, and that I have to do as he says. She went on about how I am under his control until I marry. And, of course, it goes without saying that I am under *her* control, as well."

Francesca, who was well-acquainted with the dowager duchess, nodded sympathetically. "It is no wonder that you were upset."

Callie let out a gusty sigh of relief. "I knew that you would understand!"

"I do. It is very hard having your relatives tell you what to do."

Now that she had unburdened herself and had met with Francesca's ready sympathy and understanding, perversely, Callie thought perhaps she did sound a bit childish. She gave the other woman a sheepish grin and said, "I am sorry. There is no reason to inflict all this upon you. It is just . . . I am so tired of the rules and restrictions. Grandmother has been living with us the whole winter, talking about how old I am and still unmarried. Even Aunt Odelia tonight told me I was on the verge of becoming an ape-leader!"

Francesca made a face. "You must not let Lady Pencully bully you into anything. I know that is easier said than done, for, frankly, Lady Odelia scares me silly. I find 'tis best simply to avoid her as much as possible."

"Yes, but she is not your great-aunt. Anyway, I don't mind her so much. At least she does not go on and on about one's duty and being responsible and not letting the family down. Not doing anything that might reflect badly on the duke or on the family."

"Families can be a terrible burden," Francesca said in a heartfelt voice. "My mother pushed me to make a good match my first year out."

"What did you do?" Callie asked curiously.

Francesca shrugged. "I disappointed her. But it was neither the first time nor the last, I assure you."

"I get so tired of trying to please other people."

"Perhaps you have been trying to please too many other people too much of the time," Francesca suggested. "Perhaps you need to think about yourself, instead."

"That is exactly why I came to you!" Callie cried. "I knew you were the person

112

to help me."

"I don't understand," Francesca said, puzzled. "I will certainly help you if I can, but I am afraid my opinion counts for little with either Rochford or the duchess."

"Oh, no, I do not want you to talk to them. I want you to help me find a husband."

CHAPTER FIVE

Francesca stared at her visitor blankly. "Pardon me?"

"I have decided to marry, and everyone assures me that you are the person to turn to when one is looking for a husband."

"But, Callie . . ." Francesca looked dubious. "I thought that you were upset because your grandmother and Lady Odelia were pushing you to marry. It sounds to me as if you are simply trying to please them again."

"No. Truly, I am not," Callie told her earnestly. "You see, it is not that I am against marriage. I am not a bluestocking who would rather spend my life quietly reading than marry. And I am not independent like Irene, or wary of tying my life to a man's. I want to marry. I want to have a husband and children and a home of my own. Don't you see? I do not want to spend the rest of my life as Rochford's sister or the duchess's granddaughter. I want my own life. And the only way I can have that is to marry."

"But, surely, if you wanted to be on your own . . . you are over twenty-one and in possession of an ample fortune."

"Are you suggesting that I set up my own household?" Callie asked wryly. "And have the entire *beau monde* asking what has happened to set Rochford and me at odds with each other? Or listen to my grandmother lecturing me on my ingratitude, and my duty to my brother and to her? I have no wish to break with my family. I only want to have a life apart from them. To be free from the restrictions. But I would still have them all even if I had my own household. I would have to hire an older companion, preferably a widow, to live with me, and I would still be a young unmarried woman, unable to go anywhere or do anything on my own. You know what it is like, Francesca. It is not until you are married that you have the slightest freedom at all. I would so love to have a green ball gown. Or one of deep royal blue. Or any color other than this everlasting white!"

Francesca began to chuckle. "I remember that feeling. But you can hardly want to marry just to be able to wear royal blue."

"Sometimes I think I might," Callie retorted, then sighed. "But of course it is not just that. I want to be married. I feel sometimes as if I am bobbing along going nowhere, simply keeping pace, waiting for my life to begin. I want to start my life."

Francesca leaned forward earnestly. "But, surely, my dear, you must have an ample amount of suitors. I would think you would only have to beckon and a dozen men would be on your doorstep, asking Rochford for your hand."

"Oh, I have had no lack of suitors," Callie admitted with a sigh. "But all too often they have been fortune hunters. There are other men, I think, who are actually reluctant to even approach me because of who I am. They do not want to be seen as opportunists, or they think that I would never consider them because they haven't the proper amount of wealth or a noble-enough name. People assume, without even meeting me, that I am very high in the instep. And I am not, you know."

"No, you are not."

"And others are frightened off by Rochford. It is all very well when the suitor is a fortune hunter or someone I cannot bear, but Sinclair is so intimidating that he scares off perfectly nice young men, as well."

"The duke can be a trifle daunting,"

Francesca admitted dryly.

"Humph. That is putting it mildly. If I take him to task about it, he just puts on his 'duke' face —" Callie drew her pretty features into a haughty mask "— and tells me that he has my best interests at heart."

Francesca could not help but laugh. "Yes, I know that face well. He uses it whenever he does not want to be questioned."

"Exactly."

"Do you . . . perhaps . . . have some particular man in mind for a suitor?" Francesca asked delicately.

"Oh, no," Callie responded quickly, though her mind leapt unbidden to Lord Bromwell. Could he be someone whom she would want to marry?

There was something compelling about him, something more than his good looks or warm smile. When she was with him, she felt different — brighter, happier, as if she glowed. But, of course, she knew that it was foolish to even think of him and marriage in the same thought. Why, she barely knew the man, and, anyway, her brother clearly disliked him.

Callie shook her head for emphasis.

Francesca cast her a shrewd look, but said nothing. When Callie did not continue, Francesca began carefully, "Do you not think that you might want to wait a while? You are not, after all, past the age of marrying. Why, Irene and Constance both married after twenty-five, and you have not yet passed three-and-twenty. You need not jump into anything. The right man for you may well appear."

Callie smiled impishly as she asked, "You mean that I might yet fall in love? Be swept off my feet by a handsome stranger?" Again her thoughts slid involuntarily to the stranger she had met tonight, but she quickly pulled them back. This was not, she reminded herself, about him. Not at all.

She shook her head, saying, "I used to think that such a thing would happen to me. When I was seventeen or eighteen, looking at my first Season." She shrugged. "But it did not take me long, being in the *ton,* to realize how unlikely that was. I have met many eligible men, and there have been none who have stirred my heart. Oh, I have fancied one or two, at least for a little while. I flirted a little, and danced with them, listened to their flatteries, and for a week or two I would think 'perhaps this man will be the one.' But he never was. After a time, I began to see this thing that was wrong about him, or notice a trait that grated on me. Before long, I began to wonder what I had ever seen in him."

Her face turned a trifle sad as she went on, "I think perhaps the people in my family simply are not the sort to fall in love. Look at Rochford — he has been the object of every matchmaking mama in the city, and he has never fallen prey to love."

"No, I suppose he has not, has he?" Francesca murmured.

"And can you imagine the duchess ever forgetting herself so much as to indulge in such a plebian emotion? I am sure she married my grandfather only because it was the most advantageous match."

Francesca had to chuckle. "It *is* difficult to picture the duchess carried away by love."

"Sometimes I wonder if there is something missing in us. But perhaps it is easier to be as Sinclair and I are. My mother loved my father greatly. She never stopped grieving for him until the day she died. I think she was almost happy to die so she could be reunited with him. It seems as though all I can remember of her is sadness. She passed through the days like a ghost, a shell whose heart had been stolen from her." Callie shook her head. "I think perhaps it is better to be heartwhole."

"Perhaps," Francesca agreed. "Still, when one looks at Constance and Dominic . . ."

A broad smile spread across Callie's face. "They are so obviously in love, the very air seems brighter around them. It must be thrilling to feel that way about someone."

"Yes, it must," Francesca agreed.

Callie looked a little wistful. "Have you ever been in love that way?"

"I thought I was," Francesca replied wryly.

Callie glanced at her and quickly colored. "Oh! I am so sorry. I did not mean — how thoughtless and rude of me. I quite forgot that you had been married."

"Mmm. More and more nowadays, I forget it, as well," Francesca told her.

There was something in the other woman's face that told Callie that Francesca preferred to forget her marriage altogether.

"I am sorry," Callie said again, leaning forward impulsively and taking Francesca's hand.

She had never known Francesca's husband very well, as he had died the year of Callie's first Season, and he had only rarely come to Redfields with Francesca when she visited her family there. But Callie had the distinct impression, though she wasn't sure why, that her brother disliked the man, and she had heard her grandmother remark on one occasion that Francesca had had occasion to rue the day she married Lord

Haughston.

"Do not fret yourself," Francesca told Callie with a squeeze of her hand. "Anyway, we are not here to discuss me. We are talking about you."

Callie released the other woman's hand and sat back, politely following Francesca's change of subject. "All right. Will you help me?"

"Of course I will. You should not even wonder about that. However, I am not sure what I can do that you and your grandmother could not do just as easily. The duchess knows everyone in the *ton*. And you certainly need no assistance on matters of style or charm."

"It is very kind of you to say so. But my grandmother has assured me that you have a golden touch when it comes to finding someone a mate. Why, just look at the last few months. Since last Season you have brought together two couples — and very happy ones, as well."

"I think the fact that Constance and Irene found the loves of their lives had more to do with them and their husbands than it did with me." Francesca let out a little chuckle. "Indeed, I had intended Constance for a different man altogether."

"I suspect that you downplay your own

role in the matter," Callie responded. "I am well aware that in all things regarding Society, you are an expert. I am certain that there is no one who could be of more aid to me in this endeavor than you. My grandmother knows many eligible men, 'tis true, and she is more than diligent about introducing them to me. But her standards are not mine. Her considerations are solely wealth and family and title, without any regard to looks or compatibility or temperament. I doubt that she even wonders whether a prospective husband has a sense of humor. But you know what people are like, not just their place in Society. Why, you realized how well suited Gideon and Irene were — even before she saw it."

"Ah, but I was not determined *not* to see it, as Irene was," Francesca told her.

"But you understand what I am saying, don't you?"

Francesca nodded. "Yes. You wish to find a husband who suits *you,* not your grandmother."

"Exactly. Not my grandmother or my brother or the *ton.* Just me."

"I hope that you are not putting too much faith in my abilities," Francesca said. "But I will certainly help you in any way that I can."

"Good." Callie grinned at her. "I am so glad you said that, for, you see, I have another — even larger — favor to beg of you."

Francesca's brows rose inquiringly. "But of course. You have only to ask."

" 'Tis terribly rude of me, I know, but I — it would be ever so nice if we could begin our search soon. And I must ask — that is, would you be so kind as to . . . to allow me to stay with you?" Bright spots of color stained her cheeks, and before Francesca could even speak, she hurried on. "Sinclair intends to return to the estate when he finishes his business in London. But I would like to stay here and begin my project at once. I cannot remain at Lilles House without a chaperone, of course, and while my grandmother might be persuaded to stay with me, well — frankly, I do not want her to. I don't want her looking over my shoulder the whole time, telling me about this man or the other, any more than I want to retire to Marcastle and listen to her lecture me about doing my duty."

"Perfectly understandable," Francesca replied. "Of course you may stay with me. It will be quite fun. We can plan our campaign and go shopping. Look over all the suitable candidates. It will be good to get a head start on the Season, and I will enjoy having you here. But will that meet with Rochford's approval?"

"I am sure it will," Callie told her, looking surprised. "Why ever would it not? Sinclair is not happy with me at the moment, but I do not think he would go so far as to deny me a visit with you. I am sure that you are someone whom he would accept as a chaperone for me. And what could my grandmother possibly say after she has been singing your praises to me?"

"Very clever. I will call upon the duchess tomorrow to extend my invitation."

"Thank you!" Callie exclaimed. "You are so very, very kind."

"Nonsense. I will thoroughly enjoy having you here. It is quite dull, really, until the Season begins, and having a friend here will make it ever so much livelier. Besides, we shall have a project!" Francesca smiled. "Now," she said decisively, rising to her feet, "I think it is time we got a little sleep. Won't you stay here the night? I shall send a note 'round to the duchess that you are here with me so that they will not worry, shall I?"

"I left a note for Sinclair on my pillow, so that they would not worry about me if they woke and found me gone." Callie smiled at her a little shamefacedly. "No doubt they will probably worry anyway. I should not have left so impulsively. It was just that I felt as if I might burst if I had to stay there another instant!"

"I understand exactly how you felt," Francesca assured her. "And it was thoughtful of you to leave a letter. Why don't I just pen another little note telling him that you reached my house, and are quite safe and well?"

"Thank you. You are very kind." Callie grinned a little mischievously. "Especially since you are doubtless laying the way for a visit from my brother bright and early tomorrow morning."

Francesca was not surprised to find that Callie's words were prophetic. Her maid awakened her the next morning with word that the duke himself was downstairs.

"Looking dark as thunder, too," Maisie added. "Fenton didn't dare tell him you were not receiving yet, so he set him in the front drawing room. The way he looked, though, we had better make quick work out of getting you ready or he'll be up here, knocking on your door."

"Do not worry," Francesca assured her. "The duke would never commit such a vulgar breach of etiquette, even if the house were burning. He would say, 'Pray tell your mistress that there is a slight problem with a fire downstairs.' "

Maisie giggled as she pulled out a simple morning dress and held it out for Francesca. "If you say so, my lady, but I warn you, he's looking that grim."

Francesca sighed. She had a sinking feeling that Rochford would not approve of Callie's notion of staying with her, even until the Season began. Despite what Callie had told her, she had never gotten the impression that Rochford would regard her as a proper chaperone for his younger sister. Indeed, if anyone had asked her how the duke viewed her, she would have said that she imagined he found her frivolous. Rochford had always held a weightier view of the world than she.

Francesca washed her face and slipped into the dress her maid had chosen, then let Maisie quickly brush her hair and twist it up into a simple knot. It was not her usual sort of toilette before receiving callers, and she hated to appear anything but her best before Rochford, but it could not be helped.

She found the duke standing at the window of the drawing room, staring out into the street, his hands linked behind his back. His dark blue coat and fawn trousers were as impeccable as ever, his Weston boots as polished, his cravat as expertly tied, his short black hair as neatly cut and styled, but the face he turned to her was, as Maisie had reported, grim, and his dark eyes beneath the sharp black brows were worried.

"Rochford. Good morning," she said, coming forward to give him her hand.

"I apologize for the early hour, Lady Francesca," he replied stiffly, moving to her and bowing over her hand.

"Do not worry. I realize that you are . . . concerned." She sat down and waved him toward the sofa that faced her chair.

"Yes." His jaw tightened. "I — I trust that Lady Calandra is well."

"Oh, yes. She is still asleep. I thought it best if you and I had a discussion together first."

He nodded, avoiding her eyes as he said, "I appreciate the note you sent. I would have been most worried this morning if I had not already known that she was safe and sound at your house."

Francesca knew that it was an indication of the duke's inner turmoil that he, usually the most urbane and smoothest of conversationalists, was speaking in such a stiff and uncomfortable way. She could not help but feel a rush of sympathy for the man.

Before she could speak, he went on, "It was very good of you to take her in, and I must apologize for her imposing on your good nature in this way."

"Nonsense," Francesca told him firmly. "It was not an imposition, and Callie is always welcome in my home. I am very glad that she felt she could come to me."

His expression grew even more wooden, if that was possible, as he said, "I presume that Callie told you that she and I . . . had a disagreement."

"She did."

He looked over at her, seemed about to speak, then released a sigh and let himself sag back against the sofa. "The devil take it, Francesca," he said gruffly. "I think I have misstepped badly with the girl."

"Yes, you may have."

He cut his eyes toward her, and for a moment amusement lifted his features, so that he looked more himself. "My dear Francesca, you might at least have made a pretense of protesting my admission of incompetence."

Francesca chuckled. "Ah, but what would be the point in that?"

She leaned across to him, putting her hand on his arm sympathetically. "Do not worry. I am sure that you have not ruined yourself with your sister. Callie clearly loves you, and it worries *her,* too, that you and she were at odds."

"I hope you are right," he replied with more fervor than he normally showed. "I know that I was too severe. I handled the whole thing badly. I wanted only to protect her."

Francesca shrugged. "I have been told by Dom that that is simply the way brothers are. It is very nice at times. I can tell you that as a sister. I can also tell you that there are moments when a brother's protectiveness can be excessively annoying. Callie is a levelheaded young woman, you know, nor is she just out of the schoolroom. I am sure that she would not do anything foolish."

"It was not Callie I did not trust," Rochford retorted darkly. "It was the man with her."

Francesca frowned. "Who was it that was so terrible? Callie thought that he was an eligible young gentleman."

He started to speak, then glanced at her and just as quickly looked away. "I suppose he is. But he does not wish me well, I think." He shook his head, as though dismissing it all. "It was nothing, really. It was just that when I saw him there with her . . .

129

Well, I may have spoken too harshly. I can only hope that Callie will not hold it against me forever."

"I am sure she will not." Francesca answered almost absently, her mind busy picking over the fact that he had not given her the man's name.

Why was Sinclair reluctant to reveal the man's identity? She cast about for someone who was known to be an enemy to Rochford, but, quite frankly, she could not come up with anyone. Rochford was not the sort of man whom anyone wanted to cross. Indeed, people were typically much more interested in currying favor with him than setting him against them. And, actually, he had not said that the man was an enemy, only that he did not think the man wished him well.

All she could think was that, in that typically masculine and very annoying way, Rochford felt that whatever was wrong with the man was something he deemed too indelicate for feminine ears. It was, she thought, easy to see why Callie had become irritated.

"I have a thought," she offered. "Something that might help you and Callie to . . . get over this little rough patch."

"Indeed." He turned his eyes on her

somewhat warily.

Francesca laughed. "Do not look at me with such suspicion, I beg you. 'Tis nothing terrible. I invited Callie to stay here in London with me, at least until the Season starts. Indeed, through the Season, if it is all right with you or you do not wish to return to London for the whole time. I think that Callie is a little bored at Marcastle, and the duchess . . . well . . ."

She trailed off, and Rochford could not keep from grinning. "Ah, yes, the duchess."

"Callie is a lively young girl, and I am sure it must be tiring for the duchess to have to look after her," Francesca continued diplomatically. "And Callie, while she appreciates all that her grandmother has done for her, chafes a bit under her control, I think."

"Yes, I know, and it is no wonder. Grandmother rarely finds a situation that she cannot worsen by lecturing. I know she has been wearing on Callie's nerves this winter. I have no idea why she took it into her head to spend so long with us instead of taking the waters at Bath with her friends."

"She is, it seems, growing anxious about Callie's unmarried state."

Rochford let out a groan. "She is enough to make a person swear off marriage altogether just to spite her." He cast Francesca a faintly abashed look. "You will think me ungrateful, I know, to speak in such a way about her, after she has done so much for Callie and me — taking us on when she should have been settling down to a well-deserved old age of leisure. But one cannot live one's life according to her dictates."

"Do not expect sympathy from me, Rochford. You know my parents," Francesca responded lightly. "Still, as devoted and dutiful as I know the duchess to be, I think she would welcome a little respite from chaperoning a lively young woman. I, on the other hand, would welcome the company. The city is always dull at this time of year. Callie and I could visit the shops and attend the theater. It will be ever so much more enjoyable to have someone with me."

The duke narrowed his eyes as he looked at her. "Did my sister put you up to this?"

Francesca laughed. "You are far too suspicious. Of course Callie is not averse to the scheme, but I can assure you that I would very much enjoy her company, as well. Sometimes it is a trifle lonely here by myself."

He gazed at her consideringly. Then, somewhat to Francesca's surprise, he shrugged and said, almost off-handedly, "Of course, if you and Callie wish it, I am quite willing for her to stay with you. You know, despite what Callie may have said, she does not really have to obtain my permission to visit a friend for a few weeks. She is, after all, over twenty-one. And I am not a tyrant."

"I am sure you are not," Francesca replied, then added, with the charming little catlike grin that was her trademark, "But do not forget, I have known you long enough to point out that you can be a trifle, shall we say, imperious?"

"Oh, really?" His straight black brows soared upward. "I challenge you to produce an example of it."

"I could produce a hundred of them," she retorted. "I remember when I was ten and rode my pony onto your drive and frightened that horrid peacock that used to parade about the front lawn of your house. And you told me that Dancy Park was your land, and you would not have me disturbing your bird."

"Good Gad, I had forgotten about that peacock," he said, and laughed. "Damned noisy thing. Did I really say that? I am surprised I did not cheer you on. Well, if you are going to dig back so far for examples, I should point out that you were a rag-mannered child, and I am sure that if I told you what to do, you no doubt needed to be told."

Francesca protested, laughing, and they were bantering in this lighthearted way when Callie came hurrying into the room. She stopped, taking in the scene, and smiled with relief.

When the maid had brought in her tea and toast and had told her that the duke was downstairs this early in the morning, Callie had feared the worst. Dreading the prospect of another scene with Rochford, but determined not to allow Francesca to bear the brunt of his displeasure, she had dressed as quickly as she could and almost run down to the drawing room. Now, surveying the tableau before her, she told herself that she should have remembered that Lady Francesca was an expert at turning almost any social disaster into a triumph. No doubt charming an irate duke was an easy task for her.

"Hallo, Rochford," Callie said a little shyly, still feeling a bit uneasy with him after their argument the night before, and entered the room.

He turned, smiling, at her voice. "Callie, my dear."

A knot in Callie's chest untwined, and she went to her brother, holding out her hands to him. "Oh, Sinclair, I am sorry for leaving the house like that last night. I am sure I worried you and Grandmother, and I should not have."

He took her hands in his and smiled down into her face. "Your grandmother does not even know about it. The footman brought me the note from Lady Haughston as soon as he received it, so I knew you were here and safe. I told the footman to inform your maid not to awaken you this morning, and I went to your room and retrieved your note. Then I left this morning before the duchess came down to breakfast. She will doubtless be somewhat surprised to find that you decided to accompany me on such an early call, but . . ." He shrugged and looked down at the dress that Francesca had lent her the evening before. "So unless you think that Grandmother will recognize that this dress is not yours, there should be no problem."

"One muslin morning dress is much like any other," Callie replied. "If she should notice, I will simply tell her that I had forgotten and left it at Lilles House last Season, and that is why she has not seen it on me recently."

"Clever minx." The duke grinned down at her fondly. "I suppose your ease in fabricating tales should make me nervous. But I think I will choose to ignore it. Now, Lady Francesca tells me that she has been good enough to invite you to stay with her until the Season starts. I told her I felt sure that you would enjoy that."

"Yes, I should, very much," Callie replied, smiling broadly. "I like Marcastle, but . . ."

"I know, I know, country life is beginning to pall. It is certainly all right with me if you stay here, though I must warn Lady Francesca that you will drag her through every shop on Bruton Street."

"Indeed, you wrong me!" Callie objected, but she was laughing.

"Well, you had best get on your cloak and bonnet so that we can go home and you can set to packing for your visit. No doubt you will also have a list for the housekeeper of things that she must send in addition."

"Oh, no," Callie retorted. "I shall simply purchase new things."

With another sparkling grin, she turned and left the room, hurrying on light feet back upstairs. Rochford turned to Francesca.

"Do not say I did not warn you."

"I think that I will be able to hold my own when it comes to shopping," Francesca responded, smiling.

"Callie has her own allowance, and she

can draw on her monies for clothes and such," he told her. "But, of course, I will direct my man of business to provide an adequate amount for her household expenses."

Francesca stiffened. She could feel a flush rising in her cheeks. *Was it possible that Rochford suspected her financial straits? Had he guessed how perilously close to destitution Lord Haughston had left her when he died five years ago? How closely she still skated to the edge of poverty, eking out a living from the "gifts" given her by grateful parents for guiding their daughters through the dangerous shoals of the Season?*

"Nonsense," she told him coolly. "I would not allow a guest to pay for her upkeep. Whatever can you mean?"

Rochford drew himself up to his full height, which was considerable, and looked down at her with an expression of frozen hauteur — so exactly the "duke face" that Callie had described last night that Francesca almost giggled despite her embarrassment.

"My dear Lady Haughston," he said, as if he had not known her since she was a child in leading strings. "Do you honestly believe that I am so rag-mannered as to foist my sister upon you — and you need not protest, because I know quite well that it was Callie who asked to stay with you, not the other way around — and then expect you to house and feed her, all at your own expense?"

"Of course I do not —" Francesca began, then stopped. "I mean . . ." How was it that Rochford could always make one feel as if one were in the wrong, no matter how certain one was that she was right? His steady, haughty gaze made her want to twist and squirm, and she could not help but wonder if she had indeed offended the man.

"Very well, then," the duke said, giving her a nod. "It is all settled."

"But —"

"I will have my man of business make the appropriate arrangements with your butler," he concluded. "Now, I must bid you farewell."

He spent the short period until Callie came back downstairs thanking Francesca again for taking in his sister, apologizing for the early hour of his call, and in general keeping up a steady stream of social niceties. Then, with a graceful bow, he left the house with his sister, leaving Francesca to wonder exactly which of them had managed to outsmart the other.

CHAPTER SIX

Her return to Lilles House was not as bad as Callie had expected. Her brother did not speak again of the incident that had set this whole thing in motion, and she, too, was happy to talk about other things. And since Sinclair had kindly and cleverly hidden from the duchess that she had not slept in her room the night before, she did not have to endure a long lecture from her grandmother.

The duchess was somewhat surprised to hear that they had called upon Lady Haughston so early, and even more so when she was told of Francesca's invitation to Callie to stay with her. She protested that she could not imagine why Callie would prefer to stay in London in the dull months before the Season began rather than return to Marcastle. But her argument was merely perfunctory, and Callie was sure that she had seen a glimpse of relief in the duchess's face.

By the end of the day, her grandmother was musing about going on to Bath to visit her friends for the next few months, instead of returning to Marcastle with Rochford.

It was easy enough to supervise the packing, as Callie would take essentially what she had brought, along with the addition of some clothes that were here at their town house. There were a few things that she decided to have shipped from home, as her brother had predicted, so she had to write out a list for him to give the housekeeper at Marcastle. But it took only a little time and effort, and she was able to take leave of her grandmother and brother that evening and go to Francesca's.

Sinclair accompanied her, as she had known he would, but he did not stay long, merely greeting Francesca, bidding Callie farewell, and taking Francesca's butler aside for a brief talk that seemed to leave both of them well-satisfied.

Callie and Francesca spent the rest of the evening ensconced in Francesca's comfortable little sitting room, discussing their plans for the upcoming visit. The first order of business, they agreed, was to shop for clothes. After all, one could scarcely begin the Season in frocks from last year, and if one was starting the Season early, then it only stood to reason that one must have one's clothes early.

Thus, they set out the very first morning of Callie's stay for Bruton and Conduit Streets, home to the finest milliners and modistes, not returning until late that afternoon, both of them tired and chilled by the damp cold of the day, but thoroughly satisfied.

"I think we have visited every milliner in this city," Callie commented with a sigh, gratefully taking the cup of tea that Francesca's efficient butler had brought within moments after their return.

"If we have not, we soon will," Francesca promised. "I still have not found exactly what I want for summer afternoons. But I thought we did very nicely with the dresses."

"Yes, though I do wish I could wear something besides white," Callie grumbled. "I would so love a green ball gown — or even one of palest pink."

Francesca laughed. "Just be glad that white looks fetching on you, with that glorious black hair and strawberries-and-cream skin. Think of how awful it is for us blondes. *We* look positively insipid."

Callie smiled at the other woman. "I am quite sure that you never faded away in *any* dress. Everyone knows that you have been the reigning beauty of London since your presentation."

"Thank you, my dear, that is lovely to hear, although I am sure it is not true. Anyway, I thought that the blue accents on the satin ball gown quite made up for its being white."

"You are right." Callie thought of the sketch she had chosen for the gleaming white satin — an overskirt looped up over a froth of white tulle ruffles, each high point of the drapery anchored with a baby blue rosette, with a blue satin sash around the high waist, and blue ribbons bordering the cap sleeves of the bodice. "And the lace and seed pearls on the other ball gown are lovely, too. Besides, I should never complain about anything when I am shopping with you. It is ever so much nicer than going with my grandmother. She always insists on raising the necklines."

"Oh, dear." Francesca made a moue of distress. "Will I be in trouble with the duchess now? I did not think any of the gowns were immodestly low."

"They were not," Callie assured her. "Everyone, even the youngest girl making her first Season, shows more of their bosom than Grandmother allows me. I cannot imagine why. In her time, they wore much more daring necklines. But even she will not dare to say anything about a dress that you approved. She has always told me that you have the best sense of style of anyone in the *ton.*"

"That is a compliment to treasure. Everyone knows the Duchess of Rochford is the epitome of elegance."

The two women spent a few more minutes happily going over their fashion coups, enjoying the bargains in ribbons, buttons, trims and shawls from Grafton's almost as much as the pelisses and dresses from the finest modistes. Fenton had brought in a tray of small cakes and sandwiches along with the tea, and they hungrily downed them as they talked, washing everything down with sweet milky tea.

Finally, reaching the end of the repast as well as of their recounting of their purchases, Francesca set her teacup down and said, "Now, if you are tired and do not wish to, you must tell me, but I had thought that we might begin our little project this evening by going to the theater."

"Oh, no, I am quite revived," Callie assured her, her dark eyes brightening with interest. "That sounds delightful."

"Good. I shall send a note round to Sir Lucien. One can always count on him as an escort," Francesca said, getting up and suiting her action to her words by sitting down at the small desk beside the window and beginning to scribble a note to her friend. "I thought it would give us a chance to do a spot of reconnoitering. See just what bachelors out there are worth meeting. And, of course, we need to decide exactly what requirements we are looking for in a husband for you."

"I am not choosy, really," Callie told her. "He does not have to be wealthy or come from the highest of families. My grandmother is always telling me that I am distressingly egalitarian." She sighed. "Though I suppose a certain amount of wealth and name are necessary to make sure he is not marrying me for my money and family."

"And looks?"

"Are not that important, either, although it would be nice if he were not terrible to look at. He need not be handsome — but I like a strong face. And intelligent eyes." The image of gray eyes under straight dark brows came unbidden to her mind. She had never realized, Callie thought, until she met him, but the Earl of Bromwell's face was precisely the sort of masculine visage that drew her. But, of course, she reminded herself, she was not foolish enough to choose a spouse on the basis of looks.

"He must be easy to talk to," Callie told Francesca firmly. "And have a sense of humor. I could not abide a husband who was always serious. Nor do I want a scholar. So many of Rochford's friends bore me to tears, the way they go on and on about history and such." She cast the other woman a sheepish glance and chuckled. "I must sound quite shallow."

"Not at all. I am sure Rochford's scholarly friends would have the same effect on me." Francesca blew on the note to hasten the drying of the ink, then folded and sealed it.

"But I don't want a dullard, either," Callie pointed out. "I mean, Rochford is not boring until he gets around one of those men with whom he corresponds. Scientists and historians and such. But I would not want someone who did not know how to make a clever rejoinder or could not understand what Sinclair is talking about, either." She paused. "Oh, dear, I am beginning to think that I have a great many more requirements than I thought."

"And well you should. You are, dear girl, a prize in the marriage mart. It should require a special man to win you. Besides, it makes it far easier to winnow through the prospects. Why, simply refusing dullards will cross out a large number of the men of the *ton*."

"You are wicked," Callie told her, laughing.

"Merely truthful," Francesca responded as she rose from her desk and went to pull the bell cord to summon a servant. "There, I have invited Sir Lucien to dine with us before the theater."

Even though Sir Lucien was her dear friend and most faithful escort, Francesca knew that it was always best to insure his company with a supper invitation. A confirmed bachelor and a man of impeccable style and taste, Sir Lucien's pockets were usually to let — due partly to the small size of his income and even more to the fact that he spent the major portion of that income on his clothes and the small but fashionably located rooms he let. Therefore, he was accustomed to dining out frequently, using his primary assets of good looks and good taste to maintain a steady supply of invitations from a number of hostesses.

The invitation sent, the two women went upstairs to prepare for the evening ahead. After all, the purpose of an evening at the theater was not the play, but the opportunity to see and be seen, and one needed to look one's best just as much as one would at a party.

A short nap with a cool lavender-soaked rag across her eyes was enough to refresh Callie and return her to her usual looks. She followed it with a bath, then dressed with the help of her maid, Belinda, choosing her favorite white evening dress, piped around the bottom of the overskirt and along the neckline with white braid. She wished that she could wear the dark green morocco slippers she had ordered just this afternoon, but, of course, they would not be finished for another few days, so she had to settle for a pair of brocade slippers. Her only jewelry was a single short strand of pearls with matching earrings. An elegant fan and long gloves would complete the outfit.

She sat down in front of her vanity, and her maid swept her hair up in a knot at the crown of her head, letting it fall down from the knot in several long curls, carefully formed with Callie's brush. In the front, around Callie's face, she allowed the shorter hair to frame her features in natural soft curls. Belinda had, Callie knew, been inspired to make her best effort on the hairdo because of the presence of Francesca's maid, Maisie, who was reputed to be an artist with hair. Callie thanked her, smiling, then went downstairs to join Francesca.

She found Sir Lucien sitting with her hostess, talking while they enjoyed a glass of sherry before supper. Sir Lucien sprang to his feet when Callie entered the room and executed a graceful bow.

"Lady Calandra! You can imagine my pleasure at being allowed to escort two such lovely ladies to the theater. The gods have indeed smiled upon me."

"Sir Lucien." Callie smiled at the man fondly.

Sir Lucien was urbane, witty and handsome, the perfect escort — and, Callie suspected, more interested in one's frock than in the woman inside it. Of course, no one would speak of such things before a young unmarried girl, but it had not taken Callie long to sense that Sir Lucien's flirtation and flatteries were more an enjoyable game to him than anything that contained real feeling. While he had a great appreciation of beauty in any form, whether it was a face or figure or the cut of one's dress, she had never witnessed in him the flash of heat that flared in some men's eyes when they looked at her. Lord Bromwell, for instance — there had been an intensity to his gaze, a palpable warmth that emanated from his body when he drew her close to kiss her.

"I am so glad you came," Callie told Sir Lucien, firmly putting aside her wayward thoughts of Lord Bromwell. "Although I fear our gain must be some other poor hostess's loss."

Sir Lucien gave a graceful shrug. "I was planning to attend Mrs. Doddington's musicale this evening, and I can only thank you for saving me from that. The woman always has excellent refreshments — poor Lethingham's been trying to steal her cook from under her nose for years. But her taste in music is execrable. And she always insists on her daughters contributing a set, which is more than one should have to bear, really."

He kept up this sort of light, entertaining chatter through much of dinner; it was, after all, one of the reasons why he never lacked for invitations — he could keep any dinner or party from becoming utterly dull. For Callie, fresh from the very quiet months at Marcastle, it was a welcome and informative reintroduction to London society. Sir Lucien knew the latest gossip about everyone and everything that happened in the *beau monde* — what gentleman was on the verge of having to flee the country to avoid debtors' prison, what lady's newest offspring was said to look remarkably unlike her husband, and which scion of what noble house was rumored to have challenged someone to a duel over a hand of cards.

He did not question Callie's early return to the city. To Sir Lucien's way of thinking, any sane person would leap at the chance to trade any bucolic estate, no matter how grand, for a stay in London. But later, when they had settled into their box in the theater, and Callie and Francesca had begun to discuss the possibilities around them in the audience, Sir Lucien became curious.

He leaned forward to look Callie full in the face and said, "My dear girl, unless my ears deceive me, you seem to be — is it possible — vetting the gentlemen here as marriage material?"

Callie blushed a little, but Francesca replied flippantly, "But of course, Lucien — what else do the ladies of London do? Every Season is another market."

"But Lady Calandra?" He raised a brow. "Can it be that you have decided to break the hearts of half of London and settle down in the married state?"

"I doubt it would be that tragic an event," Callie countered, smiling a little. "But, yes, I am considering it."

"Do you have a lucky man in mind? Or is

this Season to be an open tournament for your hand?"

"Lucien . . ." Francesca said warningly. "I do hope you are not planning to cast that news about. We shall have every adventurer in the city on our doorstep."

"My dear Francesca!" The man placed his hand over his heart, assuming an appalled expression. "How can you say so? Of course I will not say the slightest word, if you and Lady Calandra do not wish it. Besides . . ." A mischievous grin played about his lips. "It will be far too much fun to watch it all play out." He turned, raising the lorgnette that hung by a black silk ribbon from his lapel and making a survey of the audience. "Let us see, who are you considering? Bertram Westin? He is a devilishly handsome sort, but I have heard that he is far too fond of the cards."

"No, I have never really liked the man," Callie replied, casting a look around. She had been doing so as unobtrusively as possible since they arrived. She hoped it did not appear as if she was looking for someone in particular, though she was honest enough to admit to herself that she would not be displeased to see that Lord Bromwell was attending the play.

Not, of course, that she was considering

him as a prospect for marriage. Still, she had not been able to get the man out of her mind for the past few days, and she could not keep from surveying the crowd now and again, just to see if he had entered the theater.

"There are Lord and Lady Farrington," Francesca said, raising her fan to speak behind it. "The third box from the stage across from us. Their oldest son will inherit a fortune." She frowned. "Though one rarely sees him about. I wonder why."

"Shy, I hear," Sir Lucien supplied the answer. "It is said that he prefers, um, relationships of a more, shall we say, commercial nature? 'Tis easier than facing a line of young ladies, you see."

"Oh, dear," Francesca said. "Well, I suppose we shall have to cross him off the list."

"What about Sir Alastair Surton?" Sir Lucien asked, his glasses stopping on a man in the audience below them.

Callie let out a groan. "He is forever going on about his horses and his dogs. I like riding as much as anyone, but I would like some of my conversation to be about something else."

"True," Lucien agreed. "He is rather dull. I fear the selection is small until the Season starts."

"We are simply making a preliminary survey. A reconnaissance. Is that not what you call it?"

"Not I. Not much of a military sort, myself," Sir Lucien remarked.

Francesca reached out to give his arm a playful tap with her fan.

"You know, Lady Calandra," Sir Lucien said dryly. "You need not look far to find the perfect spouse. He is sitting right here in this box."

"You are putting yourself forth as a candidate?" Francesca asked, raising a brow skeptically. "Everyone knows you are a confirmed bachelor."

"Perhaps I simply have not had the right incentive," Sir Lucien protested, the twinkle in his eyes belying his words. "You must admit, ladies, that it would be difficult to find a more agreeable or entertaining man than myself. I am a marvelous dancer."

"That is true," Callie admitted, smiling.

"And who is better at talking to all one's old boring female relatives?"

"No one," Francesca agreed.

"And," he added triumphantly, "you would always have someone to advise you on your ball gowns."

"What more could one ask?" Callie said.

"The only problem is that you would have

153

to get married, Lucien," Francesca pointed out.

"That is a drawback," he conceded, then offered Callie a brilliant smile. "But in the case of one as beautiful as Lady Calandra, it would surely be worth the sacrifice."

Callie laughed. "Careful, Sir Lucien. Someday someone is going to take you up on one of your jests, and then what will you do?"

He cast a laughing sideways glance at her as he murmured, "There is always a trip to the Continent."

A smile still lingering on her lips, Callie turned to glance out over the audience again. Her eye was caught by movement as the door to one of the boxes opened and two men entered it, casually chatting. One of them was the Earl of Bromwell.

Callie's heart began to pound, and she quickly glanced away. She kept her face turned firmly from the box, letting some time pass before she made another slow survey of the house.

It was, indeed, her Cavalier of the other night, dressed more sedately in black jacket and breeches, a blindingly white shirtfront and cravat showing between the lapels of his jacket. He had taken off his greatcoat and now sat in one of the chairs, the other man beside him. His arm was on the ledge of the box before him, and he was half turned toward his companion. She could not see his expression. But she remembered well enough how he looked — the smile that started with a crinkling around his eyes and spread to his lips, the gray of his eyes that changed to silver or the dark color of a storm cloud depending on the emotion that touched his face.

Callie turned toward her friends. "Who are those gentlemen in the box to our right — almost in the center of the theater? One has dark hair, and the other is lighter, almost blond."

Francesca turned to scan the audience. "The box beside Lady Whittington and her daughter?"

Callie turned to check, and this time she found Lord Bromwell and his companion looking straight at her box. Color rushed into her cheeks. The earl smiled faintly and nodded to her.

"Yes," Callie said in a constrained voice and quickly looked back down at her hands.

"Do you know him?" Francesca asked, astonished.

"Not exactly. I — he was at Lady Pencully's party."

"Who wasn't?" Sir Lucien asked rhetorically as he, too, swiveled his head to gaze at the two men. "I do not recognize the dark one, but the other is Archibald Tilford." He glanced back at Callie. "He is not anyone for you to consider. Pleasant chap, but he lives on a stipend from his cousin — wait." Sir Lucien paused, frowning a little, and turned back to look once again at the other box. "Yes, that just might be his cousin. The Earl of Bromwell. If it is, *he* would definitely be a contender. I have met him only once, a few years back. Yes, that could be he."

"The Earl of Bromwell . . ." Francesca said consideringly. "I don't think — oh." She stiffened slightly. "Do you mean the brother of Lady Swithington?"

Sir Lucien nodded. "He is rarely in London. He went north to his estate in Yorkshire when he inherited — oh, a good ten years ago. Not long after I left Oxford. The old earl's pockets were pretty much to let when he died, but they say the son has recovered their fortune. Better than that, actually. I hear the man is positively wallowing in money now."

"How did he make all this money?" Callie asked.

Sir Lucien gave her a droll look. "My dear, I haven't the faintest idea. But I do know that the family does not like to discuss it.

156

The whiff of trade, you see."

"I cannot imagine why people feel they need to hide the fact that one makes money. Sinclair always says that he sees no reason why gentility should have to include poverty."

"For some, I fear, gentility is one's only asset," Sir Lucien replied.

"Alas, not a very marketable one," Francesca added wryly.

Francesca continued to study the man in the other box. He and his companion were no longer looking in their direction but were once again chatting. From time to time the earl glanced down at the playbill in his hand.

Finally Francesca said in a careful voice, "Do you wish to add him to your list of prospects?"

Callie shrugged, doing her best to look unconcerned, as if her stomach had not turned somersaults when he looked over at her. "I — the other night at the party he seemed . . . pleasant."

She looked over at Francesca. There was something in the other woman's eyes, an expression of — she was not sure what. Uneasiness, perhaps? Francesca glanced at Sir Lucien, then down at her hands.

"What?" Callie asked, straightening. "Do you know aught about this man? Is there some black spot in his past?"

"No. Indeed, I do not know him at all," Francesca assured her, shifting a little in her seat.

Callie narrowed her eyes, studying her, and Francesca went on, "I know his sister . . . slightly."

"You know something bad about her?"

"I — truly, I do not know her well," Francesca said. "I — she has lived for the past few years in Wales, I believe, at the estate of her aging husband. I have heard, however, that he has recently departed this world, and she is a widow. No doubt, she will now return to London to find another wealthy husband."

Callie recognized a distinct trace of venom in Francesca's voice, and she wondered at the cause of it. It was unlike Francesca to display even that much ugly emotion. She was normally one to turn aside a barb when someone else made it, or to couch her own remarks, even disparaging ones, in a light and witty way. But, clearly, she did not like the earl's sister. Callie would have liked to pursue the matter, but, just as clearly, it was not a topic that Francesca wished to discuss.

"Ah, look, the play is about to start," Francesca said, turning toward the stage with an air of relief.

Callie settled down to watch the play, as well, telling herself that she would delve into the subject of the earl's sister later, during the intermission, when Sir Lucien would doubtless leave to get them all refreshments.

The play was not a particularly exciting one, and Callie had trouble keeping her mind on the stage. She was aware of an urge to glance over at the earl's box, but she would not allow herself to do so. It would not do to let him see that she had an interest in him. But she could not keep her mind from going where it would, and her thoughts kept turning to the man.

Why had her brother objected to him? Francesca and Sir Lucien, two of the mainstays of the *ton,* had not even recognized him, and they were much more likely than Sinclair to know all the gossip. The earl could not be a well-known rake, which had been Callie's fear after the way Sinclair had reacted to his being with her on the terrace. If the earl was a man who was in the habit of seducing maidens, Callie was certain that Sir Lucien would know that fact, even if by some stretch of the imagination Francesca did not. Callie was also sure that Sir Lucien would have, at the very least, found a delicate way of warning her away from the man.

So, if there was no scandal attached to his name, why did Sinclair dislike him? He must know Lord Bromwell. But, according to Sir Lucien, the earl spent his time in Yorkshire on his estates, so Callie had no idea how Sinclair would even be acquainted with him. The duke had no land in Yorkshire that Callie knew of; certainly she had never gone there with him.

Perhaps at some time Sinclair had done some sort of business with the man. Sinclair, unlike most noblemen, not only paid active attention to the welfare of his many lands, he also was wont to invest his money — as well as Callie's own, smaller, fortune. She supposed that Sinclair could have thought that the earl had done something ethically wrong in his business. Callie was certain that Sinclair would not dislike the man simply because he was involved in making money, even though many of the aristocracy did consider such a thing crass.

Or, Callie thought, perhaps Sinclair had merely reacted to the situation. He had been anxious about her welfare; he had been looking for her. And when he had found her alone on the terrace with a man, perhaps it had alarmed him so much that he simply assumed the man must be a scoundrel, even though he did not know him.

That, she thought, seemed the likeliest thing. If Sinclair had leaped to such a conclusion, that meant that when time passed and he looked back on the situation, he would probably realize that he had acted hastily and without any real knowledge. And Sinclair, being the fair sort he was, would admit that he had been wrong to judge the other man so quickly and on such little evidence. If he could be made to see that he was wrong, Sinclair would always admit it and apologize. Surely that would be the case with the Earl of Bromwell.

On the other hand, Callie could not forget that Sinclair had called the other man by name. And that meant, of course, that he *did* know him, even if Francesca and Sir Lucien did not. It had seemed to her that the earl had recognized Sinclair, as well.

She was still worrying over the problem when the lights of the theater came back up, and the audience began to rustle and move about. Sir Lucien volunteered to go out into the lobby and bring back glasses of ratafia for the two women. As soon as he left, Callie turned toward Francesca, determined to steer the conversation back to Bromwell's sister, but Francesca had scarcely gotten past a few generalities about the play when there was a knock upon

161

their door.

Callie suppressed her irritation as Francesca called out a polite invitation to enter. It was in general the custom to pay calls back and forth among the boxes at the play or opera. Callie had been hoping to get in a few words with Francesca before visitors began to arrive, but obviously that was not to be the case.

Like Francesca, she turned toward the door with a welcoming smile. It opened to reveal the blond man whom Sir Lucien had identified as Mr. Tilford. Next to him stood the Earl of Bromwell.

CHAPTER SEVEN

Callie's hand clenched on the handle of her fan, and her pulse began a tumultuous run, but she managed, she thought, to keep her face coolly polite.

"Lady Haughston," the blond young man began, somewhat tentatively. "I hope you will not find me too presumptuous. We met at Lady Billingsley's soiree last Season. Mr. Archibald Tilford."

Since Francesca had not known the man's identity, Callie felt sure that she had no memory of the meeting, but the man looked so nervous and uncertain that Francesca took pity on him and smiled, nodding graciously to the gentlemen.

"Of course. Mr. Tilford. Do come in."

"Thank you. Most kind," Tilford said quickly, looking relieved, and he and his companion stepped into the small room.

The box, Callie noticed, which had seemed quite roomy with just the two of them in it, now appeared rather small. There was nowhere to look except at the man who had occupied her mind so much over the past two days.

Callie had thought that perhaps the Cavalier costume had romanticized Lord Bromwell, made him appear more dashing and handsome than he actually was. In truth, she thought as she covertly studied him now, Bromwell was, if anything, even more handsome in the simpler clothes of the present day. His long, lean body needed none of the padding the doublet provided, and the narrower trousers that were currently fashionable emphasized the strong musculature of his legs. There was no need for the jangle of spurs or the sword at his side to add to the masculine aura that hung about him.

"Lady Haughston, please allow me to introduce my cousin Richard, Earl of Bromwell," Mr. Tilford went on.

"How do you do?" Francesca greeted the other man politely, offering her hand to him. She and Callie had both stood and turned to face the men as they came into the box. Now Francesca gestured toward Callie. "Lady Calandra Lilles."

There was a twinkle in Bromwell's eyes as he turned toward Callie, executing a respectable bow. "Lady Calandra and I have met . . . if you remember, my lady."

"But of course," Callie replied, pleased that her voice came out relaxed and natural. "How could one forget Lady Pencully's masquerade?"

"Ah, then I must be excused for not recognizing you, Lord Bromwell," Francesca commented. "As we were all in disguise."

"But some are memorable even in disguise," the earl replied smoothly. "As you were, Lady Haughston — a shepherdess, if I remember correctly."

"Indeed, sir, I was."

"And Lady Calandra came as Katherine Parr, though she is far too young to have been that lady when she was queen."

"Is that who you were?" Francesca asked, turning toward Callie. "And here I assumed you must have been Anne Boleyn."

"A Tudor lady, really," Callie said. "That was all I intended. 'Twas Lord Bromwell who raised me to royalty."

"It was immediately apparent to me that that was where you belonged," he replied.

There was another tap on the door, and two more young men entered, which rendered the box full to capacity, especially when Sir Lucien came in a moment later, carrying glasses for Francesca and Callie.

It seemed natural for Bromwell to move to the side, allowing the others more room, and his movement brought him closer to Callie, so that he stood between her and the outer ledge of the box.

"I had heard that the duke had left London," he commented casually. "I was surprised to find you here tonight."

"I am visiting Lady Haughston," Callie replied. "She kindly invited me to stay with her until the Season begins, when my family will return."

Now that he was this close, she had to tilt her head back a little to look up at him. His eyes, she noticed, were a dark gray in the low lights of the theater, the color of storm clouds. He was studying her, and she wished she knew what he was thinking. Had he thought of her the past few days? Had his surprise upon seeing her been mixed with pleasure?

He had come with his cousin to visit their box, even though it was clear that Mr. Tilford had only a slight acquaintance with Francesca. Surely that indicated an interest on the earl's part. And while Callie knew quite well that it could have been Francesca's blond beauty that drew the men, she did not think it was vain of her to suppose that Bromwell had come to see her.

After all, he had not stayed near Francesca but had maneuvered his way closer to her.

Callie glanced away to hide the spurt of pleasure that the thought aroused in her.

"I am very grateful to Lady Haughston," the earl told her. "I had feared that I might not see you before I had to return to the north."

"Is that where your estates are?" Callie asked, as though she had not received an accounting of the man and his holdings from Sir Lucien an hour earlier.

"In Yorkshire. I know that I am an oddity among the *ton.* I will be leaving London when everyone else is starting to arrive for the Season. But I find the spring and summer too important a time to leave the estate." He quirked an eyebrow. "Now you will look shocked and say surely I do not mean that I oversee the lands myself."

"Indeed, no," Callie replied. "I think it is only wise to pay attention to one's estate. How else are you to insure that your land is being used properly? Or that your tenants are treated fairly?"

"You are an uncommon lady, then. I am usually told that I am lacking in gentility."

"I can see by your grin that such an evaluation does not bother you overmuch."

"I generally am not concerned with other

people's opinions of me," he admitted. "Another reason I do not fit well into the *ton.*"

"Not everyone is so narrow-minded," Callie protested.

He smiled. "I am very glad that you are not."

She glanced down, slightly flustered by the way his smile made her feel inside. It was not the sort of reaction she was accustomed to feeling toward any man. She was not a girl fresh out of the schoolroom; she had spent five years in Society. She was well used to flirtations and meaningful glances and beckoning smiles. Long ago she had learned to put little stock in compliments, and she had never been one to turn breathless because a man looked at her.

But with this man, everything was different. He had only to look at her to make her heart race in her chest, and when he smiled at her, her insides fluttered. Callie wondered if he had any idea that he played such havoc with her senses.

Bromwell cast a glance over at his cousin, then turned back to Callie. "I must take my leave now. I can see that I am making poor Archie nervous. He worries that I will embarrass him by staying too long. He fears that I have lost my town bronze in the years out of London . . . if, indeed, I ever had any."

"I feel sure that you exaggerate, my lord."

He shrugged. "I have never been well-versed in the art of polite conversation. I am too prone to voicing my honest opinion."

"That *would* be a drawback in social settings," Callie agreed lightly. "But it seemed to me that you did well enough at talking the other night. As I remember, you were quite artful in your flattery."

"Ah, but with you, you see, 'tis easy enough to pay pretty compliments, for one need only speak the truth."

"You see?" Callie quirked a brow. "Artful."

He smiled. "Now that we have been formally introduced, dare I hope that you will allow me to call upon you?"

She smiled and glanced down, a gesture that was more coy than she was accustomed to being, but she needed to buy herself a little time.

She could not deny the happy upsurge of her spirits at his words. It was gratifying to know that he wished to see her again, and she knew that she wanted to see him again, as well. But she also was very aware of the little fingers of doubt that tapped at her. Sinclair had told her not to see Bromwell again. If she allowed the earl to call on her, she would be going directly against Sinclair's wishes, something she had never done before, at least in any serious way.

If only she knew the reason for Sinclair's adamant dislike of the man. Was there something hidden beneath his handsome exterior, some inner weakness or sickness of the soul that made Sinclair react so strongly to her being alone with him? She knew that it was possible for a man to be quite other than he seemed. Over her years in the *ton*, Callie believed that she had become a good judge of character, but there were some men who could fool even the most cynical and suspicious of people. Moreover, she had long ago learned that the façade that gentlemen presented to ladies was often quite a different picture than what other gentlemen saw. It would be safer to do as her brother had ordered her.

And yet . . . His smile did something to her insides that no other smile ever had. And when she remembered the way he had kissed her, her loins were flooded again with heat. Her whole body had yearned toward him; she had wanted to press herself into him, to feel his hard muscle and bone sinking into her softer flesh. It was enough to make her blush, just thinking of it. She wanted to see him again. Quite frankly, she wanted to feel his lips on hers once more. Perhaps it was immoral of her, she thought. No doubt it was undutiful and disobedient. But right now, she did not care. For once in her life, she was going to do what she was not supposed to do.

She lifted her face. "I would like to see you again, my lord," she told him boldly. "However, I think you forget — I am staying with Lady Haughston. 'Tis she you must receive permission to call on."

A faint smile played about his lips, and there was a light in his eyes that warmed Callie's blood. "Indeed, I did not forget. But it was *your* feeling on the subject that I wanted to determine."

With that, he bowed to her, then turned and made his way to the door, where Francesca stood, chatting politely with Mr. Tilford and one of the newer arrivals. As Callie watched, the earl spoke to Francesca, clearly making his goodbyes with a bow. Francesca smiled at him, and when he said something else to her, she glanced quickly over at Callie. Then she turned back to the earl, a smile on her face, and said a few more words. Callie felt certain she had given the man permission to call on them.

The rest of the evening dragged. The play

could not hold Callie's interest, and she had to resist the temptation to turn and look over at the earl's box when the intermission came after the second act. There were more visitors to their box at that point, and she chatted with them in a superficial way, but her mind was elsewhere.

She was happy when the play ended and they were able to return home. Callie was quiet on the ride, and she noticed that Francesca was, as well. When Sir Lucien teased them about their unusual silence, Francesca smiled faintly at him and admitted that their day of shopping had left her somewhat tired.

"Then I shall not keep you ladies up any longer," Sir Lucien promised.

True to his word, when they arrived at Francesca's house, he escorted them inside, then promptly took his adieu. However, when they had climbed the stairs to their rooms, Francesca made a gesture toward her bedroom, saying, "Why don't you come into my room for a moment? We can talk."

"All right," Callie agreed, and walked past into Francesca's bedchamber.

A little anxiously, she wondered what Francesca's purpose was. Had Sinclair specifically told her not to allow Callie to see the earl? Was Francesca regretting her decision to allow Callie to stay with her?

"Is aught amiss?"

"No. Oh, no." Francesca smiled. "I hope you did not think I meant to lecture."

Callie shook her head, returning the smile. "I know you would not lecture me. But I thought perhaps you had misgivings about my staying with you."

"No, of course not!" Francesca exclaimed. "I am delighted to have you here. I was just wondering . . ." She hesitated, a delicate frown creasing her forehead. "That is to say, I am not sure whether Rochford would quite like the Earl of Bromwell calling on us."

"Do you know aught against him?" Callie asked, coming closer. "Did you dislike the man?"

"No, on the contrary, I found him quite pleasant. He was well-spoken and polite. Very handsome, as I suspect you noticed." She cast a teasing glance at Callie.

Callie could not keep from blushing, but she said only, "I was aware of it."

"I know almost nothing about him — only what Lucien told us," Francesca went on. "I had never met the earl until this evening."

Callie knew that she should tell Francesca that Sinclair had told her not to see the earl. She should reveal that her brother had warned the man away from her. It was not fair to Francesca to let her unwittingly go against the duke's wishes.

But Callie could not bring herself to do so.

"If you do not know him," she began carefully, "why do you think I should not see him?"

Francesca shook her head. "It is not that I think you should not. It is just that I am . . . uncertain." She paused, then asked bluntly, "Is the earl the man over whom you argued with Rochford?"

"Yes," Callie admitted. She could not lie to her friend. "Sinclair was looking for me, and he found us out on the terrace. But there was nothing wrong with it. We did not go out there together. I had been foolish enough to allow another man to maneuver me outside, and then, when I wanted to go back in, he grew quite obnoxious, and he seized me by the arms."

"Callie!" Francesca exclaimed. "Did he —"

"He tried to kiss me!" Callie told her, her cheeks flaming with embarrassment and anger at the memory. "I was furious. But then Lord Bromwell came up and sent the man packing. He — we — well, I took a moment to regain my calm. And that is when Sinclair came looking for me and found me with the earl."

"Did you explain to Rochford?" Francesca asked.

"I tried," Callie recalled indignantly. "He would not listen to me. He would not give either of us a chance to explain. Nor would he give me any reason for doing so — and now you say you think he would not like it, but *you* will not say why, either."

Francesca pressed her lips together and turned aside. Callie felt a strong suspicion that Francesca wanted to say more but would not allow herself to.

"What do you know?" she asked Francesca quickly. "Why won't you tell me?"

"I don't know why Rochford reacted that way. And it is not my place to say." Francesca looked distinctly uncomfortable.

"Perhaps you do not know, but you suspect something," Callie persisted. "Surely I have a right to know. I am the one who is affected."

"Yes, of course, but . . ." Francesca grimaced. "This should lie between you and Rochford."

"But he will not tell me anything."

Francesca sighed and finally said, "I would guess that it is the earl's sister who concerns your brother more than the earl himself. If

175

Rochford holds something specific against Bromwell, then I have no idea what it is."

"He objects to — what did you say her name was? Lady Smittington?"

"Swithington," Francesca said, and once again Callie detected a certain bite to her tone when she spoke of the woman. "Lady Swithington. Daphne."

"Then you know her?"

Francesca nodded. "Yes, she was in London when I made my come-out. She was a widow at the time. Her first husband was quite a bit older than she, and he had died a year or so before. There was . . . a great deal of talk about her. She was scandalous in her behavior. Everyone whispered about her. I am not sure how much of it was actual truth. As you know, young unmarried girls, especially those fresh to London, are not privy to all the rumors, especially the more licentious ones. But her reputation was that of a woman of loose morals. Even before her husband's death."

"She had affairs?" Callie asked.

Francesca nodded. "Yes. So it was rumored."

"But surely Sinclair cannot blame her brother for her behavior!" Callie declared indignantly.

"No, I am sure he does not. But perhaps

he feels that the earl is cut from the same cloth," Francesca suggested.

"But that is simply speculation. He doesn't *know*."

Francesca shrugged. "I have no idea what Sinclair knows about the man. I can only say that I have heard nothing about him," Francesca pointed out. "But you know how fragile a young woman's reputation is. Perhaps Rochford does not like the idea that anyone might connect your name with someone who is not of the highest morals. Or perhaps he feels that he would not want you to marry the man because of the scandal that has been attached to Lady Swithington's name. And if you cannot marry him, then it would be best that you have nothing to do with him."

"But that is so unfair!" Callie exclaimed, throwing her arms wide in a gesture of frustration. She began to pace up and down the room, saying, "It is wrong to color Lord Bromwell with the same stain, just because he is her brother." She turned and stared searchingly at Francesca. "Is that what you think of Lord Bromwell? That he is wicked?"

Francesca looked at her, pained, and finally shrugged. "No — I do not know what he is. I barely know the man. He seems a fine person, but I know that what he appears to be is not necessarily what he is. He is Lady Daphne's brother, so it seems possible that he may be of the same ilk as she. On the other hand, I am quite certain that not all members of a family are alike. I have two brothers. One is a wonderful man. The other was wicked." Francesca's lovely face hardened. "And I would hate to think that anyone assumed that I was like Terence simply because we were related."

"There! You see?" Callie said triumphantly. "It is wrong to assume that Lord Bromwell is wicked, too."

Francesca seemed to struggle with her answer, finally saying, "Yes, it would be wrong, if that is what your brother is doing. But we cannot know his reasons, really, and if he is so opposed to your seeing this man . . ."

"But what about *me?*" Callie cried out. "What about what *I* want? Why should my brother be allowed to make decisions for me? I am a grown woman. Why should I not be the one who decides whom I shall see? With whom I will spend time?"

"Yes, of course, you should be," Francesca agreed.

"I am not going to do something foolish," Callie pointed out. "I am quite capable of realizing that a man is trying to take advantage of me. Do you not agree?"

"Yes, certainly."

"So it seems to me that it is not Sinclair's view on this man that matters, it is mine."

"I am sure that Rochford is trying to protect you," Francesca put in.

"No doubt he is," Callie retorted. "But I am growing very tired of people who are trying to protect me telling me what I can and cannot do."

"Of course you are."

"And I should like to be allowed to make my own decisions."

Again Francesca nodded. "I know, my dear. I know."

"Then are you going to allow me to do so?" Callie asked. "Or are you going to tell me that he cannot call here?"

Francesca's brows flew up in surprise. "Oh, my dear — I was not saying that. I thought I should warn you. I was not certain if you were aware of how Rochford would feel about it."

"I am not certain, either," Callie told her. "Sinclair was angry that night, but it was so unlike him. . . . Looking back on it, I have wondered if it was not simply that he was worried because he could not find me. Perhaps it had nothing to do with the earl himself. Perhaps he would have reacted the same way about any other man — or, at least, a man he did not know well."

Francesca shrugged. "That could be true."

"He regretted getting angry, I think," Callie told her. She paused, then added, "Still, I cannot lie to you. Sinclair did tell me not to see Lord Bromwell again."

"I see. But you intend to?" Francesca asked.

Callie straightened, lifting her chin a little. "I — I want to decide for myself about the man. It is not Sinclair's place to order my life. I love my brother, but I will not live a certain way just because he tells me to. However, I can certainly understand it if you do not want to cross Sinclair."

Francesca's chin came up in a way that mirrored Callie's. "I am not afraid of the Duke of Rochford."

"But if you do not wish to allow Lord Bromwell to call here, I will not be angry with you."

"Thank you, my dear," Francesca replied. Her voice was calm, but her eyes sparked with temper. "But I would be angry with myself if I allowed the duke's, or anyone's, opinion to dictate who *I* allow in *my* house. I told Lord Bromwell that he is welcome to call here, and he is. And if your brother does not like it — well, he will just have to deal with the fact you and I are not under his command."

"Thank you, Francesca." Callie beamed at the other woman. She rushed impulsively across the room to hug her. "I am so glad I came here."

"I am, too," Francesca replied, patting her on the back.

With another hug, Callie bade her friend good-night and went to her room. Francesca turned and walked across to the window. She was tired, and yet she still felt restless. She pushed aside the edge of the heavy drapery and gazed out into the dark night.

She wondered if she had done the right thing. It would be wrong of her to do anything that would open Callie up to being hurt. She could not help but worry that Lord Bromwell might turn out to be the same sort as his sister. And how much of her own decision not to bow to Rochford's commands stemmed from her belief that Callie had the right to do as she pleased and how much from a long-simmering resentment?

Francesca told herself that she would chaperone Callie and Bromwell closely. She would watch for any sign that Bromwell was a roue, a blackguard. Nothing, she promised, would harm Callie while she was under her roof.

Still, she worried that she should let Rochford know about Lord Bromwell and about Callie's feelings. But she could not betray Callie in that way — any more than she could write or speak to Rochford about that time fifteen years ago. And it was no wonder, she thought, remembering that time, that Rochford had avoided telling her why he and Callie had argued.

That left her with only one other option — to tell Callie what she knew. But how could she tell Callie that Rochford doubtless wanted her to stay away from the earl because he did not want his sister involved with the man whose sister had once been Rochford's *own* mistress?

CHAPTER EIGHT

Two days later, Lord Bromwell came to call on them. He stayed for less than thirty minutes, which was the appropriate duration for an afternoon call. Francesca remained in the room the entire time, and during the last ten minutes that he was there, Lady Tollingford and her daughter Lady Mary also came to call. So there was no chance for any sort of private conversation between Callie and Lord Bromwell, and the conversation never swerved from socially approved topics, such as the weather, the play they had seen the other night, and the upcoming gala that the Prince was holding in a fortnight for a visiting prince from Gertensberg.

Callie had expected nothing more. A first call was simply the prelude, the opening shot in an extended campaign of courting, and was as much a chance to pass inspection by one's chaperone, parent or guardian as anything else.

Lord Bromwell, tall and wide-shouldered in his well-cut jacket of dark blue superfine and close-fitting fawn breeches, had easily passed the inspection. He was handsome and polite, and obviously knew the social niceties despite his years of living away from the City. Yet there was no slickness to his manner or speech, no indication that he sought to curry favor or to present a false front.

Callie knew, looking at Francesca, that this afternoon's call had eased some of her earlier uncertainty. No one understood the ins and outs of the *beau monde* better than Lady Haughston, and if anyone could spot an adventurer or what Francesca's brother Dominic would call a "rum 'un," it would be she. But Callie could see Francesca relaxing a little more with each passing minute that Bromwell spent there, her smile growing easier and more genuine, her words drifting from polite chitchat into more genuine conversation.

And Callie, when Bromwell threw a quick grin at her, his gray eyes full of wicked charm, could not help but grin back, a heady excitement beginning to bubble in her chest.

The next day Lord Bromwell called on

them again, this time to take them for a ride in his curricle through Hyde Park. It was five in the afternoon, the most fashionable hour for Londoners to promenade through the park. Many strolled, others rode horses, and a large number rolled through in their finest equipage, showing off their clothes, their conveyances, their teams and, in many cases, their handling of the reins.

It was a trifle cramped, for Bromwell's sporting vehicle was small and built more for speed than comfort, usually carrying no more than two people. However, Callie could see that Francesca was not about to let her go off in even an open carriage through Hyde Park alone with Lord Bromwell. Callie wondered again if Francesca did not know more about her brother's reason for disliking Bromwell than she had let on. It did not seem likely that Sinclair would react so strongly to him just because the man's sister had an unsavory reputation. It had seemed more personal to Callie than that.

But if Francesca did know something more, why had she not told her? Callie found it hard to believe that Francesca believed anything bad about Lord Bromwell, given that she was still willing to receive him. She must not know anything,

Callie reassured herself. Her friend must be behaving in a very circumspect manner simply because she did not want Rochford to take her to task.

Still, Callie could not but wish that Francesca would not take her chaperone's role quite so seriously. They could scarcely talk, at least in any but the most superficial way, with Francesca sitting between them on the curricle seat.

Over the course of the next week, it seemed that Lord Bromwell turned up everywhere they went. He called on them twice more. Then he was at Lady Battersea's rout and again at Mrs. Mellenthorpe's large formal dinner, not to mention the Carrington soiree.

However, to Callie's frustration, Francesca stayed by her side throughout each evening, so that there was never any occasion to have a moment alone with the man. The closest she got to him was when he bowed over her hand when greeting or leaving her. Francesca was, she thought, carrying things a bit far. What, after all, could happen between them in the midst of a crowded party?

Callie was no longer used to such rigid chaperonage; it had been several years since she was a young girl in her first year, and even her grandmother allowed her almost free rein at a party. Not, of course, that Francesca refused to "allow" her to be by herself; she simply made it a point to always be about if Lord Bromwell was there. Callie suspected that if they should chance to be at a ball together and Bromwell should ask her to dance, Francesca would make a point of being right there when they stepped off the floor. There would be no slipping away to a tête-à-tête in an alcove or on the terrace outside.

Callie supposed she should be grateful. Not even her brother could be upset about her being at the same party as Bromwell when she was under Francesca's watchful eye the whole time. Still, she found herself chafing under the gently-handled restriction.

On Saturday, she and Francesca attended the Fotheringham rout. Like most such events, it was something of a crush. Callie looked around in vain for Lord Bromwell, and after half an hour she decided, with some disappointment, that he would not be coming. She was standing with Francesca, chatting to Irene and Gideon, who also had decided to remain in London, when she turned her head and saw Bromwell walking through the double doorway into the large reception room.

Callie went still, her fingers clenching around the stem of her fan. At Bromwell's side, her hand tucked familiarly in the crook of his arm, was a blazingly attractive red-haired woman. Tall and statuesque, with a wealth of auburn ringlets done up *a la Meduse,* she was dressed in a black satin evening gown, richly decorated around the hem and neckline with black lace and jet beads. The low-cut neckline showed off her elegant white shoulders and chest, her full breasts swelling up over the froth of black lace. Though a somber color, it was a perfect foil for her vivid red hair, pale skin and light blue eyes. Her mouth was perhaps too thin for perfect beauty, but such a small imperfection was scarcely noticeable in the eye-catching picture she presented. There was a soft smile on her lips, and she turned once or twice to look up at the man beside her, smiling at him with clear affection.

Callie felt a coldness growing in her stomach as she watched Bromwell turn his head to smile back down at the woman. As though sensing the change in Callie, Francesca turned and glanced across the floor, following Callie's gaze. Francesca stiffened, and a soft curse escaped her lips.

Callie glanced at her, as did Irene and Gideon.

"Who is —" Irene began then stopped. "Oh, yes, I remember now. She was at the ball at the Park when we got engaged, wasn't she? Lady . . ." She paused, trying to recall the name, and turned toward Gideon.

"Do not ask me," her husband told her. "I don't remember the woman."

It seemed absurd that any man would not remember this woman, but Callie suspected that with Gideon it was true. He was clearly so smitten with Irene that he barely looked at any other women.

"Swithington," Francesca said in a rather brittle voice. "Lady Daphne Swithington."

"Oh!" Callie was surprised and a little chagrined at the relief that swept through her. "She is Lord Bromwell's sister."

"Yes. Apparently she has come to town for the Season." Francesca sounded anything but overjoyed at the prospect.

Callie glanced over at her friend. Surely there was something more bothering Francesca than just the fact that Lady Swithington's reputation had been unsavory. After all, from what Francesca had said, it had been many years since whatever scandalous behavior the woman had engaged in, and she had been out of Society since then. While her entrance had caused a stir around the room, no one was turning away or giving her the cut direct. Even if Lady Swithington were still ostracized, Callie did not think that it would cause Francesca, who was not at all high-in-the-instep, to turn as frosty as she was now. Callie could not help but wonder if perhaps Francesca's late husband might have been one of the many men with whom Lady Daphne had been reputed to have had an affair.

Though they nodded to one or two people as they passed, Lord Bromwell and his sister did not stop until they reached Callie and her companions. "Lady Haughston, Lady Calandra, pray allow me to introduce my sister, Lady Swithington," he began.

Francesca's smile was icy as she replied, "Yes, Lady Swithington and I are old acquaintances."

"Oh, yes," the other woman added, her smile much less reserved than Francesca's. Up close, Callie could see that the woman was older than she had appeared from across the floor. Tiny wrinkles fanned out from the corners of her eyes, and when she was not smiling, there were deep grooves bracketing her mouth. "Lady Haughston and I know each other well, do we not? And Lady Calandra." She turned her smile on Callie, adding, "I am so happy to meet you at last. I knew your brother, of course, but you were just a wee thing then." She let out a small, self-deprecating laugh. "Now I am showing our age, am I not, Francesca? How terrible of me."

Francesca's smile had vanished entirely. Ignoring the other woman's words, she went on, her voice like glass, "I believe you have met Lord and Lady Radbourne."

"Yes, of course. At your engagement party, was it not?" Lady Swithington smiled brilliantly at the other couple. "I was just out of mourning then, but I felt it was not amiss to attend, given that dear Lady Odelia invited me. She is our father's cousin through marriage, you see, and has always been so kind to us. Hasn't she, Brom, dear?" She turned to her brother, smiling affectionately.

"Yes, Lady Odelia is a darling," Bromwell replied in a sardonic voice, and his sister tapped him playfully with her furled fan.

"Bromwell . . . you will give everyone the wrong idea."

Gideon let out a chuckle. "Not likely — we are all related to Lady Odelia, as well."

"Now that Lady Daphne is here," Bromwell said, "I hoped that we might make up a party to Richmond Park next week. No doubt our cousin Mr. Tilford will go with us. It would give me great pleasure if all of you would attend, as well." He looked around at the others. "Lord and Lady Radbourne? Lady Haughston?" His eyes came last to Callie, but it was on her that they stayed. "Lady Calandra?"

"It sounds very nice, if the weather holds," Callie put in quickly, for she had the suspicion that Francesca might say no. "I have been growing restless, I confess. A long ride sounds just the thing."

"Yes, doesn't it?" Francesca agreed with distinctly less enthusiasm. "However, I am afraid that neither Lady Calandra nor I have any mounts stabled in the city. I find it difficult to find much time for riding, so I only ride when I am at Redfields. And as only Lady Calandra came to London to visit me, the Lilles horses are not here, either."

"No need to worry about that," Bromwell said. "I was at Tattersall's this week, and I have not sent the animals I bought to the estate yet. I should welcome the opportunity to see them in action."

"And we have some of our horses, as well," Lord Gideon put in. "I am sure that among us we will have enough for everyone."

"Then of course," Francesca gave in gracefully. "It sounds delightful."

Callie felt sure that Francesca did not

mean her words, but she was not about to quibble. The prospect of a ride out to and through the wide green spaces of Richmond Park sounded most enjoyable. Nor was it just the fact that such an expedition would offer a much freer social situation than a party. She had been feeling cooped up in the City, for she loved to ride and did so often whenever she was at one of their estates. Even in the City, she was accustomed to taking a sedate ride along Rotten Row a couple of times a week, and she had sorely missed the exercise and the fresh air.

So it was arranged that they would go to the park on the following Tuesday, provided there was no dreary rain to spoil the expedition. Bromwell and his sister stayed to chat for a few more minutes. Francesca was much more silent than was customary for her, but Lady Daphne easily took up the slack, giving a droll account of her trip from her late husband's far-flung estate to London, which seemed to have been plagued with every delay from having to turn back for a trunk left behind to a broken wheel to being stuck in a west country inn for three days because of a late snowstorm.

After a time, Irene and Gideon excused themselves, and a few moments later Bromwell and Lady Daphne did, as well, Lady

Daphne warmly taking Callie's hand in hers and murmuring that she looked forward to getting to chat with her on the outing. Bromwell bent over Callie's hand in his usual way, his lips brushing soft as velvet across her skin. Her fingers tightened involuntarily on his, and he looked at her as he straightened, his eyes suddenly hot and intimate.

After they had walked away, Callie leaned closer to Francesca, saying softly, "You need not go to Richmond Park if you do not wish to. Irene and Gideon will be there, and surely that is ample chaperonage for me. It will be perfectly all right. I will say that you fell ill the morning we are to go."

"And let Daphne revel in the idea that I hadn't the courage to spend a day in her company?" Francesca retorted. There was a steely glint in her deep blue eyes that Callie had never seen there before. "Nonsense. I will manage perfectly well." She set her jaw, muttering beneath her breath, " 'Showing our age' indeed! As if she were not six years older than I if she is a day!"

Callie smothered a smile behind her fan. She could not remember ever before seeing Francesca display the slightest feminine venom. Confident in her own beauty and place in society, she did not flare with

jealousy or envy. When other women behaved in such a manner to her, she usually
skewered them with deft skill, but without
employing bitterness or dislike. It was
somehow reassuring to see that Francesca
was as capable as the next person of giving
way to a spurt of ill-tempered dislike.

Lady Daphne had seemed to Callie to be
a pleasant, friendly person, though Callie
certainly had no intention of mentioning
that to Francesca — any more than she
would ask Francesca why she disliked Lady
Daphne so much. It was far too rude and
personal a question, especially given the fact
that Callie suspected the answer probably
had to do with Francesca's husband, who
had been rumored to be a libertine. It was
too bad, really, for Callie would have liked
very much to know exactly what Lady
Daphne had done to Francesca to engender
such a feeling in her.

However, looking at Francesca's face,
Callie knew that her curiosity was not going
to be satisfied. Even the most delicate probing was not going to elicit anything from
Francesca tonight. So Callie put her questions aside and let her mind drift to the far
more enjoyable topic of spending the following Tuesday in the company of Lord
Bromwell.

"Well, well . . ." Lady Swithington murmured as they strolled away from Calandra and Francesca. "So you have an interest in the duke's little sister. How fascinating." She cast a sideways glance up at her brother's face.

"I should have told you beforehand," Bromwell told her apologetically. "But when we saw them as soon as we arrived, it seemed such a perfect opportunity. I wanted to see her face when she met you."

"Why?" Daphne's mouth tightened. "Surely you did not expect one of the proud Lilles to show any sort of remorse."

"I just wanted to see if she had any idea what her brother did to you," he replied. "I felt she did not. It was so many years ago. Still, I was curious."

"And what did you find out?"

He shook his head. "She knows nothing. I am certain of that." He turned to look at her. "I could not say the same about Lady Haughston."

"Pffft." Daphne made a low dismissive noise, fanning out the sticks of her elegant ivory fan. "Francesca. She was always gooseish."

She waved her fan languidly as they made their way through the crowd until they reached the other side of the room. They turned and looked back. Now and then, as the crowd of people moved about, they could see Callie and Francesca still standing in the same spot, talking.

"So . . . what exactly is your plan regarding little Lady Calandra?" Daphne asked in an arch tone. "I hope you do not expect me to believe that you are seriously courting her."

"Oh, I am quite serious about it," her brother responded, a certain grimness in his tone.

"But not for marriage."

"Surely you know me better than that," he replied. "I would not offer you such an insult as allying myself with the Lilles."

"I do know you," she agreed, smiling a little smugly. "What do you intend, then? It would be only fitting for the duke to have to pay in like measure."

Bromwell gave her a startled look. "What do you mean? Surely you do not think that I would seduce the girl and cast her aside."

Daphne shrugged, her face hardening. "It seems an apt enough revenge for what her brother did to me. Not as harsh, surely, as getting her with child and refusing to marry her."

"No. But I am not a man such as Rochford," Bromwell replied, frowning. "I am sure you would not really wish such a fate on any other woman."

Daphne smiled sweetly at him. "I forget, sometimes, how good you are. Of course you are right. I would not wish any other woman to suffer the shame that I did with Rochford. It just seems so unfair that the duke never had to pay in any way." She watched her brother as he continued to gaze across the floor, his eyes intent on Lady Calandra. She frowned a little as she said, "It would not hurt if one of the proud Lilles were to be taken down a peg."

He nodded. It was the same sentiment he had expressed to his cousin Archie not long ago. Still, a frown creased his forehead. "But hardly fair to Callie."

"Callie?" His sister's brows rose precipitously.

"That is what they call her, Lady Haughston and Lady Odelia. Calandra is far too formal a name for her."

"Do not tell me that you have conceived an affection for this girl," Daphne snapped.

"No, of course not." His frown deepened. He looked at his sister, adding, "She is a pretty chit. But of no consequence to me."

"I am glad to hear that. It is never wise to trust a Lilles," Daphne told him bitterly.

"I know."

After a moment, Daphne went on, "What *are* your intentions, then, regarding Lady Calandra?"

"To worry the duke a little," he responded, one side of his mouth quirking up in a smile that held little humor. "I would like to see him dance a bit on that hot griddle, wondering what I intend to do. What I will tell his sister about him. Whether I will turn her against him — even take her from him. Or if I just might do the same as he, engage her affections, then spurn her. A man without honor expects the same behavior from others, I've found."

"He certainly will not like your courting her," Lady Daphne agreed.

"Indeed, he will not. He has already warned me off."

"Really?" She looked intrigued. "What did he do? What did he say?"

"He was his usual arrogant self," her brother replied. "He told me to stay away from his sister. As though he had only to speak and the rest of the world would obey."

"What did you do?"

"I thought about planting him a facer," he

199

admitted, a wicked twinkle in his eyes. "But I knew Lady Odelia might object, as it was her birthday ball. Gentlemen brawling on one's terrace are apt to bring down the tone of a party." He shrugged. "Anyway, I realized that it would be more fun to tease him a bit first. Let him see that the world does not dance to his tune . . . not even his sister. Eventually, I imagine, once he has heard that I have disobeyed him — that *she* has disobeyed him — he will come storming back to town, roaring like a baited bear, and then . . ." His mouth lifted in a smile. "Then *he* will come to visit *me*."

His gray eyes glinted silver with satisfaction.

"You mean he will call you out?" Daphne looked distressed. "But, Brom, no! He is reputed to be an excellent shot. You could be killed!"

"You forget, my dear — I am also an excellent shot."

"Yes, I know you are," she said, her voice almost smug. "But still . . . to risk your life . . . that is too much."

"In any case, I doubt very seriously that it will come to that. Rochford has never fought a duel. I doubt that he will start now."

"But with enough provocation . . ."

Again he shrugged. "I think it much more likely that we will settle it on the spot, with our fists." He smiled grimly, and his hand tightened into a fist with anticipation.

"Are you sure?" Daphne asked. "Last time . . ."

He waved her objection away. "Last time I was seventeen. Calling him out was a schoolboy gesture. I know enough now to realize that it will be much more satisfactory to knock him onto his arrogant backside."

"Well, of course, dear, if that is what you wish to do," Daphne conceded in the tone of one giving a little boy a treat. She tucked her hand through his arm happily. "It sounds just the thing."

The following Tuesday dawned crisp and clear, a pale golden sun shining in the February sky. It was an almost perfect day for riding out of the city to the royal park. Callie, thrilled at the prospect of the expedition actually taking place, chattered through breakfast to Francesca, who was obviously much less excited. Still, Lady Haughston was too kind to depress Callie's spirits, so she smiled and nodded, agreeing that the day was lovely, the company would be most pleasant, and that it was wonderful, indeed, that riding habits not only showed off one's figure nicely but were also one of the few articles of attire that did not have to be white.

Callie's riding habit was of hunter green velvet and never before worn, as she had ordered it from the modiste in her spurt of shopping when she came to stay with Francesca. Unlike the fashion of modern dresses, its jacket was longer and fitted snugly to her waist, frogged in black down the front and at the cuffs. The hat that went with it was also green, trimmed in black, and it sat jauntily on her head, tilting down in the front in a slightly rakish way.

Studying her, Francesca thought that Callie looked utterly charming in it, and she could not help but think it was worth putting up with Lady Daphne for a day so that Callie could present such a fetching picture for Lord Bromwell.

It was a merry party that set off for Richmond Park an hour later. As well as Lord and Lady Radbourne, Lord Bromwell and his sister, and Francesca and Callie, there were Bromwell's cousin Archie Tilford, Miss Bettina Swanson and her brother Reginald, a smiling young man just down from Oxford. Miss Swanson and her brother rode in the Radbournes' elegant landau with Lord Radbourne, who had been quick to give up his mount to Francesca to ride.

"I am sure that he will be grateful to have a better rider on his back," he told Francesca with a smile. Lord Radbourne, because of his unfortunate upbringing, had never become the skilled rider that many of his aristocratic contemporaries were.

"And for you, my lady," Bromwell told Callie, taking her arm and leading her over to a dainty white mare. "I thought Bellissima would suit." A smile lit his eyes and then was quickly gone. "The name is certainly appropriate for you. She is biddable, but not docile, and from good bloodlines. I was not sure what sort of rider you were."

"I can sit a horse," she told him with an arch smile.

"That must mean that you are veritable centaur, and I will doubtless suffer great shame for putting you on an unworthy mount."

Callie chuckled, reaching up to stroke the mare's nose. "I am sure that Bellissima is not at all unworthy. Are you, you lovely creature?" She turned back to Bromwell. "Thank you, my lord, I am sure she is an excellent choice, and I shall thoroughly enjoy her."

"I hope so." He paused, then added,

"Please, call me Bromwell, or Brom. All my friends do."

Callie looked at him. His words made her feel a trifle giddy, even breathless. "Surely we do not know each other that well, my lord."

"Do we not?" She saw in his eyes the shared knowledge of their kisses, the heat that had swarmed through them. Then he broke their locked gaze, saying in a lighter tone, "But I hope that we shall."

He turned aside, saying, "Here. Let me give you a hand up." He held his hands out to her and vaulted her up into the saddle, then moved to adjust her stirrups, stripping off his leather riding gloves so that he could work more easily.

Callie felt his arm brush against her leg as he worked at the stirrup, and even through her riding boot and heavy habit, the touch stirred her. She watched his fingers as he adjusted the strap. They were long and supple, moving with a quick sureness, and she found herself wondering how those hands would feel touching her neck, her arm, sliding up to cup her face.

She glanced quickly away and down at her own hands, gripping the reins tightly. She could feel a blush stealing into her cheeks. It was absurd, she told herself, the way her thoughts seemed to run away with her whenever she was around Bromwell. She felt sure that he must sense it; there was a knowing look in his eyes when he gazed at her — or perhaps it was simply that he remembered the way she had reacted the two times he had kissed her. She had kissed him back in a manner that she could only term abandoned.

Could he think that she was other than she was? That she was a woman of experience in such matters? Did her brother dislike Bromwell because he knew his reputation to be that of a roué? A libertine? Could it be that Bromwell was pursuing her because he assumed that she was a woman of loose morals? She knew, guiltily, that she had given him reason to think so — being out by herself in the middle of the night as he had found her that first night. And then letting him kiss her without even a protest — indeed, melting in his arms.

Anxiety curled in her chest into a hard, cold lump. She did not want to believe that was the reason behind his pursuit of her. And, after all, how likely was it that a roué would spend so many afternoons and evenings in tame chaperoned visits and parties? Surely a man interested in nothing but a wanton woman would find the path much easier elsewhere. Yet still he pursued her. She could not help but think that such behavior evinced a deeper interest than any a libertine would feel. On the other hand, she was realistic enough to realize that perhaps that was simply what she wanted to think.

She looked away from Bromwell, over at the others, who were also mounting their horses. Her gaze fell on Lady Swithington, who was studying Callie. In the other woman's pale blue gaze she saw a look of cold and intense dislike.

CHAPTER NINE

Callie's hand clenched involuntarily on the reins, and her mare shifted nervously beneath her. By the time Callie settled her down and looked back at Bromwell's sister, Lady Daphne was smiling sweetly at her.

"What a vision you are on that horse, Lady Calandra," the older woman said. "That black hair of yours and on a white horse — la, I fear you put the rest of us to shame."

"None could eclipse your beauty, Lady Swithington," Mr. Swanson assured her.

"Indeed not," Archie Tilford chimed in. "That is to say, not that Lady Calandra is not exceedingly beautiful, as well. Indeed, none could be lovelier." He glanced around, his face beginning to redden. "Of course, Lady Haughston, Lady Radbourne, Miss Swanson, you are no less lovely. I mean, can one really compare Aphrodite and Helen of Troy? Except, of course, that there are five of you, not two, and, uh . . ."

Lord Radbourne let out a sharp laugh, hastily turned into a cough, which seemed to cause Lady Radbourne to turn away and clamp her hand over her mouth, her shoulders shaking.

"Leave off, Archie, do," Lord Bromwell told his cousin bluntly. "We haven't long enough for you to work your way out of that one. Ladies, suffice it to say that you are all at the absolute pinnacle of beauty, and I daresay there is not a gentleman in London who would not trade places with us right now. And now, I think, we should get on our way."

Nodding in agreement, they started off, some in front of the carriage and some behind it. It required concentration to move through the crowded streets of London, and they were spread out, so there was not much conversation at first.

Callie was glad of the silence, for she was lost in her thoughts. Her mind kept returning to the glimpse of dislike — was it too much to call it hatred? — that she had seen in Lady Swithington's eyes. Had she really seen it, or had it been merely a trick of the light? She could not imagine how she could have mistaken it. But why would Bromwell's sister despise her?

Her thoughts kept her occupied for some time, but conversation increased as they reached the outskirts of the city, and she put the incident aside, determined to enjoy the afternoon before her.

The party fell into groups of two and three, talking and laughing as they rode into the country. Callie had been concerned about Francesca and Bromwell's sister being thrown together, but she noticed that from the first Lady Swithington chose to ride beside the carriage, flirting with young Reginald Swanson — and trying her utmost to flirt with Lord Radbourne, as well.

Callie glanced over at Irene, who after one look at the carriage, simply rolled her eyes and continued to blithely chat with Francesca, riding beside her. Callie could understand her lack of concern; Gideon, rather than flirting back, looked patently bored, and his gaze wandered more to his wife some distance away than to Lady Daphne riding beside him.

Bromwell positioned himself at Callie's side, and, somewhat to Callie's surprise, Francesca was content to let them ride alone together, for she stayed with Irene. Since Mr. Tilford seemed to have appointed himself those two ladies' guardian, it left Callie alone with Bromwell for most of the ride.

Though for the past week or more she had been eager to have exactly that opportunity, now she found herself suddenly shy and unsure of what she should say. It was a new position for her, as she had always been a lively girl. Her grandmother's constant admonition to her before a party had always been not to talk too much and draw attention to herself, though it was not, Callie was the first to admit, an admonition she had endeavored very much to follow.

She realized that her reticence stemmed from the fact that for perhaps the first time in her life, it mattered very much to her that her companion found her pleasing. Finally, having rejected a comment on the weather as much too commonplace and one on the beauty of the scenery as entirely insipid, she began, " 'Tis an excellent mare you purchased."

Immediately it occurred to her that what she had said was probably worse than either of the other possibilities, but Bromwell turned to her and smiled, and her inner criticisms vanished in a flood of warmth.

"Do you like her? I hoped you would," he replied. "I thought of you when I bought her."

He stopped abruptly, an odd look in his

eyes, as though what he had said surprised him, then went on quickly, "That is to say, I had thought of a trip to Richmond Park, and I had hoped that you and Lady Haughston would be able to join us. I bought her for the estate, of course, but it occurred to me that you could use her for the ride to the park."

"I am very glad that you did," Callie told him, and reached down to pat the horse's neck, hiding the rush of pleasure in her face at his words. "She is a smooth goer, but she is very lively, as well."

"I was not sure but what she might be too lively," he confessed. "But she was too good to pass up. And I can see that I needed to have no worries about your ability to handle her."

"My father put me up on a pony as soon as I could walk," Callie said, smiling a little. "He was an avid horseman. Indeed, one of the few things I remember about him was his walking beside me on my pony so that he could steady me if I needed it."

Bromwell looked at her, frowning a little. "He died young? I am sorry."

Callie nodded. "Yes, he contracted a fever one winter, and within a few weeks he was gone. I did not even see him before he died. My mother was afraid that I might come down with it, too."

"I am sorry," he repeated. "I hate to have brought up painful memories."

She smiled at him. "Thank you. But they are not painful. In truth, I barely remember my father. I was only five years old when he died, and I have only a few memories of him, some of them quite vague. Sometimes I am not sure whether I remember his face from actually seeing him or from the painting of him that hung in my mother's room. I envy my brother because he knew him so much longer, you see."

"For some of us, 'tis not a joy to know our fathers longer," Bromwell responded with a wry twist of his mouth.

Callie glanced at him. "Did you not — I mean . . ." She stumbled to a halt, aware that her question was probably too personal.

"No, I did not," he replied flatly. "I did not care for him while he was alive, and I did not miss him when he died." He shrugged.

"I am so sorry!" Callie exclaimed, reaching out toward him, then, remembering the others around them, quickly drawing her hand back.

"No, I am the one who is sorry. 'Tis considered disloyal, I imagine, not to say that one honors one's father. But I am not good enough at pretense to say that I did. He was a hard, cold man who cared for little but himself, and I would warrant that one would be hard-pressed to find many who knew him who regretted his passing. However, I should not have introduced such a dismal topic into our conversation." He smiled at her. "And I shall dismiss it right now. Let us talk about you. How was it that your training on horseback continued after your father's death? Was your mother an avid horsewoman, as well?"

"Oh, no." Callie let out a chuckle. "My mother did not particularly like to ride. But she knew I loved it, and she wanted to do as my father had wanted. That was very important to her. She loved him very much. So the head groom tutored me, as he had done before my father's death, and so did Sinclair. My brother." She looked at him. "That is why my brother is so . . . protective of me. In many ways, he was as much a father to me as a brother. He has become accustomed to watching over me."

"I do not fault your brother for his care for his sister," Bromwell replied. "Indeed, I would do much to protect *my* sister, as well."

At his words, he glanced over at the woman in question, who still rode beside the open carriage. She was laughing at some witticism of Mr. Swanson's, her lovely head thrown back, her white throat arched becomingly. Her black riding habit was severe, but she needed no ornamentation for her beauty, and, as with the dress she had worn the other night, the somber shade was a perfect foil for her own vibrant coloring.

As they watched, Lady Daphne reached down and playfully tapped Mr. Swanson on the shoulder. The young man flushed to the roots of his sandy hair. Callie glanced over at his sister, who had a rather sour expression on her face. Gideon, on the other hand, was ignoring all of them, jotting down something in a small book in his hand.

Callie, who had heard many tales of Lord Radbourne's flouting of societal rules, smothered a smile. She returned her gaze to Bromwell's face. He frowned a little.

"People sometimes misjudge Lady Daphne," he said. "She is a very warm and vivacious person."

"She seemed quite nice," Callie offered, not sure what to say. "She is very beautiful."

Bromwell cast her a smile. "Yes. And she takes pride in it. But it has cost her dearly in many ways. Women often . . . are disinclined to befriend her."

Callie thought about the little Francesca had told her about Lady Swithington. Could her reputation have been exaggerated? Distorted? Was she merely overly flirtatious? Callie knew how easy it was to bring on the censure of London Society. And a beautiful woman often stirred jealousy in the bosom of those females less fortunate than she.

On the other hand, it was also possible that Bromwell's words were simply a loving brother's defense of his sister. She had seen love render a person blind to another's faults. And she could not help but remember that flash of hard dislike she had seen in Daphne's eyes as they set out. What did that mean? It certainly did not match with the friendly, flattering words she uttered or the sweet smile she directed at Callie.

Still, whatever the truth, Callie could not help but respect Bromwell's loyalty.

"You are the only children in your family?" she asked.

He nodded. "Yes, and our estates are somewhat isolated. So Daphne and I were, I suppose, the only friends each other had, really. My father considered none of the families thereabouts our equals in birth, so we were discouraged from socializing with them — not that any of them were really

215

close enough to see often, anyway. And my sister was several years older than I —" He shot her a twinkling look. "Not that I would let her hear me say that. But I was not much of a companion for her. She had to look after me a great deal. And, of course, by the time I was seven or eight, she was far more interested in clothes and hairstyles than in helping me search out bugs and other wildlife in the gardens. By the time I was eleven, she had gone to London to make her come-out, and then she married."

"It sounds as if you must have been alone a lot."

He nodded. "A good bit. Fortunately, I was always a solitary sort, anyway."

"I was not," Callie responded. "I did not have any children my age about, either — I spent most of my time with the servants. My nurse, Cook, the upstairs maids. It scandalized my grandmother."

"Your mother, too, I imagine," Bromwell commented.

Callie shrugged. "My mother did not . . . involve herself too closely with my upbringing."

He looked at her, surprised. "She was unloving?" He paused, then said, "I am sorry. I should not have pried."

"No, it is all right. I don't mind talking

about her. I cannot do so, really, with my family. It makes Sinclair feel sad, I think. You see, as with our father, he knew her much longer than I did. He remembers her the way she was before our father died. She was a very warm and loving person, and when my father was alive, she often popped into the nursery to see us. I can remember going for walks in the garden with her. She used to point out all the plants and flowers to me, and tell me their names. She loved the garden. She would cut flowers in the summer, then let me help her arrange them in vases."

"She sounds like a wonderful mother," Bromwell protested.

"She was. And I know that she loved me. But after my father died, she changed. She loved him a great deal, and after his death, sorrow sapped her of all life and joy. It was almost as if she had died with him, except that her body was still there among us. She still loved me, but she was not . . . terribly interested in anything. She stopped her gardening. She never cut flowers and arranged them anymore. And though she walked enough, she rarely took me — or anyone else — with her. She wandered along the paths all alone, and stopped to sit on the benches and just . . . sit there and stare, not really looking at anything."

Callie turned to him. "You must think me terribly selfish, complaining because she was not attentive enough to me when she had suffered a great tragedy."

"No, I do not think you are selfish," he assured her quietly. "You suffered a tragedy, too. You lost your father — and with him, you lost much of your mother, as well."

"Yes." Callie was surprised, and a little embarrassed, to feel tears spring into her eyes. It had been many years since her father's death, even since her mother's passing, and she had not been moved to tears over them in a long time, but somehow this man's quiet understanding of the pain she had felt awakened a feeling of such mingled sorrow, gratitude and tenderness within her that tears welled up in her eyes.

She blinked the tears away, glancing out across the fields as she steadied her emotions. "You understand, then."

"Well enough. My mother died soon after I was born. My nurse was like my mother — though, of course, when I grew old enough for a governess, she was no longer my nurse. But still, I slipped down to see her whenever I could. She was the sister of one of our tenant farmers, a widow whose child had died shortly after my mother. We

218

were well-suited in that way. Her brother had a son about my age, Henry. He was the only friend I had aside from Daphne. So, yes, I understand."

"Do you ever see Henry now?"

"Oh, yes." He grinned. "Scandalously, he is still probably my only friend. He is my steward. His older brother holds their farm, but Henry was always quick. He learned numbers and reading from me when we were young, and I sneaked books to him. When I came into the title, I hired him as my steward. My father's man had been steadily robbing him over the years, my father, of course, being too much the gentleman to stoop to checking over the accounts. The farms had suffered, and he, as well as my father, had earned the dislike of most of the tenants." He stopped. "Sorry, I did not mean to run on about such boring matters. No doubt you will rue the day you agreed to come on this trip."

"Not at all," Callie replied honestly. "I have heard my brother talk a good bit about his business affairs — at least the estate management. I do confess that his dealings on the 'Change do not interest me much. But the farms are altogether different. They aren't just numbers, which I do not like much. They are people, you see, with faces

219

and histories and all sorts of connections. And *that* I like very much. I have long stood up with Sinclair on the estate days, and greeted everyone and welcomed them at Boxing Day. You have to remember that I spent much of my time with the servants and, when I got older, riding about the estates with a groom. I know all the farmers and their families, at least at Marcastle and Dancy Park. I confess that I am not as familiar with his other holdings. I never spent as much time at them."

"Good Lord, how many residences does the man have?"

"Well, aside from the cottage in Scotland, which has not much land with it — he goes there only by himself, for fishing and, I think, to get away from being so much the *duke,* you see — he has the manor house in the Cotswolds, which was part of my mother's dowry. That, he says, will be part of *my* dowry, but he manages it for me. And then there is the estate in Cornwall, which hasn't much of a house, just a grim-looking old keep that Sinclair says is scarcely worth keeping up, but there are tin mines on the land, so he has to go there to oversee them. And another manor house in Sussex. That is all, I think. Well, except for Lilles House in London, but that isn't an *estate.*"

"All?" Bromwell let out a crack of laughter, tilting his head back. "You have put me in my place. Here I have congratulated myself on pulling my Yorkshire estate out of its debts and purchasing a house in London."

Callie's cheeks flooded with red. "Oh! Oh, no, truly I did not mean to boast. Whatever will you think of me? It is only because of his being a duke, you know. Well, I mean, he is quite handy, apparently, at managing all those things. But there are so many estates only because of some past duke marrying some heiress or other and her lands coming into Rochford control, and of course, we started out as barons, and then every time one of my ancestors got another title, there would be another estate. . . ." She ran down, looking abashed. "I am making it sound even worse, am I not? But they are my brother's, you see, and not mine."

"Except for the manor house in the Cotswolds," he put in, his eyes twinkling.

Callie let out a low groan. "I am sorry. Truly, it is not —" She stopped, not sure exactly what she could deny.

The earl laughed. "No, do not apologize. I do not take it as boasting. 'Tis only the truth. You are a woman of very high estate."

Callie rolled her eyes. "I hate to be thought

221

of that way. It makes me sound so . . . so priggish."

"You? I do not think anyone could think of you as priggish. You are, dear lady, delightful."

"No, I fear I am a rattle. My tongue is always running away with me. My grandmother would tell you that it is one of my worst faults."

"Your grandmother sounds most disagreeable."

Callie laughed. "I am unfair to the woman. She is simply proud of the family into which she married, and one cannot fault that. She has always done her duty, even when it entailed raising an unruly young girl when she was long past the age of having to deal with children, and she expects everyone else to do their duty, as well. It is only that what they want or what they enjoy has nothing to do with the matter."

"And what *do* you want?" he asked.

"I'm not sure. Not to have to marry some stuffy sort because he is a duke, then have the requisite number of children to please his family. All because I am the sister of a duke." She let out a sigh. "Sometimes I wish . . . I don't know . . . that I could be plain Miss Somebody, possessing no fortune at all."

"I think you would find possessing no fortune vastly uncomfortable."

"I know. I must sound like an ungrateful child. I am sure that I would not be at all happy having to pinch pennies or . . . or trim hats or sew clothes or something just to make enough money to live. It is only that I feel sometimes as if all anyone sees when they look at me is Rochford's sister, not a person in her own right. Not *me*."

"I can promise you," he said, turning to look into her face, "when I look at you, I see you and only you."

Callie, gazing back at him, felt suddenly as if everything else in the world around them had fallen away. There might have been no road, no companions, no wintry countryside. All she could see were his eyes, silver in the sunlight and edged with thick dark lashes, and all she could feel was this breathless, burgeoning . . . *something* inside her, spiraling up in her until she thought it must explode.

In his eyes, she saw a myriad of emotions flash through him with the same force and rapidity as her own. He turned his face away abruptly, taking a quick breath. Callie, too, glanced away, struggling to control her visage, to hide from the world what she feared must shine out from within her like a flame.

"Ah, there's the Park," Bromwell said suddenly, relief tingeing his voice.

Callie nodded. They turned off onto the path into the park. The land rolled gently into the distance, no buildings in sight, just a wide expanse of land framed with trees on either side and beyond, past where the land dipped down. It was not the verdant field that it would be later in the spring, and the trees were still leafless, apart from the evergreen yews and larches, but it was still a scene of sylvan beauty, lit by the pale winter sun. As if to complete the peaceful rural scene, a band of red deer at the edge of the trees raised their heads to look at them with interest, then lithely bounded off.

With a laughing glance at Bromwell, Callie dug in her heels and gave her horse its head. The mare bounded forward, clearly eager to run. Behind her, Bromwell let out a shout and came pounding after her. They tore along the path, leaving the rest of their party far behind.

Callie delighted in the rush of air against her cheeks and the surge of the horse beneath her. Their speed matched the rush of emotions inside her, sending her spirits soaring. The wind caught at the charming little hat, tugging it from her head and sending it tumbling backward, but she only laughed, too caught up in the moment to care.

Bromwell pulled even with her, and though she urged her mare to the utmost, he flashed a grin at her and passed her. After that he began to pull up, and so did she, slowing to a walk. They had outstripped the others, now hidden from them by a fold of land. It was, Callie thought, a good thing that they were shielded, for Bromwell turned his horse's head toward her, coming close, his face taut and bright with purpose. His arm went out as he reached her, looping around her waist, and he pulled her off her horse and onto his, setting her in front of him.

His other arm wrapped around her back, supporting her, and his hand went up to her cheek, then slid back into her hair. His heat enveloped her; his chest rose and fell rapidly. He said nothing, but his intent was clear on his face, his eyes glinting with it.

Callie turned up her face to his, as breathless as he. They were perfectly still for an instant, their eyes locked on each other. Then his mouth came down to cover hers.

Fire flowed through her, searing her skin and settling deep within her. She trembled in his embrace, aching and eager, as his mouth both filled and fueled her hunger.

Her hand went up and curled around his neck, urging him closer. He groaned, his lips digging into hers. He kissed her until she thought she must burst from the heat and desire spiraling up in her.

"Callie . . . Callie," he murmured, pulling his mouth away to trail his lips across her skin and down over the curve of her jaw. His hand left her hair to slide down her neck and onto the fabric of her riding habit. "I have been wanting to do that all day. Sweet heaven, I have been wanting to do it for a fortnight."

Callie chuckled, turning her face into his shoulder, and whispered, "I have, too."

Her response brought a low groan from him, and she felt his body flare with an added heat as he pressed her closer to him. He kissed her again, his hand sliding down the front of her bodice.

Finally he raised his head. "We cannot. They will be in sight soon."

He hesitated, gazing down into her face. His eyes darkened, and for an instant Callie thought that he meant to ignore his own words, but then he turned his head away with a soft curse. He kissed her again, once, brief and hard, then slid her off his lap and down to the ground. He dismounted quickly and turned to her.

"We should look for your hat."

"Mmm," Callie agreed distractedly. She found it difficult to think of anything but the soft, swollen tingling of her lips or the heavy achy feel of her breasts . . . or the insistent throbbing deep within her loins.

She looked up at him, and Bromwell's breath caught in his throat. Her face was flushed, her lips rosy and moist, her dark brown eyes wide and lambent. A strand of her hair had come loose when her hat was torn from her head, and it straggled down beside her face, clinging to her cheek. She was the very picture of a woman interrupted during lovemaking, and it made desire claw at his gut like a wild animal.

For a moment he could not speak. His fingers curled up into fists, and at last he said, somewhat shakily, "Callie, do not look at me so, or I shall lose what honor I have."

She blinked, forcibly pulling herself back from her sensual daydream. Her eyes sharpened with awareness as she curved her lips up into a deliciously provocative smile. Then she turned away, smoothing down her habit, and walked over to pick up the white mare's reins.

They walked back the way they had come, saying nothing. Each was too aware of what had just happened, and of the hot juices still flowing through them, to be able to speak casually. Callie fumbled with her hair, trying to pin the loose strands back into place, and Bromwell reached over to take the mare's reins from her, so that her hands were free. His fingers brushed against her hand, and where their flesh touched, even that briefly, heat sparked through them.

When they crested the small rise, they saw their group in the distance, gathered in a sheltered spot at the edge of the trees. The coachman and the groom were unloading the picnic basket from the back of the carriage, and the others were scattered around nearby.

Callie breathed a sigh of relief to find that she still had a few minutes to regroup before she had to face the sharp gazes of the other women in the party. She spotted her wayward hat a moment later, and Bromwell picked it up, presenting it to her with a flourish.

"Is my hair all right?" she asked anxiously as she found the hatpin, which had fortunately remained stuck in the hat as it was pulled off, and affixed the saucy bit of material and net to her head.

"You look lovely," he told her, smiling down into her face.

"Do not look at me like that," she chastised him, though she could not keep from smiling back at him. "As it is, everyone is no doubt wondering madly about what we were doing when we were out of sight."

"I imagine they might have their suspicions. But we were not gone long enough to have done much. And I can assure you that neither my sister's nor my cousin's tongue will wag."

"Nor will Lord and Lady Radbourne or Francesca speak of it," Callie agreed. "And with luck Mr. Swanson is too enamored of your sister to have noticed anything."

He chuckled. "I imagine that is true. Which leaves only Miss Swanson, who is, I think, very young and unsophisticated."

They continued walking in silence for a moment; then Bromwell said, "I hope you will not think that I meant any disrespect to you. I am not usually given to seizing young women and hauling them off their horses."

"Indeed? Are you not?" she murmured, casting a sideways glance at him. "Yet you seemed most expert at it."

His mouth twitched. "You are a saucy girl. I am trying to make an apology to you."

"You need not. I, um, rather participated in what happened." Callie could not bring herself to look directly into his face as she said the words; her cheeks were flaming as it was.

He glanced at her, surprised, and she looked up. His sharp cheekbones were edged with color, and she thought at first that what she had said had embarrassed him, but then she noted the light in his eyes, and she realized that her words had once again stirred his desire.

"My dear Lady Calandra . . ." he murmured. "You will make a spectacle of me yet."

"I?" she asked. "And how would I do that?"

"When I am around you, I find myself at every turn on the verge of —" He stopped abruptly.

"The verge of what?" Callie asked, confused.

"The verge of committing an act such as I just did, for one thing," he replied. "Of showing to the world just how ungentlemanly are the feelings I have for you, for another."

She stared at him, then caught the meaning of his words and blushed vividly. "Lord Bromwell!"

"You see? I lose even the art of making genteel conversation with you."

"I see. So you are saying that if you are

'ungentlemanly,' it is my fault?" Callie raised her brows at him.

"I can see no other explanation for my mad behavior other than that you drive me to it," he agreed lightly, a faint smile playing about his lips. "But surely you must know that. I think you must be in the habit of driving men mad."

"Nay, I do believe that you are the first," she retorted dryly.

"I cannot imagine that. It seems to me that everything about you is designed to do just that." He looked at her, his steps slowing as he went on, "Your hair. Your eyes. The way your lips curve when you smile, so that all I can think of is touching those lips with mine."

Callie's color heightened, her breath coming more rapidly. "Brom . . ."

He stopped, and so did she, turning toward him. For a moment the very air between them seemed to vibrate with heat and hunger. Then, with an effort of will, Callie turned away.

"I fear you are not helping us —" she told him somewhat shakily, "— in our attempt to appear normal when we rejoin our friends."

"You are right." He took a breath and released it in a sigh. He started walking forward again, saying lightly, "So . . . Lady Calandra . . . 'tis a lovely winter day for a ride, is it not?"

She let out a little laugh and fell into step beside him. So, talking of nothing, they walked back to the others, and by the time they reached their party, outwardly they seemed as always, only a little windblown from their ride.

Inside, however, was an entirely different matter. Inside, Callie did not think she would ever be quite the same.

CHAPTER TEN

The women of the party were seated upon a blanket on the ground, the men still standing as they waited. Francesca and Lady Daphne, Callie noticed, were seated as far apart as they could get and still remain on the blanket, and there was a faint flush to Francesca's cheeks, telling Callie that she was not in the best of humors. Miss Swanson and Irene were seated between them, the latter looking determinedly inexpressive and the former seeming blissfully unaware.

"Ah, Lady Calandra! And Bromwell. You naughty children, to have escaped like that," Lady Daphne said brightly, and pointed a mockingly admonishing finger. "You will set tongues wagging with that sort of behavior."

"Not unless someone sets out to spread such rumors, Lady Swithington," Francesca commented sharply, sending the other woman an icy look.

"Well, of course, none of us would remark

233

on such a thing," Lady Daphne replied, looking wounded. "We all know what it is to be young and lively, do we not?" She smiled archly at the men.

"I think you will find that you need not be concerned about Lady Calandra's reputation, Lady Swithington," Irene interjected calmly. "Everyone knows that Callie's character is above reproach."

"Of course it is," Bromwell agreed as he strode over to sit down beside his sister. Callie took a seat next to Francesca.

Francesca turned to her with a smile. "It is an excellent day for a ride. Did you enjoy your run?"

"Oh, yes." Callie followed Francesca's welcome change of subject. "Lord Bromwell's horse is such a lovely creature. He is clearly a superior judge of horseflesh."

"Yes, he is," his sister agreed proudly. "Brom has always taken care of such matters for me . . . and for my dear late husband, as well."

The conversation predictably veered off into a discussion of horses, and Callie sat back, letting the words flow around her, now and then tossing in a comment. She did not let herself think about what had happened between her and Bromwell earlier. That would come later tonight, when she was back in her room alone and could hug the knowledge to herself, letting the memories wash over her again.

After a cold luncheon, Callie and Francesca went for a walk, accompanied by Archie and Miss Swanson, while the others stayed behind to rest and chat. Later, after a rambling ride through the park, they turned back toward the road to London, pleasantly tired.

"Such a delightful outing," Lady Daphne declared.

She was joined in her raptures about the day by Miss Swanson, who vowed that it was the most pleasant time she had had in London yet, and Mr. Swanson chimed in with his opinion that it had all been "capital."

"We must have another outing," Lady Daphne went on, smiling. "Now, what would be amusing? I know! The perfect thing — Vauxhall Garden."

Miss Swanson clapped her hands in agreement, and Mr. Swanson and Mr. Tilford both agreed that it sounded excellent. Francesca smiled stiffly and made a vague murmur.

"Tuesday next?" Lady Daphne pressed. "Do say yes, Lady Calandra."

Callie cast a glance at Francesca, who she

suspected had no desire to go anywhere with Lady Daphne, given the tenseness of her posture.

"I am not sure," Francesca temporized. "I believe that I may have a previous engagement."

"But Lady Calandra can come, surely," the other woman countered, looking not in the least displeased by the prospect of Francesca's absence. "There will be a large party of us, after all. That should be ample chaperonage for these youngsters. Lord and Lady Radbourne will be there, will you not?" She looked appealingly at Irene and Gideon.

Irene glanced from Lady Daphne to Francesca and Callie. "Why, yes, I daresay."

"There, you see." Lady Daphne smiled triumphantly.

"Of course Lady Calandra is free to do as she wishes," Francesca told her stiffly.

Callie turned to Francesca, torn. She wanted to go, but she felt a little guilty about it, as if she were deserting Francesca. "I — that is, I should go with Lady Haughston to, um . . ."

"Nonsense." Francesca smiled and reached over to pat Callie on the arm. "There is no need for you to sacrifice yourself. I recall now that it is simply a visit with an old friend. You go on and have fun."

"Then it is settled. What fun it will be." Bromwell's sister smiled brilliantly, and she and Miss Swanson settled into a discussion about dominoes and masks to wear to the event.

Callie fell back to ride beside Francesca and Irene. She said in a low voice, "Francesca, I can send Lady Swithington a note saying I cannot come."

Francesca smiled at her. "No, I should feel quite terrible if I made you forego your pleasure just because I cannot bear to be in that woman's company a few more hours. I would not countenance Lady Swithington as a chaperone, heaven knows, but if Irene and Gideon are there, it will be perfectly proper. And I know you want to go."

"I will make sure that decorum is maintained," Irene agreed, leaning forward to speak across Francesca.

It was common knowledge that a good deal of overly free behavior took place at Vauxhall Gardens. But as long as there were gentlemen in one's party to discourage the bold young men who liked to stroll along the boxes, ogling unattached women, and a married lady to lend countenance to the whole affair, it was an enjoyable evening's entertainment.

Callie had been there before in the company of her brother, and it had always seemed to her a magical sort of place, with its paths and fountains and false ruins, all bathed in the warm glow of lanterns strung along the walkways and in the surrounding trees. If that were not enough, there were the orchestra in the pavilion, dancing, wandering singers, and sometimes even acrobats who might juggle or walk along a tightrope strung over their heads.

She looked forward to the prospect of seeing it when she was not under the watchful eye of her brother, and the idea of strolling along the paths in the company of Lord Bromwell appealed to her even more.

Callie smiled over at Irene. "Thank you." She looked at Francesca again. "If you are sure."

"Yes, I am sure." Francesca smiled. "I do not think even your grandmother would question your going there with a large party that included Irene and Gideon. And if you do not go without me, then I shall be forced to endure an evening in that woman's company, which I vowed an hour ago I would not do."

Callie cast a questioning glance at Irene, who merely shrugged and raised her eyebrows slightly.

"All right," Callie agreed, then smiled affectionately at Francesca. "Thank you."

"Do not be foolish. There is no reason why you should be deprived of your pleasures just because I allow that woman to overset my nerves." She smiled at Callie. "And now I think I shall go for a little run myself and see if I can clear out my poor temper."

She urged her horse into a trot, and soon left them and the rest of the party behind her. Callie watched Francesca ride past the others and settle into a slower pace in front of everyone else.

Callie turned to Irene. "Do you know why she was upset with Lady Swithington?"

"I'm not sure, other than the fact that Lady Swithington can be a bit of a trial. However, I have seen Francesca smile and get along with far worse, my sister-in-law included."

Callie, who was acquainted with Lady Wyngate, the wife of Irene's brother Humphrey, smothered a smile.

"I understand that Lady Swithington's reputation left something to be desired," Irene went on. "But that was years ago. I do not even remember her. And as she has been away in Wales or some such place since then, she cannot have aroused much scandal there. Or, at least, none we heard of. She is a flirt, that much is clear." Irene seemed placidly unconcerned by the fact, given that her husband had been the object of the other woman's flirtation. "But I cannot see why that would have bothered Francesca. I was the one who wanted to slap her."

"You did?" Callie asked in surprise.

Irene laughed. "Well, I would have, except that Gideon kept sending me such piteous looks, hoping for rescue, that I could not help but be a trifle amused by it all."

A smile curved the other's woman's mouth, and for a moment there was such a slumbrous sensual light in Irene's eyes that Callie had to glance away, feeling that she had seen something far too private. Then the look fell away, and Irene shrugged.

"I think Francesca may have been upset by the fact that Lady Swithington kept talking about you. It was hardly the sort of thing that one could object to — how lovely you were, what delicate manners you have, how well you sit a horse. Lady Daphne was hoping to further her brother's suit, I suppose, but it might have been wiser not to say anything, as it only reminded everyone that you were not there, but were with her brother. In other company, or if you had been some other, less well-known, young woman, it might have led to gossip."

Callie felt her cheeks warm. "Was there talk? I did not realize we were gone so long. I — it was just so enjoyable to ride." She looked off to the side, unwilling to face Irene's clear golden-brown gaze.

"No. Of course not. Your reputation is such that it would take behavior far worse than that to shake it. And in any case, you were soon in sight again." Irene paused. "Lady Swithington mentioned your connection to the duke more than once, as well. Francesca probably thought she was being encroaching."

Callie nodded. She was still of the opinion that there must be something more than little things such as Irene had mentioned to make the usually equable Francesca so dislike Lady Swithington. But Callie was not one to gossip about her suspicions, even to Irene.

The ride home was uneventful. Lord Bromwell did not single Callie out again. She knew that his action was wise; it would not do for him to show so strong a preference for her company after having ridden all the way over to the park by her side. Still, she could not deny the fact that she missed his presence, or that she would have liked more memories to store up and go over in her mind that night as she lay in bed.

He said goodbye to her in a formal way, only the warmth that tinted his eyes revealing any special feeling for her, then remounted and left with his sister and friends. Irene and Gideon also took their leave, refusing Francesca's offer to stay and partake of a late tea with them.

Francesca and Callie, after a look at each other, agreed that they wanted to do nothing but rest and clean up, partake of a light supper and go early to bed. Callie was glad for the time alone. Fond as she was of Francesca's company, right now she wanted only to be alone with her thoughts. She soaked in the tub, her maid appearing periodically to warm up the water from a kettle. Then, wrapped in her dressing gown, she sat on a low stool in front of the fire, brushing out her hair and letting it dry.

She hugged her memories of this afternoon to herself, remembering each word and gesture, lingering over the kisses they had shared, recalling the look in Brom's gray eyes when he gazed down into her face. It made her blush when she thought about what they had done and the way she had reacted to him. Even thinking about it, her blood heated once more. She had never felt this way before, and it was both delightful and alarming.

She had no idea what was going to happen or even what she wanted to happen. She knew only that she was enjoying her life more than she ever had before, that she awoke each morning with a sense of eagerness and excitement.

It would have to end. She knew that. And she also knew how little likelihood there was that it would end well. Sinclair would be bound to return to London sooner or later — or some busybody would take it upon herself to write to Callie's brother and grandmother and let them know that the Earl of Bromwell was busily paying court to Lady Calandra. Callie had no idea what her brother would do when he found out she had been defying his direct orders not to see Bromwell, but she was not eager to find out.

She dreaded the thought of an argument with her brother, and she had no idea what she would do if he ordered her back to Marcastle for the rest of the Season. She would not allow him to dictate her life to her, but on the other hand, she could not bear the thought of a rift between them. What would she do if it came down to that? If she had to choose between Sinclair and Bromwell?

That, of course, led to the larger question

of exactly what she would be choosing if she chose Bromwell. He was showing her marked attentions, but where were they leading? Indeed, where did she want them to lead?

She was not sure what Bromwell felt for her. He appeared to be smitten with her; all the signs were there. But she could not dismiss a certain uneasiness caused by Sinclair's warning against the man. Sinclair was not unreasonable, nor was he someone who was easily upset. If he felt so strongly that she should not see Bromwell, she could not help but wonder if there was something wrong with the man, something she could not see, could not tell. Was Bromwell not serious in his pursuit? Was he playing some sort of game?

He had said nothing about his intentions, but it was still too early for that. Why, she did not even know what her own intentions were. If Bromwell were to ask for her hand tomorrow, she had no idea what she would say.

She felt about him as she had never felt about a man before. His touch made her shiver; the thought of seeing him again made her almost giddy. And when he kissed her, she ached in an utterly new and wonderful way. Any day when she did not see him seemed far emptier than her days had been in the past, and whenever he entered the room, it was as if a light had gone on inside her. Was that love?

Or was it simply infatuation? Passion?

Callie did not know. All she was certain of was that she wanted to continue feeling this way.

True to her word, Lady Swithington invited them to join her party in a visit to Vauxhall Gardens the following Tuesday. She did not entrust the matter to paper, but called upon them herself to issue the invitation. Francesca, smiling stiffly, reiterated her commitment to the fictitious meeting with her old friend, but added that she hoped that Callie would attend.

In fact, Francesca felt a ripple of unease about the whole endeavor. She knew how much Callie wanted to go, but she hated to think what the Duke of Rochford's reaction would be to his sister spending time in the company of his notorious former mistress.

Of course, it was entirely the duke's own fault, not Francesca's, that he was in such a precarious position regarding Lady Swithington. She could not, she thought, be expected to protect him from what had been, after all, his own folly. It was her duty, though, to protect Callie, and in Francesca's opinion, Lady Swithington was not a fit person for Callie to associate with.

However, everyone in the beau monde seemed to have forgiven — or at least forgotten — the reputation Lady Daphne had earned before her marriage to Lord Swithington fifteen years ago. Moreover, Francesca was not sure how well known the woman's liaison with the duke had been. The duke was in general a very discreet and conservative sort of man, and while Daphne's determined pursuit of him had been quite public, Francesca felt sure that few people had actually witnessed, as she had been unlucky enough to, the sight of Rochford and Daphne emerging from one of their trysts.

Francesca had not heard of Lady Daphne's not being received by any of Society's hostesses. Lady Odelia Pencully, a force in the *ton,* was peculiarly fond of the woman. So Callie would have some difficulty understanding why she could not associate with Lady Swithington, should such an association suddenly be forbidden. And Francesca could not reveal why Rochford would dislike Callie's being around Lady Daphne without telling her the very thing that the duke would not want Callie to know.

She ought to attend the party herself, Francesca knew, but she had found it almost unbearable to be in Lady Swithington's presence the other day at Richmond Park. She had thought that fifteen years would have healed all wounds, but in truth, being around Daphne had instead reminded her all over again of the reasons why she disliked her. Every time Daphne had mentioned Rochford, Francesca had grown stiffer, until she had felt as if she might break.

And, after all, Irene and Gideon would be there, as well as several other people. It was not as though Callie would be with Lady Daphne and her brother unchaperoned or associating closely with the woman. And Callie would be wearing a concealing domino and mask. No one would even know she was there. Nothing would happen to Callie or to her reputation. And if Rochford was upset by it, well, she reasoned somewhat snippily, then he should have been more careful about what he did fifteen years ago.

So resolved, Francesca did not attend the party nor try to dissuade Callie from doing so. Still, she could not quite suppress a twinge of uneasiness as, the following

Tuesday, she watched Callie climb into the carriage Lady Swithington had sent.

Callie, however, felt not the slightest discomfort. She waved goodbye to Francesca, then settled back for the short ride to Lady Daphne's house, where the party was gathering for the trip. She was wearing an evening gown of white with silver lace trim, and over it a black satin domino, lined in white satin. She had borrowed the domino from Francesca, as she had not brought one with her from Lilles House, and she thought it was both elegant and dramatic. The hood was folded back a turn to reveal the accent of white lining, and as the hood was wide, much of the lining was visible, a rich contrast to her tumbled black curls. With the half mask in place, she looked, she thought, both sophisticated and mysterious.

She giggled a little at the thought, for the truth was that inside, Callie felt anything but sophisticated and mysterious. She was brimming with excitement, like a girl at her first ball, and she thought her feelings must glow from her like a lamp.

A doorman stood outside Lady Swithington's gray stone home, which was festively ablaze with lights, and he bowed and opened the door for Callie. Inside, a butler showed her into the drawing room, where a merry group stood talking and laughing. Besides Lady Swithington, the Swanson siblings were there, as well as Mr. Tilford, and two more young men and a young woman whom Callie had never met.

"Lady Calandra!" Daphne swept forward to meet her, holding out both hands to take Callie's. "I am so pleased that you are here. Come, let me introduce you to the others in our little party."

The men were dressed in the latest styles, with the most up-to-date affectations and ornamentations. One wore a nosegay as big as his fist in the buttonhole of his lapel, and the other's watchchain contained so many fobs that it was a wonder the chain did not break. Their speech was peppered with cant, and they amused one another with frequent witticisms that left Callie wondering why they thought themselves so funny.

However, Miss Swanson and the other young woman, a blond girl possessed of a high-pitched giggle, seemed to find the two young men inordinately charming, and they hung upon their every word, letting loose peals of laughter whenever one of them made a *bon mot.*

Lady Daphne, wincing a little as the blond girl let forth a particularly piercing shriek of laughter, introduced Callie to the others.

The blond woman turned out to be Miss Lucilla Turner, and the gentlemen were Mr. William Pacewell and Mr. Roland Sackville. No sooner had they been introduced than Callie found herself unable to remember which man was which, but as she quickly realized that she had little interest in speaking to either of them, it did not really matter.

She nodded at Mr. Swanson and his sister, relieved to see someone she knew, and looked around the room for the rest of the party.

"Ah, I see you are looking for my brother," Lady Daphne said with a knowing smile. "He is not here yet. He will meet us later at Vauxhall. You know how it is. Young men are so busy."

"I see." Callie smiled, doing her best to hide her disappointment. "I presume Lord and Lady Radbourne have not arrived yet?"

"No, but it is early yet. Let me get you some refreshment while we wait for them."

Lady Daphne motioned to a servant, and in short order Callie had a glass of ratafia in her hand. She sipped at it and talked to Lady Daphne, feeling a little strange and out of place. Callie was not a shy person, but the absence of anyone she knew well made her quieter than normal, and she found the young men's self-conscious posing and boisterous talk off-putting.

The minutes crawled by, but still Irene and Gideon did not appear. Lady Daphne had begun looking repeatedly at the clock and frowning, then smiling and saying airily that she was sure they had just been delayed and would be there shortly.

Finally, however, after Miss Turner had asked yet again when they were going to leave, Lady Daphne sighed and said, "Well, I suppose it would be best if we went on to Vauxhall. After all, it is not long until Lord Bromwell is to meet us there."

"But what about Lord and Lady Radbourne?" Callie asked.

"I have no idea why they have not come. But no doubt they are merely a trifle late. I shall leave word with the butler for them to join us at Vauxhall."

"Perhaps I should wait for them," Callie began uneasily. She knew that Francesca would not like her going off with Lady Swithington and the others without Irene and Gideon along.

"Heavens, no," Lady Swithington replied gaily. "What if one of them has fallen ill and they do not come at all? Then you should miss all the fun. Or they may simply decide, being so late, that they will meet us there and will not even come to the house. You would not wish to stay here all evening by yourself."

That was certainly true. Callie had no desire to sit in a strange house alone for hours, doing nothing. She knew that she should probably tell Lady Swithington that she would just go back to Francesca's. But she could think of no way to tactfully tell Bromwell's sister that Francesca — and no doubt her own grandmother and brother — would not consider Lady Daphne an adequate chaperone. Surely Irene and Gideon would arrive eventually, and then she would have missed it all for nothing. Besides, she wanted very much to see Bromwell and walk along the romantic lighted pathways with him.

Anyway, she reminded herself, she could hardly ask all the others to wait even longer while Lady Daphne's carriage took her back home first. So she summoned up a smile and said, "You are right. We had best go on."

The four women rode in Lady Swithington's carriage, while the men hailed a hansom to transport them, and they started out for the gardens. Callie's doubts ebbed as they rode along. The conversation with just the four women in the carriage was much quieter and more pleasant, and with every passing moment, she grew more eager to see the sparkling gardens and, most of all, to be with Bromwell.

Vauxhall was as magical in appearance as ever, and Callie's unease disappeared as they stepped out of their carriage and started inside. The men purchased their tickets and reserved one of the supper boxes that lined the main promenade.

They strolled along the wide walkway until they reached their box, located near the pavilion where the orchestra would soon play. They took their seats and began to watch the passing parade. There was something wonderfully freeing, Callie thought, in being in domino and mask. She could look at everyone who walked by, secure in the knowledge that no one would know who she was and there would be no talk that could make its way back to the duchess.

A waiter brought out their supper of wafer-thin slices of ham, along with chicken and various salads, and poured freely from containers of the arrack punch for which the Gardens were famous. It was a potent brew and though Callie merely sipped at it, she soon found herself relaxing under its influence, and she settled down to enjoy herself.

It was great fun to watch the people, who came in all shapes, sizes and classes. There were many young bucks, some of them dandies, others with the athletic builds of Corinthians, and there were a good many unattached women, as well, who boldly flirted with the men. Callie watched them in some fascination, blushing now and then at some of the warm comments that were tossed back and forth.

Somewhat to her surprise, some of the young men were bold enough to ogle her and the other women sitting in their supper box. Miss Swanson and Miss Turner responded to their bold looks with a rash of giggles. Lady Daphne did not giggle, but Callie was a trifle shocked to see that lady lift her fan and look back over it flirtatiously at one or two of the brash young gentlemen.

Callie expected the men of their company to send the others on their way. She could well imagine how Sinclair would have responded to such impudence. Of course, when she had come here with her brother, simply his presence in the box had been enough to keep any young man from directing such inappropriate looks her way.

The orchestra struck up in the pavilion, and people took to the dance floor in front of it. For politeness's sake, Callie stood up with Mr. Tilford and then with Mr. Pacewell — at least, she thought it was Mr. Pacewell — but he trod clumsily upon her foot, and his breath stank so much of alcohol that she decided after that to sit out any dances, at least until Bromwell arrived . . . if he arrived. She was beginning to have her doubts.

Still Lord and Lady Radbourne had not come, and neither had Brom. Callie began to find her pleasure in the evening decreasing. The conversation in their box was growing louder and more boisterous as the evening progressed and more and more arrack punch was consumed. The girls' giggles increased, and the men's laughter grew heartier. Their words became slurred, and they tended to set their glasses of punch down too hard, and once Mr. Sackville, or perhaps it was Mr. Pacewell — the drunker they became, the more difficulty Callie had in telling them apart — missed the table altogether with his cup, and it fell to the earth and spilled. Everyone except Callie seemed to find this mishap hilarious. Indeed, Mr. Swanson laughed so hard that he staggered back and knocked into a chair, turning it over, and subsequently wound up sitting on the ground, as well, which set everyone off into even further gales of laughter.

Callie sipped at her glass and tried to ignore everything that was going on about her. But it was growing more and more difficult by the moment. Mr. Pacewell — or whichever it was of them who had not spilled his drink — was leaning over Miss Turner, boldly staring down the front of her dress, as he murmured into her ear, his lips almost touching her.

Callie glanced away quickly and looked over at Lady Swithington. However, if she had hoped that that lady would restore some semblance of decorum, she quickly saw that she was wrong. Daphne was sitting at the front edge of the box, her arms on the ledge before her, leaning forward to talk in low tones to a man who stood outside. The man was leaning in toward Daphne, as well, a smile playing about his mouth, and as Callie watched, he reached out and ran his forefinger along her hand, trailing it up her arm to her elbow.

Callie looked away again, rather uncertain as to where she could direct her gaze. She took a nervous gulp of her drink, then gasped as the potent mixture roared down her throat.

Where was Bromwell? Why had he not come? She wished desperately that he was there. He, she thought, would set everything in order. At least, she thought a little falter-ingly, she hoped that he would. What if, when he arrived, he acted the same way as the other men? What if he joined in the drunken revelry, boldly eyeing the women in the other boxes and on the walkway?

Another man had stopped to lean into their box and talk, and before long, Callie saw to her horror that Lady Daphne and Miss Swanson had invited the strangers to join them. Callie pushed her chair back as far as she could against the side wall and away from the others, and contemplated what she ought to do.

She had given up all hope that Irene and Gideon were going to appear, and she was growing doubtful about Brom. The evening had developed into a veritable romp, and she was keenly aware that she should not be there. The problem was that she did not know how she was to get away. The thought of making her way alone through the throng outside the box made her shudder. This was not the sort of place where a woman alone was safe from crude remarks and lascivious glances — and, she suspected, far worse.

However, she hardly knew any of the men in her party. She was not at all certain, given the way they had been acting, that any of them could be trusted to protect her from the advances of another man — or, indeed, trusted at all. Even if she could rely on them, she was not sure that any of them were sober enough to help her, anyway.

Callie set down her glass on the table beside her and rubbed her forehead. Her own thoughts were a little muzzy, and she wondered how much she had drunk of the strong punch. One glass — no, two, for she rather thought that whenever she set a half-empty glass down, it was soon replaced by a full one. Lady Daphne had been assiduous in making sure that everyone stayed well-refreshed.

Even as Callie thought this, a waiter was at her side, filling up her glass again. She shook her head at him, but he seemed not to notice, simply topped off her glass and moved away. Callie sighed and tried to clear her thoughts. She was going to have to stop sipping at her drink, no matter how nervous she felt. She was going to need a clearer head to deal with the situation.

"What, all by yourself?" a male voice slurred, and one of the two strangers whom Daphne had let into their box sat down heavily in the chair closest to Callie's. "Can't have that, pretty young thing like you."

He smiled at her in what he doubtless

thought was a charming way.

"I am perfectly content by myself," Callie told him in a frosty tone.

For some reason he seemed to find her remark amusing, for he chuckled. "My, my, bit high in the instep, aren't you?" He reached for the glass she had set down earlier and offered it to her. "Can't have fun like that, can you? Here, have a nip. It'll set you up right."

"No, thank you."

He shrugged and drained the glass himself. Then he leaned closer, peering into her face. "Whassa matter? Don' you want some fun?"

Callie recoiled. His breath stank of alcohol, and his eyes were bloodshot. "No," she told him firmly. "Now, please, move somewhere else."

She was not normally rude, but it was clear that no polite rejoinder would have any effect on him. He regarded her for a moment, his eyes narrowing, and for an appalled moment she thought he was going to say something vicious. But then he shrugged and hauled himself to his feet, reeling away toward the others.

Callie saw with dismay that while she had been occupied with the man, several of their party had left their box. Neither Miss Swanson nor Miss Turner was there, and the two dandies were gone, as well. She turned to look out across the promenade and was a little relieved to see that the four young people had decided to dance; they would come back soon. As she watched, they were swallowed up by the crowd of dancers.

She looked around at the occupants of the box. Mr. Swanson, it seemed, had reached his limit, for he was sitting slumped over one of the tables, eyes closed, snoring heavily. Mr. Tilford picked up a cup, filled it with punch, then toddled out the rear door, apparently seeking more lively companions.

Callie glanced at Lady Swithington. She was sitting between the two men whom she had invited into the booth, talking and laughing and flirting with them over her fan, now and then folding it to lay a light, teasing tap upon one or the other of them.

One of them took her hand and raised it to his lips, lingering far longer than was acceptable, but Daphne made no move to take her hand away. She simply laughed throatily and leaned closer to whisper something in the man's ear.

"Lady Swithington," Callie said urgently. "I — I must leave. I am sure that Francesca will be worried about me."

It took Daphne a moment to focus on

Callie. "But, my dear, it is still early yet. You cannot mean to leave so soon."

"I — Lord and Lady Radbourne have not come, and I — I fear I should not be here. If you could send for your carriage . . ." She was not sure how she would safely reach the carriage, but she felt that she must leave, and soon, before the situation grew even worse.

Lady Daphne laughed, waving her hand airily. "Now, now, you can't leave yet. Why, Brom has not even arrived. You must not let Lord and Lady Radbourne spoil your fun."

"I am — I do not think that Lord Bromwell is coming," Callie replied, trying to keep her voice even. "It is quite late."

Lady Daphne rose, saying with a laugh, "The evening has scarcely begun. You cannot go yet. Come." She held out a hand toward Callie. "Come with us. We are going to dance. Poor Willoughby needs a partner, don't you, Mr. Willoughby?"

The man in question peered at Callie, then shook his head. "No, she won't go. Too Friday-faced."

"Lady Swithington . . ." Callie began again. "I truly do not wish to dance."

"You see?" the drunken man said, nodding sagely. "Told you."

"I wish to leave," Callie went on. "And I

imagine that Miss Swanson and Miss Turner should go, as well. They are in that crowd, completely unchaperoned."

"Well, of course, of course, if that is what you wish," Daphne replied magnanimously. "Just as soon as Brom comes. Though I doubt that Miss Turner and Miss Swanson will welcome your dragging them away, as well," she added with a chuckle. "Now, if you are sure that you won't come dance with us . . ."

She turned away, looping her hands through both men's arms and flashing a dazzling smile at them. "Come, gentlemen. I am eager to dance."

The man who was not Willoughby chuckled and murmured, "Eager for much else, as well, I trust."

Lady Swithington laughed, seemingly not in the least offended by his suggestive words, and said, "We shall see, won't we?"

"Lady Swithington!" Callie cried out, appalled, as the group made their way toward the door.

Daphne appeared not to hear her as she swept out of the box, closing the door behind them. Callie stood there, staring after her in astonishment. Slowly, she turned, taking in the scene. She was alone except for Mr. Swanson, passed out in his chair. Indeed, she had never felt quite so alone. She looked out at the increasingly boisterous scene in front of her. Lady Daphne and her two swains had disappeared into the crowd, nor could she spot any of the others who had come with her tonight.

Callie frowned and sat back down in her chair to think. What was she to do? She wanted very much to simply run through the crowd to the entrance and there jump into a hansom cab to take her home. However, she could not help but be concerned about Miss Swanson and Miss Turner, who had clearly had more of the arrack punch than was good for them — and were rather foolish to begin with, if one was being truthful. The men who were with them were hardly people on whom one could rely. She should have done something more to stop them, she thought. And it seemed irresponsible to simply leave them here.

"Well, what are you doing all alone, pretty one?"

Callie jumped, startled, and turned to see a middle-aged man leaning on the open ledge of the box. She rose, her heart pounding, and her hands clenching into fists at her side.

"Please go away. My brother will return soon," she improvised, her mind roaming over the possibilities the box offered in the way of weapons. One of the empty bottles would be best, she thought, and she started to edge toward the table where Mr. Swanson sat, his head on his arms.

"Brother, is it?" His smile conveyed his disbelief. "He should have more sense than to leave a lovely like yourself all alone. Perhaps I should come in and keep you company 'til he gets back."

"No. You should not." Callie reached the table, and her hand curled tightly around the neck of the bottle.

The man laughed. "Oh, ho. 'Tis a dust-up you're after?" He placed his hands upon the ledge, as though he would climb over it into the box.

Callie heaved the bottle at him and was surprised to see that it hit him, although on his chest, rather than his face, where she had aimed. The man stopped, looking at her in surprise.

"Here," he said resentfully. "No call to do that." He straightened his jacket and shot her a disgruntled look, then turned and staggered off.

Callie let out a sigh of relief and moved farther away from the front of the box. She looked around and found another bottle to use in case she needed a weapon again. She straightened and turned to find another man looking into the box.

A startled shriek escaped her, and she raised her bottle.

"Callie? Is that you?" the man said and, putting his hand on the ledge, lightly vaulted into the box. "What the devil are you doing here by yourself?"

"Brom!" The bottle dropped from her hand, and with a little sob, Callie ran to throw herself into his arms.

CHAPTER ELEVEN

Bromwell wrapped his arms around her tightly. "Callie, what happened? What's wrong?"

"Oh, Brom . . ." She clung tightly to him. "Nothing happened. There's nothing wrong, really."

And, strangely enough, she thought, it was true. Now that Bromwell was here, everything was all right. She no longer felt anxious or afraid, not with his hard chest against her head, his heart beating in steady rhythm beneath her ear.

"Where is everyone?" he asked. "Why the devil are you here by yourself?"

"I'm not," Callie said lightly, releasing her hold on him a trifle reluctantly and taking a step back. With a wry smile, she gestured toward Mr. Swanson's slumped form.

The earl turned to look at him, his frown deepening. "Bloody hell! Is the man incapacitated?"

Callie nodded. "I think everyone had too much of the punch, frankly. I feel a bit fuzzy-headed myself."

"But where is my sister? Where are Lord and Lady Radbourne and the others? Why did they go off and leave you here alone?"

"I don't know why Irene and Gideon are not here. They never arrived. And everyone else has gone to dance." She gestured vaguely toward the promenade area. "I was beginning to think that you were not going to come, either."

"Of course I was coming. Daphne said . . ." He stopped, his frown deepening. "How long have you been here?"

"I'm not sure. It seems like forever."

"Obviously long enough for Mr. Swanson to be in his cups," Bromwell added dryly.

"Yes. We were here well before ten, for Miss Swanson was very eager to arrive before the orchestra began its second performance."

Bromwell gazed out at the promenade area for a long moment, then let out a sigh and said, "I cannot imagine what possessed my sister to leave you here with only Mr. Swanson. Was he like this when she left?"

Callie nodded and gave a wry smile. "He was not much protection."

"I should think not." He grimaced. "I

apologize for not arriving sooner. I must have mistaken the time Daphne said. It will be a wonder now if Lady Haughston allows me to darken your door again."

"It might be best if Lady Haughston did not know exactly what transpired here tonight," Callie said. "She will only worry. And I am sure there is no likelihood of it happening again."

Because she would never again make the mistake of accepting one of Lady Swithington's invitations, Callie added silently.

Bromwell nodded, seeming a trifle distracted. "Well . . . I shall discuss this later with Daphne. Right now I think it would be best if I saw you home."

"Yes. I would appreciate that," Callie agreed. She hesitated. "Although Miss Swanson and Miss Turner are still here. We should make sure that they are all right."

"Surely they are not alone, as well."

"No, they went to dance with Mr. Pacewell and Mr. Sackville."

"Pacewell and Sackville. Good Gad, those two peacocks?" Bromwell rolled his eyes. "They are fools, but the ladies are unlikely to come to any harm with them. The important thing is to see you home, and after that I will return and find the others."

Callie smiled. "Thank you."

He allowed a smile finally and his hand came up to cup her cheek. "I am deeply sorry, Callie, that you have been subjected to this debacle."

"It was not so bad," she lied. Indeed, looking up into his eyes, she found the memory of her earlier anxiety fading rapidly.

"It is good of you to say so, but I know full well that this evening was not the kind of situation that you are accustomed to. I shall speak with my sister about it."

"I do not wish to cause any hard feelings between you and Lady Swithington."

"Do not worry." He smiled again. "We shall not disown one another. But I fear that Daphne has been too long out of Society. She does not, perhaps, recall, how restrictive the rules are governing the behavior of a young unmarried lady. Nor is she accustomed to the sort of strong punch they serve here. She clearly was not thinking. Now, pull up the hood of your domino and we shall brave the mad throng outside."

Matching his deeds to his words, he reached out and took the edges of her hood in his hands, gently pulling it up over her black curls. His hands lingered for a moment on the material as he gazed down into her face. Then, as if coming to himself, his hands dropped away and he turned, politely offering Callie his arm.

She laid her hand on his arm, and they left through the back door, walking around to the wide promenade in front of their ornately decorated box.

They paused, and Callie gazed around at the scene. Now that her anxiety was gone, she was able to enjoy the way the gardens looked, and she wished that Bromwell had been there the entire evening. Then she could have enjoyed everything without worrying. She turned toward him entreatingly.

"Could we not just walk around a bit before we go? I have seen very little of the gardens."

He looked torn. "It is not the thing, your being without a chaperone."

"But I am not in any danger," Callie protested. "You are with me."

"There are those who would say that *I* am the danger."

She smiled. "But we both know that you are not."

Only minutes before, she remembered, she had wondered painfully if Bromwell would have acted in the same manner as all the others. But as soon as he had arrived, she had known that it had been foolish to even consider such a possibility. She was not exactly sure what had happened here tonight, or why. Lady Swithington's actions had been exceedingly odd — more than she was going to admit to the woman's brother — and Callie could not escape the suspicion that the way events had unfolded had been somehow calculated by Lady Daphne, though she could not understand her reasons for it.

But whatever Lady Daphne had done, whether by accident or design, Callie was positive that Lord Bromwell had had nothing to do with it. She was also sure that had he been there throughout the whole evening, he would not have permitted things to get out of hand. The astonishment, even anger, on his face had told her everything she needed to know.

He smiled back at her, his expression softening. "All right. We shall walk around a bit. It is time for the fireworks, and it would be too bad to miss that."

Callie agreed, and they set off along the promenade. Bromwell left the main path, choosing one of the walkways branching off through the trees. Lanterns hung along the paths, illuminating them with a soft glow, and were scattered throughout the trees beyond, twinkling like little stars through the branches. Now and then they came upon a "ruin," artistically lighted, or a sparkling fountain.

There was a pop, and they stopped and looked up to see the first of the fireworks splash across the sky. The fireworks continued, a dazzling display of colors. They strolled on, stopping now and then to admire a particularly glorious burst of light.

As they walked, the paths grew narrower and more empty of people, until they were by themselves. In the distance, Callie heard a female giggle, followed by the sound of running feet. After that, they were left alone in silence.

They reached a stone bench, set beside a small pond, and they sat down to watch the spectacular end of the fireworks. Then, finally, the display was done, leaving only silence and the acrid scent of gunpowder lingering in the air.

"It was lovely," Callie told Bromwell. "Thank you for staying."

"I am only sorry that the remainder of your evening was spoiled," he replied, smiling at her.

She shook her head. "It does not matter."

He reached out and stroked his forefinger down her cheek. "You are so beautiful. I wish . . ."

"You wish what?" Callie asked when he did not continue.

Bromwell shook his head. "I'm not sure. Only that things were different."

Callie frowned a little. "What things? What do you mean?"

"Nothing. Do not listen to me. I fear I am in a mood tonight." He stood up, going over to the edge of the pond.

Callie rose and followed him, reaching out to take his hand in both of hers. "What sort of mood? Can I help in any way?"

"Would that you could." He turned and looked down at her, his eyes roaming over her face hungrily. "I have been thinking of you ever since our ride to Richmond Park. Indeed, ever since I first saw you. Sometimes I think you have bewitched me." His voice was hoarse, the words seemingly pulled from him.

Heat spread through Callie, and she thought that he must feel it in her hands.

"I did not mean to," she told him, her voice a trifle shaky.

"I know. That is part of your allure. You are unstudied, natural, yet you pull a man toward you with only a look."

"I have never noticed that I was so irresistible," she remarked, struggling to retain a light tone.

"Then perhaps it is only I who feels your power." He brought her hand up to his lips and kissed it. His lips were like velvet on her skin, sending a shiver through her. "In truth, I would be glad for that."

He turned her hand over and laid a kiss in her palm. Unconsciously, Callie's hand curled into a fist, as if enclosing his kiss there. She was very aware of the blood pulsing through her veins. She could feel it pounding from her heart and thundering through her.

She wanted his arms around her again. She wanted to taste his mouth, to be enveloped by the warmth and scent of him, to feel his hard body pressing into hers as it had the other day at the park. She had not known temptation with any other man, but with this one, she felt consumed by it.

He lifted his head and looked at her.

In the next instant Callie was in his arms and their lips were melded together. Fire flashed to life inside them, fierce and demanding. He crushed her to him, his mouth digging into hers, and Callie wrapped her arms around him, wanting only to be closer and ever closer. He groaned, and she could feel the tremor that ran through his hard body. His lips left her mouth and trailed across her cheek to her ear, nibbling at the sensitive lobe and teasing it with his teeth.

He murmured her name, his voice thick

with desire, as he kissed her ear, her face, her throat. Her skin flamed to life wherever his lips touched, and she trembled, full of inchoate yearnings.

With some last vestige of reason, he broke their embrace and pulled her off the path and deep into the shadows. Callie went with him easily, driven by the hammering pulse deep in her loins. They kissed again and again, and his hands slipped beneath her domino, roaming over her body. She could feel the heat of his skin even through her dress, and when his hand slid up onto the rise of her breasts above her dress, his touch was searing. He caressed the soft orbs, his fingers sliding between her skin and her clothes, and Callie wished fiercely that she could feel his hands all over her body in the same way.

He spread the sides of her domino apart and laid his lips against the soft, quivering flesh of her breasts. Callie sucked in a quick breath of surprised pleasure, and she dug her fingers into his coat, holding on as though anchoring herself in the world that was now spinning around her. Her own body was a stranger to her — her loins throbbing, and a hot damp ache growing between her legs, so pleasurable that it was almost painful. She wanted to be with him, to know him in some deep primitive way. She realized that, shockingly, she longed to wrap her legs around him and press herself against him in the most intimate manner.

Bromwell's hands went down her back and curved over her buttocks, his finger digging into the soft mounds of flesh and pushing her against the hard ridge of his desire. Callie trembled, her breath rasping in her throat, aware that she was teetering somehow on the brink of a precipice, eager and uncertain and just a little frightened all at once.

He made a low, frustrated noise and broke from her. "Sweet Lord, Callie . . ."

Wrapping her domino tightly around her, he pulled her to him and tightened his arms around her, leaning his forehead against her hair. She could hear his breath rasping harshly in his throat; she was enveloped in his heat. They stood for a long moment, their pulses gradually slowing.

"If we continue this," Bromwell said at last, "I shall forget all honor entirely." He pressed his lips into her hair. "I must take you home."

He was right, she knew, and yet Callie did not want to leave. She wanted this moment to go on forever. She wanted to race onward to the finish that her body so ardently desired.

It occurred to her that she had been standing outside, hidden only by the shadows, kissing Bromwell in a way that anyone would label as far bolder than any of the behavior of the other women in the supper box tonight. It was hypocritical of her, she supposed, to have been so shocked at Lady Daphne's public display with her swain, yet fling herself into passionate kisses with Daphne's brother.

She had acted in a most immoral way, she was sure. Yet she could not bring herself to regret it. Indeed, at the moment the only regret she felt was that she could not continue to kiss him.

Callie opened her eyes and leaned her head back, looking up into Bromwell's face. His lips were slightly reddened and sensually relaxed, his eyes dark and heavy-lidded. Just the sight of his face, so clearly stamped with desire, stirred her.

There was a difference, she thought, between her and Lady Daphne. Daphne had been playing fast and loose with a man she barely knew; Callie suspected that almost any man who had passed by would have served. But Callie could not imagine feeling like this with any other man in the world. It was Lord Bromwell, and he alone, who sparked this passion in her.

She took a shaky breath and let it out, feeling once again that she was teetering on the edge of something, and that, she thought, was even more frightening. For if she fell here, she knew, it was not her virtue that would be lost, but her heart.

Bromwell and Callie said little on the ride home. Uppermost in their minds was the passion that still hummed between them. It was not something that either wanted to discuss, and it required a careful concentration to keep it at bay.

He walked her to Francesca's door, stepping inside only to take his leave of her. Then he turned and trotted back down the steps to the hansom cab, his face settling into grim lines. A few quick words to the driver sent them back to Vauxhall Gardens at a fast pace.

When they reached the gardens, Bromwell headed purposefully toward his sister's supper box. He was greeted by the sight of several intoxicated young men, as well as the decidedly tipsy Miss Swanson and another young woman he had never met. His sister was sitting on the lap of a man he had never seen, the fellow boldly nuzzling her neck.

Once again he cleared the front wall of the box in a lithe jump rather than taking the time to enter through the rear door. Walking straight to his sister, he wrapped his hand around her upper arm and pulled her to her feet.

She let out a gasp, turning toward him with a snarl before she realized who he was. "Brom! Hello, dearest. I wondered where you were."

"And did you wonder where Lady Calandra was?" he asked, his voice hard and clipped.

"I presumed . . ." A smile curved her lips as she cast him a sly upward glance ". . . that she was with you."

"It is fortunate for you and for everyone else here that she was," he shot back, his eyes bright with a cold, fierce anger.

Daphne blinked, stunned into momentary silence.

"I say!" The man upon whose lap Daphne had been sitting rose to his feet, swaying. "Who the devil do you think you are? I ought to call you out for speaking to . . . to . . . the lady that way."

"I am 'the lady's' brother, and I assure you that I answer only a gentleman's challenge. Your sort I am more likely to take out back and thrash a little respect into."

"What? By God, sir!" The other man raised his arms into a position that faintly resembled a pugilist's stance. "Say that to my face! I dare you."

"I believe I just did," Bromwell replied. His lips curling in disgust, he grabbed the man's lapels and yanked, pulling him off his feet and half onto the front ledge of the supper box. With his other hand, he grasped one of the man's legs and shoved him up and over the edge, where he tumbled to the ground.

He then advanced toward two other men, who were sitting beyond Daphne, drunkenly gaping at him. At his approach, both took to their feet, stumbling hastily to the back door and out.

"Cousin!" Archie Tilford rose to his feet and executed a perfect bow, which was marred only by his tipping too far forward and having to grab the back of a nearby chair to keep from falling on his face. "Glad to see you. Good thing, sending those chaps off. Didn't like them."

"Bloody hell, Archie, why did you not do something earlier?" Bromwell asked in exasperation.

"Well . . ." Tilford considered the question. "Not the sort of thing I do, you see.

Sort of thing *you* do."

Bromwell grimaced and turned toward the elegantly dressed Mr. Pacewell and Mr. Sackville, now looking somewhat worse for wear. "And you two! Is everyone here completely foxed?"

They all glanced around at each other, as though unsure.

"Good Gad," Bromwell said in disgust. "Archie, you and your friends haul up Mr. Swanson and take yourselves home. I will see that the ladies get back to my sister's house."

The men hastened to do as he said, pulling the limp form of Swanson from his chair, looped his arms over their shoulders and half walked, half dragged him from the supper box. Miss Swanson, now in tears, and Miss Turner gathered up their dominoes and masks, which they had long since discarded, as well as their fans. Miss Turner, it seemed, had lost one of her shoes and seemed to have no idea where it might have gone.

Bromwell shot his sister a fulminating glance. "Well, you will simply have to borrow a pair from Lady Swithington. When we get back to her house, she will write a note to both your parents — or whatever poor benighted souls have guardianship of you — and say that due to the lateness of the hour and everyone's exhaustion, the two of you are spending the night with her. Hopefully that will serve to salvage your reputations — providing no one who knew you saw you here tonight out of your disguises."

This speech sent Miss Swanson into further wails, and even Miss Turner's foolish expression began to give way to trepidation. The earl ignored them, turning back to his sister and raising his brow.

"Very well, Brom," she told him testily, grabbing up her own things. "I am ready. Goodness, but you have turned into a prim sort. Is that Lady Calandra's influence? I must say, it is not appealing."

"Stop." His face was tight, his eyes hard. "Do not even mention her, or I fear you will hear much more than you wish to. We will discuss this later, after your charges have been put to bed."

With a shrug, she wrapped her domino around her and swept from the box, the girls hurrying after her. Bromwell escorted them home in silence. Miss Swanson was still sniffling and dabbing at her eyes with a handkerchief, and Miss Turner seemed subdued and even, perhaps, a trifle ill. Lady Daphne kept her face turned to the window, even though the curtain cut off all view of the outside.

Once they were inside, Lady Daphne's maid took the two girls up to bed, while Daphne sat down with a sigh and wrote out notes to their parents as Bromwell had instructed her. Once she had sent the notes off with a footman, she turned to her brother, crossing her arms.

"Very well. Out with it before you choke," she told him shortly.

"What the devil did you think you were doing?" he burst out. "Leaving Lady Calandra alone like that? Don't you realize what damage you could have done to her reputation?"

"Really, Brom, when did you turn into such a puritan? I was trying to help you."

"Help me? By exposing Callie to drunken bounders? By abandoning her in the midst of Vauxhall Gardens?"

"Now that is doing it a bit too brown, don't you think?" Daphne retorted. "You make it sound as though I left her in the middle of the promenade. She was inside a supper box."

"Where any passing stranger could glance inside and see that she was alone," he shot back. "Oh, except, of course, for the man who was dead drunk on the table!"

"I knew you would be along soon," Daphne explained reasonably, "and that she would not be there for long. I did not intend for that foolish Swanson boy to pass out. How was I to know he could not hold his liquor? I simply wanted to arrange it so that you and she were alone together." Her face softened, and she came toward him, holding out her hands to him. "Come, Brom, pray do not be displeased with me. I wanted only to aid you in your endeavor. I saw how close an eye that Haughston woman kept on Lady Calandra. I simply tried to arrange a situation where you could have her to yourself for a little while." Daphne smiled a little smugly. "Long enough for you to accomplish your purpose."

"What? Ruining her good name?" he asked, not reaching out to take her hands. "Daphne, how could you think I would want you to do that? I told you I had no intention of destroying her reputation. Why should she be harmed? It was her brother who hurt you. He is the one who should pay for it, not Callie."

"What does it matter if she is hurt?" Daphne shot back. "She is a Lilles, just as he is, and I am sure that she is as haughty and cold as the duke. Or that bitch Francesca Haughston! They are as alike as two peas in a pod. Such fine ladies, such delicate airs, as if they had never had a wicked thought in their heads. Oh, no, they are far too refined to even think of lying down with a man."

Her face was hard and bitter, and her brother regarded her with some shock. "Daphne! I have never heard you speak so . . . look so . . ."

"Try living trapped in Wales for the last fifteen years with some horrid old man!" she cried. "Never able to come to London or have any fun. A trip to Bath was considered his utmost treat! And all the while I was getting older, losing my looks. . . ." Tears welled in her eyes and spilled down her cheeks.

"Daphne . . ." Her tears touched him, dissolving much of his anger, and Bromwell went to her, putting his arm around her. "I am sorry. I hate that you had to marry an old man whom you did not love. And then to lose your unborn child after making that sacrifice . . . It was terrible, and you should not have had to do it. I wish that I had been older, wiser. I should have done something besides rush in there and try to call Rochford out. I wish to God that I had been able to help you. But you are not old, and you are still the most beautiful woman in London."

Daphne relaxed against him at his words, and she turned her face up to him, smiling despite the tears glittering like diamonds in her eyes. "Really? Do you truly think I am the most beautiful woman in London?"

The thought of Callie flashed into his head, but he pushed the image aside, saying stoutly, "Of course I do. You are. You always have been. You know that."

"There. I knew you could not love her more than you do me," she said with satisfaction, wiping away her tears with her fingers.

"Love her more than you! Of course not," Bromwell said, reaching into his pocket and handing her his crisp white handkerchief. He released her shoulders and stepped away. "How could you possibly think that? I do not love her at all. I simply do not want an innocent person hurt. The Duke of Rochford is the only one I care to harm. I told you that when we talked before. I never meant to ruin her. Only to bring Rochford out of his den and force him to deal with me."

"And what did you think would happen to her?" Daphne asked. "How could you harm Rochford without harming his sister? If you dance attendance on a woman, she is bound to expect something of you. A gentleman does not lavish attention on a woman unless he is trying to seduce her or he expects to ask for her hand. It is certainly an embarrassment if he does not then make her an offer. All of the *ton* will gossip about it."

"But I have only begun courting her. I have not —" He stopped.

"You have not what? Called upon her practically every day?" Daphne asked. "Invited her to go riding at Richmond Park or taken her out in your curricle? Or popped up at every party she has attended?"

Bromwell frowned. "I have perhaps hung about her more than I had intended," he admitted. "I had not expected her to be quite so assiduously chaperoned, I think. I had thought I would be able to spend more time with her alone."

"That is precisely why I arranged that little interlude at Vauxhall Gardens," Daphne exclaimed triumphantly. "So that you could have the opportunity to be alone with her. If there is no whiff of scandal, why should Rochford be alarmed?"

He sighed and ran his hand back through his hair. "I don't know what to say. If you are right, then I have already harmed her."

"That is right," Daphne agreed. "So . . ."

"Perhaps I should stop."

"What?" Daphne gaped at him, thunderstruck. "You mean, end this? Do nothing to her? To Rochford?"

His mouth twitched in a grim semblance of a smile. "I have hopes I still will hear from Rochford."

"But Lady Calandra? You are going to stop pursuing her?"

"I am not sure," he said, looking distracted. "I must think on this."

His sister opened her mouth to speak again, but he was no longer paying attention. Turning, he strode toward the door and down the hall, leaving Daphne staring after him.

Bromwell took his greatcoat and hat from the footman and went outside. He jammed the hat down on his head, and threw on his coat as he trotted down the steps and onto the sidewalk. A breeze fluttered at the edges of the fabric and stole beneath it, but he did not bother to do up the buttons as he strode along the street, scowling.

Should he stop calling upon Callie? Something twisted inside him at the thought, and he knew that he did not want to end this. He thought of her smile, her dancing dark eyes, the thick lustrous black curls that made his fingers itch to touch them. The idea of never seeing those things again, never again enfolding her in his arms or pressing his lips to hers as he had tonight, made him want to smash his fist into something.

Yet if he continued to see her, how would it end? In all likelihood with himself and Callie's brother at each other's throats. It would be pistols at dawn or, at best, them going at each other with their bare fists. The one way it was certain not to end was with what polite society would expect — Bromwell proposing marriage to her. He let out a snort at the picture of Rochford's reaction should Bromwell ask him for his sister's hand in marriage.

Rochford would never allow it. And, of course, Bromwell knew that he would never ask it. Ally himself with the family of the man who had disgraced his sister? It was unthinkable. It would be a betrayal of Daphne, a thoroughly dishonorable thing to do.

If he had no intention of marrying Callie, though, he should not continue seeing her. Daphne was right, of course. His pursuit of Callie had been determined. Everyone, including Callie, would expect a proposal of marriage from him if he continued to court her in this way. Even after the few weeks that he had been calling on her, it would cause gossip if he suddenly stopped seeing her.

The thought of Callie being subjected to the whispers of the gossipmongers twisted his gut, but he knew that it would be much, much worse if he waited. Every day, every nosegay delivered to her house, every dance they shared at a ball, would increase everyone's certainty that he was on course to propose to her. Therefore, when he stopped seeing her, it would make the gossip all the stronger.

And if it ended with Rochford exploding in anger and rushing to town to confront him, then the scandal would be even graver. It would probably follow Callie all her life.

Bromwell's scowl deepened. Why had he ever thought that wooing Callie would be such perfect revenge on Rochford? He should have just settled his account with the man with a swift right uppercut to the jaw then and there. After all, none of this had anything to do with Callie. She had done nothing to deserve it, and yet she would be hurt worst of all by it.

He remembered his words to Archie, how he had shrugged off the idea that Callie was an innocent and did not deserve to be hurt. He had gotten angry with Daphne just now for doing something that could hurt Callie's reputation. Yet he had set out to get his revenge without caring at all how badly she might be hurt by his scheme. He had been a fool, he thought, a shallow, callous fool.

There was no way he could make up for the harm he had already done to her. The only thing he could do was to ensure she was not hurt any more. He would not call upon Callie again. But why did doing the right thing leave him feeling so empty inside?

CHAPTER TWELVE

Callie was somewhat surprised and disappointed when Lord Bromwell did not call upon her the following morning. However, she did not think anything of it. She was not feeling very hearty herself. Her head hurt, her stomach was a bit queasy, and the winter light streaming in the windows of Francesca's morning room made her eyes hurt. It was all due, she knew, to the strong arrack punch that she had drunk the evening before. Callie had never drunk anything more than white wine with dinner or perhaps a glass of ratafia or sherry. Given the way she felt, she thought that she would prefer to stick to that course in the future.

Francesca asked her a few questions about the evening. Even though Callie had planned to tell her nothing about the events at the Gardens, she realized that she must reveal that Lord and Lady Radbourne had not been there, as they were close friends, and the subject was bound to come up when next they saw Lady Irene.

Therefore, after telling her a bit about the beauty of the lights and the fireworks, Callie finally said, "Lord and Lady Radbourne did not come."

"What?" Francesca, who had been darning a stocking as they talked, dropped the darning egg in her lap and sat up straighter. "They were not there?"

"No."

"But what — who — oh, dear, I knew I should have gone," Francesca moaned.

"Do not worry. It was all quite uneventful. Lady Swithington was there, and Lord Bromwell. It was quite a big party. Miss Swanson and her brother and another young lady were there, also."

"I cannot imagine why Irene would not have notified us if she could not go," Francesca said, looking worried. "Well, at least you had on a domino and mask. You kept it on all evening, did you not?"

"Oh, yes. No one would have recognized me," Callie assured her. "I did not even go out to the dance floor," she lied.

Francesca nodded, looking somewhat relieved, but a frown still married her forehead. "You know, I believe that I shall pay a call on Irene this afternoon."

"You think perhaps one of them was ill?"

"I am not certain what I think," Francesca replied thoughtfully. "But I would like to discover why they were absent. Irene is not the flighty sort. Would you care to come with me?"

Callie declined. She did not feel like going out, and she was hopeful that an afternoon nap with a lavender-scented cloth over her forehead might help her headache. Besides, she found that she often preferred to stay at home, given Lord Bromwell's frequent calls.

As it turned out, he did not come to call in the afternoon, either. But the nap in her darkened room did help restore her, so that when Francesca returned, Callie was feeling much more the thing and greeted her cheerfully.

Francesca, however, looked a good deal less than cheerful. Indeed, her deep blue eyes were snapping, and there was a pugnacious set to her delicate chin.

"That Swithington woman!" she said scathingly when Callie asked her if aught was amiss.

"What do you mean?"

"I mean," Francesca said, biting off each word, "that Irene told me that Lady Swithington wrote her a note on Sunday saying that she was sorry to tell her that the party to Vauxhall Gardens had been called off, but that she hoped very much that they would plan for it again in a few more weeks."

"Oh." Callie was not very surprised, though she had been hoping that the whole thing would turn out to have been an unhappy accident.

Francesca continued to pace the room, talking angrily about Lady Swithington's deception, but Callie listened to her with only half an ear. Her mind was occupied with thinking about what Lady Daphne had done.

It was clear now that Bromwell's sister had arranged things the night before to turn out as they had. She had not wanted the restraining influences of Lord and Lady Radbourne — or perhaps it was simply their respectability she wished to avoid. She also clearly had not wanted Callie to know that Gideon and Irene would not be among their party, for she had pretended ignorance at their absence and kept assuring Callie that the pair would doubtless come later. So it was not simply that she had wanted to be free to indulge in her own scandalous behavior, she also wanted Callie to be there and a part of it.

But why? It made no sense to Callie. The

only result she could find was that it made her distrust Brom's sister.

Brom had obviously not known about whatever his sister had planned. He had been shocked and angry when he found her alone in the supper box. He had also expected Irene and Gideon to be there. And, Callie thought, he had given no indication that he could not have been with them earlier. In fact, he had seemed rather surprised at the length of time they had been there, and when Callie had commented that she had been afraid he was not going to come, he had looked surprised and said something like, "Daphne said —" and then stopped. Callie felt rather certain that he had been about to remark that his sister had told him not to come any earlier.

Callie could not escape the conclusion that for some reason Daphne disliked her intensely, despite the sweet way Daphne acted toward her. Could it be that she hoped to somehow influence her brother against Callie?

If Callie had not tossed a bottle at that fellow last night, might he have climbed over the ledge of the box and tried to take advantage of her? And what might Brom have thought if he had arrived at the supper box to find Callie all alone in the arms of another man?

Callie gave a little shiver. If that had been Daphne's reason for the way she acted last night, she must be a very cold and uncaring person, to sacrifice another woman that way. It also seemed a most uncertain sort of outcome. Things were just as likely, surely, to turn out as they had, with Bromwell arriving and being annoyed with his sister for leaving Callie alone.

She was glad that they had no social engagements for this evening. She did not feel like going out, especially if there was any possibility of running into Lady Swithington. It was rather nice, really, to spend a quiet evening at home, and she managed to get letters written to both her grandmother and her brother. However, she had to admit, at least to herself, that she did miss Lord Bromwell. She tried to remember when was the last time that an entire day had gone by without her seeing him.

Callie awaited his call the following day with anticipation, but, surprisingly, he did not come by. Late in the afternoon, Francesca asked, "Where is your friend Lord Bromwell? I must say, I have become rather accustomed to seeing him."

Callie shook her head, aware of an odd little pain in her chest. "I do not know."

Francesca frowned a little, but said lightly, "How odd. Well, we must take him to task for his neglect next time we see him."

But they did not see him — not that evening when they attended Mrs. Cutternan's soiree, nor the next afternoon when they received callers. Callie determinedly kept a polite smile on her face as they chatted with their visitors, doing her best not to appear as though she was waiting each moment for Lord Bromwell to appear. But she could scarcely attend to what was being said. All she could think of was Lord Bromwell and whether he would call on her later in the afternoon, and if not, why not.

Had she said something wrong? Done something wrong? Had he thought she acted imprudently the other night, that she should have left Vauxhall as soon as the party turned boisterous? Or that she should not even have gone there without Irene and Gideon in attendance?

But surely he could not be so unfair as to blame her for going there with his own sister as chaperone. If Lady Swithington had not been acting with such abandon, if she had exercised more control over the party, it would not have degenerated into such a romp. Would he actually blame Callie when it was obviously his sister who should have been more responsible?

On the other hand, she reasoned, perhaps it was not that at all. Perhaps it was her behavior after they left the supper box. She had not wanted to go straight home but had asked him to linger. Had he thought her too bold? Had she not appeared shaken enough by her experience? Had she seemed too worldly? Too experienced?

Or was it that Bromwell thought she had behaved like a wanton? The memory of the kisses they had shared by the fountain were enough to bring blushes to her cheeks. She could not help but wonder if he had found her too brazen, too bold. It was unfair, of course, for certainly he had participated in their kisses and caresses fully as much as she. But she knew full well that men were often unfair in their moral judgments of women. A young man could have relations with a woman and no one thought anything of it. A young woman, however, would be ruined if she lay down with a man. A man might want to sleep with a woman, but if she gave in, then he would not want to marry her. It was a tale she had been told ever since she came out.

She could feel Francesca casting worried glances her way from time to time. When their last visitor left, Francesca turned to her and said quietly, "Perhaps Lord Bromwell has been called away from town for some reason. There might have been an emergency at his estate, and he did not have time to leave a message."

"Yes, I suppose so," Callie answered, summoning up a smile. "Or perhaps he is simply the fickle sort. I have heard that some men are."

"He did not seem so," Francesca replied, her frown deepening. "I had come to think — oh, well, there is no use in talking of it now, is there? We must wait and see if he writes and tells you what happened. Or perhaps he will simply arrive tomorrow with a perfectly reasonable explanation."

Callie was not sure what an adequate explanation would be, as it seemed to her that whatever had happened, he could have sent round a note by now to explain his absence. However, she was eager to end the conversation, for it was growing more difficult with each second to keep her worry and fears from showing. She was afraid that if Francesca continued talking about the matter much longer, she might start to cry.

Fortunately, Francesca seemed as happy as she to drop the subject and began to chat about what they should wear to the opera that night. Callie joined in, grateful that

Francesca was able to bear more than her share of the conversational burden.

They went to the opera with Irene and Gideon, occupying Lord Radbourne's luxurious box. Callie paid especial attention to her attire and hair, unable to suppress the hope that she might see Bromwell tonight. If he was there, it was vitally important that she look her best — and that she appear lighthearted and carefree.

He was not there, however, and Callie was not sure whether to be unhappy or relieved. For if he was at the opera, it would mean that he had not been called away or been ill or any other such thing; it would mean that he simply had not wanted to call on her.

The next afternoon, she decided to make a round of calls. She had been staying home all too much recently, waiting for Lord Bromwell to visit, and she did not want to spend another afternoon that way. There was a little niggling worry inside her that he would come by and she would be gone, but she refused to give way to it. If he did call, it would serve him right that she was not there. He would see that she was not sitting about pining for him.

Still, when she returned, she could not keep from sifting through the calling cards that had been left her in absence, just to see if Bromwell's was among them. It was not.

Francesca had tactfully not mentioned Lord Bromwell since their brief discussion of the subject the afternoon before. Callie could only admire the woman's ability to find so many other things to talk about other than the one that was so glaringly obvious.

The next evening was Lady Smythe-Furling's ball. She was not known for the excellence of her parties, but it was the only social entertainment that evening, and Callie was now determined to go out at every opportunity. She wanted desperately to keep herself occupied, to dance or chat or do something, anything, to chase away the depressing thoughts and doubts.

Almost as soon as they entered, however, Callie wished that they had not come. As she made her polite curtsey to Lady Smythe-Furling and her two daughters, she glanced across the room. And there, standing at the edge of the dance floor, talking to Lord Westfield, was Bromwell.

Her heart skittered in her chest, and she struggled to keep control of her expression. He was here! Hope surged within her, no matter how she struggled to keep it down. He would see her, she thought; he would turn and smile, and then he would walk over to her, and everything would be all right again. She could stop her incessant worrying.

But he did not turn or look at her. She strolled away, careful not to stray toward the part of the room where he stood. She refused to seek him out. If he wanted to talk to her, he would come to her.

He did not.

She danced with her host, and with the husband of Lady Smythe-Furling's oldest daughter. She danced with Francesca's good friend Sir Lucien — and was very grateful for his presence at her side for much of the evening. She felt certain that Francesca had put a word in his ear, but it was, Callie thought, kind of him to oblige her and devote his evening to easing her discomfort.

She was also grateful that her dance card was full and she was able to appear, at least, to be enjoying the party. She chatted, she laughed, and she even managed to flirt a bit — it was easy with Sir Lucien, who was able to carry on a flirtation almost entirely by himself, truth be known.

Inside, however, she ached. Bromwell was here — the man who had kissed her passionately only a few nights before, the man who had devoted himself to her over the past few weeks — and he had not even come over to say hello to her. It was just as well that he had not, she thought, for she was not sure how she would have maintained her composure. It had been difficult enough to do so without having to face him.

The hours moved with excruciating slowness. All Callie wanted was to go home and throw herself upon her bed and cry, but she would not allow herself to leave early. She would not give anyone the opportunity to whisper about how upset she had been.

She knew that there were already whispers. Lord Bromwell had been so assiduous in his attentions to her recently that it was obvious to everyone there that he was not speaking to her tonight. She had felt the glances that were directed her way; she had seen the conversations stop in midsentence when she had looked toward someone. It made her pain much worse to bear — and at the same time, it made it all the more imperative that she not reveal that pain.

Francesca, she noticed, began to act tired long before she normally did, now and then covering a yawn with her fan, then apologizing prettily to those around her for her sleepiness. Callie suspected that she was doing it for Callie's benefit, so that they could slip away from the party early.

It did not surprise her when Francesca announced that she simply could not remain any longer, and so they made their good-byes. Callie let out a sigh of relief as she sat down in the carriage and leaned back against the soft leather seat.

"Thank you," she said softly to Francesca.

"It was a dull party, anyway," Francesca replied airily. She reached over and put her hand on Callie's arm. "Are you all right, dear?"

Callie nodded. "Yes, of course. A little puzzled, I admit, but . . ." She finished her statement with a shrug.

Francesca nodded. Callie felt sure that she was not convinced by that answer, but Francesca was too well-bred to pry. Instead she merely said, "I suppose one should never underestimate the vagaries of men. However, I am convinced that Lord Brom-well's behavior must have been influenced in some way by his odious sister."

Callie could not keep from chuckling. "Dear Francesca. Trust you to make me laugh."

"Yes. My mother once told me that I am able to make even the most serious matter trivial." She paused and added drolly, "I do not believe she meant it as a compliment."

Francesca, with her accustomed sensitivity, did not say anything on the rest of the drive home, and when they reached her house, she simply bid Callie goodnight and went into her morning room to "see to a few matters," leaving Callie alone.

Callie hurried up the stairs, the long-suppressed tears welling up in her. Her maid was waiting for her there, but Callie dismissed her with a few brief words, ignoring the girl's puzzled expression.

Then, at last, for the first time tonight, she was alone. She stood there for a moment, letting down the barriers that she had kept raised all evening. She had refused to let herself feel, to even think about her pain, determined to present a cool and undisturbed face to the world. But now, at last, she let it sink in: Lord Bromwell's ardor had cooled. For whatever reason, he was no longer interested in her. And she was going to have to live without him.

A deep, primitive sound came up out of her throat — part moan, part sob — and she threw herself across her bed and gave way to tears.

The next morning, Callie was listless and red-eyed, but she refused Francesca's offer to decline all callers.

"No, I must see them sometime, and I

refuse to let anyone pity me. They will gossip, I know, about the fact that Lord Bromwell has grown tired of my company, but at least I do not have to give them further food for gossip by going into a decline."

"You are a very brave girl," Francesca said. "Unfortunately, I suspect that we will be inundated with callers."

As it turned out, the number was not quite as large as Francesca had feared, but their afternoon was filled, and Callie was kept busy pretending that she had scarcely noticed Lord Bromwell's absence, and that she cared about it even less.

It was a great relief, however, when it grew too late for calls and they were able to settle down to tea. Callie did not feel like eating, really, but no one would be allowed to disturb them, at least, at this hour.

Francesca had just begun to pour their tea, however, when the house echoed with the sound of a loud knock at the front door. Francesca and Callie glanced at each other, surprised, but continued with their tea. It was more surprising when Francesca's butler appeared at the door a moment later, looking torn.

"Ah . . ." He hesitated, then continued in a rush, "His Grace, the Duke of Rochford, is here to see you, my lady." Clearly, the duke was someone whom even Fenton did not dare turn down.

Francesca and Callie looked at each other, alarm dawning on their faces. It was, Callie thought, a dreadful end to a perfectly dreadful day. Sinclair must have gotten wind of Bromwell's visits and had come to take her to task for it.

"Yes, Fenton, show him in, of course," Francesca said, suppressing a sigh, and rose to her feet. Beside her, Callie did the same.

A moment later the duke strode into the room. He was dressed for riding, and it was apparent from the less-than-pristine condition of his boots that he had come straight to Francesca's home without stopping at Lilles House to change. His dark hair was disheveled, his face grim, and there was a light in his eyes that did not bode well for either of the occupants in the room.

"What the devil has been going on here since I left?" he demanded curtly. "I received a letter from Grandmother saying you have been seen everywhere about town with the Earl of Bromwell. She said several of her correspondents have even hinted that we must be expecting an 'important announcement' soon."

"I am sorry if Grandmother's letters annoyed you, Sinclair," Callie replied coolly.

"But I really do not believe it was necessary for you to come in person to inform me of that fact."

"Blast it, Callie!" he exclaimed. "Don't adopt that innocent guise with me. I told you not to see that man again! And you —" He rounded on Francesca. "My God, how could you have been so lax, so irresponsible, as to allow that man to dance attendance upon my sister?"

"I beg your pardon?" Francesca's voice iced over. "You have the impertinence to upbraid me over whom I permit to call on me at my home?"

"Could you not see what he was about?" Rochford growled. "Didn't you know better than to allow a man who hated me to try to fix his attention with my sister?"

"If you disapprove so of whom I receive at my house, then no doubt you will wish to remove Callie from my care," Francesca shot back. "If I am so lax in my standards, so uncaring of who I see or speak to, I can only be surprised that you allowed Callie to visit me at all."

The duke looked startled; then his brows drew together in a rush, but before he could speak, Callie stepped forward, saying crisply, "No one is 'removing' me from anywhere. I am a grown woman, and I will stay where I choose." She turned toward Francesca. "Unless, of course, you no longer wish me to remain with you because of my brother's rude behavior."

Francesca unbent enough to smile at Callie. "You are always welcome here, Callie. You know that." Her quick sideways glance at the duke did not extend a similar invitation to him. She turned back to Callie. "Now I think it would be best if I left you and the duke alone to discuss the matter."

"No, Francesca, truly, you need not leave —" Callie began.

Francesca stopped her with a shake of her head. "I do not believe that your brother feels the same say. Clearly the Earl of Bromwell and his family are a *personal* matter for the duke."

She turned, sweeping Rochford a cool glance, and left the room, closing the door discreetly behind her. The duke watched her go, his jaw tightening even more. He swung back to face his sister, but Callie jumped in before he could speak.

"How could you have spoken to Francesca that way?" she asked, her eyes snapping. "You were absolutely abominable, acting as though you had some right to tell her what to do! Who she could see or not see! Really, Sinclair!"

"I am perfectly aware that I exercise no control over Lady Haughston," her brother retorted stiffly. "However, I would have thought that she had better sense than to allow any man to hang about you so much that it is the talk of the City. Especially Bromwell, of all people!"

"Francesca was not to blame. She was very careful to provide me with chaperonage the entire time I have been here. No one would dare intimate that I have done anything scandalous."

"No, of course not," Rochford retorted impatiently.

"And how was Francesca to know that you would take it so amiss if an eligible gentleman paid court to me? She did not even know Lord Bromwell until I came here."

"I thought it was enough that I explicitly told *you* not to see him," Rochford retorted. "Obviously you paid no attention whatsoever to me."

"I am not a child to be told what to do and whom to see, without any reason given for your orders! If there was something wrong with Bromwell, you should have told me what it was."

Rochford shifted on his feet, looking uncomfortable.

"What? What is so wrong with Lord Bromwell?" Callie pursued. "Why do you despise the man?"

"I do not despise him," Rochford replied stiffly. "I have no feeling toward the man, bad or good. It is he who despises me. He has done so for years. I feared that he would try to attach himself to you in order to harm you . . . just to hurt me in some way."

"Why?" Callie asked. "He has never said anything to me about hating you. I do not think he has ever spoken about you at all. Why would he dislike you so much that he would pursue me just to wound you?"

"It is not the sort of thing one discusses with a lady," her brother began stiffly.

Callie's dark eyes sparked with fire. "Then I fear that you and I have nothing else to say."

She started toward the door.

"Blast it, Callie! I am trying to protect you."

"I am sure that is very noble. But if protecting me means treating me as something less than an adult, than a person, then I do not want your protection."

Rochford's lips tightened. Callie sighed and, unexpectedly, tears sprang into her eyes. She started once again toward the door.

"Wait." He turned, reaching out for her. "Callie, stop. Do not go. I will tell you."

She turned and looked at him, waiting.

"Fifteen years ago, Bromwell challenged me to a duel." He paused, then added, "For dishonoring his sister."

CHAPTER THIRTEEN

Callie stared. "What? How could he think that?"

A faint smile touched the duke's lips. "You do not ask me if the accusation was true?"

"Of course not. Really, Sinclair . . . what kind of a ninny do you take me for?" Callie replied astringently. "I know that you would not dishonor any woman, much less a lady. I am not naïve enough that I do not realize that you have had . . . relationships with women. But I am certain that they were perfectly aboveboard and . . . well, professional."

He chuckled, shaking his head. "Why did I ever think you would be overset by such news?"

"I do not know. But I do wonder why Bromwell would have believed such a thing of you. He is not a stupid man."

Rochford shrugged. "He was very young at the time, and he was badly misinformed.

He did not know me. He did not know that I was not the sort to force myself upon a woman — or to seduce a woman of virtue. And it would not have been hard for him to believe that I had . . . formed an attachment to Lady Daphne. Half the men of the *ton* were . . . fascinated by her."

"And were you?"

"No." Her brother shook his head. "Indeed, at the time, I was interested in quite a different lady, but . . . Lady Daphne was interested in me. She was a young widow and was clearly intent on marrying more money than she had the first time. She was always a grasping sort, and she believed that no man was immune to her beauty. She seized on me as her next victim. But I had no interest in marrying her — or having anything else to do with her. When I made it clear to her that her hopes were in vain, she was furious with me." He shrugged. "She was not used to being turned down. In retaliation, I suppose, she convinced her brother that I had played fast and loose with her affections. From what he said to me, I believe that she may have told him she was carrying my child."

"No!" Callie gasped. "So he challenged you?"

Rochford nodded. "To pistols at dawn.

He would not listen to me."

"Did you meet him?"

"Of course not." The duke grimaced. "Bromwell was nothing but a lad. Seventeen or eighteen, just a student at Oxford. I could scarcely let him throw away his life like that. And certainly I had no intention of deloping, when I had done nothing wrong."

"You were not exactly aged yourself," Callie pointed out. "Fifteen years ago? You were only twenty-three."

"That may be, but I had had to grow up quickly because I came into my inheritance young. I had been running my estates for five years by then. I felt worlds older than that young hothead. But . . ." He sighed, shaking his head. "I did not handle the situation well. I was angry at Daphne for her lies and angry at . . . well, everyone, I suppose. I was short with the boy. I spoke to him sarcastically, contemptuously. I made it clear that I thought him a young puppy, not worthy of meeting on the dueling field. In short, I embarrassed him. And it was at my club, in front of a number of others. The young are very full of pride. He hated me, not only for what he perceived as my wrong to his sister, but also for humiliating him in the eyes of the *ton*. He went back to Oxford, but he held on to his anger, nursing it."

Callie went to her brother and put her hand on his arm. "Sinclair, I am so sorry. I wish that you had told me."

"It is not the sort of story one wants to tell one's sister. It was not something in which I showed to advantage."

"Lord Bromwell has hated you ever since?" Callie asked. She understood everything now — why Brom had pursued her, why he had stopped so abruptly. His only purpose in all of it had been to hurt her in order to get back at her brother. "Did he never learn the truth?"

Rochford shrugged. "I have heard from others now and then that he still despises me. Lady Daphne found someone else to marry her. I believe she never had a child, but that is easy enough to put down to an accident, another bit of tragedy befalling her. She was always a skillful liar. Her brother was not the only one whom she fooled."

His face was grim, and Callie squeezed his arm sympathetically. "I am sorry. No one who knows you would believe you would play fast and loose with a woman, surely."

"Perhaps they did not believe I acted dishonorably toward her. But there were those who believed that I was involved with her."

"The woman in whom you were interested?" Callie asked him tentatively.

He gave her a faint smile. "She fell in love with another, I am afraid. I cannot blame all of that on Daphne. One cannot help where one loves, I have found."

Callie frowned, swept with sadness. She had never thought about the possibility that her brother might have been in love once, or that he might have lost that love. It had, frankly, never occurred to her that any woman would not have leapt at the chance to marry him. She felt a little guilty, as well, that she had simply assumed Rochford was too cool and aloof for love, and that that was why he had remained single.

Rochford, as though sensing the thoughts stirring in her mind, spoke, returning to the subject of the earl. "In any case, I suspect that Bromwell may never have learned what his sister is really like. Love can blind one to all sorts of things. And neither of them has really lived much in the *ton*. I believe that he went abroad after he finished at Oxford, and then several years ago, when he inherited, he chose to live on his estates. Daphne's second husband was wise enough to keep her close. She has not been much in society for several years. And I doubt that anyone is too likely to discuss his sister's morals in front of the man. Perhaps he is still able to believe her an innocent victim."

"He does, I think," Callie said. "He did not tell me anything of what happened, but he has spoken very highly of his sister. Indeed, I met her. She was . . . very pleasant."

"Oh, Daphne excels at subterfuge. There are those who like her — Great-Aunt Odelia, for one. I cannot blame Bromwell. I would despise any man whom I thought had hurt you in any way. As I feared *he* would hurt you."

"You should have told me."

"I know. I realize that now. I am too accustomed to regarding you as my baby sister. I forget that you are a woman — a very wonderful and intelligent woman."

"Perhaps not so intelligent," Callie replied, with a wry smile. "I did not see through Lord Bromwell's deception. I believed that he was genuinely courting me. But now I understand why he was so assiduous in his attentions. But you need not worry. He has ceased calling upon me. I think that he must have sought his revenge on you in that way. He was very attentive, in order to make everyone take notice, and then, when he abruptly stopped, everyone was able to witness my embarrassment. I was the object of gossip. It was, in a much smaller way, the sort of thing that had happened to his sister."

"I am so sorry, Callie." The duke wrapped his arms around her, pulling her into a hug. "I would have given anything for you to avoid that hurt."

Callie leaned her head against his chest for a moment, letting herself rely, just for a bit, on his strength, soaking up the feeling, as she had when she was a child, that Sinclair would somehow make everything better.

But then she pulled back and smiled up at him. "Do not worry. Clearly I would have been wiser to do as you said. I cannot escape the realization that I was hurt through my own rashness. Anyway, I am not so very hurt. I am chagrined, most of all, at my own foolishness. It is nothing more than a little social loss of face. Embarrassing, but nothing more. My good name is unsoiled. I can put up with a bit of gossip about me. It will all blow over in a few weeks. There will be some on-dit or other that will take precedence over my problem."

"I feared that he had much worse intentions when I heard that he was courting you." Sinclair smiled. "I should have realized that you would have the good sense not to let yourself be maneuvered into a compromising position."

Callie, thinking of the kisses and caresses that she had shared with Bromwell, could not quite meet her brother's eyes. "I do not know that he ever intended to do any more than make me a bit of a laughingstock."

"I am glad to learn that he was not wicked enough to force his attentions upon you. Despite his dislike of me, I did have a certain respect for the man for his loyalty to his sister, however misguided he might have been."

A silence fell on them. Rochford was clearly uncomfortable talking about such things with his sister, and Callie, rather guiltily aware of just how much freedom she had allowed Bromwell, had no desire to speak for fear the guilt would show in her voice.

Callie shifted a little. Rochford cleared his throat.

"I — um, I need to return to Marcastle. I left rather abruptly, and there are still several things that must be done. I also have some matters that require my attention at Dancy Park. So I shan't be staying." He looked at her, a faint smile quirking up his lips. "Do not worry. I will not try to compel

321

you to return with me. I can see that you are well, and that you are quite able to take care of yourself. It was foolish of me to come tearing up to London."

"A little," Callie agreed with a smile. "Still, I am glad that you care about me enough to do so."

"Of course. Your well-being is what matters. I did not come here because of 'family duty' or the 'honor of the name' or any of that."

"I know."

"But . . . if you would like to, um, get away from the city for a while, you are welcome to come home with me." He cast a concerned glance at her.

"You mean until the talk about me dies down?" Callie asked. She shook her head. "No, I think not. I do not like being the object of whispers or amused glances — or pitying ones, either. But I refuse to run and hide just because of a little embarrassment. It would only give the matter more importance, anyway. It will be better, ultimately, if I stay and face it down."

Pride was evident in his smile. "I suspected you would say that."

"Francesca is quite helpful in that regard. It is much easier than it would be if I were alone — or with Grandmother." She looked at him sternly. "You must apologize to Francesca for those things you said, however. It was not her fault. She did try to warn me a little — in a delicate way — by pointing out that his sister's reputation was not the best. She said that she thought you might not like it — which of course I already knew. Now I understand why she was, perhaps, a little reluctant to explain further."

"Yes, I imagine that she was."

"She was meticulous about chaperoning me, even though I am sure that often it was a dreadful bore to her."

"I realize that my words were uncalled-for. I had not told her that you were not to see him. And, in any case, I am aware that she has no control over you. I spoke out of fury. I will, of course, apologize to her. However, I fear that Lady Haughston's opinion of me has been set for some years now."

They found Francesca in the formal drawing room at the front of the house, sitting at the piano, not playing anything, but staring sightlessly across the top of it, her hands unmoving in her lap. They stopped in the doorway. Then the duke started forward into the room.

"Lady Haughston."

Francesca turned at the sound of his voice and rose to her feet, wearing an air of cool civility like a cloak. "Your Grace."

The corner of his mouth twitched with annoyance, but he said only, "You are right to be upset with me. I must apologize for the way I acted earlier. I had no right to reprimand you, as you pointed out. Naturally you and my sister are free to see whom you wish. In my defense, I can only plead my desire to protect Calandra. I hope you will forgive me."

Francesca's nod was regal as she replied, "Of course. You need not worry. I have never taken your criticisms to heart."

"I am relieved to hear it," he told her dryly. "I am returning to the country now. Callie would like to remain here with you, if that is acceptable."

"Certainly. Callie is always welcome here." A stranger might not have noticed the slight emphasis Francesca put on Callie's name.

"Thank you." He bowed. "Then I will take my leave of you."

Callie walked her brother out. When they reached the front door, he cast a glance back toward the drawing room where Francesca stood.

"Do not worry," Callie told him with some amusement. "I shall do my best to soften Francesca toward you. Anyway, I have never known her to hold a grudge long. She is a most forgiving person."

"Is she?" He smiled faintly. "Do not trouble yourself over it, Callie. Lady Haughston and I are . . . accustomed to each other."

He took his leave of her, and Callie watched him go, her forehead creased in a small frown. For the first time, she wondered exactly what lay between her brother and Francesca. She had always just accepted that Francesca was a part of her life, a friend of the family. She would have said that Sinclair and Francesca were friends, but now that she thought about it, she realized that there was something different in their manner toward each other.

There was not the easy, jesting affection that Francesca shared with Sir Lucien or with her brother Dominic. Nor did Francesca display the lightly flirtatious manner she often adopted with other men of the *ton*. There was, Callie reflected, even in the midst of a pleasant conversation, a sort of brittle quality between the two of them.

She recalled now the surprised expression on Francesca's face when Callie had told her that she was one of the few people to whom Sinclair would have entrusted his sister. And just now her brother had sardonically referred to Francesca's opinion of him as being "set" long ago, and he had not, she thought, implied that her opinion of him was a good one.

Callie might have termed them friends, but now she was not sure that either of them would have said the same thing. On the other hand, she was positive that they did not dislike each other. Until tonight, Francesca had never made a genuinely slighting comment toward or about Sinclair that Callie could remember, and she was certain that whenever Francesca's name came up in conversation, her brother always listened with interest. At nearly any ball that they both attended, Sinclair would always dance a waltz with Francesca. With another man, that might not have indicated anything, but Callie knew that her brother was not much given to dancing.

But what did any of this mean?

Still puzzling over the matter, Callie walked back inside and down the hallway to the smaller sitting room, where she suspected her friend would have returned. Her instincts were right, for Francesca was seated upon the couch. Unusually for her, she held a needlepoint frame in her lap.

As Callie entered, Francesca glanced up

at her and smiled, then returned her attention to her needlework. "You and the duke have resolved the problem?" she asked lightly.

"Yes." Callie paused, then asked, "Why did you not tell me that Lord Bromwell disliked my brother so?"

Pink tinged the other woman's cheeks, and Francesca glanced at Callie, then away. "I didn't — I was not sure that Lord Bromwell disliked Rochford, or how much he disliked him. I thought that certainly he might . . . because of . . . of the duke and, um . . ." She trailed off uncertainly.

"And Lady Daphne?" Callie supplied.

Francesca's astonished gaze flew to Callie's face. "He told you?"

Callie shrugged. "There was little way around it. He knew I would not let him slide out of explaining to me why he was so strongly opposed to my seeing Lord Bromwell. Why he was so frightened of what Lord Bromwell might intend regarding me. And once he told me about Bromwell's issuing him a challenge —"

"What!" Francesca's needlepoint dropped, unnoticed, from her hand and slid onto the floor. "He challenged Sinclair to a duel?"

"Yes. Did you not know?"

Francesca shook her head so hard that her

golden ringlets bounced about wildly. "No! He must have been mad! Everyone knows what a dead shot Rochford is."

"He was too angry to think, I suspect," Callie replied. "Sinclair said he was only seventeen or eighteen, and he thought . . . well, he believed that Sinclair had played the cad with his sister, seducing and abandoning her. That is what he accused him of, though of course Sinclair did not put it quite so bluntly."

Francesca let out a short, wordless sound of disbelief. "As if anyone would have to seduce Lady Daphne!"

"Bromwell loves his sister very much. I have heard him talk of her. I feel sure he did not realize the sort of person that his sister was. He was young and away at school."

"Of course. And no doubt Daphne told him that she had been wronged. She was hoping to force your brother's hand, I am sure. She wanted very much to be the Duchess of Rochford."

"Clearly she did not know Sinclair well enough," Callie commented.

A brief smile touched Francesca's lips. "No. I suppose she did not, after all. Rochford does not respond well to being pressed." She shook her head. "What happened? Did Rochford tell you? Surely he did not fight the boy."

"No, of course not. But he said that he regrets the way he handled it. He was scornful, apparently. He thinks he hurt Lord Bromwell's pride. Brom — that is, Bromwell — must have nursed a grudge against him all these years. And when he had the chance to inflict a little revenge upon Sinclair, he seized it." Callie shrugged. "He wooed the duke's sister, then unceremoniously left her, exposing her to the *ton's* gossip."

"Oh, Callie, I am so sorry." Francesca reached out to take her friend's hand, and Callie saw that her blue eyes were swimming with tears. "I had no idea that he carried such a grudge against the duke. I never heard about the challenge. I was . . . busy with my first Season, and Lord Haughston had just asked me to marry him. I was so wrapped up in my own concerns that I suppose I did not listen to all the gossip." Francesca saw no need to add that she had, at that time, been doing her best to avoid any mention of anything to do with the Duke of Rochford.

"I was a little suspicious of Lord Bromwell at first," Francesca went on. "But mostly because he was Lady Swithington's brother, and I thought he might be like her. Greedy, ambitious, licentious. I was suspicious of his reasons for courting you because I thought he might harbor some resentment against Rochford, but I did not feel I could speak to you about your brother and Bromwell's sister. It did not seem appropriate. And I had no idea of the strength of Bromwell's feelings. Or that he would seek vengeance upon the duke through you. I am terribly sorry. I should not have let him come to call here. I should have kept a closer eye on him."

Callie smiled and squeezed her friend's hand comfortingly. "You are very sweet, but I do not think there was anything you could have done. I knew that Sinclair did not like him, did not want me to be around him. If anyone is at fault, it is I — for being headstrong and obstinate, refusing to take my brother's advice. I was foolish — and too ready to believe that Lord Bromwell cared for me."

"He is despicable," Francesca declared. "To set out to break your heart! I promise you — I will plot some quite devious and painful social downfall for him."

Callie laughed, as she knew Francesca had meant her to. "No, indeed, 'tis not so awful. He did not break my heart. I told you when I first came here that I am not a romantic. I did not fall dreadfully in love with him. As I told Sinclair, the worst I have suffered is a little trifling embarrassment. Why, it is not even the full Season yet. Half the people I know are not even here, and in a few weeks there will be something much more interesting to gossip about than me and my little fall from pride."

Francesca still looked troubled, but she let the matter drop. Callie was grateful. She knew that her words were not entirely truthful, and it was hard to keep up a pretense of good cheer.

She did believe that the gossip about her would die down quickly enough, and though she did not like the fact that people were talking about her, she could bear it without much difficulty. But she had lied about the heartache that she felt. The truth was that her heart had been sore without Brom. It had not been only her pride that had been hurt.

She had not fallen in love with him. She reminded herself of that fact frequently. But she could not deny that her days were far duller without him in them. She missed talking to him and seeing his face. She missed his smile, his laugh, the way his presence filled a room. The other night, when she had seen him across the room, her heart had leapt in her chest. The problem was, she thought, she was lonely without him, and unhappy. Every morning when she woke up she would feel again for a moment as she used to, and then she would remember that Brom was missing from her life, and a quiet sadness would settle upon her.

However, she was determined that the world, at least, should not see that she was unhappy. Gritting her teeth, she went about her usual social routine. A Lilles, after all, had to keep up appearances.

Therefore, as the days wore on she paid calls or received visitors every afternoon, and she accompanied Francesca to parties, smiling and chatting with friends and acquaintances as if she did not have a care in the world. And if there were nights when she cried herself to sleep, or mornings when she wished that she did not have to get out of bed, she did not let on.

One evening, at the theater, Sally Pemberton, a rather sharp-faced blond girl, came in with her mother to visit them in their box, and once the requisite amount of small talk had passed, she said archly, " 'Tis odd, is it not, how rarely one sees Lord Bromwell these days."

"Really?" Callie glanced at her. "I am afraid I had not noticed."

"Not noticed! But, my dear, the man was practically in your pocket, was he not? Every party, every dinner. Why, the way he danced attendance on you, I vow I quite expected to hear a happy announcement very soon. And now . . ." She shrugged. "Well, one cannot help but wonder what has happened."

"I have learned that it is a fool's game to take a young gentleman seriously — either in what he says or in what he does. It is precisely because of a young man's fickleness that a woman is always wise to keep a firm grip upon her heart." Callie smiled serenely at Miss Pemberton.

And if she had to curl her hand into a fist in her lap, fingernails digging into her palm, to keep any emotion from showing in her face, or if she cried into her pillow again that night . . . well, at least the Miss Pembertons of the world did not know it.

Francesca, she felt sure, suspected that Callie's nights were restless; she could hardly have missed the mornings when Callie came down to breakfast with eyelids still swollen from tears or smudged with faint blue beneath them from lack of sleep. But, tactfully, Francesca refrained from comment.

Callie knew, too, that Francesca turned down a number of invitations, choosing only enough to make it clear that Callie was not sitting home nursing a broken heart. Her friend also, Callie noticed, remained by her side through most of any party, quick to steer the conversation in a new direction if it entered troubling waters, or to skewer with a few well-chosen words any person with the audacity to repeat whatever gossip still circulated about Callie and Lord Bromwell. For that, if for no other reason, Callie thought, Francesca would always have a special place in her heart.

She did not see Bromwell at any of the parties she attended. She thought he might have left London. He had only been visiting, after all; he obviously preferred living on his estate. But she heard his name now and then at parties, and Sir Lucien told Francesca that Bromwell had been seen frequently at Cribb's Parlour, a drinking establishment favored by the "fancy," as gentlemen with a keen interest in the sport of pugilism were known. He had also, according to Francesca's friend, spent several afternoons at Jackson's Saloon, where he had been given the honor of stripping to the waist and sparring with Gentleman Jackson himself.

Callie could not help but wonder if Bromwell was staying in London so that he could see for himself what sort of damage he had inflicted on Rochford's sister. This thought served to stiffen her spine and send her to one or two parties that she had been reluctant to attend for fear she might run into him.

More and more members of the *ton* were arriving in London almost daily, it seemed, and Callie knew that it would not be many more weeks before the Season was well under way. The number of invitations they received each day was rapidly growing, and they were spending more and more evenings at one party or another.

She thought of the months ahead and the exhausting whirl of parties and calls, and she quailed inside. She was not sure she could stand living through this spring and into June, going to a constant round of social engagements, when all the while she felt somehow both leaden and empty inside. As for her original plan of using the Season to find a husband — well, that idea carried no importance for her any longer. Looking back on it, she wondered why she had ever thought that she wanted to marry, much less spend the time and effort it would require to actively seek out a likely prospect for the endeavor.

She thought with longing of going to Marcastle to stay with Sinclair — or, even better, to Dancy Park. She could spend her days riding about the estate or taking long tramps through the countryside. There were friends to visit there — Dominic and Constance. Everything would be quiet and calm, and there would be no prying eyes searching her face for signs of sorrow or embarrassment. She would not have to worry about what she would do if she saw Lord Bromwell walk into a party.

But she knew that she could not leave yet. It was too soon, and gossiping tongues would stir. No one left at the height of the Season except with good reason, and everyone would be certain that her reason was a broken heart. She would have to stay at least another two months now, until May, she decided, and she almost wept at the thought.

"I thought we would attend Lady Whittington's musicale tonight," Francesca announced one afternoon.

Callie barely suppressed a groan.

"Yes, I know," Francesca commiserated. "They are dead bores, usually."

"Usually?"

"Well, always. However, they have one distinct advantage. They do not last past ten o'clock, ever, and one also does not have to converse most of the time. You can pretend to be listening to the wretched music."

"If one is adept at acting," Callie agreed. "But you are right. Having to be out only two hours is a very welcome thing."

So with somewhat less reluctance than she usually felt, Callie dressed for the evening, letting her maid spend a few extra minutes taming and arranging her curls, and she and Francesca went to the musicale. Francesca, as usual, arranged it so that they swept in later than most of the crowd; such behavior was always marked down as simply the way Lady Haughston was, but Callie was well aware of the fact that it greatly reduced the time that she would have to spend keeping up her pose of cheerful indifference to Lord Bromwell's absence.

They met Lady Manwaring and her sister, Mrs. Beltenham, just inside the foyer, and they strolled into the music room together, pausing to look about for seats. Callie's gaze went to the west wall of the room, opposite the windows, and her heart skittered in her chest.

Standing there, his elbow resting negligently upon a marble pedestal and looking straight at her, was Lord Bromwell.

Callie felt as if she suddenly could not breathe. It had been over a week since she had last seen him and two since she had spent any time with him, and she was struck all over again by his hard, spare handsomeness. He straightened as their gazes locked, and Callie thought, feeling a little panicky, that he was about to walk over to her.

She could not bear that. Not here, in front of all these people. She turned quickly away, touching Francesca's arm. "I — I am feeling a bit of a headache. If you will excuse me . . ."

"Oh, dear. Do you want to leave?" Francesca asked quickly. "Perhaps you are coming down with something. I hear that there is a fever going about."

"No, no, I think it is just a . . . um, a trifle warm in here. Pray do not worry. Just sit and enjoy the music. I shall return shortly."

Callie turned, not daring to glance back at Bromwell, and fled from the room.

CHAPTER FOURTEEN

Callie hurried down the hallway, paying little attention to where she went. A door stood open to a small library, and she slipped inside, closing the door after her. Letting out a sigh of relief, she sank down into a wingback chair. Her legs, she noticed, were trembling.

She wished she had not fled. Had anyone noticed? She suspected that someone must have. She only hoped she had not looked as distressed as she had felt.

It was so much harder to maintain her air of indifference when Bromwell was there. When he had first stopped calling on her, she had half expected to see him every time she walked into a party. She had been prepared, braced to run into him . . . as well as still hopeful that when she saw him, somehow everything would return to the way it had been.

But now she had become accustomed to

his not being around. She had let her guard down, and the sight of him had been a shock. Moreover, now that she knew why Brom had pursued her and then rejected her, there was no hope in her heart, only pain at the sight of him.

She would have to go back, she knew. She could not hide in here for the entire musicale — or even for more than a few minutes. People would notice her absence, and there would be talk. If she let on how much Lord Bromwell had hurt her, then all of her careful work for the last two weeks would be for naught. Callie closed her eyes and tried to school herself for the ordeal ahead.

The door opened suddenly, and Callie jumped at the sound, her eyes flying open. Lord Bromwell stood framed in the doorway.

She stared at him for a moment, every nerve in her body tingling. Then she rose to her feet, her hands curling into tight fists at her side as though ready to literally fight.

"Lord Bromwell," she said, relieved that her voice came out much steadier than she felt.

He stepped into the room, closing the door behind him, but did not come any closer. "I thought — are you all right?"

"I am fine," Callie replied coldly. "If you

hoped to find me brokenhearted over you, I fear you are doomed to disappointment."

"Of course I did not hope to break your heart!" he flared up, his eyes flashing silver. "I —" He broke off, his face stamped with frustration, and began to pace the room. "Blast it! I never thought about you. I only thought to tweak the duke's nose a bit."

Callie stiffened. "I am well aware that your only interest in me was to hurt my brother. However, I do not think that a few whispers about my losing a suitor will do much to damage Rochford. No doubt you regret the fact that you were not able to besmirch my name," she added in a voice that dripped sarcasm. "It would have been a much greater scandal."

Bromwell stopped in his pacing and whirled around to face her. "I never intended to do that! Is that what you think of me? That I am the kind of man who would shame a lady, just to get revenge on her brother?"

"What else am I to think?" Callie shot back, taut with fury. Her muscles trembled as the anger and hurt, long tamped down, came welling up in her. All the pain, all the tears, all the worry and doubt, swept through her, filling her with such rage that she could no longer keep it from flooding out. "Why else did you pursue me? That is what my brother believes. It is why he warned me not to have anything to do with you. You wanted to put a blot on our good name, and what easier way to do so than that?"

"Oh, really?" Bromwell took a long stride closer to her. "And if that was my purpose, how do you explain the fact that I did not 'besmirch' you?"

"Rotten luck on your part, I suppose," Callie snapped.

His hand lashed out, grasping her upper arm, his fingers digging in. "Rotten luck?" he repeated incredulously. "Is that what you believe? In what way did I have bad luck? It certainly was not in lack of opportunity — and you were certainly not unwilling." He jerked her to him, his eyes blazing down into hers. "I'll warrant you still are not unwilling."

He bent and kissed her, his mouth laying claim to hers with a savage intensity that she knew should have frightened and repelled her. But it did not, she realized with dismay. Instead, the harsh, possessive, ravening kiss ignited a fire inside her. It geysered up, shooting throughout her body, turning her skin to flame, and settled in a hot, aching mass deep in her abdomen.

His arms went around her, pressing her into him. She wrapped her own arms around his neck, and they strained against each other, their mouths clinging, devouring. His hands moved over her body hungrily. Growing frustrated at the cloth that thwarted his desire to touch her, he bunched the dress in his hand, pulling it up and up until at last his fingers were able to slip beneath her skirts.

He spread his hand across the soft flesh of her thigh, separated from him only by the sheer cotton of her undergarment. His hand slid upward, seeking the moist heat of her center, and the path of his fingers sent shivers of passion through her. As his mouth possessed her, he caressed and stroked her leg, sliding back to curve over the soft mound of her buttock, then around to the front, easing between their bodies.

Callie gasped and moved involuntarily in surprise as his hand boldly slid across her abdomen and delved down between her legs. Never had she imagined being touched in such a way, but she found that it excited her almost beyond measure. She moved, wanting more . . . *needing* more.

Brom made a noise deep in his throat, hunger tearing at him as he found the damp, heated cleft between her legs. His fingers stroked and flexed, aching to touch her skin without the thin cloth between them.

Breaking the seal of their mouths, he kissed his way down her throat and onto the supremely soft flesh of her breast, which rose above the neckline of her dress. He tasted her skin with lips and tongue, tracing hot wet patterns across the smooth flesh and gently grazing it with his teeth.

Callie trembled, sure that she would go mad beneath the touch of his fingers and mouth. The pleasure was stunning, sending the heat within her skyrocketing. She ached to feel him all over her, to take him inside her. She was aware of a deep, primitive longing to circle her hips against him, to open her legs to his hard masculine force.

With his other hand, he reached up to tug at the neck of her gown, working down the dress and the chemise beneath it until at last her breast was free. He grew still, gazing down for a long moment at the soft white orb and the pinkish-brown circle of her nipple.

Then he bent and circled the center with his tongue, causing it to grow even harder. Softly he blew on the nipple where his tongue had touched, and it tightened even more, plucking a cord that ran straight down into her abdomen and flooded her with desire.

Slowly, thoroughly, he loved her with his mouth, using teeth and tongue and lips to arouse the tight bud of her nipple. Finally he settled down to suckle at her nipple, pulling with strong, deep strokes even as his fingers moved in the same rhythm between her legs.

Desire clawed at his loins like a wild beast, and he wanted to pull her to the floor and take her, to rip the clothes from her and sink into her, surging to his completion. He felt her skin flame beneath him, felt her move and gasp and softly moan at the pleasure he was evoking in her, and it filled him with such heat and hunger that he thought he would explode.

Callie's breasts were full and aching, her loins throbbing with an incessant beat. She arched up against him, wordlessly seeking more. Something was building inside her, intense and demanding.

With a low, soft curse, he broke from her and turned away. She swayed where she stood, staring after him, stunned and bereft. She wanted to follow him, to throw herself at him and beg him to take her, to give her the satisfaction her body so craved. Only some last small vestige of pride enabled her to remain where she was, silent.

Brom leaned over the library table, his hands braced, his chest rising and falling with deep fast breaths. Callie stared at his back. She was trembling all over, her mind benumbed, and she felt incredibly soft and aching, vulnerable, like a creature outside its shell.

Slowly she came to herself enough to pull up the neck of her dress and smooth down her skirts into some semblance of modesty. She moved away shakily, saying, "Well . . . you must be happy now that you have humiliated me."

"Humiliated *you?*" he answered through gritted teeth. "I am the one who cannot walk out of this room."

Her body was still hot and aching, still yearning for satisfaction, but she was not about to argue with him about which of them suffered most from desire. "This is to no purpose," she said tightly, bringing her hands up to cool her burning cheeks.

She could feel the sorrow rising in her, pushing its way through the heat of her desire. "I will not let you use me against my brother," she told him, struggling to keep her voice steady. "Whatever mad feeling you may be able to call up in me, it will not be enough to make me ruin my good name and

346

his. I will make certain that we are never alone together again."

"I did not mean to do that," he gritted out. "And you need not fear me. Or what I want from you." He swung around to look at her, his face stark and etched with pain. "I did not consider what would happen to you when I started this, and for that I apologize. I wanted only to tease the duke, to make him worry that I might do to you what he did to my sister. I had some hope that it might even bring him to confront me personally — to finish what started fifteen years ago.

"But I never set out to hurt you," he went on. "And, God knows, I never intended to — to wind up wanting you so much it's driven me near mad. I did not expect to spend every day counting the minutes until I could be with you again. Or to become the sort of fool who would attend a dull thing like Lady Whittington's musicale just on the chance that I might get to see you again."

Callie stared at him, torn between hope and despair. "But if that is how you feel, then why did you stop coming to call on me? Why —"

"Because there can be no future for me and the sister of the Duke of Rochford!" he exclaimed, shoving his hands up into his hair and pressing against his head as if to keep it from exploding. He swung away, crossing to the wall and turning back. "Your brother destroyed my sister! He led her on. He seduced her and got her with child, and then he refused to marry her."

"Sinclair would never have done something like that!" Callie cried. "He is a man of honor. He would never hurt a woman that way. I know it. He told me. He never touched your sister."

Bromwell's lips twisted into a grim smile. "Of course you would believe that."

"It is the truth."

"No. My sister told me the truth. I know what happened."

"She lied to you," Callie said bluntly.

His eyes flared with anger. "No."

"Are you saying that she has never lied? She lied to me. She told me that Lord and Lady Radbourne would be with us that night at Vauxhall, but they were not. When we asked Lady Radbourne about it, she said that your sister told them that the party had been canceled. She tricked me into being there without any sort of chaperone, and then she left me there alone. She tried to —"

"I know! I know. She was trying to help

me. She thought that she would please me. She knew how I wanted you, and she wanted to help me. It is different. She would not have lied to me about . . . about *that*."

"And my brother would not lie to *me*."

He looked at her, regret and sorrow in his eyes. "Then you see how it is. You are as loyal to your brother as I am to my sister. There is nothing for us."

Callie caught her breath in pain as Bromwell walked away. He opened the door, then paused and turned back to look at her. "I am sorry, Callie, for hurting you. I —" He shook his head and went out the door, closing it behind him.

Callie raised her fist to her mouth to stifle the whimper that rose from her. She drifted to a chair and sank down in it, fighting the tears that threatened to overwhelm her.

She could not stay here. She no longer cared whether people gossiped about her reaction to Lord Bromwell. She had to get away to grieve in private.

Swallowing hard, she left the library. In the foyer, she found a footman and sent him to tell Francesca that she was leaving. By the time the other footman had located Callie's cloak and helped her into it, Francesca came hurrying out of the music room, looking worried.

"Callie, dear, are you sick? We shall go at once."

Callie nodded, murmuring, "You need not leave."

"Nonsense," Francesca replied quickly, already motioning to the footman for her cloak. "I could not stay here, worrying about you. I told Lady Manwaring that you had fallen sick. She will make our apologies to Lady Whittington."

Callie nodded and pulled up the hood of her cloak, grateful for the concealment it offered. Francesca whisked her out to their carriage and climbed in after her.

"What happened?" she asked as she settled into the seat beside Callie, reaching out to take her hand. "I saw Lord Bromwell leave the room after you did. Did he speak to you? Is that why —"

"Yes — oh, yes!" Callie burst out, no longer able to hold in her emotions. Tears began to stream from her eyes. "It is impossible! It was foolish of me to even retain the hope that —" She broke off, a sob escaping her. "Oh, Francesca! He will never be disloyal to his sister any more than I would break from Sinclair! It does not matter what I feel, or even what he feels for me. It is utterly hopeless."

"Oh, my dear." Tears of sympathy glimmered in Francesca's eyes, and she put her arms around Callie as Callie collapsed against her in a storm of tears.

Lord Bromwell stood up as his sister entered the drawing room. He had left the musicale and walked straight to Daphne's home, his emotions storming within him.

"Brom!" Lady Daphne exclaimed, coming forward with both her hands extended to take his, smiling at him with such delight that he felt a stab of guilt.

He had not been here often recently. He had not wanted to see anyone, including his sister, and he had spent most of his time at his club, drinking, or at his house, drinking, punctuated by bouts of pugilistic exercise at Jackson's. Pounding on something, or someone, seemed to be the only thing that brought him any relief.

"I was afraid that you were still miffed with me about that little fiasco at Vauxhall Gardens," Daphne went on, squeezing his hands. "Come, sit down with me."

"I know that you did what you thought best," he equivocated.

"Yes, I did." She smiled radiantly at him, taking his answer for approval. "You know that you are all I care about."

He managed a smile. "Well, I believe that

351

I rank somewhere in the vicinity of clothes and jewels."

"Oh, you!" Daphne gave him a playful push on the arm. "Shall we do something together tonight? Have you plans? I have heard of a very nice gambling club. Of course I would never think of going there by myself, but with an escort, it would be quite another matter."

He shook his head. "I am not in a gaming mood, I fear. Save that for one of your battalion of beaux. I have come to tell you that I am leaving London."

Daphne stared at him. "Leaving London? Whatever do you mean? Where are you going?"

"Back to the estate," he answered. "I am better there."

"But what about Rochford? What about Lady Calandra?"

"I have ended that," he said, standing up and crossing the room to the fireplace. He picked up the poker and pushed the logs about a bit, staring broodingly into the flames.

"I had heard that you were no longer pursuing his sister," Daphne said. "But I did not think that was the end of the matter."

He stuck the poker back in its place and

turned to face her. "The duke did not come to confront me, and I saw no point in continuing."

"No point!" Daphne burst out, rising to her feet. "I thought you were going to avenge what he did to me!"

"What would you have me do, Daphne?" he asked.

"Something more than cause that girl a little public ridicule!" she shot back.

"Isn't that enough to do to an innocent woman?" he retorted.

"No!" Daphne cried fiercely. "It's not! It is not enough to pay for what her brother did to me!"

"I cannot change what happened to you," Bromwell told her earnestly. "I wish to God that I could. I would do anything to take that pain from you, to erase it from your mind and heart. But I cannot. And hurting Callie further cannot make you happy."

"I want you to ruin her!" Daphne seethed, her lovely face contorting with rage.

Bromwell stared at his sister, shocked by her words. "Daphne! You cannot mean that. Your hurt and bitterness over what the duke did to you are keeping you from thinking clearly. You would not really wish me to inflict damage on an innocent young woman's reputation. I thought when we talked the other night that you realized as much yourself. That you would not want me to be the sort of man who would do such a thing."

Daphne drew a long breath, then smiled at her brother a little shakily. "No, of course, you are right. I would not want any harm to come to the girl. Not really. I just — I could see that you wanted her, and . . ." She turned away from him, reaching down to reposition a pillow on the sofa.

"Still," she went on, picking up another pillow and fluffing it, playing with the fringe along its edges. "I hate that you are leaving. I have seen you so little the last few years. I had looked forward to our having this Season in London together."

"I know. But I have duties at the estate that need seeing to. And there is little for me to do here beyond corresponding with my steward and my business agent."

"Oh, such dull stuff. You need to have fun. Not work so much. You are a gentleman."

"I am a gentleman who needs something to do," he responded.

"I know!" Daphne brightened. "Why don't you go to Lord Swithington's hunting lodge? You can rest there for a few days before you return to the estate."

He smiled, glad to see that she had gotten over her disappointment. He hated to see the way the past had embittered her, her desire for vengeance eating away at her once-happy nature. "But, Daphne," he pointed out, "it is not even hunting season. There is nothing to do there."

"But that is entirely the point, is it not?" she responded brightly. "You can tramp about the countryside. Read by the fire in the evenings."

"I can do all those things at home."

"Yes, but that is so far away. At the cottage you will not be so far from London. I could drive up there in a few days and join you. As soon as the Wentwhistle ball is over. I must be here for that. I promised Mrs. Wentwhistle only yesterday that I would not fail her. But that is only a few days away. The day after the ball, I will drive up there, and we can spend some time together. Wouldn't that be fun? Just the two of us, like when we were children. We can talk and talk . . . about everything. Since we have been here, I have been thinking how much I have missed you all these years."

He chuckled. "Daphne, we visited one another two or three times a year ever since you married Lord Swithington."

"Yes, I know, and no doubt you think it silly of me," she told him, pursing her lips in a little moue. "But it has been so nice the past few weeks, living close to you. And I do not want it to end just yet. Please, do say you will, or I shall be certain that you are still displeased with me about our trip to Vauxhall."

He smiled at her. "All right. I know that you are accustomed to having your way. I will only end up saying yes eventually."

"Of course you will," she agreed with a charming laugh, coming forward to tuck her hand in his arm. "It will be such fun. You'll see. Now, I shall just write a note and tell the caretaker to expect you the day after tomorrow. How is that?"

"Fine," he answered. "It will be fine. It will take a day to get my affairs in order, anyway."

"Wonderful," Daphne purred. "You will see. You shan't be sorry."

The following morning Francesca announced that Callie had done quite enough maintaining face for the present.

"I think that you should stay home for a while," she told her as they sat at the breakfast table.

Callie, who had eaten little, mostly pushing her food about on her plate, looked at Francesca with an eagerness she could not disguise. "Do you think so? Truly? There will be talk."

"There is always talk," Francesca retorted. "But you have shown everyone that you are not hurt, that you scarcely notice or care that one of your admirers has fallen out. It has been two weeks now that you have carried on, and I should think that is adequate to set most of the tongues to rest."

"But I know that people must be gossiping about how I behaved last night," Callie said, grimacing. "I wish that I had been better able to control myself."

"Pray do not worry about that. What happened last night will only add verisimilitude to our story. You were suddenly struck ill. That is why you left the party. For that to be believable, you must continue to be ill for at least a week, I should think. Perhaps even two. Who knows? Perhaps your illness will require a return to the country to recuperate."

Callie smiled faintly. "That sounds very nice, I must say. But I am not sure I wish to be at death's door."

"Well, perhaps not. Everyone will plague you with questions about it. Elaborate lies can be so difficult to maintain. Perhaps just a week or so, then, and after that you may venture out a little. But I shall insist, of course, on your taking care. You must not exhaust yourself and cause a relapse." Francesca smiled, her cheek dimpling in that way she had that made it almost impossible not to return her smile.

"Very well," Callie gave in. "You have convinced me. I will not deny that seeing no one will be a vast relief."

"Then it is done," Francesca decided with a nod. "I shall fulfill our social obligations alone for the next few days — though I feel that I should reduce them, of course. After all, I must devote myself to taking care of you, or else what sort of friend would I be?"

So that afternoon Callie retired to her bedroom with a book, leaving Francesca downstairs to entertain whoever happened to call. She was, as she had told Francesca, greatly relieved not to have to pretend a calm and good cheer that she most certainly did not feel. Indeed, she was not certain that she would have been able to maintain such a front.

Her eyes were still swollen and red-rimmed from her bout of crying last night, followed by a long night with little sleep, broken more than once by a fresh outpouring of tears. It was a wonder, she had thought this morning, that she had any tears left in her body, yet she had found herself blinking away the moisture in her eyes as she looked at the dress that Belinda had laid out for her — it had been the one she wore the first time Bromwell had come to call on her.

She had missed his presence for the past two weeks, but the exchange between them the night before had left her desolate. She knew now, beyond any doubt, that he would never be part of her life again. She had come so close to love. It made the loss that much keener.

Or perhaps, she thought, it was too late. She was beginning to wonder if perhaps she had, at last, finally fallen in love . . . with a man who would never marry her.

Francesca was sitting at her desk early the next afternoon, wondering how it was that paying her bills had gone so smoothly for the past month, especially when they had eaten so well and had not scrimped on coal or candles, either. She suspected strongly that it had something to do with the duke's agent having come to discuss Lady Calandra's expenses with her butler. She could not decide whether Fenton had managed to squeeze a good deal more money out of the duke's agent than was deserved or the duke had instructed his man to pay more than was necessary, which left her uncertain with whom she should be cross. Of course, she knew that she would never get the truth out of Fenton, who was the most closemouthed creature ever.

When the butler entered the room, she thought for a fleeting second that her thoughts had conjured him up, but then he announced that Lady Pencully had come to call and was awaiting her in the formal drawing room. This news was enough to drive all thoughts of numbers straight out of Francesca's head.

No matter how old Francesca was or how long she had been managing her own affairs, Lady Odelia never failed to make her feel as if she were a schoolgirl again. Somehow, when Lady Odelia raised her lorgnette to gaze at her, Francesca was always sure that the woman spotted everything that could possibly be wrong with her.

She wished, in a quite cowardly way, that she had not decided to pretend that Callie was feeling ill. For all her youth, Callie never seemed to feel intimidated by her great-aunt.

Francesca took a peek in the small mirror beside the door to make sure that her hair was in place and there was no errant ink smudge on her face before she left the room, smoothing down her skirts as she went. Lady Odelia was always impossibly early in her calls, Francesca thought, so she could not even hope that other callers might interrupt the visit.

"Lady Odelia," she said, smiling brightly and offering the older woman a polite curtsey as she entered the drawing room. "How very nice to see you. I am surprised that you have not yet left the city. Do you intend to stay for the Season?"

"Hallo, Francesca." The older woman gestured toward the seat beside her, as if she were the hostess here rather than Francesca. She was dressed, as usual, in garments at least ten or fifteen years out of date, her graying hair dressed up in a high sweeping hairdo decorated by feathers. "Sit down, girl, don't make me crane my neck to look at you."

As Francesca sat down, Lady Odelia continued, "I haven't decided yet, actually. I was not planning to, but I have felt quite invigorated since my party. Nothing like turning eighty-five to make one wonder if one really should be rotting away in boredom in Sussex."

"Many people enjoy a visit to Bath, especially in the summer," Francesca offered.

"Yes, well, I haven't come here to discuss travel plans," Lady Odelia said briskly.

"No, of course not," Francesca agreed, wondering if the old lady had come up with some other scheme for which she sought Francesca's help. Her last one had involved marrying off one of her great-nephews, Lord Radbourne. Of course, that had turned out well all around, but still, Francesca could not help but feel a little leery; Lady Odelia was quite adept at putting other people to work for her.

"Your man Fenton tells me that my great-niece is ill," Odelia went on.

"Yes, she is." Francesca hoped that Lady Odelia could not see that she was lying, another of the things that Francesca was always sure Lady Odelia could do. "She came down ill the day before yesterday at Lady Whittington's musicale."

"Ill — or just missing that rapscallion Bromwell?" Lady Odelia asked shrewdly.

"Lady Calandra had no expectations of Lord Bromwell," Francesca replied smoothly. "Why, she barely knows the man. I believe she first met him at your birthday ball."

"Yes, well, time isn't always what matters," Lady Odelia pronounced. "Damn the boy. I don't know what got into him. I understand he has gone back to his estates. I had hopes for him and Callie. Ah, well . . ." The old lady shrugged. "She won't be wanting for suitors long."

"No, I am sure not."

"What are you doing tomorrow?" Lady Odelia asked abruptly.

Francesca froze. "Um . . . I am not sure," she murmured, stalling for time. She did not know why it was that her mind, usually so agile in concocting polite social lies, always seemed to jolt to a stop around Lady Pencully. "What time tomorrow?"

"The whole day. I have been meaning to visit the Duchess of Chudleigh. Your mother's godmother," she added, as if Francesca would not know whom she meant.

"Oh," Francesca replied, with a sinking sensation in her stomach.

"Thought it might be a good idea for you to come along. She lives in Sevenoaks, you know, only a short ride. She would quite like to see you, I imagine, and you will be able to write your mother and tell her how the duchess is doing. She was in rather ill health this winter, you know."

"I believe Mother mentioned it," Francesca agreed weakly. The prospect of spending the day either enclosed in a carriage with Lady Odelia or sitting with the two ancient women as they shouted back and forth to each other — for the duchess was quite deaf, but refused to use an ear trumpet because she claimed it made her appear old — had no appeal for her.

However, as Lady Odelia had made sure to hint at, visiting the old lady would be what her mother would expect of her. It was her duty, and, like Callie, Francesca had been raised to do her duty. She knew that she could not look Lady Odelia in the eye and tell her that she was not going to visit her mother's aged godmother, no matter how much she would like to. Even if she could bring herself to do it, Francesca knew that Lady Odelia would soon wear her down with argument and wrest an agreement from her. She might as well give in gracefully.

"Well, I suppose that Callie will be all right by herself for a day," Francesca began reluctantly.

"Of course she will," Odelia told her stoutly. "She has a whole houseful of servants to look after her. She will be fine."

"Very well," Francesca capitulated, suppressing a sigh. "I will go with you tomorrow."

"Excellent!" Lady Odelia beamed at her. "I shall be here to pick you up at nine o'clock."

"Nine?" Francesca repeated hollowly. "In

364

the morning?"

"Yes, of course, in the morning." Lady Odelia sent her an odd look. "It will take the whole day — best to get an early start."

"Naturally."

Her mission accomplished, Lady Pencully did not remain long. She soon took her leave — no doubt, Francesca thought sourly, going off to bully some other poor person into doing something for her.

Francesca went upstairs to tell Callie, who immediately chuckled.

"Well, I am glad that my misfortune pleases you," Francesca told her with mock indignation. In truth, she was pleased to see Callie laugh for the first time in days.

"I am sorry, truly," Callie told her, her eyes twinkling. "I know it will be a misery for you. But I am so happy that you decided I should be sick."

"You should be," Francesca retorted, unable to keep from smiling. "Else I would have dragged you into going with us."

Callie gave an exaggerated shudder.

"Are you sure you do not want to go anyway?" Francesca teased. "We could say you had a miraculous recovery. 'Twill be very boring for you here alone, after all."

"Better lonely than riding half the day in a carriage with Lady Odelia," Callie retorted heartlessly. "Do you think she will bring that horrid snuffling dog of hers?"

"That ancient pug!" Francesca looked horrified. "Do not even think it."

Callie dissolved into giggles at her expression, grateful for the opportunity to laugh. She was not someone who enjoyed dwelling on her sorrow.

Tomorrow, she thought, she would have to find some task to do, something to put her mind on other than her own problems.

So the next day, after she awoke and had a quiet breakfast alone downstairs, Callie rang for her maid and spent the next few hours going through her closet, choosing what dress or slippers she might refurbish with a bit of ribbon or some flowers, and what she should give away or just assign to the ragbag.

Unfortunately the job did not take long, as she had only the clothes she had brought with her from home or had only recently bought, so there was little to repair or toss out. By noon she was finished. If she had been at home, she could have gone through the attic, cleaning out old unusable things and getting pleasantly distracted by this or that old dress or well-worn toy. But she could scarcely do so in Francesca's house.

After that, her mind began to turn in its

too-well-traveled path of thinking about Brom. She was not going to do that, she told herself, and went to Francesca's morning room to look for a novel to read. Perhaps a lurid tale from Mrs. Radcliffe's pen would occupy her mind.

She was searching through the shelves when Fenton came into the room, his anxious face most unlike his usual unruffled expression. "My lady . . ."

"Yes, Fenton, what is it?"

"There is a man here. He says that he has an urgent message for you. He says, my lady, that . . . His Grace the Duke has been injured."

CHAPTER FIFTEEN

Callie stared at the butler, the blood draining from her face. "What? My brother?"

She pushed past Fenton into the hall and saw a man standing in the entryway, his hat in his hand. He looked travel-stained and tired. Callie rushed down the hall toward him.

"You have word of the Duke of Rochford?" she asked before she reached him. "Is he hurt?"

"He is alive, my lady," the man said hastily. "But he was in an accident. Here is a letter for you." He extended a folded and sealed sheet of paper to her.

Callie took it. Across the front of it was written *The Lady Calandra Lilles.*

Quickly she turned the note over and ripped open the seal. With hands that trembled, she unfolded the letter. At the top right-hand side were written the words *Blackfriars Cope Cottage, Lower Upton* and the date. Her eyes dropped to the salutation and she began to read:

Dear Lady Calandra Lilles,

I am sorry to report to you that the Duke of Rochford was in a carriage mishap on the road near my cottage. My husband and his man carried him to our house, and the doctor was called. His left leg and several ribs were broken, but other than that, he is well. He is awake and asked me to write and ask you to come. The doctor does not want to move him.

Sincerely yours,
Mrs. Thomas Farmington

Callie let out a little sigh of relief and looked up at the messenger. "He is truly all right?"

"I haven't seen him, miss. I only know what Mrs. Farmington told me. But she said to tell you he was fine."

"I will go at once. If you can tell me exactly where this Lower Upton is . . ."

"It's in Buckinghamshire, my lady. Mrs. Farmington told me to hire a chaise to take you there as soon as I brought you the message."

"Thank you. That would be very good. I

will just pack a few things, and we can be on our way."

The man nodded and left, and Callie turned to find the butler standing a few steps behind her, his expression once again suitably under control.

"Good. Then you heard?" At Fenton's nod, she went on. "I will pack a small bag and leave immediately. I will leave you a note to give to Lady Haughston."

"Very good, my lady. I will send your maid to you."

Callie nodded and flew up the stairs. Her thoughts were tumbling around in her mind, and her heart was pounding. How badly was Sinclair hurt? Mrs. Farmington had taken care to reassure her that he was all right, but the woman doubtless would have been reluctant to have written a bald statement of the truth if his condition was very bad. He could be seriously injured, even close to death. And though he might only have broken a few bones, Callie was well aware of how quickly such a thing could turn into a dangerous fever and illness, even death. Even if a worse illness did not develop, Callie was sure that he was probably in great pain and in need of the care of someone besides strangers. She was determined to reach him as soon as possible.

Buckinghamshire was not terribly far away, she thought, as she began opening her drawers and throwing clothes onto the bed to be packed. She should be able to get there by tonight.

Belinda popped into the room, her eyes big in her white face. "His Grace is injured, my lady?"

"Yes, but I am sure he will be fine," Callie said stoutly. "He has broken a few bones. I am going to him at once."

"Yes, miss, I'll set to packing right away."

"Just put enough things for a day or two into a bag," Callie told her. "I am leaving immediately. But I fear that I might be there some time, so pack a trunk with more clothes, and you can bring it there to me on the mail coach as soon as I send you word to come. I do not know what the situation is. If it turns out we are able to move him, we will return to Lilles House."

While Belinda packed her a bag, Callie sat down to write a quick note to Francesca, explaining where she was going and why. Fenton would tell Francesca the general story of what had happened, Callie knew, but she thought it best that she relate the exact details and tell Francesca where Sinclair was. She ended the note with a promise to send word as soon as she saw Sinclair and could more accurately describe his condition. Even though Rochford and Francesca had not parted on the best of terms the last time he was here, Callie was certain that Francesca would want to know how he was.

That task done, she folded and sealed the note, and handed it to Fenton to give to Lady Haughston as soon as she returned. By that time Belinda had finished with her bag and the messenger had returned with the post chaise. Callie did not take the time to change into a traveling dress; she simply replaced her soft slippers with a sturdier pair of boots and threw her heavy cloak around her shoulders.

She climbed into the post chaise, and they set off only slightly more than half an hour after she had received the message. Callie settled a little breathlessly into her seat and for the first time allowed herself to think of something other than the practical problems of rushing to her brother's side.

Her mind went first to his injuries. She pulled Mrs. Farmington's note from the pocket of her dress, where she had stuffed it after she read it, and perused it again, more slowly this time. She could get nothing more from it regarding his injuries, unfortunately, and she was left to wonder how the accident had occurred and how badly he had been hurt. The dry recital of a broken leg and a few ribs did not really give a good picture of Sinclair's condition. Of course, the woman had doubtless written the note in haste; Callie could not really carp about her not providing enough details. But Callie did wish she knew more about the matter. Had the break been severe? She had seen or heard enough about injuries around their estate to know that there was a great deal of difference between a simple broken bone, easily enough set, and a leg that had been broken in more than one place or had bone piercing the skin.

She shuddered at the pictures she was conjuring up and tried to think of something else. Had Sinclair been driving himself in his curricle? Or had he been in the grand ducal carriage driven by Haskell, their head coachman? Neither of them was the sort to have an accident, so she assumed that it was probably the fault of another driver, but Mrs. Farmington had not mentioned anyone else being hurt. But then again, the woman had clearly not taken the time to explain the accident in detail.

And what was Sinclair doing in Buckinghamshire, anyway? He had told her that he was going home to Marcastle, and though her geography was perhaps a little hazy, she was quite sure that they never passed through Buckinghamshire when they traveled from Marcastle to London. In any case, her brother had left far too long ago to have still been traveling home.

He could, she supposed, have been delayed somehow, but if he had been detained in London, he would have let her know. That did not make sense. Or he could have started toward Marcastle, then changed his mind and decided to travel somewhere else, though such impulsivity was not a mark of her brother's character.

Sinclair usually did what he said, so the odds were that he had gone back to Marcastle and finished his business there, then left on some other sort of business. He had said that he would probably go to their house at Dancy Park, but, again, Buckinghamshire did not lie between the two places. There must be some other property that he had decided to visit; she supposed that if he had been going to his land in Cornwall, he could have traveled that way if he did not want to go through London. It would not usually be like Sinclair to avoid spending a few days in London on the way, so that he could visit with her. But perhaps, she thought sadly, he was still displeased enough with her for disobeying his orders that he had not wanted to see her.

But then again, maybe he had simply decided to visit a friend, or even look at a property to purchase. And, of course, it made no difference why he was there. The subject was, however, something that was far less worrisome than how bad his injuries were or how much pain he was in, or how long it was taking to get to Blackfriars Cope, which were the other things that occupied her mind throughout the afternoon and evening.

They broke their journey only to change horses, and on those occasions, Callie got out of the carriage to stretch her legs. At one of the inns where they stopped, she ordered a light meal of cold meats, cheese and bread, but she had little appetite for it and wound up leaving most of the food on the table.

She knew they were traveling as fast as they could, for they changed horses often enough that they were fresh, but still the trip seemed to take an eternity. It became even slower after it grew dark, because then she did not have the distraction of the landscape to look at from time to time. Time would have passed more quickly, she knew, if she had been able to sleep, but she could not manage even to doze off briefly. Her mind was whirling with doubts and fears and painful images of Sinclair lying in a bed, pale, bruised and bandaged.

More than once, Callie wished that Francesca had not gone away with Aunt Odelia today. Nothing would have been as bad if Francesca had been there to talk to and help her. She felt sure that Francesca would have come along to keep her company. But it was not just the company and the comfort she missed. Francesca was quite good at getting things done. She always knew just what to do, and with a smile and a few words, she could manage to get the best possible results out of people.

When the carriage pulled to a stop, Callie assumed that they had reached another inn and were about to replace their team, but when she pushed aside the curtain to look out, she saw that they had pulled up in front of a country house. It was not quite the little vine-covered cottage she had envisioned upon reading Mrs. Farmington's note, as it was a sturdy two-story building with a stone lintels above the door and windows, but it was certainly no busy inn, and she realized that they must have reached their destination.

"Is this Blackfriars Cope?" she asked the messenger, who had ridden all the way on top of the coach and who now jumped down to give her a helping hand out.

"Yes, my lady. Looks like they're still up waiting for you." He looked toward the house, where the windows above the front door and to one side of it were bathed in a golden glow.

"Thank you," Callie told the man, and though she felt sure that Sinclair must have given him money for the post chaise and the changes of horses, along with his own payment, she pressed a gold coin into his palm, as well. A light rain had begun to fall, chilling and sharp, and she pulled the hood of her cloak forward to protect her face as she hurried up the front steps and sounded the door knocker.

It was a few moments before the front door opened to reveal a short stout woman dressed in a plain muslin dress, with a white apron on top of it. "Aye?"

"Mrs. Farmington?" Callie asked eagerly.

"Aye, that it is."

"I am Lady Calandra Lilles. Is he still awake? Where is he?"

"In the study, miss," the woman replied, turning to point down the hallway to where light spilled out of an open door.

"Thank you." Callie rushed down the hall, scarcely noticing the sound of the front door closing behind her. She pushed back her hood and took off her gloves as she went, tossing them onto a hallway table, then burst into the room Mrs. Farmington had indicated.

She came to an abrupt halt, staring at the scene before her, unable for an instant to make any sense of it.

Lord Bromwell was half reclining on a sofa, one booted leg stretched out in front of him on the sofa and the other leg bent, his foot planted on the floor. He was braced against the end of the couch, turned a little so that his torso was partly in the corner. His jacket and ascot lay discarded on the chair closest to him, and his waistcoat hung open, his shirt unbuttoned partway down his chest. Beside him on the floor sat a silver tray upon which stood a glass decanter half-filled with a dark liquid, and in one hand he held a glass containing the same liquid.

For a moment the two of them stared at each other blankly. He recovered first, exclaiming, "Callie!" He set his glass down with a thunk on the tray and rose to his feet in a smooth motion marred only by his swaying a little on his feet.

"What is it?" he asked, looking alarmed, and started toward her. "What happened? Are you all right?"

"What are *you* doing here?" Callie blurted out, finally recovering her wits enough to speak. Had Bromwell been involved in her brother's accident? Had it not been an accident after all, but a fight between the two men? "I don't understand. Where is Sinclair? Is he all right? What happened?"

"Sinclair?" he repeated blankly. "Who is —" His eyes widened. "You mean your brother? Rochford? Why the devil would he be here?"

"But the note!" Callie exclaimed and started to reach for her pocket to pull out the letter she had received, but she stopped in mid-action, her head suddenly whirling. Dozens of oddities tumbled in her mind, falling into place — the elegant handwriting on the note supposedly written by a country woman living in a cottage, the fact that this same woman had addressed the letter in precisely the correct way one addressed a letter to a duke's daughter, the unlikelihood of her brother being in Buckinghamshire at this time, the fact that the journey had been so well-arranged and paid for, yet her brother had not even scribbled a note to her or written his name to assure her that he was well.

"You tricked me!" she gasped, feeling the blood drain from her face, leaving her light-headed and queasy.

Bromwell continued to stare at her blankly. "What? What the devil are you talking about?"

But Callie was no longer listening. She was realizing that she was miles from anywhere, alone, late at night, in the company of a man and without any chaperone except Mrs. Farmington — if that was even her name — who was doubtless in Lord Bromwell's employ. Her reputation would be ruined. Then, on the heels of that thought came one even more horrifying — all this would not have been arranged only to ruin her reputation. He must mean to take her virtue, as well.

She thought she had reached the depths of emotion the other night when she realized that there was no hope for a future with Brom, but she found out now that she could feel far worse. Bromwell not only would not marry her, did not love her and would never come to love her, but he thought so little of her that he would callously ruin her. He had lied to her. He intended to use her to achieve some sort of twisted vengeance against her brother, without any regard to her pain and humiliation.

"Oh, God!" she choked out, tears welling in her eyes, and she raised her hand to her mouth, feeling sick. "What a fool I've been! I have been missing you, mourning you, when all the while you have been sitting here, *plotting* —"

She broke off and ran from the room. She heard him call her name behind her, but she did not stop or even glance back. Her only thought was to reach the post chaise before it left. She would tell them what had happened. Surely they would not callously leave her with him.

There was no sign of the woman who had opened the door, but Callie shrieked for help anyway. She could hear Bromwell running down the hall after her, heard him curse and call her name. She flung open the door and raced outside, then came to a dead halt.

The carriage was gone.

Panicked, she looked to the right and the left, but there was no sign of it anywhere. Clearly it had left as soon as she went inside. No doubt the driver had had instructions to do so. Probably Mrs. Farmington had gone with them — and even if she had not, Callie had no hope that she would help her. Sobs rose up in her chest, threatening to burst out, but Callie shoved them down.

She started to run.

"Callie!" Bromwell, who had come to a halt in the doorway behind her as she stared around the yard, started after her again. "Come back here!"

It was raining harder now, pelting onto her head, stingingly cold, but she did not bother to pull up her hood. She simply lifted her skirts up to her knees and ran as fast as she could. He had been drinking, she thought; perhaps he would not be able to catch her. He might stumble and fall. If she could reach the trees, perhaps she could elude him.

She quickly realized the futility of her hopes. Within a few yards, he had caught up with her, and he grabbed her arm, pulling her to a stop. Callie twisted and pulled, trying vainly to tear herself from his grasp.

"Let go of me!" she cried, blinking back her tears, as much from anger and frustration now as from sorrow. "Rochford will kill you! Nay, I will kill you myself!" She reached over with her other hand and scratched at his arm, digging in her nails.

"Bloody hell!" he exclaimed, grabbing her other wrist and pulling it away from his arm. "What the devil is wrong with you?

Have you gone mad?"

"I never would have believed this of you!" she spat. "I never would have thought that you would stoop this low!" She struggled against him wildly, shrieking wordlessly as she twisted and pulled, lashing out at him with her feet. She managed to jerk one of her arms free, not even noticing the pain, and swung at him, hitting his cheek.

"Blast it! Callie, stop this!" He whirled her around and wrapped his arms around her from behind, pinning her arms to her sides, and lifted her from her feet.

She struggled for a moment longer, but the sobs she had fought against could no longer be held back, and she began to cry in great, gulping breaths and finally went limp in his arms. The chilling rain poured down over them, soaking them.

Bromwell set her down and swept her up in his arms like a child. He bent his head to hers, murmuring, "Callie . . . sweetheart . . ."

His lips brushed her hair for an instant. Then he turned and carried her back into the house. She lay against him, weak and unresisting, chilled to the bone and numbed from the onslaught of emotions.

Inside the house, he set her on her feet, calling, "Mrs. Farmington!"

He unfastened Callie's sodden cloak and

let it fall to the flagstone floor. Her hair was wet and had fallen from its pins during their struggle, and now it fell over her shoulders, water dripping from it. Beneath the cloak, her dress had gotten wet, as well, and her boots were covered in mud.

"Mrs. Farmington!" he shouted again. "Blast it, where is the woman?"

He was even wetter than Callie, for he had worn no outer garment. His white shirt clung to him, soaked through, and his hair was plastered to his head. He shivered, his fingers trembling as he reached out to unfasten the buttons of her dress.

"Here, you must get out of this dress," he told her.

"No!" She jerked away from him, though she was too weary to run or fight any longer.

He sighed. "Then sit down on this bench."

He took her arms and hauled her over to the wooden bench that sat to one side of the entry. He pushed her down onto the seat, none too gently.

"Stay here," he ordered.

Callie would have liked to disobey him, just for principle's sake, but she found it too hard to move. She leaned her head back against the wall. She was terribly cold, she knew, but she felt too numb and disconnected to do anything about it. She shuddered, her teeth beginning to chatter.

Bromwell reappeared, holding a knitted throw, which he wrapped around her tightly. "There. That should warm you up a bit."

He stripped off his wet shirt and waistcoat, and tossed them onto the floor. Callie's eyes widened warily. But he made no move toward her, only wrapped another afghan around himself like a shawl. It made such a comical picture that in any other circumstances she would have been tempted to laugh.

He slicked his hair back, squeezing the water from it, then reached down to do the same to Callie's hair. She raised her hands to push his hands away, but there was little strength in her, and he ignored her feeble attempts. Then he knelt in front of her and began to unlace her boots.

"Stop," she said.

"Hush. You are freezing and wet, and I refuse to let you catch your death of cold simply because you have run mad."

"I have not run mad," she protested weakly.

He sat back on his heels and quirked an eyebrow at her. "No. Of course not. You show up here — though I cannot fathom why or how you knew where I was. You begin raving about your brother, and then you start shrieking and run straight out into the rain, pelting off God-knows-where. And when I try to stop you, to find out what is the matter, you attack me. What in all that is anything *but* mad?"

When she made no answer, only looked at him mutinously, he said, "Very well. We will leave your shoes on." He pulled her to her feet again. "Come here."

"Where?" She set her jaw, looking mulish.

"Oh, blast!" He swooped her up in his arms again and strode off down the hall to the study, ignoring her wriggling protests.

He set her down on her feet in front of the fire and picked up the poker to stir the flames higher. The heat felt wonderful against her skin, and Callie could not refrain from letting out a sigh of pleasure. She sat down on a stool in front of the fire screen, automatically turning her head so that her hair fell loose down the side closest to the heat.

Bromwell strode over to the decanter and glass that still sat on the tray, and filled up the glass again. He returned to Callie and thrust the glass into her hand. "Drink this. It will warm you faster than the fire."

She looked at him suspiciously, and his mouth tightened. "Drink," he ordered, "or I shall pour it down your throat."

With a grimace, Callie took a gulp of the liquor. It burned all the way down her throat, and she gasped, but it warmed her from the inside, and she felt immediately better. He took the glass from her and drank, then handed it back to her and squatted down in front of the fire beside her.

Callie took another, smaller, sip of the drink and stole a sideways look at Bromwell. He had shrugged off the cumbersome throw he had wrapped around his shoulders, and the firelight played across his bare shoulders and chest. There was something primitive about him as he squatted there, his arms resting on his knees, warming himself in front of the fire, his hair tousled and wet, drying in the heat.

Her throat was suddenly dry, and Callie was humiliatingly aware of the warmth that was stealing through her loins, a warmth that had nothing to do with the fire and everything to do with the man in front of her.

He turned his head and caught her looking at him. She glanced quickly away, blushing, but he reached out and took her chin in his fingers, tilting her face back to look at him. He did not speak, only let his eyes roam over her, taking in her wet disheveled curls and the damp dress that clung to her breasts, revealing the thrust of her tightening nipples against the cloth. His mouth softened a little, and his eyes sparked with heat. His thumb caressed her chin, moving up to skim across her bottom lip.

The touch of his skin on the sensitive flesh of her mouth sent sparks skittering through her, and she realized, aghast, that she was tempted to take his hand and press her lips against it. Despite everything, some primitive urge deep inside her had responded to the desire in his eyes and wanted to see it flame even higher.

She shot to her feet. "No! Do not think that you can seduce me. I will not succumb to you. I will not be a willing part of your scheme to stain my name!"

He rose, too, facing her, and the heat in his eyes now was more anger than desire. "I would never do that. You know I would not."

"Really?" Her voice dripped sarcasm. "Do you expect me to believe that you lured me here to talk?"

He opened his arms in a gesture of bewilderment. "I did not lure you here at all! I have no idea what you are talking about, nor have I since the moment you walked through that door, babbling about Rochford."

"How can you say that?" Callie cried. Somehow it hurt all the worse because she wanted so much to believe his words. "I am not a fool. I received a letter telling me to rush here because my brother had suffered a carriage accident, and when I arrived, there was no one here but you."

"What?" He continued to stare at her. "Callie . . . I sent you no letter. I have no idea what you are talking about. I would never — I swear on everything that is dear to me, I would never try to lure you here and take advantage of you. How can you even think that?"

Callie looked into his eyes, the silver-gray warmed with the gold of the fire, and in that moment she was suddenly sure that he was telling the truth. And she was equally sure who must have arranged the trick that had been played on her.

Silently, she reached into her pocket and pulled out the folded note she had received. With fingers that trembled a little, she held it out to him.

Frowning, Bromwell took the letter and opened it. Hidden inside her pocket, beneath her cloak, it had not been soaked. It was only slightly damp, and the words were still legible. Looking at Bromwell's face, Callie knew that he recognized the handwriting. He read it through twice and handed it back to her.

Avoiding her eyes, he said, "That was not written by Mrs. Farmington. She is the housekeeper here, and I am not sure that she is even literate. Your brother has never been here. I came to this house when I left London after . . . after we talked at Lady Whittington's musicale."

"What is this place?"

"It is indeed named Blackfriars Cope," he told her, and finally he looked her in the eye. "It was Lord Swithington's hunting lodge."

He looked in that moment sad and tired and older than he was. With a sigh, he turned away, adding, "And the hand looks very much like Daphne's." He picked up the glass from the hearth and drained it. "I am sorry, Callie. I cannot tell you how sorry I am."

He moved away, going to the desk and setting down the glass. He turned back to her, saying, "Perhaps she thought that she was helping me somehow. She knew that I — felt more for you than I should. Perhaps she believed that I would welcome the chance to be placed in such a situation with you." He shook his head. "I do not know what is wrong with Daphne. She has acted . . . in ways that I have never seen her act. She has said and done things that are not like her at all. She — all I can think is that she has become so obsessed with what she suffered that she has lost all sense of reason. She is driven by the need to avenge the wrong that was done to her."

"Brom . . ." Callie went to him and laid her hand upon his arm, looking up earnestly into his face. "Sinclair swore to me that he did not get your sister with child. He told me that he did not even have an affair with Lady Daphne."

His eyes sparked with anger, and his arm stiffened beneath her hand. He shrugged it off, moving across the room. "Of course he would deny it."

"My brother is an honorable man. He feels badly about the way he treated you. He knows that he mishandled the situation. He was not, you know, all that many years older than you were. But he swore to me that what you accused him of was untrue. I believe him. I do not believe that he would lie to me."

"We have talked of this before. Of course you believe him. He is your brother."

"Have you ever heard anything else ill of him?" Callie asked. "Ask anyone, and they will tell you that the Duke of Rochford is a gentleman. He would not seduce a lady and then abandon her, least of all if she was carrying his child. Your sister did not have that child, did she?"

"No. She lost it not long after she married Lord Swithington. But that proves nothing," he flared. "Women often miscarry."

"Were you there when it happened?"

"No, of course not. I was back at Oxford." He looked stony. "That does not mean it did not happen."

Callie said nothing, merely looked at him, and after a moment his eyes dropped. But she had seen the doubt that flickered there. She knew that he must be struggling with the dawning realization that what he had believed for the last fifteen years had been a lie, that the sister he loved and trusted had deceived him.

"That does not matter now, anyway," he said gruffly. "We cannot resolve the matter. It is not ours to worry about."

"It certainly affects us," Callie retorted sharply, nettled.

"I know." He met her gaze squarely this time. "Do not think that I am dismissing the situation in which Daphne has placed you. Whatever her reasons, I know how much she has wronged you, and I refuse to allow you to suffer. That is what we need to be concerned with. We must make sure that your reputation is not damaged."

"There must be a village nearby — this Lower Upton. They have an inn, surely. I will go there and take a room."

"Your carriage is gone," he pointed. "I have a horse in the stable, but he is the only one. You cannot go riding off through strange countryside alone in the middle of the night. He would carry us both, or I could walk alongside you as you rode. But in any case, that would scarcely solve the problem. Whether you arrive after —" he paused and glanced at the clock sitting above the fireplace "— midnight, riding a horse, alone or with a man, and take a room by yourself, it will look exceedingly odd. We are trying to avoid rumors, not engender them."

"But who is to know?" she argued. "The people of the village do not know me. I will use a false name."

"It is better that no one even sees you," he responded flatly. "Does anyone know that you are here?"

"I cannot imagine who would. The messenger brought me this note, and I left straight away in a post chaise he hired. There was no one with me when he arrived, only the servants, and they are very loyal to

Francesca. Even Francesca was not there. She had gone on a visit with Aunt Odelia." She stopped, an odd look crossing her face.

"What?" Bromwell asked. "What is wrong?"

"Nothing, really. I just wonder if that, too, was by design. If Francesca had been there when I received the news about Sinclair, she would no doubt have accompanied me, which would have spoiled the plan."

Bromwell sighed and said, "Lady Odelia is fond of my sister and me. She says we make her laugh. I am sure that your great-aunt would have done nothing to harm you, but if Daphne had artlessly suggested that she go visit someone, and added that Francesca would doubtless love to go with her, she would probably have agreed. She might have guessed that Daphne had something up her sleeve, but I doubt she would have thought that it was anything so ruinous."

Callie nodded. Furious as she was at what Daphne had tried to do to her, she was almost as resentful about the careless hurt the woman had brought to Bromwell.

"In any case," she went on briskly, hoping to distract him from the pain of discovering the full unpleasantness of his sister's character, "Francesca does know where I am and what I was told, for I left a note for her so that she would not worry. But she is the only one, and I am positive that Francesca would never whisper a word that would harm me. I would trust her always."

"Then if no one sees you in the village, there is no reason why anyone should ever find out you were here," Bromwell said. "I think there is but one thing to be done. You must spend the night here."

CHAPTER SIXTEEN

"Here!" Callie exclaimed. "But that would *surely* ruin my reputation."

"Who is to know that you were here unless you or I tell them? I assure you, Mrs. Farmington will not say a word for fear of losing her position here. Tomorrow I will ride into town and hire a chaise for you. You can return to London, and no one will be the wiser. Unless —" he looked worried "— Francesca has spread the word about that the duke is injured and here."

"I do not think she would," Callie said. "Francesca is no gossip. And I doubt she would have received visitors or gone out tonight. She would have been exhausted from having spent the day with Aunt Odelia. Besides, she will be awaiting word from me about Sinclair's condition."

"Good. Then no one will know," he said.

Callie nodded slowly, thinking about the fact that they would still be alone in this house together. She remembered how the firelight had rippled across his bare chest, turning his skin golden and highlighting the smooth curve of his muscles beneath his skin.

"I promise you, I will do nothing to you," he told her quietly. "But if it will make you feel easier, I will sleep in the stables, so that you are truly alone in the house. Mrs. Farmington has clearly already returned to her cottage in the village. And you can lock the doors and windows."

"No, you need not do that." Callie was not about to tell him that she had been worrying more about the pull of attraction she felt toward him than his trying to have his way with her. "I believe you."

"Thank you," he said simply

Their eyes held for a moment; then they both looked away, feeling suddenly awkward. Bromwell cleared his throat and glanced about the room, as though he would find some sort of answer there.

"I imagine you would like to get some sleep," he began finally. "Shall I show you to your room?"

"Yes, please."

"I, uh, perhaps I can find you something to, um, sleep in," he went on as they left the room, color tinting the high ridges of his cheekbones. "One of my shirts or . . ." His voice trailed off.

Callie thought of sleeping in one of Brom's shirts, and her loins prickled with desire. It seemed far too intimate, almost as if he would be there with her. She wondered if any scent of him would still linger on the material.

They started along the hall to the staircase, which lay near the front door. Callie saw the small cloth bag that she had brought with her lying beside the door. She supposed it must have been there earlier, though she had not noticed it in her panic as she ran out the front door.

"Look. It is my bag." She went forward to pick it up, but Brom took it from her hand. "That man must have brought it in. I did not notice."

"Good. Then you will have your clothes." He looked away as he said it.

Everything seemed awkward now, Callie thought. She wondered if he, like she, could not stop thinking about the fact that they were alone together. There were no chaperones and no one to tell tales. No one would know what transpired tonight except them.

He led her up the stairs and along the hallway, stopping at the last door. "Here is your room. I fear it is rather cold. Let me light you a fire. Excuse me a moment."

It was indeed chilly in the room, which had clearly been unused for a while. Bromwell set down her bag and lit the lamp on the table beside the bed, then left the room. He returned a few moments later, carrying some firewood and kindling in his arms. Callie noted that he had also taken the time to put on a shirt, though he had not bothered to tuck it in, so that it hung loosely outside his trousers.

He knelt in front of the fireplace and began to build a fire. He coaxed the flames into life, and before long the fireplace was giving forth warmth. Callie, who had stood watching him, huddled in the light blanket he had given her, went over to the hearth.

He smiled at her. "I hope you have not caught a chill." He reached out and smoothed back a stray curl of her hair, which had caught upon her cheek.

Callie found herself wanting to lean into his hand like a cat, to close her eyes and give herself up to the wonderful feeling of being with him, of feeling his skin touch hers.

His hand fell away, and he moved across the room to the window. He parted the curtains with his hand and stood there looking out into the dark night.

After a moment, he said, "I believe I told you that my mother died when I was young. My nurse used to call Daphne my 'little mother.' She looked after me, played with me. We were all we had growing up. My father was . . ." His lip curled in distaste. "I have always sworn that I would never be such a one as my father. He had no understanding of or love for children. He expected us to behave as adults, and there was no quarter given for youth or a lack of strength or skill."

"I am sorry," Callie said, her heart melting in sympathy.

He looked over at her and smiled. "I did not mean to ask for your pity. I wanted to explain about Daphne. She protected me from him. His punishments were stern, even cruel, and she tried to shelter me from them. She would hide me, make excuses for me, even take the blame for something I had done because she could not bear to see me hurt. I have much to be grateful to her for."

"I know." Callie's smile was sad. She understood his love for his sister. Daphne had been the only one who loved him. She knew that he could never give up his sister, no matter how wrong she was in her actions.

"She had to bear a great deal. I was too

young to shelter her in any way. My father insisted that she marry advantageously. She was beautiful, and there were many men who wanted her. She married a man years older than she, a man she did not love, and she did it for us, to keep our estate from being swallowed up in my father's debt. I remember hearing her weep in her room the night before her wedding day. And then, when she was finally free of him and could have a new life, a good life, she fell in love with Rochford. I hated him for her unhappiness. For her having to marry another old man and wither away for the last fifteen years, so far from everything she loved."

He turned to Callie, frowning. "And now . . . now I feel as if I do not know her. The things she has done to try to harm you. This ruse. That night at Vauxhall Gardens. I can scarcely believe that this is my sister, that she would stoop to such tricks. Her heart seems filled with bitterness and hatred. And now I . . . now I cannot help but wonder if I ever really understood her at all. Were all those things she told me lies? Was she the same then, and I just did not see it? Was I simply too young and foolish to recognize the truth?"

The look on Bromwell's face was so wretched that Callie went to him and put her hand on his arm. "I am sorry," she told him softly again, gazing up into his face.

Her dark eyes glowed with compassion, large and warm in her delicate heart-shaped face, and he was struck all over again by how beautiful she was. Her face, he thought, was perfect in every way, framed in a riot of black curls. Her lips were full and red, and he could not help but remember how her mouth had felt against his. And though he was across the room from the fire, his skin was suddenly searing.

The wrap had fallen from her shoulders when she reached up to touch him, and his eyes dropped down to her shoulders and chest. The scoop neckline of her plain dimity gown revealed only a slice of skin along the rounded tops of her breasts, but the material, still slightly damp, clung to her form. His heart was hammering, his breath suddenly faster in his throat. As he gazed at her, her nipples tightened, thrusting against the cloth in a blatant show of desire.

Suddenly he found it very difficult to think. He knew he should tear his gaze away from her, but somehow he could not. His body was pulsatingly aware of her hand upon his arm, now burning where it touched.

"I, um . . . should go," he said vaguely.

"No. Do not," Callie replied. She was aware that everyone would tell her that what she was doing was wrong, but it felt absolutely right to her. The pain of the past few weeks seemed to have melted away all fear, all doubt. The heat in his eyes as he had looked at her had opened up some deep, primitive longing in her. She wanted to feel again what she had felt with him before. She wanted to experience everything that had lain beyond that, unexplored.

She slid her hand up his arm and onto his chest, aware of the smooth curve of his muscles beneath the fabric of his shirt. The quick, harsh intake of his breath, the sudden sharpening of his face, stirred her. He wanted her, and that knowledge made her hungry.

"Stay here with me," she murmured.

"Callie . . ." He released a shaky breath. "You are playing with fire."

She smiled slowly, sensuously, her eyes heavy with meaning. "Ah, but I like the heat."

Looking at him, seeing the desire that washed over his features, she felt heady with power, filled with the triumphant knowledge that she could move him, and she ached to test the limits of that power. She loved the sensations sizzling inside her, and she wanted more, wanted it all. She wanted him.

"I have thought about kissing you these past days," she told him, emboldened by the energy pulsing through her. "Have you not thought about it?" She stretched up on tiptoe to place a featherlight kiss upon the line of his jaw.

She felt the shudder that ran through him. "Good God, Callie, I have thought of little else." She turned her head, brushing a kiss along the other side of his jaw. "You are mad to do this."

"Perhaps I am, a little," she agreed. "Do you mind?"

"I fear that *you* shall mind — tomorrow."

"I will not," Callie promised, pressing her lips to his chin.

She stretched upward, her soft lips beckoning his mouth, sweet and promising. He knew that he should pull away. A gentleman would never take advantage of a woman this way. But he could not seem to make his legs move, and he certainly did not feel like a gentleman at the moment.

Callie pressed her lips against Brom's, gently, like the merest breath, then came back to taste again, lingering this time before she pulled away. She looked up into his eyes, dark now with desire, and waited. She could feel the heat emanating from his body, the tension that ran up and down the length of him. His hands were clenched into fists, as if to hold on tightly to the shreds of his control.

Her eyes steadily on his, she went up on tiptoe again, her mouth turning up to his. He let out a groan deep in his throat, and his arms clamped around her as his mouth came down to meet hers. Passion, long held back by both of them, came flooding out, swift and unstoppable.

Their arms strained to pull them closer as their mouths clung desperately. They pulled away only to tear at their clothing, coming back together an instant later, unable to bear another moment apart, moving in a constant turning dance of desire that brought them closer and closer to the bed.

His boots were soon gone, and his shirt unbuttoned and tossed blindly onto the floor. The myriad buttons down her back proved more difficult, but they, too, were conquered, though several of the small buttons were popped from their moorings in the process. In one smooth motion he stripped her dress down her body, revealing her lithe form, clad only in her thin undergarments.

Callie's breasts pushed up against the cotton chemise, swelling over its ribboned neckline, the nubs of her hardened nipples visible through the thin fabric. He stopped, his eyes dropping to the sight of the full white orbs, the edge of the chemise skimming just above her nipples, keeping them tantalizingly out of view. Slowly, almost reverently, he traced his forefinger along the neckline, his skin grazing her soft white flesh. Callie quivered beneath his touch, a soft moan escaping her lips.

With the same deliberation, his fingers hooked into the top of the chemise, edging the material downward. The cloth rubbed over her sensitive nipples, tightening them further, as he slowly tugged it down until at last her nipples popped free, hard and pointing, dark rose in their arousal.

He pulled the chemise down sharply then, little noticing and caring less for the faint ripping sound of the fabric. Her breasts fell free of the garment, firm and deliciously rounded, full white globes that seemed made for his hands. He could not keep from reaching out and cupping them, taking the weight of them in his hands, savoring the silken smooth feel of her skin. His thumbs moved over her nipples, circling and teasing the hard buds.

With each movement Callie felt desire curl and knot within her, her loins melting, turning her hot and liquid. She could not keep still. Her flesh jerked and quivered beneath his touch; her legs moved restlessly, pressing together as though to still the relentless yearning that was growing there.

She wanted each moment to last forever, yet at the same time she was filled with an urgent need, an eagerness that wanted to find and grasp and have everything at once.

Callie reached out, finding the waistband of his breeches, and began to unbutton them. She could feel the insistent movement beneath the cloth, the physical proof of his need, and she could not resist sliding her hand downward over the material, caressing the throbbing ridge beneath it.

Brom let out a low moan, which emboldened her to explore further, gliding lower to edge between his legs, then back up to slip between his trousers and his skin, down past the top unfastened button. It was completely unknown to her, the feel of satin-smooth skin and rough hair, the eager, leaping surge of flesh, and it was strangely exciting.

He seized her lips in a fierce kiss, his mouth devouring hers as she made her tentative sensual exploration, and he caressed her breasts, gently squeezing and stroking. Desire sparked through her, jumping and twisting with each movement of his hands.

Suddenly, as though he could wait no longer, Brom released her, moving back a little and reaching down to unbutton his breeches and sweep them down his body. Callie barely had time to react before he was untying her chemise and petticoats, pulling them from her and throwing them toward a chair.

He went down on one knee, startling her, and she realized that he was untying her boots. He lifted her foot to pull one off, and she put a hand on his shoulder to steady herself. He looked up at her as he raised the other foot and pulled the boot from it, and his eyes were intense and bright with promise. Callie suddenly found it difficult to breathe.

Brom slid his hand up under the lace-trimmed leg of her pantalet, following the curve of her calf and moving up onto her thigh. He hooked his fingers into her garter and slowly drew it, and her stocking, down, his hands gliding over her now-bare flesh with infinite slowness. Callie swallowed hard; her skin tingled under his touch, and her legs felt unaccountably weak, as if they might give way beneath her at any moment. With the same care, he removed her other stocking.

Then he rose to his feet, his hands sliding up her legs and over her pantalets until he reached the waistband. Slowly, his eyes holding hers, he tugged at the ribbon, untying the bow. His hands slid under the loosened waistband, shoving the thin cotton garment out of the way as his hands smoothed down over the lush curve of her hips. The pantalets fell the rest of the way to the floor, and she stood before him completely naked at last.

His eyes roamed down over her body, his face slackening with hunger. Callie thought she should have felt embarrassed to have him look at her like this — and perhaps she was, a little — but to her surprise, his gaze stirred her as though it was his fingers that roamed over her flesh. She could feel the moisture gathering between her legs, the tender flesh throbbing.

"You are so beautiful," he said hoarsely, and he bent to pick her up in his arms and carry her the last few steps to the bed.

He laid her down upon the mattress and stretched out beside her, propping himself up on one elbow. His other hand went to her chest, spreading his fingers on the flat plane of her rib cage, then traveling, curving over her breasts, then onto her stomach, caressing her abdomen, her hips, and at last moving down the side of her leg. His fingers slipped then between her legs, separating them, and slid down the inside of her thigh. Slowly, his hand began to retrace its path upward.

Callie's breath came short and fast as his fingers trailed higher, teasing the tender inner skin of her thighs, moving ever closer to his goal. Then, at last, he reached the center of her femininity, the lush secret folds that guarded her. Heat poured through her as he touched her there, gently separating and exploring that most intimate place.

She bit her lip, so sudden and sharp was the exquisite pleasure, and arched against his hand. She had never dreamed that anything could feel quite like this, that her body could surge and melt at the merest touch of his finger.

Callie groaned and moved beneath his hand, and he smiled down at her, his face heavy with sensual triumph. He bent and touched his lips to her breast, and she gasped at this new sensation. His lips moved across the soft white flesh, kissing and nibbling gently, teasing with the tip of his tongue, until he came to the hard button of her nipple. There he stopped and concentrated his attention, circling and teasing, until finally his mouth came down upon it and he began to suckle her in long, luxurious strokes.

A shudder shook her body at the combined pleasures of his mouth and fingers. Callie felt as if every part of her was on fire, and the molten center of that flame lay deep in her abdomen, where she pulsed and burned with a desperate need. She writhed beneath his ministrations, digging in with her heels and clutching at the coverlet beneath her.

"Please, please," she begged, feeling as if she must die, must explode.

He moved over her, and she opened her legs to receive him. He slid his hands beneath her hips, tilting her up, and she felt the tip of him probing at the tender intimate flesh. She arched up gladly to meet him, and he slid into her slowly, carefully, his body taut with the strain of holding back.

She had heard that there was always pain the first time, but she felt none, only a wonderful fulfillment as the full length of him slid inside her, stretching and filling her. Callie let out a low cry of pleasure, calling his name, and he buried his face in her neck, breathing in her scent, as he began to thrust in and out. She wrapped her arms and legs around him, moving in time with his long, sure strokes.

His breath was harsh and ragged in her ear, and his searing heat enveloped her. Callie felt herself surrounded by him, immersed in him, and she reveled in the sensation. Tension was building deep in her abdomen, growing with each movement he made, knotting and re-knotting ever tighter, until at last it exploded in a glorious burst of pleasure so intense that she cried out.

Brom shuddered and groaned, pumping into her wildly as he hurtled to his own peak with her, and together they collapsed, spent and exhausted and utterly replete. Brom murmured her name as he rolled from her, his arms still wrapped around her; then he reached out with one arm and grabbed the coverlet, pulling it over and around them like a cocoon. And together they drifted into sleep.

Callie came slowly awake, aware first that it was very hot and, secondly, that something very heavy was weighing her down. Her eyes fluttered open, and she found herself gazing at a large expanse of firm flesh, with hair prickling her nose. She blinked, and in another moment she was fully awake. The heat came from Brom's large body, which she lay against, her cheek on his chest. And the heavy weight was his arm thrown across her.

Memories of the night before came flooding back in on her, and she smiled to herself. A woman of greater virtue, she thought, would doubtless have been embarrassed, even ashamed. She, however, was bursting with happiness; there was no room in her for any other feeling.

Despite the heat, she lay there for a moment longer, luxuriating in the new feeling of her body, alive with the imprint of last night's pleasures and pleasantly sore.

Finally she eased out of bed, letting the coverlet fall back over Brom's body. She glanced about the room ruefully. Their clothes were scattered all over. Remembering the few faint ripping sounds as they undressed, she suspected that her garments might not be in wearable condition anymore. It was a good thing that she had brought several additional frocks in her bag.

The fire had died to ashes, but she scarcely noticed the cold as she made her way over to the window. The room was still dim, but the light that came in through the slit in the draperies made her think that it was already long past sunrise. She pulled aside a corner of the thick drape and looked out. It was indeed morning; the landscape was washed with sunshine. She let the curtain fall and turned back to the room.

Her dress lay in a heap in front of a chair; her petticoats were tossed over the foot of the bed; her boots were several feet apart. And her chemise was a crumpled little ball near the door. She made her way around the room, picking up her clothes.

As she turned back toward the bed, she saw Bromwell, braced on one elbow, watching her. She gasped, dropping the garments in her surprise.

He smiled. "Ah, now that is much better. Those clothes were hiding far too much."

"What are you doing?" she scolded. "You scared me!"

"Watching you," he replied.

"Why did you not speak? I didn't know you were awake."

"I know. That made it all the more enjoyable," he replied, grinning unrepentantly.

She bent down to retrieve her clothes, holding them in front of her, her cheeks high with color.

"Nay. Do not hide yourself," he said. "I like to look at you."

Callie smiled a little, feeling strangely shy and yet excited, too, the now-familiar warmth stealing through her loins. " 'Tis scarcely fair, as you are modestly covered."

That was not quite true, as the cover had slid down to his waist, and she could see the full expanse of his chest and arms, which, she would be the first to admit, was a very nice sight.

Brom grinned and reached down to flip the covers aside. "There. You may look as much as I."

Her cheeks flushed as her eyes of their own volition ran down his body, taking in the tanned, firm flesh, the smooth curve of muscle, as well as the unmistakable sign that he was already aroused.

"Oh!" she said, her eyes widening and her blush deepening. But she found that the sight of his thickening staff deepened the heat that was already alive in her.

"Yes," he admitted, grinning. "I am a slave to you."

"A slave to your own base desires, I should say," she told him saucily, but she dropped the garments and strolled over to the bed, her faint embarrassment overridden by the tingle of pleasure that went through her as his eyes, heavy-lidded with desire, roamed her body.

"Only where you are concerned," he assured her, reaching out to grab her arm and pull her the last few inches to the bed.

He turned to sit on the edge of the mattress, bracing his heels, and put his hands on her hips, pulling her up against him. Callie smiled into his eyes and put her hands on his shoulders, moving them slowly down and back up, then lower over his chest. She could feel his arousal pushing against her abdomen, and it made her smile wickedly.

"You enjoy that, don't you?" he growled, nuzzling into her neck. "The thought of making me suffer."

"No," she disputed, trailing her fingernails lightly down his chest. " 'Tis the thought of ending your suffering that makes me smile."

He laughed, his breath hot on her neck, and nipped lightly at the taut cord. "*That,* my lady, you are welcome to do."

With those words, his arms went around her and he pulled her back onto the bed with him, rolling over quickly so that she was beneath him. Pulling her arms above her head, he anchored them with one hand and proceeded to kiss his way down her body. His lips lingered over her skin, taking his time as he explored her. She writhed, tugging at her hands, but he continued to hold them trapped beneath his.

"Nay, not yet," he murmured. "First it is my turn to pleasure you. Then you may have your way."

He made slow, sweet love to her with his mouth and hands, bringing her closer and closer to that wild, delicious burst of passion that she had experienced the night before. But each time, as she drew near, trembling and eager, he retreated, only to bring her to the heights again.

As his mouth loved her breasts, his fingers sought out the hot, throbbing center of her desire, gliding over the slick folds and smoothing over the tiny nub deep within them. She arched up against him, almost sobbing in her need. At last his fingers tightened on her, rhythmically stroking, until she tensed all over and a high, small cry issued from her mouth as pleasure washed through her in deep waves.

Callie lay, looking up at Brom through dark, slumbrous eyes. He leaned down and kissed her gently on the lips, then moved between her legs.

"Oh, no," Callie said huskily, smiling up at him. She braced her hands on his chest and pushed him over onto his back.

He went easily, grinning up at her. "What? That is enough for you? You want to stop?"

"No, not stop. Postpone. It is my turn now, remember? You said that I could have my way with you next."

His grin broadened. "So I did. Tell me, my lady, what do you have planned?"

"I think that I shall make it up as I go along," Callie retorted. "I am just learning, you remember."

He linked his hands behind his head, assuming a relaxed pose, despite the unmistakable evidence of his desire springing up between his legs. "Feel free to improvise, then."

Callie moved over him, straddling him, and his eyes darkened with desire. She slid her hands across his chest, exploring his thoroughly masculine body. Her hands were firm upon him, finding the different textures of hard bone and springing muscle, smooth skin and wiry hair. Her fingers glided over his flat nipples, teasing them to hard life; then she bent and applied her mouth to them as he had done to her, lashing and stroking and circling until they were engorged and hard as pebbles, their color a deep, dark rose.

She sat up, shifting her body a little on his, and a low moan escaped him at her movement. Callie smiled sensually and moved again, feeling him stir and throb against her. She rubbed her body over him, exciting herself as much as him as flesh slipped over flesh, the wiry hair on his chest

418

delicately abrading her supremely sensitive nipples.

His hands went to her hips to move her down onto his swollen shaft, but Callie smiled and shook her head. "Oh, no, not yet. I have not had my way nearly enough. Why, I haven't even kissed you."

She went down on all fours above him, moving up a little until her face was over his. She gazed down at him. His skin was stretched taut over his facial bones, his mouth full and sensual, and his eyes blazed with feverish light. He had long since given up his casual pose with his hands locked behind his head. They now gripped the cover beneath him, tightly holding on to his control.

Callie bent and kissed his forehead lightly, brushing her lips against his skin. She made her way down his face, kissing the tender skin of his closed eyelids, the sharp cheekbones that fascinated her, the strong masculine jaw and chin, settling finally on his mouth. She kissed him deeply and long. She could feel his muscles bunch and gather beneath her, and she knew that he was twitching and burning as she had done earlier.

She raised her head and slid off his body. He made a noise of protest and reached for her, but she pushed his hand away and began to kiss her way down his chest as her hand slid farther down his body. Her fingers glided light as air over his chest and stomach, then down onto the sharp outcropping of his hipbone and onto his thigh, furred with curling hair. He stirred, his legs moving restlessly, and made a low noise.

Her fingers teased back up the inside of his thigh, until her fingertips found the heavy sac between his legs. She hesitated a little timidly, then gently moved her fingertips across it. He sucked in his breath and moved his hips involuntarily.

"Do you like that?" she whispered, pressing her lips against his throat.

His answer was a low, urgent noise.

"I shall take that as agreement," she said, and cupped him in her palm.

He shivered beneath her gentle movements, and she grew bolder, sliding her fingers up the underside of his manhood and curving her fingers around it. She moved slowly, exploring the satin-smooth skin that overlay the hard member, which was throbbing now with desire.

Then, with a low growl, he put his hands on her arms, and in one swift motion, she was on her back and he was over her, between her legs and smoothly sliding into her. Callie let out a soft sob, so sweet was the feeling of his filling her again. She wrapped herself around him, holding on tightly as he rode hard and fast to his completion, taking her with him into the dazzling explosion of their desire.

They lay for a long time in a blissful state, floating somewhere between sleep and consciousness. Callie was curled on her side, her head on Brom's arm, and his arm draped over her. She felt deliciously spent and lazy, and her mind drifted in a pleasant haze.

Finally, however, with a sigh, Bromwell moved his arm away, saying, "I must go into town and hire a post chaise."

"Later," Callie murmured, snuggling back against him.

He chuckled and stroked his hand down the side of her body. "Vixen. You cannot tempt me from my purpose."

She turned her head, casting a sparkling glance his way. "Is that a challenge?"

He laughed and planted a kiss upon the point of her bare shoulder. "No, for I know I should not win that one."

He kissed her mouth then, more slowly, but pulled away after a moment, saying, "No. I must go. We must get you back to

London before anyone knows you are gone."

She nodded, realizing the truth of his words, though she was reluctant to give up this moment. Once she left Blackfriars Cope, everything would change.

Bromwell did not bother to scoop up his clothing, only grabbing his boots as he left the room to return to his bedchamber and dress. With a sigh, Callie, too, arose. It was chilly in the room, so she wrapped herself in the same light blanket that Brom had given her the night before when he brought her in from the rain.

She picked up her bag and pulled out the change of clothes that her maid had packed. Fortunately she had had the foresight to pack a simple morning dress that buttoned up the front, so that it was easy enough to put on without help. It was rather wrinkled, but there would be no one to see, and it would soon enough be wrinkled from traveling, anyway.

Brom came in a few minutes later, once again dressed, bringing with him a pitcher of water for the washstand, and told her that he was going down to see if the housekeeper had shown up for work this morning.

Callie quickly washed and dressed, brushing out her tangled hair with some difficulty and pinning it up into a simple knot at the crown of her head. Then she hurried down the stairs and made her way toward the back of the house, following the sounds of crockery and metal pots.

She found Brom in the kitchen alone, setting down plates and eating utensils at a large wooden table. He looked up at her and grinned a little sheepishly. "Mrs. Farmington is not here. But I have made tea, and found butter and jelly, and I've managed to slice off a few pieces of bread for toast."

"That sounds perfect," Callie said, beaming.

The toast was a trifle burned on one side and soft on the other, and the tea was terribly strong, but it was, Callie thought, the best breakfast she had ever eaten. He described his culinary efforts, sending her into giggles, and as they talked and ate, he kept reaching out to caress her hand or smooth a piece of hair back from her cheek, as if he could not go too long without touching her.

They had just finished eating and were reluctantly rising from the table when Callie heard a sound in the yard outside. She turned her head, listening. "Is that a horse I hear?"

Callie glanced out the window, but she could see nothing but the side yard and the stables.

Brom went still. "Yes. Someone riding fast."

They started out of the kitchen and were halfway down the hall when there was a thunderous knock at the door. Callie and Brom glanced at each other. She felt suddenly uneasy.

The pounding continued, and Brom strode to the door and yanked it open. The Duke of Rochford stood framed in the doorway.

CHAPTER SEVENTEEN

The duke was dressed for riding. His clothes were travel-stained, his boots splattered with mud. He carried his hat and a riding crop in one hand. And his face was stamped with a cold fury.

"Then it *is* true!" he snarled.

Stepping forward, he smashed his fist into Bromwell's jaw. Bromwell staggered backward and fell through the wide double doorway into the drawing room.

"Sinclair!" Callie shrieked. "No!"

She ran to Bromwell to help him up, but he shrugged off her hand as he rose lithely to his feet. His eyes glittered silver as he looked at Rochford, and he reached up to wipe away a trickle of blood from his cheekbone, where Rochford's knuckles had smashed into him.

"You want to fight?" Bromwell asked in a dangerously soft voice, and a corner of his mouth quirked up.

"Brom, no!" Callie cried.

"I want to kill you," Rochford replied shortly, tossing his hat and crop onto the bench in the foyer.

"Sinclair!" She whirled toward her brother in exasperation.

Neither man paid her the slightest attention as they began in unison to pull off their jackets and toss them aside, then roll up their sleeves.

"Would you two stop for just a minute?" Callie asked. "Please? Would you listen to me? Sinclair, I am all right. There is no need —"

"There is every need," her brother told her shortly, not even looking at her.

"Callie, stay out of this," Bromwell told her at the same moment.

"Stay out of it!" Callie stared at him. "How can I stay out of it? You are going to fight my brother? How can I possibly stay out of it?"

But it was clear to her that they were going to continue to ignore her no matter what she said. She glanced around the room, searching for inspiration as the two men moved closer together, warily circling each other, their hands up and curled into fists.

Then, like lightning, Bromwell jabbed with his left hand, but Rochford as quickly moved aside so that the blow fell on his shoulder rather than his face. Bromwell followed with an overhand right that landed flush on Rochford's jaw and sent him backward into a tall cabinet. There was a crash, and a porcelain figurine toppled out and smashed on the floor behind him.

Bromwell came rushing after him, but Rochford neatly twisted away and, grabbing Bromwell's arm, threw him against the cabinet in turn. Bromwell charged back, punching, and the two men came up hard against the sofa and tumbled over its back onto the seat and then down to the floor, still grappling and punching, the fine rules of pugilism discarded.

Callie screamed at them to stop, but to no avail. She ran to the fireplace and grabbed the poker, then turned back to the men. They were rolling across the floor, knocking into the tables and chairs, and she ran to them, poker raised. But she could not bring herself to hit either of them with it.

She was standing there indecisively, the poker still held up in her hand, when a cool female voice behind her said, "Really, Rochford . . . brawling in the drawing room? Before breakfast? How terribly primitive."

Callie swung toward the direction of the voice and stared, her jaw dropping. There

427

stood Francesca at the foot of the staircase, looking calm and unruffled in a pale blue frock.

Callie could think of nothing to say, so stunned was she by the unexpected vision. Apparently Francesca's appearance had been enough to halt the men in the midst of their fight, for they, too, had stopped and were staring in equal astonishment at Francesca.

"Really, Rochford, do get up. You look exceedingly foolish there on the floor. As do you, Lord Bromwell. I must say, I would think you men could find something better to do than break up the furniture. I am sure whoever owns this charming house will be most upset at the damage you have caused."

When no one answered her, Francesca strolled forward, stopping in the doorway and looking down at the men.

"Both members of the 'Fancy,' I presume?" she went on as the two men got to their feet, looking bewildered. "It does seem to me that you could have pursued your interest outside. You made such a dreadful amount of noise that you woke me up. Now I shall have great dark circles under my eyes, I am sure, especially after the late night that Callie and I had, driving here through the dark."

Francesca paused, then added magnanimously, "I am glad, however, to find you all in one piece, Rochford. I did not think you would like having a broken leg and ribs overmuch."

The duke at last found his voice. "What the devil are you prattling about, Francesca?"

"Why, your injuries, of course," she replied sweetly. "We came as soon as we received the letter saying how badly you had been injured. You can imagine our surprise when we arrived, and you were nowhere to be found."

"You — you mean you were here with Callie?" Rochford asked, astonished.

"Yes, of course, we came posthaste as soon as she received the note from — what was the name, Callie?"

"Mrs. Farmington," Callie supplied, struggling to suppress the smile that wanted to spring to her lips.

"Yes, Farmington, of course. Well, I could hardly allow Callie to make the trip all by herself. We were most puzzled, of course, not to find you here, but Lord Bromwell was kind enough to allow us to put up here for the night. It was excessively late, you know, and I rather think the inn was not the sort of place where I would feel comfortable."

"I don't understand. What note are you talking about? Why are you here? And why is *he?*" He scowled over at Bromwell.

"I live here," Lord Bromwell offered. "Or, at least, I am staying here for a week or so."

"And Callie and I were brought here by the note. I just told you this, Rochford. Do you still have it, Callie?" Francesca asked. "Why don't you run up to our room and fetch it, dear, so you can show it to your brother? Mayhap it will make more sense to him."

Callie nodded and hastened to up to her bedchamber. In her absence, Rochford looked suspiciously from Francesca to Lord Bromwell, who crossed his arms and stared back at him arrogantly. Francesca simply regarded him with the same cool, faintly derisive gaze.

When Callie returned a moment later, she handed the note to her brother, and he read through it quickly, frowning. When he was done, he looked up at her and then at Francesca.

"But what does this mean? Who sent this to you?" He swung toward Bromwell, scowling. "Was this a trick of yours?"

"No!" Callie exclaimed quickly. "He knew

nothing about it. He was quite as astonished as I was. Or Francesca," she added quickly.

"We were quite tired, so we decided to go on to bed and try to clear the whole matter up this morning. But then you came in howling like a madman."

"Why didn't you tell me Francesca was here?" Rochford turned to Callie.

"I tried to!" Callie exclaimed, crossing her arms combatively. "If you will remember, you refused to listen to anything I said."

"Oh." The duke looked somewhat abashed.

"Now it is your turn, Rochford," Francesca said. "What are you doing here?"

"I received a letter also," he replied. "It said that my sister was here with Lord Bromwell. That they had eloped."

"I see." Francesca's normally warm blue eyes turned to chips of ice.

"Yes, I think we all do," Lord Bromwell said heavily. He turned away and busied himself with picking up an overturned chair and table, and setting them aright.

Francesca's gaze was locked with Rochford's for a long moment. Then she turned to Callie. "Come, my dear, shall we get our things? Perhaps Rochford will escort us back to London."

"That reminds me," Rochford said, his

431

voice once again suspicious. "Where is your carriage? I did not see it when I rode up."

"Why, in the stable, of course," Francesca replied, looking at him as if he had taken leave of his senses. "Where else would it be?"

In the silence after her words, they heard the sound of horses outside. The four of them glanced at each other in surprise, and Bromwell started toward the door.

At that moment there was a sound of feminine voices and laughter, and Brom stopped abruptly. The door swung open, and Lady Swithington stepped inside, accompanied by another woman. She was talking gaily to her friend, but she stopped in midsentence when she saw her brother standing before her, his face like stone.

"Why, Brom!" she exclaimed, looking surprised. "I did not expect you to be up yet. And Lady Calandra . . . what an unexpected pleasure." Her eyes went on to Callie and the duke standing beyond him. "And Rochford. Whatever are you doing here?" Her voice was as rich and smooth as cream, obviously pleased despite her attempt to look surprised.

"Hello, Daphne," Francesca said.

Daphne's gaze snapped over to Francesca, and her eyes widened in a much more natural expression of shock. "Francesca! What the — well, this is indeed a surprise." She stood for a moment, seemingly nonplussed, then turned to the woman with her. "I am sorry. Please allow me to introduce my friend, Mrs. Cathcart. Do you know Mrs. Cathcart, Lady Calandra? Lady Haughston?"

"Yes, I believe we have met," Callie answered, forcing herself to smile in greeting. "How do you do, Mrs. Cathcart?"

The sharp-faced blond woman was one of the worst gossips of the *ton*. Clearly, Brom's sister had staged this scene so that the scandal she had arranged would be witnessed by someone who was sure to spread it all over London.

Lady Swithington continued with the introductions. The duke had recovered enough to roll down his sleeves and offer Mrs. Cathcart an elegant bow.

"It is a pleasure to speak with you," he told her, smiling in his gracious way that was at once winning without letting the recipient forget that he or she was in the presence of a duke. "I do hope you will forgive the way I appear, Mrs. Cathcart. I fear I was not expecting visitors."

"Of course, your Grace," Mrs. Cathcart said, smiling and blushing, clearly flattered at actually being in conversation with the Duke of Rochford.

"You *are* rather . . . mussed, Rochford," Lady Daphne agreed. "And is that blood on your cheek, Brom? Whatever have you two been up to?"

The two men glanced at each other, and Francesca rushed to fill the silence. "They have been working at righting our carriage. It is no wonder that they are rather disheveled and battered. A wheel went into a ditch, and we overturned. Such a distressing thing!"

Mrs. Cathcart made appropriate noises of shock and dismay, but Lady Daphne looked at Francesca with narrowed eyes and said flatly, "How dreadful. I am surprised that you were not hurt."

"It was most jarring, I can assure you," Francesca went on blithely. "Was it not, Lady Calandra?"

"Yes, indeed," Callie said, joining into the spirit of the story. "I have a horrid bruise on my back. But luckily there were no broken bones." She gazed steadily into Lady Daphne's eyes, making sure that her meaning was clear.

After a long moment of silence, Daphne said, "My. You must have had a very trying day — and it is not yet noon. How fortunate that your carriage broke down here, where my brother could help you."

"Yes, was it not?" Francesca put in sweetly. "Lord Bromwell has been most kind to us. We have all appreciated his help. Haven't we, Rochford?" She turned to the duke, and only those who knew her well would have caught the iron undertone in her voice.

A muscle jumped in Rochford's jaw, but he said somewhat stiffly, "Yes. I appreciate his assistance."

"It was my pleasure," Bromwell added. "I am sorry that your journey was interrupted."

"You will understand, then, that we should be on our way," Rochford put in smoothly. "It was a pleasure talking with you, Mrs. Cathcart, but I fear you must excuse us."

"Wherever were you going?" Lady Daphne asked. "I had thought that you were in London."

Rochford turned his most aristocratic gaze upon her, the sort he used to stop impertinent questions, but Daphne did not look in the least intimidated. "We were going to visit friends before traveling on to Marcastle."

"Oh, really? Who were you going to visit? Perhaps I know them," Daphne went on.

The duke's eyebrows rose at this, and he

said shortly, "I doubt it."

"No more questions, Daphne," Lord Bromwell put in, and there was a harshness in his voice that his sister had never heard. "Our guests must leave now. We do not want to delay them."

"Of course not," Daphne agreed, casting a brilliant smile at everyone.

"I shall go out to the stables and tell the driver to bring the carriage round," Rochford said, his gaze going to Francesca as he said it.

"That sounds like an excellent idea," she told him, her smile cool and composed.

Rochford made a perfunctory bow to everyone and strode out of the room.

"If you ladies will excuse us, Callie and I would like to freshen up a bit before we leave," Francesca said, going over to loop her arm through Callie's.

The two of them smiled at the other women and left the room. Callie carefully avoided looking at Bromwell, afraid that something of what had happened between them would show in her face. She and Francesca went up the staircase, Francesca's arm keeping Callie to a slower pace.

When they reached the top of the staircase, out of sight of those below, Francesca released her arm, and Callie sagged against the wall.

"Oh, Francesca," she whispered.

Francesca shook her head and led her farther down the hallway. "Do you have a bag or anything?" she asked quietly.

Callie nodded, answering her in the same hushed voice, "Yes, it's in here."

She thought in that instant of what had happened in that room the night before, and a blush stained her cheeks. Brom's discarded clothes were still scattered about the floor.

"I will get it," she said quickly, and hurried into the room.

She was back in a moment, carrying her bag. "How will we explain this? Perhaps I should just toss it out the window or stuff it in a closet here."

Francesca shook her head. "We shall brazen it out. That is usually the best policy."

She took the bag from Callie and started down the stairs. About halfway down, she began in a carrying voice, "I am so glad, Callie, that we thought to bring in one of my bags. It is so difficult to put oneself in order without one's brush and hairpins. Do not you agree?"

"Yes, very much," Callie agreed, hiding a smile. *Trust Francesca.*

"This is such a charming abode, Lord Bromwell," Francesca went on as they stepped into the foyer, not giving anyone else time to speak. "Has it always been in your family?"

"It is my sister's," Bromwell said. "It belonged to her late husband."

"Ah, I see." Francesca turned toward Daphne. "How kind of you, Lady Swithington, to lend it to him. But, then, you are always thinking of others."

The gaze Daphne turned on Francesca was full of venom, but Francesca merely smiled at her and turned to Callie. "We had best be on our way, lest the duke grow impatient." She cast a droll look toward Mrs. Cathcart, adding, "Men so dislike having their plans interrupted, I have found. Do you not agree, Mrs. Cathcart?"

"Indeed, Lady Haughston," the other woman replied. "That is invariably the way. I am sorry to see you leave so soon, before we have had a chance to chat, but I quite understand."

"Just let me get my pelisse, and we will be out of your way," Francesca said, and walked back through the house to the kitchen.

She returned a moment later, carrying her reticule and wearing a dark blue pelisse over her dress. Callie quickly snatched up her cloak from the bench where Brom had dropped it the evening before, and the two women turned toward the door.

"I will walk you out," Lord Bromwell said, coming up beside them.

"There is no need," Callie murmured, forcing herself to look at him and hoping that there was nothing in her face that reflected the emotions whirling around inside her.

"I insist," he said shortly, stopping all argument, and offered her his arm.

Just looking at his face made her want to smile and weep, all at once. She wanted to reach up and soothe his cheek where Rochford's blow had cut him. She ached to kiss his lips one last time and to throw her arms around him. Tears burned at the backs of her eyes. But here in front of the others, she could do none of the things she wanted to. For all their sakes, she must keep up the charade they had started. All she could do was smile politely and take his arm, as if he were nothing more than an acquaintance.

They bade goodbye to the other two women. Mrs. Cathcart was clearly quite pleased at their encounter, for she was not one who normally moved in the elite circle that Lady Haughston and the Lilles family occupied. Lady Swithington appeared far less pleased. The smile she gave them looked as though it might break her face, and the blue eyes above it were charged with resentment. Callie's feelings toward her were, frankly, quite as unfriendly, and her nod and farewell to the woman were as brief as possible.

They walked out the front door, leaving Lady Swithington and Mrs. Cathcart behind. Callie was supremely aware of Bromwell's large body beside her; her hand trembled a little on his arm. Francesca's carriage was emerging from the barn, the duke walking beside it, and Francesca began to move toward it, discreetly leaving Callie alone with Lord Bromwell for a moment.

"Callie, I —" he began.

"No, don't, please," she said in a choked voice, turning her face up to gaze at him. She was afraid that she would begin to cry, but she had to take a last look at him. Deep inside, where the cold, hard knot in her chest resided, she knew that she would not see him again.

Despite what his sister had done, she feared that he would never turn his back on Daphne. She was his flesh and blood, whereas Callie was . . . indeed, she did not even know what she was to the man. They had shared a night of incredible passion, but he had said no words of love or commitment. And she was the sister of a man he had despised for years, a man with whom he had been exchanging punches less than an hour ago.

"I must stay and talk to Daphne," he told her.

"I know." She turned away. Her brother was watching them as he walked toward them. She could not talk any longer to Brom. She was too near tears, and if Sinclair saw a tearful goodbye, she was afraid that all Francesca's inventive story-weaving would be for naught. And the one thing that she absolutely could not bear was for the two men she loved to fight each other again.

"Callie, wait, do not go yet," Bromwell said, starting to reach for her.

"No. Pray, do not." Callie looked at him. She knew her eyes were welling with tears, but she could not help it. "I must go. Goodbye, Brom."

She closed her mouth firmly, swallowing the rest of the words that fought to surge up out of her: *I love you.*

Callie turned and hurried toward the carriage door. She saw with gratitude that Francesca had gone up to Sinclair, so she was able to walk past him and get into the carriage without his looking at her or speaking to her.

The duke saw his sister walk past, but his attention was all on Francesca at the moment. He raised a skeptical eyebrow at her, then nodded toward the team pulling her coach.

"I found the driver inside rubbing down the horses. They look rather, um, bedraggled, shall we say, for having spent the night in the stables."

"Odd," Francesca commented lightly. "Of course, they are not my horses. We had to change on the drive up, but still, my coachman is generally quite good at taking care of the animals. Perhaps he was tired and fell asleep as soon as we arrived. I know I did."

"Did you?" The duke's gaze was penetrating.

Francesca gazed back at him unflinchingly. "Yes, of course, I did. Why else should I say it? You have only to ask your sister. The hunting lodge is small, so she and I were forced to share a bedchamber."

He gazed at her for a long moment, then gave a small nod. "Very well. Let us go before that blasted woman decides to come out here and plague us with more questions."

Rochford handed Francesca up into the

carriage and strode off to mount his horse, still tied to a post by the driveway. Francesca sat down in the coach beside Callie, turning to her immediately.

"Are you all right, my dear?" she asked, reaching out to take Callie's hand.

Callie nodded, but when she reached up to wipe the tears from her eyes, Francesca noticed.

"Are you certain? You may tell me anything, you know. I promise you that no one will ever hear of it."

"There is nothing to tell," Callie said in a low voice and summoned up a smile. She did not realize how very unconvincing it was.

"Very well, then, you needn't," Francesca assured her. "We shall talk of something else, shall we?"

Callie nodded, but then, as if she could not hold it in, she exclaimed, "Oh, Francesca! I love him!"

She had realized it last night when she had looked into Brom's eyes and known that he was telling her the truth. In trusting him, believing him, she had given him her heart.

"And he will never ask me to marry him," Callie went on. "I know it."

"Are you certain?" Francesca asked.

"Surely he must realize that his sister arranged that scene. Not only putting you in a compromising position, but making sure that Rochford would arrive and find you that way! And then walking in at that exact moment, with the worst gossip in London in tow. Even I was astonished at the depth of her dishonesty, and I have despised her for years."

"I know he realizes it, but he does not want to believe badly of her. He is very close to her. He owes her a great deal, he believes. He talked to me last night about how she raised him after his mother died, about how horrid their father was and how she protected Brom from him. No matter what she did, I am not sure that he could break with her. Even if he did, how could he marry the sister of a man whom he has hated for so long? He was beginning to have his doubts about her story about Sinclair. I could see that. But he does not want to believe that she lied to him."

"She has an amazing ability to deceive men," Francesca said with a touch of bitterness. "Still, love is a very powerful thing."

"I did not say that he loved me, only that I loved him," Callie replied, and tears began to stream down her cheeks. She did not bother to wipe them away.

"I have seen the way he looks at you," Francesca pointed out.

"That is desire, not love," Callie retorted. "He has never said he loves me. And I fear that I will never even see him again."

Her last words ended on a choked sob, and she began to cry in earnest. Francesca wrapped her arm around Callie's shoulders and pulled her close. Callie rested her head on Francesca's shoulder and let her tears come.

CHAPTER EIGHTEEN

It was some time before Callie's sobs began to subside, but finally she sat up and took out her handkerchief, wiping the tears from her face. She let out a long breathy sigh.

"I am sorry. That is the second time I have cried all over you," she told Francesca. "You must think me dreadfully prone to tears."

"No. I think you are going through a very trying period. Believe me, there have been times in my life when I have done nothing but cry, it seemed," Francesca replied and patted her hand. "There is no need to apologize."

"Thank you." Callie summoned up a watery smile. "And thank you for what you did in there earlier. You saved me. I was afraid Brom and Sinclair were going to kill each other."

"I am just glad that I arrived in time."

"How did you?" Callie asked. "I have

never been so surprised as when you walked in."

"Well, when I returned from my visit to the Duchess of Chudleigh, Fenton gave me your note, saying that Rochford had been hurt and where you had gone. So I had my carriage brought 'round, and I set out after you."

"So you did not come because you had figured out it was a trap?" Callie asked.

"No. I hadn't the slightest idea. I had realized that Daphne was behind Lady Odelia's invitation. She let it slip as we were driving home. Lady Odelia said that 'dear Daphne' was right. She had not thought I would like to go, but then Daphne had assured her that I would doubtless want to see my mother's godmama. Well, you can imagine how I felt. If Daphne had been there, I would have slapped her. Of course, I just had to swallow my bile and smile. But I did not realize that Daphne had a larger plan to get me away from the house when her message arrived. I simply assumed that she had done it in order to have a good laugh at my expense."

"I see," Callie said, a smile curving her lips. "Then you came rushing up to the cottage just because you thought Sinclair was hurt. You care for him, don't you?"

Francesca seemed for once at a loss for words. She looked at Callie for a moment, then pulled herself up as straight as possible and gave her a cool look, saying repressively, "Of course I care about Rochford. After all, I have known him all my life. Besides, I assumed that you might need my help in caring for him if he was injured. I feel sure that he is a terrible trial when he is ill."

"Oh," Callie said, with a knowing smile. "I see."

Francesca frowned at her and continued, "We had slow going. It was night by then, and sometimes, in the darker patches, a groom had to walk in front of the horses with a lantern. When we finally pulled into the yard this morning, I saw Rochford's horse tied up in front. I thought that was most odd, since he was supposedly laid up in bed with broken bones. And the instant I got out of the carriage, I could hear him shouting and all the noise inside, so I knew that he wasn't hurt after all. That is when I realized this was all some sort of plot — doubtless of Daphne's making."

"It was quick thinking on your part to send your carriage round to the stables."

"I hadn't any time for considering things. I knew I had to convince Rochford that I had been with you the whole time, so the carriage could not be sitting in the yard. I told the coachman to go to the stables and take care of the horses, and I ran around to the back and came in the back door. Then I pretended to have just come downstairs."

"Thank goodness you did," Callie said fervently and reached over to squeeze Francesca's hand. "You saved us all from disaster."

"Well, I did promise to help you in any way possible," Francesca responded lightly.

"You have done more for me than I ever could have imagined," Callie told her. "And I appreciate it so much." She hesitated, then said, "But I think that I will return to Marcastle with Sinclair. I thought that I would stay through most of the Season, just to keep everyone's tongues from wagging, but it does not seem that important anymore."

"Oh, Callie . . ." Francesca's face was filled with sympathy. "I am so sorry. I wish you would stay. Not just for the company, although I confess that I will find the house quite empty without your presence. But I hate to think that you are giving up . . ."

"On finding a husband?" Callie supplied the ending to her sentence. "I fear that I am no longer interested in that. I rather doubt now that I shall ever marry."

"No. I meant giving up on finding love,"

Francesca corrected her gently.

"I do not think that I am meant to do that." Callie smiled faintly. "Do not look so sad. I do not regret the past few weeks. I would not give up what I have done and learned and felt for the world. I did not think that I was capable of great love, and I was willing to settle for something less — comfort and companionship. But I discovered what it is to truly love. I have experienced that. Now I know that nothing less would be enough."

"Callie, pray do not give up entirely on the earl. It is clear how much you love him."

"Yes, but it is not enough for *me* to love *him*." Callie's smile was sad, her tone resigned.

Francesca knew that there was nothing more to say. She nodded, aware of an old ache deep in her own heart.

After that, the two of them fell silent. As the carriage moved slowly onward, they sat, sometimes raising an edge of the curtain to look outside, but most of the time simply lost in their own thoughts. Finally, Callie, worn out from her tears, slept, wedged into one corner of the carriage.

They traveled slowly at first, for the horses were tired, and they soon stopped to change horses. Rochford even decided to leave his horse at the inn where they made the change, reluctantly handing over the care of his prized mount to Francesca's groom, with orders to bring the animal on to London the following day.

With fresh horses, their pace picked up, and by evening they were once again in London. Callie had told her brother that she wanted to return to Marcastle with him, so he left her at Francesca's house to pack while he went to Lilles House to arrange for their departure.

"I will send the carriage for you tomorrow morning," he promised Callie. "I presume that you and Lady Haughston will want to spend this evening together to make your goodbyes."

"Thank you," Callie said, going up on tiptoe to kiss his cheek.

He looked at her, surprised. "Does this mean that I am out of your black books?"

She smiled faintly. "I did not approve of your attacking Lord Bromwell, no, but I am glad that you care enough to come racing to protect me. There is no brother as good as you, I am convinced."

He smiled. "I shall hold on to those words and remind you of them next time you are vexed with me."

Rochford turned to Francesca. "Lady

Haughston."

"Rochford." She held out her hand. "I trust that next time we meet, it will be under less . . . strenuous circumstances."

"Whenever and wherever that is," he said, his mouth quirking up at the corner, "I am certain that it will not be dull."

He took her hand and bowed over it. Somewhat to her surprise, he held her hand a fraction longer than was customary. Her eyes flew up to meet his, and she found him looking intently into her face. He squeezed her hand for an instant, and said simply, "Thank you."

She gave him the slightest nod, acknowledging his words, with all the unspoken undercurrent attached to them. He strode away, and the two women turned to the task of getting Callie's things ready for her departure.

Fortunately Callie's maid had already packed a trunk of her clothes, awaiting instructions to bring them to Blackfriars Cope, so there was not as much to do as Callie had feared. It did not take them long to get it all done, as Callie was more interested in speed than in neatness. Normally she would have repaired torn ruffles and such, or made sure that all the clothes she packed were clean and ironed, but there would be plenty of time for cleaning and repairs when she was back home. Right now she wanted only to get away.

They did not need to stay up late to finish, but Callie was unable to get much sleep anyway. She tossed and turned and woke from restless, confusing dreams. She felt odd and out-of-place, as if she did not belong here in this room that had been a cozy home for her for close to two months. Once she got up out of bed and went to stand at the window, pushing aside the heavy draperies to look out.

There was little to see, only the dark street below, but after a moment she realized that the restlessness that plagued her came from a vague, deep-buried hope that Bromwell would come riding through the night to be with her. She rested her forehead against the cool glass pane, telling herself not to be foolish. He would not come.

Finally, she pulled herself away from the window and went back to bed.

The ducal carriage arrived early the next morning, shortly after Francesca and Callie finished breakfast. It was their town carriage, not the one they usually used for traveling, as it was smaller and more dashing, a brougham rather than the heavy coach and four that was now sitting at Marcastle. The coachman explained, with a slightly aggrieved air, that the master had hired a post chaise to take them from Lilles House to their estate, not warranting the town carriage large enough for all their luggage. Indeed, it was a snug fit loading Callie's baggage onto the brougham, and two smaller bags had to go inside with her.

Francesca walked Callie out to the carriage, where Callie turned and gave her friend a hug.

"Here," Callie said, taking Francesca's hand and pressing a small object into it. "I so enjoyed being here with you," she said, tears clogging her throat. "I want to give you something."

Francesca looked down at her palm, where a delicate ivory-and-jet cameo necklace lay on a golden chain. "Why, Callie, this is beautiful. But —"

"No, please. It was my mother's."

Francesca's eyes widened. "No, Callie, think! You cannot want to give this away. I cannot take it. Really." She tried to hand the necklace back to Callie.

Callie shook her head. "No, I want you to have it. It is not the only thing I have of my mother's. And I would like to think that we are linked — almost like sisters. Please?"

Francesca looked troubled. "Are you certain?"

"Yes. Absolutely. It is important to me."

"All right. If that is what you want." Francesca's palm closed over the cameo. Then, impulsively, she stepped forward to hug Callie again. "Please, do not immure yourself up there in Norfolk. Promise me that you will come back — for the Little Season, perhaps?"

"Perhaps. And you will come to Redfields, won't you? I intend to persuade Rochford to spend a good long while at Dancy Park."

"Yes. Of course I will visit there."

Francesca felt unaccustomed tears rise in her throat as Callie gave her a last smile and climbed up into the smart black carriage. Then it rolled off down the street, with Callie leaning out to wave another goodbye.

Francesca waved back, watching until the carriage turned the corner. She turned, then walked back into the house and up the stairs to her bedroom. Her maid Maisie was there, seated on a stool by the fireplace, sewing a ruffle onto the bottom of one of Francesca's skirts.

"Well, Lady Calandra is gone, Maisie," Francesca told her, then sighed and sat down at the vanity table. "I shall miss her, won't you?"

"Yes, my lady. She's a winning one, she is."

As much as Maisie liked the Lady Calandra, she would have to admit that what she would miss most of all was the hearty meals that the duke's generous allowance to their household had meant. Lady Francesca would have objected, of course, if she had known just how much money had flowed in from the duke's agent the last two months to pay for Lady Calandra's upkeep. Indeed, she would probably have sent it back to His Grace in a temper. But, fortunately, Fenton was too canny for that; the duke's man of business had dealt straight with Fenton, who would have been sure not to reveal the details of the arrangement with Lady Francesca.

Maisie smiled a little to herself as she considered the fact that Fenton was also canny enough to have set a good bit of that money aside for future use, so perhaps the larder would not prove to be too lean, at least for another month or two.

Francesca opened up the jewelry box that sat atop her vanity and pulled out a drawer, manipulating a catch so that a hidden drawer slid out of the false bottom. Carefully she laid the cameo down beside a glittering sapphire bracelet and a set of sapphire earrings.

"I cannot keep receiving gifts that I cannot bear to sell, Maisie, or we shall all starve," Francesca told her maid ruefully and closed the small cabinet.

She turned to Maisie. "This Season I must find someone I don't care about at all and marry her off."

"Yes, my lady," Maisie agreed placidly, biting off the thread and tying a knot.

It was a short journey to Lilles House, one that Callie would have walked if it had not been for her baggage. A post chaise waited in front of their house, and the servants were busy loading it, supervised by the butler. That good man took a moment away from his task to hand Callie out of the carriage and welcome her home, just as if she and her maid had not stopped by for a visit just last week.

She wondered if the servants, too, had heard the gossip and felt sorry for her. Probably, as they always seemed more knowledgeable than she about all the latest scandals.

"Callie." Rochford stepped out of the house to greet her. She noticed that a red spot on his cheek and another beside his eye had blossomed into bluish bruises since yesterday.

"Hallo, Sinclair." She smiled as he came out to take her arm, pausing to inspect the job of loading and unloading the carriages.

"We will be ready to go as soon as they transfer your trunks," he told her. "Cook has prepared an enormous hamper to take with us. She is convinced that inn food would be certain to lay us both low."

Callie went inside to speak to the cook and housekeeper, knowing they would both be hurt if she did not take the time to do so. By the time she returned, the coach was completely loaded, waiting only for the coachman to check every strap once again. Rochford had turned to offer his hand to help Callie into the carriage when there was a shout and clatter of hooves. Both of them turned to see a man riding down the street at a much faster pace than was normal — or safe.

An instant later, Callie realized that it was Lord Bromwell.

She sucked in an astonished breath, her heart suddenly hammering in her chest. It was as if her daydream had come to life — Brom racing to stop her from going.

"Wait!" he cried as he grew close, pulling his mount to a stop and leaping off the horse. "Do not go!" He tossed the reins to one of the servants and strode up to Callie and Rochford. "Thank God I caught you."

"Just barely," the duke said, eyeing the other man a trifle warily.

"I went to Lady Haughston's first. I thought you would be there. She told me you were leaving for home. I was afraid I had missed you." Bromwell's gaze flickered to Callie. "I had to talk to my sister, as I told you yesterday. She told me . . . everything. How she planned yesterday because she wanted revenge on the duke. How she —" He stopped, the muscles jumping in his jaw, before he went on. "How she lied about you, Rochford, all those years ago. I have come to apologize for . . . for everything. I am sorry. What she did was wrong and despicable."

He looked wretched, almost ill. "I hope you will accept my apologies for the trick she played on us all yesterday." His gaze went to Callie again, then as quickly away.

Why would he not look at her? Callie wondered. This was not at all the way she had envisioned Brom's return. Where was the passionate declaration of love? The assurance that he could not live without her? Indeed, it seemed that Bromwell was more interested in talking to her brother than to her.

Bromwell straightened his shoulders and faced the duke squarely. "Sir, I regret my rash and impulsive actions fifteen years ago. I was foolish to believe my sister, and I — I am sorry for wrongfully accusing you. I hope that you will find it in your heart to forgive me. If not, I can understand, though I will deeply regret it."

Rochford hesitated, then offered the other man his hand. "It is only natural for a man to defend his sister."

"I know." Bromwell shook his hand, and some silent masculine communication seemed to pass between them.

"I have broken my ties with my sister," Bromwell went on, still looking at the duke. His face reflected the pain of that decision. "I know that she cannot be in our lives after what she did. I could not expect you to agree to my marrying *your* sister if she was. And that is why I am here. I have come to ask your permission to pay my addresses to Lady Calandra."

Callie stared at him, stunned.

Rochford, oddly, did not seem as surprised. "I think you will find that Lady Calandra makes her own decisions. But you have my permission."

"Thank you." Bromwell nodded to him, then swung around to Callie.

"Lady Calandra . . ."

Callie raised her brows. "Oh? Have you noticed me finally? Am I allowed to have some say in this matter? I thought perhaps you and my brother were simply going to write out a marriage contract, decide my dowry, and all would be settled."

"Callie?" Brom began uncertainly.

"I am my own woman," she said fiercely. "And if you wanted to marry me, *I* am the one you should have asked. Not him!"

Tears burned at the backs of her eyes, threatening to break through. Callie turned and ran back into the house, slamming the door after her.

Bromwell turned back toward the duke, looking confused. "What happened? What did I do?"

Rochford shrugged, turning his hands up in the universal gesture of a male baffled by the behavior of females.

Bromwell turned and trotted up the steps after Callie. One of the footmen jumped to open the door for him, but Bromwell was already inside. "Callie!"

She was standing in the huge vaulted entryway of the house. Whatever servants were around had discreetly melted away into some other area, and she was alone before a round table. Arms crossed, she seemed to be studying the large vase that sat in the center of the tabletop. At Bromwell's voice, she turned and regarded him balefully.

"Callie, I don't understand," he said, going over to her. "I — I thought you would — I thought you would be agreeable to marriage. I was not aware that you had . . . an objection."

"I have no interest in marrying you to salve your conscience," Callie shot back, swallowing back her tears. "I have no desire to marry you because you feel that you wronged my brother fifteen years ago, or because it is the proper thing to do, or because your sister trapped us into a compromising position."

"What the devil are you talking about!" he protested, his own temper rising now. "I never said any of those things!"

"You did not have to. It is quite clear that all I am is a burden to you. You said not a word to me — not a smile or a glance — and went straight to my brother to apologize to *him!* As if *he* were the person who was most concerned with this, and I would do whatever was agreeable to him."

"No! I spoke to him because I wanted it

all done properly. I wanted to make peace with Rochford so there would be no reason for a rift between you and your brother. It was not he who concerned me, it was you. My desire to marry you has nothing to do with the duke. Nor anything to do with my sister or with gossip or what everyone in the *ton* will think."

"Then why do you wish to marry me?" she challenged.

He looked at her, astonished. "Because I love you, blast it! Because I cannot bear to live without you in my life. When I was there at the hunting lodge, before you came, I had nothing to do but look at the bleak days that stretched out in front of me. Endless, bitter, lonely days, because you would not be in them. I love you so much that my life is worthless without you. And that is why I want to marry you!"

"Oh, Brom!" The tears now sprang into her eyes and fell, unheeded. She leaped forward, throwing her arms around his neck. "That is the right reason."

He wrapped his arms around her and held her close, burying his face in her hair. "Then will you agree to marry me? Or must I go down on one knee?"

"No, no," Callie said, half laughing, half crying. "Stay just where you are. Yes, I will marry you."

He kissed her then, a long, satisfying seal to their agreement. He raised his head and looked down into her eyes. "I love you, Callie, more than I ever dreamed I could love anyone."

"And I love you," she said, looking up at him with stars in her eyes. She had come to London to find a husband, she thought, and instead she had found love.

With a smile, she went up on her toes to kiss him.

EPILOGUE

Francesca looked around the ballroom of Lilles House, decorated with what appeared to be all the spring flowers in a fifty-mile radius of London, and populated by fully half the *ton.* The cathedral earlier had been similarly crowded for the ceremony.

It was no surprise. This was, after all, the wedding of the year. It was not every day that the sister of a duke married, especially the only and much-beloved sister. No expense had been spared, either for the wedding or the wedding dinner afterward, and the *ton* had been abuzz about it from the moment the engagement was announced. Invitations had been more eagerly sought than vouchers to Almack's, and no one wanted to admit that they had not been invited.

She made her way along the line of guests toward the happy couple. They were standing with the duke and Callie's grandmother.

Francesca knew that Lord Bromwell's sister had also been invited, despite what she had done. Knowing how close Brom had been to his sister, Callie had been too softhearted to allow him to cut himself off from Daphne entirely. However, at least Lady Daphne was not receiving guests with them, and Francesca hoped that she would be able to avoid the woman altogether.

The duke was, as usual, the most handsome man in the room. He bowed over Francesca's hand, his eyes twinkling.

"Ah, the fair lady who has brought all this about," he said.

"I can scarcely take the credit," Francesca demurred. " 'Twas love that triumphed. I find it usually does."

"Especially when love has an able general such as you."

"Francesca!" Callie reached out to hug her friend. Callie's face glowed with happiness, and her large brown eyes were bright as stars.

"Hello, Callie, Bromwell. I wish you both very happy," Francesca told them, smiling. "But I can see that you already are."

"Indeed," Bromwell agreed, lifting his wife's hand to his lips to lightly kiss her fingers. "How could I be otherwise, when I am married to the most beautiful woman in the world?"

Callie blushed and smiled, and as they looked at each other, it was clear that the rest of the room barely existed for them. They had eyes only for each other.

Smiling, Francesca moved on. She must, she thought, start searching for someone to guide through the treacherous waters of the Season. It was already in full swing, and her time was growing short. She had meant to find someone as soon as Callie left, but she had gotten swept up in the wedding preparations, and she had not done her research.

The truth was, she knew, that she was not looking forward to grooming any other girl for marriage. Over the past year she had had such a splendid time, and become such good friends with each of the women she had helped, that the thought of a more businesslike arrangement held little appeal.

A few minutes later, she heard a murmur among the crowd, and she turned to see Callie and Brom taking the floor. They stopped in the center of the dance floor, waiting for the orchestra to strike up the strains of their first waltz as husband and wife. Looking at them and seeing the love that shone on their faces, Francesca could not help but blink back a tear.

Of all the couples whom she had brought

together, she thought that these two made her the happiest. Callie was like a sister to her. Indeed, she thought, once she had thought that Callie would be her sister in truth. Francesca shrugged away that thought impatiently, but she could not keep her eyes from going to the tall, straight figure of Callie's brother, who stood at the edge of the dance floor, watching his sister dance with her new husband.

The duke turned at that moment, and his gaze caught Francesca's. They gazed at each other for a heartbeat; then Francesca glanced away, breaking the connection. She stared down at her gloved hands, busying herself with smoothing down each finger.

"Well," said a woman's voice from just over her shoulder, "I am sure that you must be quite happy now."

Francesca turned and found herself staring into Lady Swithington's pale blue eyes.

"Of course I am pleased for Lady Calandra and Lord Bromwell," Francesca replied coolly. "I am sure that they will be very happy."

"Naturally." Daphne cast a sardonic glance at the newlyweds. "Such lovebirds." She turned back to Francesca. "But I meant you. I am sure you are bubbling with happiness to have found out that I lied about

Rochford." Daphne's pale blue eyes were venomous.

Francesca shrugged. "I would never have believed that Rochford had gotten you with child and refused to marry you. He is not the sort of man to do that. Anyway, I never heard that rumor at the time, so it was scarcely any matter to me."

Daphne sneered. "You certainly jilted him anyway, did you not?"

Francesca's eyes flashed. "I could scarcely marry a man who was having an affair with another woman, even if he had no reason to marry her."

She stopped, staring at the other woman's suddenly bleak face. A chill swept through her. In a shaky voice, Francesca said, "You lied about that, too, didn't you? You just made it *appear* that you two were discovered *in flagrante.* It was one of your schemes!"

Daphne's lips curved up in a self-satisfied smirk. "Of course it was not true. Rochford was most boringly steadfast. If you had been a little less in love with yourself and more in love with him, you might have realized that."

Francesca turned away from Daphne, her eyes going across the room to the Duke of Rochford. She felt weak and sick inside, her knees trembling so that she thought she might fall down.

Blindly she made her way through the throng of people, not looking to either side. Someone took her elbow in a firm grasp, and she heard Irene's voice, "Francesca? Are you ill?"

Francesca looked at her. "A little, I think."

"Here, sit down." In her brisk, competent way, Irene steered Francesca to a bench and sat down with her on it. "Let me get you something to drink."

"No. It's all right. I merely needed to sit down. I had a bit of a shock, that is all."

"What happened? I saw you talking to that odious Lady Swithington. No doubt she said something to upset you." At Francesca's nod, Irene went on, "You must not believe her. I am certain it was a lie."

"No. I do believe that this time it was not." Francesca's voice was weary and laced with sorrow. "I fear that I made a terrible mistake many years ago. I wronged Rochford."

"What do you mean?" Irene asked. "I am certain that you could not have done anything terrible."

"I did. I did not believe him when he vowed he was telling me the truth." She looked out over the crowd, seeking out his tall figure again. "Worse," she went on, "I think I influenced him to — to live the sort of life he has."

"Whatever do you mean? He has a life anyone would envy."

"But he has never married. I think that what I did perhaps made him distrust women."

Irene stared at her. "Are you serious?"

Francesca nodded. "Yes, and I must make it up to him."

"But how?"

"It is clear," Francesca said. "I must find Rochford a wife."

We hope you have enjoyed this Large Print book. Other Thorndike, Wheeler, and Chivers Press Large Print books are available at your library or directly from the publishers.

For information about current and upcoming titles, please call or write, without obligation, to:

Publisher
Thorndike Press
295 Kennedy Memorial Drive
Waterville, ME 04901
Tel. (800) 223-1244

or visit our Web site at:

http://gale.cengage.com/thorndike

OR

Chivers Large Print
published by BBC Audiobooks Ltd
St James House, The Square
Lower Bristol Road
Bath BA2 3SB
England
Tel. +44(0) 800 136919
email: bbcaudiobooks@bbc.co.uk
www.bbcaudiobooks.co.uk

All our Large Print titles are designed for easy reading, and all our books are made to last.